DUBLINERS

JAMES JOYCE

WITH AN INTRODUCTION AND
NOTES BY TERENCE BROWN

PENGUIN BOOKS

PENGUIN BOOKS

Published by the Penguin Group
Penguin Books Ltd, 80 Strand, London WC2R 0RL, England
Penguin Putnam Inc., 375 Hudson Street, New York, New York 10014, USA
Penguin Books Australia Ltd, 250 Camberwell Road, Camberwell, Victoria 3124, Australia
Penguin Books Canada Ltd, 10 Alcorn Avenue, Toronto, Ontario, Canada M4V 3B2
Penguin Books India (P) Ltd, 11 Community Centre, Panchsheel Park, New Delhi – 110 017, India
Penguin Books (NZ) Ltd, Cnr Rosedale and Airborne Roads, Albany, Auckland, New Zealand
Penguin Books (South Africa) (Pty) Ltd, 24 Sturdee Avenue, Rosebank 2196, South Africa

Penguin Books Ltd, Registered Offices: 80 Strand, London WC2R 0RL, England

www.penguin.com

First published in 1914
Published in Penguin Books 1956
This annotated edition first published 1992
Reprinted in Penguin Classics 2000
30

Introduction, Appendices and Notes Copyright © Terence Brown, 1992
All rights reserved

The moral right of the editor has been asserted

Printed in England by Clays Ltd, St Ives plc
Set in 10/12 pt Monophoto Sabon

ISBN-13: 978-0-141-18245-2

www.greenpenguin.co.uk

Penguin Books is committed to a sustainable future
for our business, our readers and our planet.
The book in your hands is made from paper
certified by the Forest Stewardship Council.

PENGUIN BOOKS

Dubliners

James Joyce was born in Dublin on 2 February 1882. He was the oldest of ten children in a family which, after brief prosperity, collapsed into poverty. He was none the less educated at the best Jesuit schools and then at University College, Dublin, where he gave proof of his extraordinary talent. In 1902, following his graduation, he went to Paris, thinking he might attend medical school there. But he soon gave up attending lectures and devoted himself to writing poems and prose sketches, and formulating an 'aesthetic system'. Recalled to Dublin in April 1903 because of the fatal illness of his mother, he circled slowly towards his literary career. During the summer of 1904 he met a young woman from Galway, Nora Barnacle, and persuaded her to go with him to the Continent, where he planned to teach English. The young couple spent a few months in Pola (now in Croatia), then in 1905 moved to Trieste, where, except for seven months in Rome and three trips to Dublin, they lived until June 1915. They had two children, a son and a daughter. His first book, the poems of *Chamber Music*, was published in London in 1907, and *Dubliners*, a book of stories, in 1914. Italy's entrance into the First World War obliged Joyce to move to Zürich, where he remained until 1919. During this period he published *A Portrait of the Artist as a Young Man* (1916) and *Exiles*, a play (1918). After a brief return to Trieste following the armistice, Joyce determined to move to Paris so as to arrange more easily for the publication of *Ulysses*, a book which he had been working on since 1914. It was, in fact, published on his birthday in Paris, in 1922, and brought him international fame. The same year he began work on *Finnegans Wake*, and though much harassed by eye troubles, and deeply affected by his daughter's mental illness, he completed and published that book in 1939. After the outbreak of the Second World War, he went to live in unoccupied France, then managed to secure permission in December 1940 to return to Zürich. Joyce died there six weeks later, on 13 January 1941, and was buried in the Fluntern Cemetery.

Terence Brown was born in 1944 and educated at Trinity College, Dublin, where he is Professor of Anglo-Irish Literature and a Fellow of the College. He is author of *Louis MacNeice: Sceptical Vision* (1975), *Northern Voices: Poets from Ulster* (1975), *Ireland: A Social and Cultural History* (1981, 1985) and *Ireland's Literature: Selected Essays* (1988). He is currently at work on a critical biography of W. B. Yeats. He has lectured on Anglo-Irish literature in many parts of the world. He lives in Dublin with his wife and two children.

Seamus Deane is General Editor for the works of James Joyce in Penguin. He is Keough Professor of Irish Studies at the University of Notre Dame, Indiana.

Dubliners and *The Dead and Other Stories*, both read by Gerard McSorley, are also available as Penguin Audiobooks.

CONTENTS

Introduction   vii
Notes on Introduction   xlvi
Note on Text   l

DUBLINERS

The Sisters   1
An Encounter   11
Araby   21
Eveline   29
After the Race   35
Two Gallants   43
The Boarding House   56
A Little Cloud   65
Counterparts   82
Clay   95
A Painful Case   103
Ivy Day in the Committee Room   115
A Mother   134
Grace   149
The Dead   175

Appendix I   227
Appendix II   229
Appendix III   233
Notes   237

INTRODUCTION

At the end of 1905 a young Irishman sent a manuscript of twelve short stories entitled *Dubliners* to an English publisher, hoping for early publication. But it was to be almost a decade before the ambitious and impecunious author would see his book in print and then only after so many delays and disappointments that the actual appearance of the work must have seemed to him something of an anticlimax. This dismal chapter in publishing history ran as follows. After an initial commitment, the English publisher, Grant Richards, developed serious qualms about the book's contents, as his author, James Joyce, submitted new tales for inclusion in the promised volume. His printer too was fearful that Joyce's realism about sexual matters would offend contemporary taste and lay both printer and publisher open to legal penalty. So author and publisher entered on a protracted correspondence in which a compromise was sought – in vain – between artistic integrity and commercial pusillanimity. By 1909 Joyce had given up on Richards and had placed his manuscript in the hands of an Irish publishing house, Maunsel and Company, where history was repeated as farce. This time the book got as far as the print stage, only for the complete edition to be destroyed at the very last moment as, once again, a printer and publisher took fright, reckoning now with the possibility of libel actions on account of its many references to living persons. Finally in 1914 Richards took his courage in his hands and issued the book without suffering any of the dire consequences he had earlier envisaged.

This delayed publication undoubtedly affected the book's reception. A work begun when the author was a mere twenty-two-year-old graduate of University College, Dublin, and completed with the composition of 'The Dead' in 1907, when Joyce was all of twenty-five, did not appear until the author's thirty-third year. By that time he was already attracting admiration as a novelist, with the serial publication of *A Portrait of the Artist as a Young Man* in *The Egoist*. This new work rather over-shadowed Joyce's collection of stories, for at that time the longer fictional form enjoyed greater critical esteem than the short story, even when it was given to the world in a coherent collection. So it was not readily recognized that *Dubliners* constituted a milestone in the history of short prose fiction and a remarkable and precocious achievement in its own right. Indeed for many years *Dubliners* continued to languish somewhat in the shadow of Joyce's other fictions – *A Portrait*, *Ulysses* and *Finnegans Wake* – generating only rather grudging critical attention when so much more ample and complex work awaited explication and assessment.

The young man who began work on *Dubliners* in 1904 was the first surviving son and eldest child of a family of ten children which blessed (if that is the word) the marriage of John Stanislaus Joyce and Mary Jane Murray ('May'). John Joyce hailed from Cork City in the southern province of Munster while his wife was a Leitrim woman from the predominantly rural province of Connacht in the west of the country. Joyce père was a man of some marked social gifts (singer, raconteur, personality, colour-ful frequenter of public houses) but signally deficient in the matter of earning a living. Despite the responsibilities laid upon him by his wife's frequent pregnancies (six girls and four boys survived the fifteen pregnancies which James Joyce believed hastened his mother's early death in

1903), John Joyce consistently lived beyond his means, and through mortgages and unwise investments managed to dissipate his family's inheritance which depended on properties in Cork. Driven to the desperate expedient of actually working for a living, John Joyce, through political connections, found himself a position as a Collector of Rates in Dublin. This post allowed him plenty of time for gossip and for enjoying the lore and backchat of the city, but paid insufficiently to meet the needs of his burgeoning family. Even this tenuous hold on the world of secure employment was broken in 1892 when John Joyce's position was discontinued and he was forced to retire on a less than ample pension (only granted after May Joyce had pled the dire state of the family finances) of about £132 per annum. In 1904, the year after his mother's death, Joyce wrote bitterly to Nora Barnacle, the young Galway woman he was to invite to share a life of social and intellectual rebellion with him in exile on the Continent:

> My mind rejects the whole present social order and Christianity – home, the recognised virtues, classes of life, and religious doctrines. How could I like the idea of home? My home was simply a middle-class affair ruined by spendthrift habits which I have inherited. My mother was slowly killed, I think, by my father's ill-treatment, by years of trouble, and by my cynical frankness of conduct. When I looked on her face as she lay in her coffin – a face grey and wasted with cancer – I understood that I was looking on the face of a victim and I cursed the system which had made her a victim. (*Letters, II*, 48)

Life *chez* Joyce had not always been so dreadful an affair as the young and self-accusing writer characterized it in this angry outburst. Joyce himself had been born on 2 February 1882, in the family home at 41 Brighton Square in the Dublin suburb of Rathgar. This square of recently built houses was located in a respectable district of the city, and the house itself was eminently suitable for a middle-class family with a private income. The family soon removed to Bray (after a sojourn at an equally respectable address in Rathmines near by), a pleasant sea-side resort in County Wicklow about ten miles south of the city, where they took a large house on Martello Terrace that was at least the social equal of the houses in Rathgar and Rathmines they had vacated. Here they lived in some style, employing not only servants but a governess for the young children. The Joyces were, in fact, comfort-ably placed members of a class new to Irish life, Catholic bourgeois of strong nationalist outlook who expected Home Rule, which was surely imminent, to enter them on their true inheritance as an elite in the emerging Irish political and social structure. Education played a crucial part in their aspirations and the Jesuit order was regarded as the agency most likely to prepare their sons for coming triumphs. James Joyce was accordingly enrolled as a boarder in the Jesuit-run Clongowes Wood College in County Kildare in September 1888 when he was six years old. Here he remained (apart of course from holidays) until the decisive year of 1891 when reverses in the family fortunes became definitive and the boy had to be removed from Clongowes because of paternal inability to meet the fees demanded there. As if this indignity was not enough to highlight the rapidly deteriorating circumstances the family now experienced, in 1893 the young James would find himself for a brief period enrolled as a pupil in a school run by the Christian Brothers. This teaching order supplied a notoriously robust education for the children of the Irish poor (John Joyce snobbishly identified their constituency as 'Paddy Stink and Mickey Mud'). Joyce never subsequently mentioned his time under their tute-lage and fortunately his Jesuit education was continued when, in April 1893, he was enabled, through the generosity of the order itself, to begin attendance at Belvedere College on the north side of central Dublin, where he was to remain until 1898.

This hiatus in James's educational progression under the aegis of the Jesuit order had occurred as two other seismic events shook such emotional security as the young boy had enjoyed to that date. The one was entirely personal to the Joyce family, the other was an event of national significance. The year 1891 saw the financial crisis which meant the removal, in early 1892 of the Joyce ménage from their family home in Bray, to a house in Carysfort Avenue on the south side of the city. It was the first visible crack in the edifice of a family life that was soon to be shaken to its foundations. For within a couple of years, the Joyces were to make a further removal, with the necessary haste which was to mark all their subsequent flits through the city, from that comparatively respectable address to the north side of the river Liffey. The river then marked, as it does now, a social divide between the indisputably respectable and the doubtfully so. Thus the young boy, who to that date had enjoyed the salubrious environs of Bray in the holidays from Clongowes, was to be exposed, not only to familial and financial insecurity, but to a Dublin of mean dwellings, low public houses and slum tenements with their teeming populations, houses of ill-repute and grinding poverty. He was to get to know too a Dublin of lower-middle-class desperation in the crowded streets of north central Dublin, Drumcondra and Fairview, a city life hitherto unknown to Irish literature.

The shock delivered to the sensitive boy by this social transition must, one imagines, have been akin to that famously suffered by the English writer Charles Dickens when his equally improvident father was imprisoned for debt and the future novelist was set to work in a blacking factory. Joyce never forgot this trauma. This is evident, it can convincingly be argued, in his lifelong fascination with the theme of betrayal which focused on the fate of the Irish political leader Charles Stewart Parnell whose political career reached its climacteric in the same year as the Joycean *démarche*. Parnell's death in October 1891 ended the hopes and expectations of those like John Joyce, members of the Catholic nationalist middle class, who had reckoned their future as intimately bound up with the success of Parnell's skilfully fought parliamentary campaign for Irish Home Rule which would have allowed the country, in a devolved government, a significant degree of legislative independence from Westminster. Thereafter Joyce father and son would associate, in a way which seemed to come from springs of grievance and resentment which were less than fully rational, the collapse in the Joyce fortunes and the immiseration endured by the family in the wake of their own undignified experience, with the sufferings heaped upon Parnell in his final months. The Chief, as Parnell was known, had been forsaken by a majority of the Irish Parliamentary Party at the behest of ecclesiastical opinion in Ireland and nonconformist prudery in Britain, when his adulterous relationship with a married woman (Katherine O'Shea) became public knowledge. The Joyce family, who should have been pillars of society in the new Ireland Parnell had fought for, found itself by contrast in a kind of exile in rented accommodation on the unfashionable north side of the city, shamefully assailed by creditors and importunate landlords. James Joyce's Parnellite loyalties and his obsession with the act of betrayal found bitter expression in *Dubliners* in 'Ivy Day in the Committee Room' with its comprehensive indictment of the casual, treacherous corruption of Irish political life in 1902, in contrast to the noble idealism of the dead Chief, Parnell. In writing such a work Joyce was bringing together a personal and national sense of betrayal and outrage that had their origins in his own experience as a boy in Dublin a decade before.

It was not only Joyce's experience of social decline and Parnellite disillusionment that found its way into *Dubliners*. This text, like all of Joyce's work, contains autobiographical matter and is rooted in an intensely accurate apprehension of the detail of the Dublin life Joyce had observed all about him as he grew to adulthood. Many incidents and characters can be shown to have their origin in real personalities whom Joyce would have known and to be based on experiences he and others had undergone (though only 'An Encounter' and 'A Mother' were based on Joyce's direct personal experience). Indeed he drew with almost clinical dispassion on the experiences and even the private diary of his long-suffering brother Stanislaus (who was to be a financial mainstay of the Joyce household in its European wanderings for many a year). It was Stanislaus who afforded a model for Mr Duffy in 'A Painful Case', as Joyce imagined what might become of him in a later life of unfruitful bachelorhood. And his brother's experience in a political by-election in which he served as a canvasser along with his father in 1902 is also the basis for some of the detail in 'Ivy Day in the Committee Room'. Stanislaus Joyce himself records, confirming how intently his brother sought accurate data for his fictional realism, that 'the detailed acquaintance with office life which some of the stories show, as well as the end of one of them, "Counterparts", he got from my diary and more fully from me in conversation'.[1] The Misses Morkan in 'The Dead' were undoubtedly based on his own great-aunts who had kept a kind of finishing school for young ladies at Usher's Island, where the story is set. This story suggests how the author of *Dubliners* did not hesitate to draw even on personal details of those closest to him for his fiction. For the girlhood of his own Nora Barnacle supplied the Galway backgound for his portrayal of young love in that searchingly emotional tale. *Dubliners* is the work of a young man who, as his brother Stanislaus records, did not scruple to read through his mother's letters a week or so after her death, offering only a curt, and as Stansilaus believed, contemptuous 'Nothing' as commentary on their contents. From quite early on there was something about James Joyce's personality which bespoke a capacity to respond to life even at its most terrible with the intrigued, calculating imperviousness of an artist for whom nothing real is beyond his purview. For in the midst of trauma, alcoholism, familial violence and disintegration Joyce maintained a cheerful resolution of temperament which came from sources of self-belief that could not be shaken by the storms which raged about him. He was, his brother wrote in a diary entry in 1903 'a genius of character' and possessed 'extraordinary moral courage'[2] which expressed itself in a scornful disregard for conventional opinion, for what Joyce termed 'the rabblement'.[3] His instinct was for the truth of life as he saw it and his moral engagement involved him in a search for modes of artistic expression which would serve that truth, whatever the consequences.

An early ideal was the Norwegian dramatist Henrik Ibsen (1828–1906) about whose play *When We Dead Awaken* Joyce wrote an admiring review article during his second year as a student at University College, Dublin where he had matriculated when he left Belvedere College in 1898. The eighteen-year-old undergraduate had the gratification of seeing his essay published in the widely read English *Fortnightly Review* (to whose editor he had ambitiously dispatched it), bringing him to the attention of the great man himself. Joyce had made an auspicious beginning.

What the developing artist in Joyce responded to in Ibsen was the 'defiant realism'[4] of his vision (he tended to ignore in his enthusiasm the symbolic qualities of Ibsen's dramaturgy) and the independence of mind which underlay it. From Ibsen he received essential instruction that 'out of the dreary sameness of existence, a measure of dramatic life may be drawn'.[5] The portrait of a dismal, enervated provincial world that Joyce draws in *Dubliners* must owe its exacting, diagnostic realism in part to Joyce's admiration for those plays by Ibsen in which the lives of the Norwegian living-dead are seen 'steadily and whole, as from a great height, with perfect vision and angelic dispassionateness, with the sight of one who may look on the sun with open eyes'.[6]

In Joyce's youthful view, Ibsen had 'chosen the average lives in their uncompromising truth for the groundwork of all his later plays'.[7] In *Dubliners* he emulated the master, and accordingly it must have been almost insufferable to him that the prudery and caution of publishers in London and Dublin delayed publication of a work which he believed, with Ibsenite zeal, represented 'a chapter of the moral history' (*Letters, II*, 134) of his country. So he wrote to Grant Richards, as that pusillanimous soul hesitated, with the conviction of an artistic Mr Valiant-for-Truth whose weapon is an uncompromising realism:

> It is not my fault that the odour of ashpits and old weeds and offal hangs round my stories. I seriously believe that you will retard the course of civilisation in Ireland by preventing the Irish people from having one good look at themselves in my nicely polished looking-glass.
>
> (*Letters*, 63–4)

Therefore, it is clear that Joyce intended *Dubliners* at the very least to be a realist's study of his native city, a work representative of Irish experience, conducted with

unflinching Ibsenite moral rigour. Writing to William Heine-
mann (to whom he had first sent the manuscript in
hopes of publication) he insisted, 'The book is not a
collection of tourist impressions but an attempt to represent certain aspects of the life of one of the European
capitals.' (*Letters, II*, 109) To his brother Stanislaus he
wrote in the same month, reinforcing the point: 'When
you remember that Dublin has been a capital for thousands of years, that it is the "second" city of the British
Empire, that it is nearly three times as big as Venice it
seems strange that no artist has given it to the world.'

(*Letters, II*, 111)

The Dublin which in the early twentieth century lay open
to the inspection of Joyce's realism was a city of some
three hundred thousand persons. It was a city which
certainly exhibited much evidence of its significance in
the scheme of things, being endowed with much splendid
architecture and an urban layout that allowed its citizens
to appreciate its magnificent setting on the river Liffey
between the open arms of a great bay and beneath the
rolling mountains of County Wicklow to the south. Many
of Dublin's most distinguished buildings dated from the
eighteenth century (the Four Courts and the Custom
House which dominated the north bank of the river, the
Bank of Ireland on College Green which had housed an
independent parliament in the last decades of that century) but the city also boasted two medieval cathedrals,
two universities, one the Elizabethan foundation of Trinity College, Dublin, the other the more recently established University College, Dublin, off-spring of John
Henry Newman's educational experiment in the 1850s.
Even after the city's nineteenth-century decline from the
glories of the late eighteenth century, when it was a seat
of native government (however restricted the franchise

which elected it), there remained several noble squares (Merrion Square, St Stephen's Green, Fitzwilliam Square) which made the city an urban masterpiece that allowed it to be compared with Bath in England and even with the Italian Venice which Joyce invoked in his letter to Stanislaus. The eighteenth-century Wide Streets Commission had also bequeathed to the city's citizens a street pattern of ready access and spacious vistas so that Dublin was very much a walker's city (note in *Dubliners* as in *Ulysses* how much time the characters spend on their feet or on brief journeys by cab or tram so that peregrination becomes almost a principle of composition) which could fairly easily be negotiated, even in the course of a day's business, by foot.

The city that Joyce chose as his literary subject matter, for all its graciousness and fortunate physical setting, had by the early twentieth century endured almost a century of decline. This perhaps accounts for the fact that the Dubliners of Joyce's text seem unconscious of the city's charms, thereby reflecting contemporary taste that had not yet been alerted to the attractions of Georgian architecture. A guide book of the period advised 'The street architecture of Dublin is not beautiful, the houses generally being of the uninteresting Georgian period.'[8] The Act of Union of 1801 at the end of the Georgian century had reduced the city's importance in the British Isles as the seat of a native Irish legislature and the economic difficulties experienced by the country at large in an era of free trade and burgeoning transport facilities had taken their toll on the city too. As the historian of Dublin's decline has it 'At the time of the union Dublin was easily the second largest city in the British Isles and among the ten largest cities in Europe. By 1860 she was merely fifth in the UK rankings and by the end of the century was to suffer the ultimate indignity of being overtaken by upstart

Belfast as Ireland's largest city.'⁹ Symptoms of stagnation and concomitant human misery were not hard to find. Because the city lacked any really productive industrial base, the two hundred thousand or more of working people that constituted the great majority of its inhabitants were forced to depend for employment on the building industry, on such concerns as biscuit-making and brewing, on domestic service, casual labouring and carrying and on work on the docks. This latter reflected the fact that Dublin was an important entrepôt for the country as a whole, but even in this sphere, the late nineteenth century saw decline and failure to meet competition from new sources (Gabriel Conroy's father in 'The Dead' was an employee of the influential Dublin Port and Docks Board which regulated the work of the port). By 1907 the port, which had been of long-standing significance in the growth of the city, had to play second fiddle in terms of growth to both Belfast and Cork in the north and south of the country. But the decline in the docks was only one element in a generally dismal picture, summarized as follows by Mary E. Daly:

> The lack of dynamism from the rural Irish economy and the failure of Dublin businesses to manufacture, and, in some cases, even to distribute the manufactured goods which rural Ireland needed, plus the apparent stagnation of the port in the third quarter of the nineteenth century all meant that Dublin failed to provide adequate employment, either for the indigenous population or even for a small proportion of the surplus population of rural Ireland.[10]

Many of the city's labouring and unemployed poor lived in the tenements for which the city was notorious. These were squalid, decaying Georgian townhouses on streets and squares on the north side of the river in central Dublin which had once been the height of fashion, but by the early twentieth century were given over to slum conditions of the worst kind. As F. S. L. Lyons has recorded, 'over 30% of these tenements consisted of single rooms; estimates of the average number living, eating and sleeping in these rooms varied from three to six, though cases of from seven to twelve were by no means uncommon. Up to one hundred people could live in a single tenement house; often there would only be one cold tap in a yard or passage, and the facilities for sewage disposal were unspeakably inadequate.'[11] Unsurprisingly, Dublin had both a disgracefully high infant mortality rate and the highest death rate in the country. We get only glimpses of the desperately poor or of the labouring masses in *Dubliners*. In 'An Encounter' we meet 'ragged girls' and 'ragged boys', probably inmates of one of the many orphanages and charitable institutions that were a necessity in such a city; in 'Araby' we hear of 'the rough tribes from the cottages'. In 'A Little Cloud' Little Chandler the hero (if such he can be called) walks after work down Henrietta Street in north central Dublin, amidst a horde of grimy children – 'They stood or ran in the roadway or crawled up the steps before the gaping doors or squatted like mice upon the thresholds. . . . He picked his way deftly through all that minute vermin-like life and under the shadow of the gaunt spectral mansions in which the old nobility of Dublin had roistered.' And in 'Two Gallants' Lenehan finds himself in a café patronized by working people whose demeanour makes him embarrassed at his own, not especially developed, gentility of manner. But if actual references to this huge underclass in Dublin's life are few in *Dubliners*, such brief allusions to a dominating social reality, widespread and apparently unmitigable immiseration, give one to understand why the characters in this grimly realistic work view even loathsome or dispiriting employment with such proprietorial concern. Mr Doran

for example in 'The Boarding House' accedes to a not-so-
tender trap which will have him married to a woman he
does not love lest in disgrace he should lose his job. And
Farrington in 'Counterparts' gets violently drunk in self-
disgust when he has been forced to 'offer an abject
apology' to his superior at work after a moment's futile
rebellion. For the unemployed and underpaid there are
only the desperate stratagems of a Lenehan (in 'Two
Gallants') 'knocking about . . . pulling the devil by the
tail . . . shifts and intrigues' or of a Mr M'Coy (in
'Grace') who borrows luggage for proposed concert tours
to be undertaken by his singer spouse only to pawn it
forthwith to augment his income. And there is too the
kind of precarious hold on gentility which allows the
Morkan sisters in 'The Dead' to keep up a show of
middle-class hospitality, at least at Christmas, even
though they live over a corn factor's premises in rented accommodation.

For Joyce in *Dubliners* concentrates his attention on a
fairly narrow strand of Dublin society: the lower middle
class, petit-bourgeois world of shopkeepers and trades-
men, functionaries of one kind or another, clerks, bank
officials, salesmen like Mr Kernan in 'Grace' who sells as
well as tastes tea for a living. Their world is one of rented
rooms and houses in less than fashionable areas of the
city, of furniture bought on the hire-purchase system, of
boarding houses, offices and public houses (in the early
years of the century the city boasted about 800 licensed
premises) where they eke out their dismal and often
insecure lives. When we have noted the hotel at which
Ségouin stays and where Jimmy dines in 'After the Race',
the Gresham Hotel where the Conroys spend the night
after the Misses Morkans' Christmas party, and observe
that Gabriel and Miss Ivors are graduates of the Royal
University, we have scaled the social heights to which

Joyce's characters attain in this book. At the bottom of
the ladder, by contrast, are the skivvy in 'Two Gallants'
and Lily the caretaker's daughter in 'The Dead' who
probably both exist on the edge of that cruel poverty
which was the lot of the majority of the city's inhabitants
and which gave an added intensity to natural lower-
middle-class anxiety about economic survival.

Such social ambition as Joyce's characters can reasonably entertain in *Dubliners* is represented by Jimmy's
nouveau riche father (in 'After the Race') who has made
a fortune in the grocery trade supplying police contracts,
Jack Power in 'Grace' 'the arc' of whose 'social rise' has
elevated him to a post in 'The Royal Irish Constabulary
Office in Dublin Castle' and by Father Flynn in 'The
Sisters' and Constantine Conroy (Gabriel's brother in
'The Dead') who have achieved the social respectability
of priesthood in a society where the taking of holy
orders offered advancement for the upwardly mobile. It
was not of course that Dubliners of the kind that Joyce
chose to write about were constitutionally deficient in
the desire to improve themselves or to advance their
children in the world (class consciousness is a recurrent
motif). Rather the Dublin of the early years of the century
was economically in serious decline and its energies were
restrained by the limits placed upon ambition by a caste
system which operated with almost comprehensive effi-
ciency.

The population of Dublin in the first decade of this
century was about 17% Protestant while the rest was Catholic. That Protestant minority included the ruling elite
whose loyalty to the union between Ireland and Great
Britain was unquestioned and certainly understandable
since the union protected their own position in a strikingly
inequitable social order. It was they who constituted the
upper levels of society in Dublin and who largely controlled

entry to the major professions of Law and Medicine. They were powerful too in banking and in business (in brewing and distilling, and in biscuit-making, for example). They would indeed have reserved for poorer Protestants many of the better-paid jobs in the government bodies which, under the authority of the Viceroy (with his residence in the Phoenix Park in the city), administered both the city and the country at large. The excluded were not only those suspected of disloyalty (those of advanced nationalist or republican sympathies) but many Catholics whose only wish for themselves was that they could work and live at a decent level in their own city. For many such only the world of clerking, serving as a shop assistant or as a low-paid official in some government office stood between them and the kind of undignified scrounging practised by the Corleys and Lenehans of this economically depressed and unjust world.

If economic life in the city for the majority of the city's inhabitants is adequately represented by the crowd of spectators who in 'After the Race' form a 'channel of poverty and inaction' through which 'the continent sped its wealth and industry', we can readily understand then why money plays a distinctive role in this text. We learn here that Eveline earns a weekly wage of seven shillings, that Mrs Mooney's young men in 'The Boarding House' pay fifteen shillings a week for board and lodgings, that Farrington is so far gone in alcoholic dependency in 'Counterparts' that he spends six shillings (having pawned his watch) on drink in one evening, which must represent a substantial drain on his family's only visible means of support. We learn too that Maria in 'Clay' has two half-crowns and some coppers (pennies) in her purse when she steps out for her evening visit. The fact that she expends almost half this sum on an intended present which she leaves on the tram adds, of course, a note of pathetic extravagance to this tale of frustration and evasion. For the world of *Dubliners* is economically exiguous, a place of venal money-grubbing, fiscal prudence and aggressive financial insistence. Little Chandler in 'A Little Cloud' still has the furniture to pay for, the electoral workers in 'Ivy Day in the Committee Room' labour for meagre payment or the small reward of a bottle or two of stout, while Kathleen Kearney's father in 'A Mother' 'by paying a small sum every week into a society ... ensured for both his daughters a dowry of one hundred pounds each when they came to the age of twenty-four'. Which doesn't of course inhibit Kathleen's mother from loudly insisting that her daughter be paid a full fee of eight guineas even when a depleted concert-hall audience makes it unlikely that the management can meet its commitments. All of which gives a peculiar relevance to the work as a whole of the gold coin in 'Two Gallants', which reveals to us the full parasitical horror of the relationships explored in that grim study of colonial degradation.

For Joyce in *Dubliners* does not fail to identify the source of much of the human misery he so clinically diagnoses. The coin in question is a gold sovereign with its associations of regal power, sovereignty, and ultimate authority. Corley and Lenehan in their circular peregrinations about the city in pursuit of their unworthy ends, traverse a public domain dominated by the buildings and the street names associated with that Anglo-Irish Protestant Ascendancy which served as the bulwark of British power in the land. It is outside the Kildare Street Club, bastion of Ascendancy influence and prejudice, that they come on a symbol of their nation's servitude and abuse as if to indict a polity in which they themselves are representative victims even as they exemplify the grosser forms of moral turpitude:

They walked along Nassau Street and then turned into Kildare Street. Not far from the porch of the club a harpist stood in the roadway, playing to a little ring of listeners. He plucked at the wires heedlessly, glancing quickly from time to time at the face of each new-comer and from time to time, wearily also, at the sky. His harp too, heedless that her coverings had fallen about her knees, seemed weary alike of the eyes of strangers and of her master's hands.

The image of Ireland as a wronged woman which this passage brings to mind links Joyce in fact with a tradition of nationalism in which Ireland has variously been entered as the Poor Old Woman, the Hag of Beare and Kathleen ni Houlihan, all legendary figures in the tragic narratives the country's history has generated. But there is perhaps a more immediate pertinence in this choice of imagery in a text where it is women who so frequently bear the brunt of male oppression, which in the sexual sphere may be the moral and actual equivalent of imperial domination in the political. Although only three of the fifteen stories offer a woman as a central character and although the first three stories, all dealing with the growth to consciousness of a young boy and the final story 'The Dead' with Gabriel Conroy's framing conclusive vision, seem to valorize the masculine viewpoint in the narrative perspectives of the work as a whole, the reader is aware through much of the book that it is women who suffer the most severe victimage in the narrow confines of this disabling social milieu. It is Eveline's mother whose 'life of common-place sacrifices' closes in 'final craziness'. (No critic has yet suggested that the famous crux 'Derevaun Seraun' may be read as a tragic instance of '*écriture feminine*'.) It is Maria who must unknowingly await the death that the auguries have forecast. It is Mrs Sinico in 'A Painful Case' who dies an undignified, accidental death, which is

the stuff of the coroner's court and of journalistic invasion
of her private, drunken misery. Throughout we hear the
accents of female distress, and we witness its terrible
silences: 'The men that is now is only all palaver and
what they can get out of you'; 'I think he died for me';
'She stood still for an instant like an angry stone image';
'When they came out of the Park they walked in silence
towards the tram; but here she began to tremble so
violently that, fearing another collapse on her part, he
bade her good-bye quickly and left her'; 'Amid the seas
she sent a cry of anguish! . . . She set her white face to
him, passive, like a helpless animal. Her eyes gave him no
sign of love or farewell or recognition.'

Employment opportunities for young women in Joyce's
Dublin were even more restricted than those for men.
The teaching and nursing professions were almost entirely
the preserves of those in religious life. Married women
did manage to gain a toe-hold on the commercial world
as shopkeepers and landladies but the capital for such
enterprises was usually supplied by inheritance or marriage. In a country where marriages were often postponed
to very advanced ages indeed, marital opportunities were
few. So outside of domestic service, a post as a shop
assistant, secretarial work, of the kind Polly Mooney
undertakes for a time in 'The Boarding House', only
Dublin's rich musical life offered any real chance of a
satisfying career. *Dubliners* as Florence L. Walzl has
noted 'is full of musicians of all ages and talent'[12] so it is
not surprising that the Misses Morkan and Mary Jane, in
'The Dead' have made their lives in the musical world
and that Mrs Kearney is crudely ambitious for her musical
daughter in 'A Mother'. Indeed Dublin's musical vitality
is the only aspect of civic life in the city to which Joyce
seems able to extend any kind of approval. While Dublin's
politics in 'Ivy Day in the Committee Room', and its

religion, in 'The Sisters' and in 'Grace' are treated with single-minded contempt, at least its musical enthusiasms are allowed a certain sentimental charm and some dignity. Yet even music has been compromised in this depressing city, by its implication in the new nationalism which is a further object of Joyce's satiric impatience in *Dubliners*, as 'A Mother' makes clear.

Not all Irishmen and women were content to acquiesce in the provincial lethargy and colonial subjugation which Joyce so intently documented in *Dubliners*. In fact in the years in which these stories are largely set, two movements brought together individuals who were earnest to ameliorate Ireland's lot through political and cultural endeavour. The first of these was the Irish Ireland movement, at its most political in the foundation of *Cumann na nGaedheal* (Confederation of the Gaels) by Arthur Griffith in 1900 to develop the ideal of self-reliance, and at its most cultural in the Gaelic revivalism of the Gaelic League (founded 1893) which sought to encourage national self-confidence through a nativism of outlook and linguistic programme. And secondly, since the 1880s, the Irish Literary Revival, the cultural brain-child of W. B. Yeats, Lady Gregory and their literary confederates, had sought to reinvigorate a depleted Irish cultural condition through contact with an ancient Celtic spirituality by means of an English language literature which might rekindle the authentic national fire.

In 1906 Joyce wrote to his brother Stanislaus about the Irish Ireland movement as it manifested itself in a new political power in the land: 'You ask me what I would substitute for parliamentary agitation in Ireland. I think the *Sinn Fein* policy would be more effective.' He added however: 'If the Irish programme did not insist on the Irish language I suppose I could call myself a nationalist. As it is, I am content to recognise myself an exile: and, prophetically, a repudiated one.' (*Letters, II*, 187) It was unlikely that Joyce's muted endorsement of *Sinn Féin's* abstentionist policy (developed concurrently with many of the incidents recorded in *Dubliners*) in contrast to the parliamentary tactics of the Home Rule Party, could long have survived his exposure to the less than attractive aspects of Griffith's political personality. While there may have been something in *Sinn Féin's* protectionist economic theories and policy of parliamentary abstention to appeal to Joyce's nationalism, Griffith's lack of social-ist feeling was a signal deficiency to a writer whose continental experience was of serious class politics in Italy. Also, to the cosmopolitan Joyce, Griffith's anti-semitic xenophobia was intolerable. He could not have failed to recognize that Griffith's newspaper, *Sinn Féin*, contained noxious matter: 'What I object to most of all in his paper is that it is educating the people of Ireland on the old pap of racial hatred whereas anyone can see that if the Irish question exists, it exists for the Irish proletariat chiefly.' (*Letters, II*, 167) *Dubliners* therefore makes little of the cultural programme of Irish Ireland which Griffith commended to his readers. The attempt to revive the Irish language receives short shrift in Joyce's telling portrait of an enthusiast in the person of Miss Ivors in 'The Dead', all coquettish mischief-making and puritan ardour. Likewise the musical opportunism of Kathleen Kearney and her mother in 'A Mother' provokes the Joycean contempt: 'Soon the name of Miss Kathleen Kearney began to be heard often on people's lips. People said she was very clever at music and a very nice girl and, moreover, that she was a believer in the language move-ment. Mrs Kearney was well content at this.'

So Joyce saw nothing in the cultural project of deliber-ate Hibernicization that Griffith and the Irish Ireland movement had in hand. It was not, however, because he held the activities of their principal rivals in the cultural field (the writers and thinkers associated with the Irish Literary Revival) in very much greater esteem. Certainly he leapt to the defence of Yeats and the Irish Literary Theatre and to the defence of Synge when their work had encountered opposition from the very forces that energized Irish Ireland: xenophobia and an aggressive puritanical nativism. But, while he recognized Yeats's genius, the elder man's way of discovering an artistic vocation through contact with the soil and in an idealization of a heroic Celtic past was scarcely his, committed disciple of Ibsen and instinctive urban socialist as he was. 'Ancient Ireland' he asserted 'is dead just as ancient Egypt is dead. Its death chant has been sung, and on its gravestone has been placed the seal.'[13] And while he may allow Yeats's poem 'Who Goes With Fergus?' to echo in Stephen Dedalus's mind in the 'Telemachus' episode in *Ulysses*, Joyce was altogether less than enchanted by the poetic effusions of those many imitators of Yeats, minor Irish poets of dubious talent, who, in his considerable shadow, composed poems of supposed Celtic Twilight spirituality and actual inanity. Little Chandler in 'A Little Cloud' imagines himself a putative part of this movement, though the fact that his dreams are all too materially of success indicates that Joyce considered the Celtic Twilight school to be opportunistic and lacking in artistic integrity. It was a means to easy literary success, especially in England. Indeed the portrait of Little Chandler in this story may be read as a satiric commentary on the Revival itself. For Little Chandler, so preoccupied with his hopes of a literary future when 'The English critics, perhaps, would recognise him as one of the Celtic school by reason of the melancholy tone of his poems . . .' fails, as Phillip Herring has recently noted[14] to make any real contact with the life of his own city in his walk to Corless's public house where he will meet his erstwhile friend Ignatius Gallaher. Surrounded by the squalor and misery of Dublin he becomes merely 'sad' in a literary and affected manner: 'Little Chandler gave them no thought. He picked his way deftly through all the minute vermin-like life.' Little Chandler, his mind turning to the possibility of a coterie of admirers in England for his unwritten verses – 'For the first time in his life he felt himself superior to the people he passed. . . . his soul revolted against the dull inelegance of Capel Street' – is a damning indictment of the artistic impulses of the Literary Revival as the youthful Joyce understood them. They are portrayed here as evasive, condescending and self-interested to a shocking degree.

Irish Ireland ideologues, Literary Revival propagandists and Joyce himself, whatever their differences, all did at least share one crucial thing: a belief that Ireland's ills had a source in English domination of the country. In fact Joyce the pacifist and almost lifelong exile produced what was unquestionably the most succinct account of Ireland's case against her powerful neighbour, in terms not even an ultra-nationalist could have deemed insufficiently harsh: 'She enkindled its factions and took over its treasury.'[15] But unlike most other Irish nationalists, of whatever stripe and however zealous, he was no less cogent and outspoken in his judgements on that other power in the land, the Holy Roman, Catholic and Apostolic Church, which exercised, in Joyce's view, an even more disabling, because unopposed, authority. Irish Ireland was robustly Catholic in its national chauvinism (the Faith of the Fathers serving as a ready rallying cry). The Revival writers, mostly Protestant by background and agnostic or indifferent by inclination, while sometimes closet anti-Catholics, had to be careful not to alienate by too obvious an anti-clericalism the majority they wished to influence. Joyce, inhibited neither by a patriotic nor a strategic regard for the faith of *his* fathers, and certainly not by a timid or prudent disinclination to give offence, addressed the religious issue with marked candour. 'I do not see' he stated categorically 'what good it does to fulminate against the English tyranny while the Roman tyranny occupies the palace of the soul'.[16]

Dubliners is a book of churches. In story after story we learn of church buildings, church institutions, pious practices and traditions, of Feast days, religious attitudes and assumptions, and of the ubiquitous Catechism which even the atheistic Mr Duffy in 'A Painful Case' numbers among his literary possessions. The first and what was to be the last stories in the collection, 'The Sisters' and 'Grace' ('The Dead' was completed and added subsequently in 1907, some time after the completion of 'A Little Cloud' which was the fourteenth of the stories to be finished in mid-1906) take religious matter for their subject and offer us peculiarly troubling images of Irish priesthood. 'Grace' is the more frankly satiric of these two anti-clerical studies. It makes its point with a kind of feline glee, producing a portrait of a priesthood so corrupted by egregious complacency that the subject damns himself out of his own mouth. There is something appalling, to be sure, about such invincible spiritual ignorance as it is represented in the preposterous figure of Father Purdon, but as with all satire there is the risk that enjoyment of the victim's surgical flaying can vitiate the moral force of the work itself. The altogether less directly satiric story 'The Sisters' allows, in its sombre and mysterious control of tone and its syntactical and verbal elisions, no such readerly evasion of the terrible import of a profoundly troubling image of the enfeebled sacerdotal.

Father Flynn is a paralytic whose past contains some unmentionable shame. Standing (or lying in his coffin) at the beginning of the book he seems to cast an oppressive shadow over the whole, as a malign presence of which we are reminded each time we encounter the pervasive signs of that ecclesiastical influence on Dubliners' lives that he so unpleasantly represents. For this realist text which attends so scrupulously to the details of Dublin's social and cultural geography also requires its dramatis personae to play representative roles, Miss Ivors as the Irish Ireland *Gaeilgeoir*, Little Chandler as the typical Revival poetaster, the personified harp as Ireland, Father Flynn as the corrupted priest. Father Flynn at the outset seems indeed to set the stage for a social tableau of representative types. In fact, Joyce himself, in a famous letter to Grant Richards, encouraged such symbolic reading of his work. 'My intention', he wrote,

> ... was to write a chapter of the moral history of my country and I chose Dublin for the scene because that city seemed to me the centre of paralysis. I have tried to present it to the indifferent public under four of its aspects: childhood, adolescence, maturity and public life. The stories are arranged in this order. (*Letters, II*, 134)

That Father Flynn suffers a debilitating condition which some critics have even identified with that general paralysis of the insane which characterizes the terminal stage of syphilitic infection, in a story which begins with a brooding on the words 'simony' and 'paralysis' (whatever we make of 'gnomon') seems in the light of this letter to invest him with central symbolic significance in the text as a whole. The quotation from the letter also encourages the critic to read *Dubliners*, not as a series of discrete stories, but as a work of complex structure in which the characters unknowingly arrange themselves in a modern version of an ancient trope: the ages of man.

Many critics of course tend to read *Dubliners* as an apprentice work by the master who produced *Ulysses* with its deliberate and extended analogues to existing, primary works of the imagination; *The Odyssey*, *Hamlet*. They have been encouraged by this letter (which apprises them of the fact that the work was conceived as an integral thing) to treat the text as if Joyce had already developed in *Dubliners* the method he was to employ in so thorough-going a fashion in the later work. A hint by Joyce's brother Stanislaus seemed further to justify an exegetical game of hunt the analogue. In 1941 Stanislaus released the information that 'Grace' was based on the triune structure of Dante's *Divine Comedy*, taking us from the inferno of the public house jakes, through a purgatory of convalescence to an ironic paradise in Gardiner Street. This account of the matter was then developed by no less an authority than Stuart Gilbert who, in 1946, argued that Joyce 'had employed in that remarkable story "Grace", a technique combining an apocalyptic background – that of the Dantean tryptich – with wholly modern motifs'.[17] Further, in a BBC broadcast talk of 1954, Stanislaus reconfirmed the presence of a Dantean parallel to the structure of the tale. Significantly, the critics were more inclined to respond interpretively to this element in Stanislaus's talk than to his categorical denial that his brother had intended, as an earlier critic had argued, that Maria in 'Clay' should be both a witch and a figure of the Virgin Mary as well as her own diminutive self. 'I am in a position', Stanislaus Joyce insisted, 'to state definitely that my brother had no such subtleties in mind when he wrote the story.'[18] *Dubliners* has therefore endured a considerable amount of rather mechanical symbol hunting as if the surface of the text, with its realistic detail and subtleties of dialogue and socio/cultural allusion, can be disregarded in pursuit of some definitive interpretation rooted in a symbology which the ingenious critic has identified. It is as damage done to those finely woven textures that constitute the work's finesse, that these exercises in misguided scholarly acumen give most offence. For it is not that *Dubliners* does not possess a complex structure and a detailed symbolism, for all the realism it also achieves, but that such readings direct attention away from a full encounter with the individual story itself to a reductive account of some altogether simpler narrative which is a poor substitute for the true Joycean experience.

There is, of course, no doubt that Joyce the disciple of Ibsen was also deeply interested in the work of the French symbolist poets whose work he knew and whose literary movement he had learnt of in Arthur Symons' pioneering study *The Symbolist Movement in Literature* (1899). But what Joyce took from symbolism was something radically different from what, for example, his fellow-countryman W. B. Yeats (to whom Symons's book was in fact dedicated) took from it. For Yeats, symbolism offered a means whereby the poet might draw back the trembling veil of the visible to reveal transcendent realities beyond the corporeal world. He defined a symbol as 'the only possible expression of some invisible essence; a transparent lamp about a spiritual flame'.[19] For Joyce, a symbol was not so essential and therefore sacred a thing, nor was it a means to definitive truths (the symbol-hunting exegetes offer a mechanical and often vulgarized version of the Yeatsian essentialism and transcendentalism, out of key with the subtle indeterminacy and this-worldliness of the Joycean method). For Joyce the symbolic power of writing lay in its capacity, as if it were a kind of revelation or manifestation, to suggest mood, psychology, the moral significance of an occasion, without (and here Flaubert is mentor and not Ibsen) obtrusive authorial presence or palpable design upon a reader. 'I am writing', Joyce told a friend in August 1904, as he embarked upon the work which would become *Dubliners*, 'a series of epicleti – ten – for a paper. . . . I call the series *Dubliners* to betray the soul of that hemiplegia or paralysis which many consider a city'. (*Letters*, 55) The term *epicleti* here derives from the Greek Orthodox liturgy and refers to the moment in the sacrifice of the Mass when the bread and the wine are transformed by the Holy Ghost into the body and blood of Christ. At this moment of consecration the everyday realities of bread and wine are charged with spiritual significance. Given Joyce's employment of this term to describe his intentions in *Dubliners* it is not surprising that commentators have made much of a similar use of a theological term in Joyce's *Stephen Hero* which he was at work on concurrently with *Dubliners*. There he used the idea of Epiphany (literally a manifestation, but theologically the feast commemorating the manifestation of Christ's divinity to the Magi) to write of an artist's duty as he saw it:

> By an epiphany he meant a sudden spiritual transformation, whether in the vulgarity of speech or of gesture or in a memorable phrase of the mind itself. He believed that it was for the man of letters to record these epiphanies with extreme care, seeing that they are the most delicate and evanescent of moments . . . .
>
> . . . First we recognize that the object is *one* integral thing, then we recognize that it is an organized composite structure, a *thing* in fact: finally, when the relation of the parts is exquisite, when the parts are adjusted to the special point, we recognize that it is *that* thing which it is. Its soul, its whatness, leaps to us from the vestment of its appearance. The soul of the commonest object, the structure of which is so adjusted, seems to us radiant. The object achieves its epiphany.

But critics have not always been so ready to take Joyce at his word here, often failing to accept C. H. Peake's assessment that 'there could hardly be a more emphatic assertion that an epiphany was an apprehension of the thing's or person's unique particularity, and not a symbol of something else'.[20] So, when *Dubliners* gives us details of rooms, pubs, streets, churches, cityscapes, when it scrupulously attends to the to and fro of conversation, the momentary gestures of an individual, it is not because these things can be read as items in a complex process of reference to abstractions, concepts, historical and mythological analogues, systems of thought or even transcendent truths. Rather it is because it is in the givenness of the real, in time and place, that psychological, social, cultural and moral realities will reveal themselves. Not of course that the details of life in a city as burdened with history and experience as Dublin, will not carry with them associations, hints of parallel situations in the Irish and European past, in legend and mythology, and carry with them too general implications for the society observed in this exacting miniaturism of focus, to give added force to the moral urgency of the writing or to augment the sense of significance revealed. But it is in the details of the work and the complex patterns which they achieve in individual stories and in the book as a whole that meaning is in fact primarily vested. To seek to experience it as any other kind of thing is accordingly to cheat oneself of the subtle particularity of a text whose meanings are inseparable from 'the most delicate and evanescent of moments' recorded with shocking precision.

So the detail of Joyce's art in *Dubliners* is not simply the realist's involvement with a congeries of fact as a reflection in prose of a world which palpably exists before and after the act of literary composition (though realism is not the least of the artistic effects achieved in this multi-levelled text), but the strategy of a symbolist who believed that the given in the hands of an artist would speak its own radiant if disturbingly uncomfortable truths about the world. It was, Joyce believed, the artist's duty to expedite that uttering forth, that manifestation, through his placing of such epiphanic moments in a context that allowed the reader to discern their possible significance. As Stephen has it in *Stephen Hero*: 'the artist who could disentangle the subtle soul of the image from its mesh of defining circumstances most exactly and re-embody it in artistic circumstances chosen as the most exact for it in its new office, he was the supreme artist'. In *Dubliners* Joyce chooses to re-embody the details of a Dublin life he knew intimately in a context where they would inter-relate with one another to compose an interpretative statement about the city as a whole. Thus it is not only that the details of the Joycean *epicleti* in *Dubliners* enjoy the added significance that historic echo, cultural association or mythological analogue can variously provide as they seek to reveal their truths, but that they occupy a text in which patternings of incident, imagery and structure intensify the possibilities of a controlling artistic vision.

Dubliners is therefore much more than a series of sketches set in a particular place linked by an authorial preoccupation with manifestations of personal and social paralysis. It is, as numbers of critics have shown, a work which achieves a complex pattern of repetitions, parallels and restatements of theme in which detail, incident and image combine to establish a vision of life in the capital which serves as a kind of metaphor for the spiritual condition of the Irish nation as a whole. At an apparently simple level, as Brewster Ghiselin suggested in a pioneering (if somewhat too ingenious) essay,[21] the idea of escape eastwards is a constant in these tales, that happy consummation denied by a paralysis of body, affect and will, in which Father Flynn's affliction seems only the paradigmatic case. Eveline frozen in immobility at the end of

'Eveline', Mr Duffy in silence and solitude halted under a tree at the end of 'A Painful Case', the snow-capped statues in 'The Dead', stony equivalent of Gabriel Conroy's atrophied emotional life, all seem more than instances of particular fate, but emblematic of a pervasive malaise. There are too the prevailing colours of the work, the ubiquitous brown bricks of the buildings, the shadows of enclosed rooms, the darkness that seems to fall in so many of the tales that are set at day's end or at night, which means what little light does get through in these tenebrous tales is candid and cruelly revelatory, like the lamplight on the gold coin at the end of 'Two Gallants'. And that coin, so shockingly highlighted in that story reminds us of how frequently coins are the material expression in the book of economic and personal relations perverted and thwarted by dishonesty, disappointment, evasion, frustration, so that the pitiful coinages of these exchanges are the counters of a corrosive spiritual desuetude. Eating and drinking seem to play their parts too in a symbolical economy where they may or may not parody (as some critics have suggested they do [22]) the celebratory feasts of the Christian church, its communions and eucharists, but certainly lack the creative conviviality that the meal as symbolic action represents in more ample societies than that of *Dubliners*. Only in 'After the Race' is a meal 'exquisite' and the word there seems only to highlight the decadence and folly of that story's climax. Elsewhere a little sherry is taken, a plate of peas and a ginger ale hungrily consumed, Mr Duffy dines alone, drink is always to hand to sedate or inflame, so that the Dickensian largess of the hospitable Christmas board in 'The Dead' serves to rebuke both the parsimony and the grossness of many of the appetitive occasions in the earlier stories: 'the broken bread collected, the sugar and butter safe under lock and key' after breakfast in 'The Boarding

House', Lenehan's 'solitary, unique ... and recherché biscuit' and the 'real cheese' in 'Two Gallants', Farrington's 'gulp' of plain porter and a caraway seed in 'Counterparts', Gallaher's crass reduction of marital relations to a crude gustatory metaphor ('Must get a bit stale, I should think, he said') in 'A Little Cloud'.

So detail in *Dubliners* is disposed like brush-strokes in a complex canvas to compose a settled impression of a society in the grip of paralytic forces. Those broader masses of colour which we may designate incident in the text also contribute to the picture, establishing its broader outlines and internal structural rhythms. The book, one observes, is framed by two stories that might exchange their titles without effecting notable damage ('Sisters' invokes the dead Father Flynn, 'The Dead' deals with a sisterly duo). Between these, stories like 'A Little Cloud' and 'Counterparts' establish patterns of similitude and contrast (in these two stories both the weak and the strong man finish at home in states of equivalent powerlessness expressed in contrasting reactions). Parallels are drawn across the pages between such texts as 'Eveline' and 'A Painful Case', in both of which a failure of nerve leaves a character in a state of terminally destructive self-denial. The frustrated boy in 'Araby' has a partner in the child-like figure of Maria in 'Clay' as they both discover disappointment at journey's end. In 'Two Gallants' a young woman is exploited by a predatory male; in 'The Boarding House' a young man is a victim of female cunning. And there is too a sense of concentrated acummulation, the basic perceptions of the Joycean vision finding more and more confirmatory perspectives as the book moves deliberately through the stages of childhood, adolescence, maturity and public life.

The publication of so complex and strategic a work as

Dubliners in 1914 with its ostensible realism and compli-
cated symbolist deployment of detail and structural pattern, whatever it may have done to aid the course of
civilization in the author's own country, most certainly
marked a chapter in the history of modern prose fiction.
For in *Dubliners* Joyce seized on certain late nineteenth-
century developments in English prose fiction and made
of them the instrument of an art that was both experimental and markedly enabling for his own development as a
writer. And in so doing he demonstrated the literary
significance of the short story as an artistic form of
remarkable economy and charged implication.

When George Russell suggested to the young Joyce in
1904 that he might contribute some stories to the *Irish
Homestead* and thereby make a little money he was only
pointing out an obvious feature of the literary market-
place as it then existed in the British Isles. An increasingly
literate (but often ill-educated) populace in Britain and
Ireland was avid for magazines and newspapers of all
kinds. Commercially minded publishers were happy to
satisfy this new appetite. Their productions often contained short tales, sketches, impressions of places and
persons, the sort of thing which might while away an
hour or two in the evening after work or enliven a train
journey from suburb to city. At popular level, the stories
of such as Conan Doyle in the *Strand Magazine*, with his
famous detective Sherlock Holmes, achieved enormous
success. Other magazines indulged a reading public that
sought sensationalist stimulation, adventure yarns and
stories of imperial exploit and derring-do (at their best,
as in the stories of Kipling, these achieved their own
special artistic integrity). The heyday of the great Victorian reviews (the *Cornhill, Fraser's Magazine*) with their
solemn essays and serialized novels in many episodes
seemed to have passed and the field for serious fiction

was largely abandoned to shorter, more populist, forms of writing in proliferating outlets that lacked the cultural authority of their more prestigious predecessors. However a few journals sought to stand against the tide, not by seeking to sustain archaic modes of cultural production but by a deliberate experimentalism. The psychological sketch in the *Yellow Book* with its prose excursions into the worlds of urban alienation and private perspectivism had set a fashion which bore fruit in the 1890s in collections of short prose pieces with titles like *Keynotes* and *Monochromes*. The issue as to the short story's artistic legitimacy became a matter for discussion in the more literary of the periodicals.[23] In 1898 for example, in the *Fortnightly Review*, Henry James opined that the short story 'has of late become an object of almost extravagant dissertation' and added his own voice to a debate about the fictional effects of brevity. 'Are there not', he wrote, 'two quite distinct effects to be produced by this rigour of brevity – the two that best make up for the many left unachieved as requiring a larger canvas? The one with which we are most familiar is that of the detached incident, single and sharp, as clear as a pistol-shot; the other of rarer performance, is that of the impression, comparatively generalised – simplified, foreshortened, reduced to a particular perspective – of a complexity or a continuity.'[24]

Even as a schoolboy Joyce seems to be have been aware of the advanced taste of the nineties. His brother Stanislaus tells us that in his last year at Belvedere Joyce began to write a series of sketches which he called most fashionably *Silhouettes* and the vignette which Stanislaus describes as one of these is something one might have expected to have come upon in the *Yellow Book* or the *Savoy Magazine*. But it also, as Stanislaus recognized, anticipated 'the first three stories of *Dubliners* . . . and described a row of mean little houses along which the narrator passes after nightfall'.[25]

Contemporary commentators on the short story were not only exercised by such issues of technique as James addressed in the *Fortnightly Review*. Questions of subject matter were also raised. Common life was deemed an appropriate theme. Indeed Henry James could reckon the end of the nineteenth century as 'the advent of a time for looking more closely into the old notion, that to have a quality of his own, a writer must needs draw his sap from his soil of origin'.[26] But it was James's fellow American, the short story writer and novelist Bret Harte (from whose novel *Gabriel Conroy* Joyce took a name and an imagery of general snow for 'The Dead') who stated this doctrine most explicitly with reference to collections of short prose sketches and tales. Considering the rise of the short story in his native America he wrote in 1899:

> It would seem evident, therefore, that the secret of the American short story was the treatment of characteristic American life, with the absolute knowledge of its peculiarities and sympathy with its methods; with no fastidious ignoring of its habitual expression, or the inchoate poetry that may be found even hidden in its slang; with no moral determination except that which may be the legitimate outcome of the story itself; with no more elimination than may be necessary for the artistic conception, and never from the fear of the 'fetish' of conventionalism.[27]

It was Joyce's genius in *Dubliners* to combine these strands of thought about the short form in a work which exploited the technical experimentalism of the psychological sketch and prose impression while sustaining an unshakeable aesthetic commitment to life as it was really lived in a provincial place as the proper subject-matter of this developing art form. The result was a work both uncompromisingly objective in its moral envisioning and tantalizingly inscrutable in its subtle significations. For

Dubliners, as well as being a chapter in the moral history of the author's race, the entirely persuasive portrait of a city, is also a study of the obliquities, evasions and uncertainties of human consciousness in its strange occupancy of a world at once so apparently answerable to language but at the same time so indifferent to its suasions.

Joyce the prose technician, in defending *Dubliners* to Grant Richards, spoke of a style of 'scrupulous meanness' (*Letters, II,* 134) as the appropriate expressive tool for his diminished subject-matter in *Dubliners*. This, in several of the stories, reveals itself as a mode of free indirect style which, purporting in the third person to offer the objective account, in fact enters the consciousness of a protagonist and makes that character's habitual formulations the stuff of narrative. Maria's euphemistic evasions in 'Clay' are only the most obvious example of such a process in a text which is much less stable in tone and register than Joyce's own description would suggest. The fact that the source of the book partly rises in the psychological sketch, with its employment of free indirect style to individualize a fictional portrait, gives a troubling indeterminacy to many of the work's key passages. It is as if such passages are half in the world of dramatized thought and feeling and half in the world of those many facts which give the book its sense of a real world made manifest in oppressive, burdening detail. There is present both the given Dublin of the turn of the century, with the social and cultural signs and symbols it embodies (which justifies in its complex reality the act of annotation that this edition attempts) and the insubstantial incoherencies of memory, desire, hope, defeat, which constitute the ambiguities and unknowabilities of the affective zone. *Dubliners* is accordingly an enigmatic text for all the realism of its apprehension of its world and for all its moral certitudes, its epiphanic realizations. It offers fragments of human experience that may or may not amount to defining moments. So where a sense of definition, of closure, is attained it is often of a kind so problematic as to constitute a new deferment of readerly gratification. In some stories, 'Two Gallants', 'Grace', we are cunningly brought to a conclusive revelation that ironizes the preceding matter, instructing us in the superficiality of our prior attention. In others, 'A Painful Case', 'Eveline', we are allowed to realize the limits of a consciousness that has been made available to us but are left with a sense only of the futility and oppressiveness of the knowledge we have gained. And in some other stories, the first three tales of childhood in particular, when it is the protagonist himself or herself who seems to apprehend a truth about the events that have occurred in the text, it is in terms so opaque as to be undecidable to the reader. How, for example, do the concluding sentences in 'An Encounter' and 'Araby' relate to the events and psychological matter they apparently climax? Why does the narrator feel that they do? What advancement of learning does the narrator in 'The Sisters' undergo as he records a disturbing fragment of conversation: 'Wide-awake and laughing-like to himself. . . . So then, of course, when they saw that, that made them think that there was something gone wrong with him. . . .'? What exactly had Polly been waiting for at the end of 'A Boarding House'? Is it simply the closing of the trap in which she had played the part of willing bait or does the arch, slightly mysterious tone in which we are encouraged to read her mental state suggest we should check our reading for hidden motives?

It is not only in its epiphanic endings or in those moments when epiphany seems at hand that *Dubliners* functions as an oddly unstable text, ostensibly all naturalistic detail and yet knowingly at work in the recesses and secrecies of consciousness where the world can seem a mere trace, a shadow amid the perplexing echoes of language. Conversations in this book are also characteristically ellipitcal, the words deployed with a sense of absences and deletion, of things said and unsaid. 'The Sisters' is obviously a heuristic entry in the book with its brooding on half-comprehended, half-stated conversations, its identification of the word 'gnomon' (in one of its meanings, a parallelogram with a part missing) as somehow textually significant. Taking that tale at its word, we are ready for the unsung stanza in 'Clay', the absent hero who is present between the lines throughout 'Ivy Day in the Committee Room', the absent lover in 'The Dead'. And we are ready too for the misinterpretations, the vulgar errors, the confusions of so much of the talk in this book where even the political activists of 'Ivy Day' cannot, it seems, remember in 1902 that Queen Victoria had visited Dublin as recently as 1900.

To read *Dubliners* as a moment in the history of the short story in English is therefore to become aware of the experimental nature of the work, of how its effects break the canons of classical realism, for all the sense of context the writing also manages. These fragmentary sketches and impressions arranged in complex pattern with detailed symbolist purport, these almost plotless stories together compose a text where consciousness seems a disjunct, isolated thing (no protagonist knows any other socially, even in the narrow world of the small city Joyce takes as subject, a clear infringement of realistic probabilities) its moral motions limited by the available linguistic resources, its spiritual condition more available to scrutiny over a few hours of trivial event than over a lifetime of significant action. Which is of course to say that *Dubliners* is also a chapter in the history of Modernism, its textual strategies already anticipating the linguistic, stylistic, temporal and structural achievements of *Ulysses*, which itself had a source in a projected tale for the volume in hand.

Dubliners is more, however, than just a particularly intriguing contribution to the Modernist movement and a stage in the development of the modern short story in English. It is a work that, for all the fragmentary, oblique quality of its procedures, its slight air of self-congratulatory hermeticism amid the sepia tints of an early photographic realism, its occasional purple patch, compels attention by the power of its unique vision of the world, its controlling sense of the truths of human experience as its author discerned them in a defeated, colonial city. Those truths provoked anger, an almost vindictive rejection of the Ireland that would or could not transcend them, the satiric shudder of recoil from the terrible and cruel squalor of so much that takes place in these tales (marital abuse, violence against a child, sexual exploitation and entrapment, casual political corruption, religious hypocrisy). But they do not, I believe, involve Joyce as artist in a rejection of the people in his stories ('my poor fledglings, poor Corley, poor Ignatius Gallaher' he calls them with proprietorial affection as he compares them to characters in Thomas Hardy's short stories, *Letters, II*, 199) who have no choice, it seems, but to endure the diminished lives they live. The emotional consequence of this kind of engagement with his material is, as Marilyn French has recently pointed out,[28] a peculiarly Joycean synthesis of irony with compassion. The subject-matter is the object of a satirist's ironic diagnostic skill, the affective contents engage his humanistic sympathies, almost despite himself, in an ambiguity of response that is as artistically complex as it is emotionally profound. And this is as true of a story like 'A Little Cloud' or 'Clay' as it is of the extraordinarily developed ironies, ambiguities and final

incertitudes in 'The Dead', with which the book con-
cludes. There is, too, even in so grim a set of stories as
these are, the comedic impulse at work, lightening the
mood of 'Grace' (whatever the central irony) where we
eavesdrop on a marvellously preposterous conversation
around Mr Kernan's sick-bed. It is as if for a moment in
the text Joyce reveals the bonding agent, comedy, which
allows him to bring irony and compassion together, to
show himself as the comic artist in the making who
would eventually give the world *Ulysses* in which some of
Dubliners' Dubliners (some of those gathered about Mr
Kernan's bed indeed) would achieve comedic fictional
apotheosis and occupy a text where variegated perspectives and a mythic method would bring to full term the
embryonic Modernism of this precociously experimental
and achieved book.

Terence Brown,
Trinity College, Dublin.

NOTES

1. Stanislaus Joyce, *My Brother's Keeper*, ed. with an introduction by Richard Ellmann, with a preface by T. S. Eliot,
London: Faber and Faber, 1958, p. 237.
2. Quoted by Richard Ellmann, op. cit., p. 18.
3. 'The Day of the Rabblement' was the title Joyce gave to an
essay he wrote in 1901 attacking the provincialism of the
Irish theatre and its pandering to a public made up of 'the
most belated race in Europe'.
4. B. J. Tysdahl, *Joyce and Ibsen: A Study In Literary Influence*, Oslo: Norwegian Universities Press/New York:
Humanities Press, 1968, p. 32.
5. James Joyce, *The Critical Writings of James Joyce*, ed.
Ellsworth Mason and R. Ellmann, London: Faber and
Faber, 1959, p. 45.

6. *Ibid.*, p. 65.

7. *Ibid.*, p. 63.

8. Quoted by C. H. Peake, *James Joyce: the Citizen and the Artist*, London: Edward Arnold, 1977, p. 149.

9. Mary E. Daly, *Dublin, The Deposed Capital: A Social and Economic History*, 1860–1914, Cork: Cork University Press, 1984, p. 2.

10. Daly, op. cit., p. 15. Interestingly Daly identifies 'a growing sense of economic crisis from the middle of the first decade of the century, one which does not appear to have been caused by agricultural recession as in the 1880s, but seems somehow endemic to the city'. Daly, op. cit., p. 64. This is of course at just the time Joyce was working on his collection of Dublin stories.

11. F. S. L. Lyons, 'James Joyce's Dublin', *20th Century Studies*, 4 (November, 1970), p. 11.

12. Florence L. Walzl, '*Dubliners*', in *A Companion to Joyce Studies*, eds. Zack Bowen and James F. Carens, Westport, Conn./London, England: Greenwood Press, 1984, p. 198. I am indebted to this study for its information on female employment opportunities in Joyce's Dublin.

13. Joyce, *Critical Writings*, p. 173.

14. Phillip F. Herring, *Joyce's Uncertainty Principle*, Princeton, New Jersey: Princeton University Press, 1987, p. 59.

15. James Joyce, *Critical Writings*, p. 166.

16. *Ibid.*, p. 173.

17. Stuart Gilbert, 'James Joyce', in *Writers of To-day*, ed. Denys Val Baker, London: Sidgwick and Jackson, 1946, p. 2.

18. Stanislaus Joyce, 'The Background to *Dubliners*', *Listener*, LI (1954), p. 526.

19. W. B. Yeats, 'William Blake And His Illustrations To The *Divine Comedy*', *Essays and Introductions*, London: Macmillan, 1961, p. 116.

20. Peake, op. cit., p. 9.

21. Brewster Ghiselin, 'The Unity of Joyce's *Dubliners*', *Accent*, 16 (1956), pp. 75–88; 196–231. Some of this essay is republished in *Dubliners*, the Viking Critical Library edition, eds.

Robert Scholes and A. Walton Litz, New York: the Viking
Press, 1969, pp. 316–32. See also Walzl, op. cit., pp. 193–
216.

22. See Florence L. Walzl, 'Symbolism in Joyce's "Two Gallants"', *James Joyce Quarterly*, II (Winter 1965) pp. 73–81
and A. Walton Litz, 'Two Gallants' in *James Joyce's* Dubliners: *Critical essays*, ed. Clive Hart, London: Faber and
Faber, 1969, pp. 62–71.

23. I am indebted in my placing of Joyce's work in the con-
text of the development of the short story form to Clare
Hanson, *Short Stories and Short Fictions, 1880–1980*,
London: Macmillan, 1985 and Valerie Shaw, *The Short
Story: A Critical Introduction*, London and New York;
Longman, 1983.

24. Henry James, 'The Story-Teller At Large: Mr Henry
Harland', *Fortnightly Review*, New Series, No. CCCLXXVI
(April, 1898), p. 652.

25. Stanislaus Joyce, op. cit., p. 104.

26. James. op. cit., p. 650.

27. Bret Harte, 'The Rise of the Short Story', *Cornhill Magazine*, New Series Vol. VII (July, 1899), p. 8. The remarkable
similarity between this description of the short story's poten-
tial and Joyce's exploitation of the form tempts one to
imagine that the young Joyce (who clearly was aware of
English periodical literature, since he sent his essay on Ibsen
to the *Fortnightly Review* in 1900) had read this essay when
he embarked on *Dubliners*. And it may indeed have been
his memory of the fact that one of Harte's stories ('The
Luck of the Roaring Camp') had, in Harte's own words,
been 'objected to by both printer and publisher, virtually
for not being in the conventional line of subject, treatment,
and morals' (Harte, op. cit., p. 7) that prompted him in
1906, as his own problems with a printer mounted, to
enquire of his brother, 'Ought I buy a volume of Bret
Harte.' (*Letters, II,*. p. 166) In 1920 the library which Joyce
left behind him in Trieste contained two of Harte's books,
Gabriel Conroy (which gave him a name for his own story
'The Dead') and *Tales of the West*. See Richard Ellmann,

The Consciousness of Joyce, London: Faber and Faber, 1977, p. 111.

28. In a public lecture in University College, Dublin, 2 February 1991.

The text used for this edition of *Dubliners* is the
Viking Critical Library edition (1969) edited by
Robert Scholes and A. Walton Litz and published
by Penguin Books (1976).
The 1969 edition incorporated further corrections
by Robert Scholes, based on suggestions by Jack
P. Dalton, to Scholes's Viking Press edition of
1968 (text of *Dubliners* corrected by Robert
Scholes in consultation with Richard Ellmann).

THE SISTERS

There was no hope for him this time: it was the third stroke. Night after night I had passed the house (it was vacation time) and studied the lighted square of window: and night after night I had found it lighted in the same way, faintly and evenly. If he was dead, I thought, I would see the reflection of candles on the darkened blind for I knew that two candles must be set at the head of a corpse. He had often said to me: *I am not long for this world*, and I had thought his words idle. Now I knew they were true. Every night as I gazed up at the window I said softly to myself the word *paralysis*. It had always sounded strangely in my ears, like the word *gnomon*[1] in the Euclid[2] and the word *simony*[3] in the Catechism.[4] But now it sounded to me like the name of some maleficent and sinful being. It filled me with fear, and yet I longed to be nearer to it and to look upon its deadly work.

Old Cotter was sitting at the fire, smoking, when I came downstairs to supper. While my aunt was ladling out my stirabout[5] he said, as if returning to some former remark of his:

—No, I wouldn't say he was exactly . . . but there was something queer . . . there was something uncanny about him. I'll tell you my opinion . . .

He began to puff at his pipe, no doubt arranging his opinion in his mind. Tiresome old fool! When we knew him first he used to be rather interesting, talking of faints and worms;[6] but I soon grew tired of him and his endless stories about the distillery.

—I have my own theory about it, he said. I think it

was one of those ... peculiar cases ... But it's hard to say. . . .

He began to puff again at his pipe without giving us his theory. My uncle saw me staring and said to me:

—Well, so your old friend is gone, you'll be sorry to hear.

—Who? said I.

—Father Flynn.

—Is he dead?

—Mr Cotter here has just told us. He was passing by the house.

I knew that I was under observation so I continued eating as if the news had not interested me. My uncle explained to old Cotter.

—The youngster and he were great friends. The old chap taught him a great deal, mind you; and they say he had a great wish for him.[7]

—God have mercy on his soul, said my aunt piously.

Old Cotter looked at me for a while. I felt that his little beady black eyes were examining me but I would not satisfy him by looking up from my plate. He returned to his pipe and finally spat rudely into the grate.

—I wouldn't like children of mine, he said, to have too much to say to a man like that.

—How do you mean, Mr Cotter? asked my aunt.

—What I mean is, said old Cotter, it's bad for children. My idea is: let a young lad run about and play with young lads of his own age and not be ... Am I right, Jack?

—That's my principle, too, said my uncle. Let him learn to box his corner. That's what I'm always saying to that Rosicrucian there:[8] take exercise. Why, when I was a nipper every morning of my life I had a cold bath, winter and summer. And that's what stands to me now. Education is all very fine and large. . . . Mr Cotter might take a pick of that leg of mutton, he added to my aunt.

—No, no, not for me, said old Cotter.

My aunt brought the dish from the safe and laid it on the table.

—But why do you think it's not good for children, Mr Cotter? she asked.

—It's bad for children, said old Cotter, because their minds are so impressionable. When children see things like that, you know, it has an effect. . . .

I crammed my mouth with stirabout for fear I might give utterance to my anger. Tiresome old red-nosed imbecile!

It was late when I fell asleep. Though I was angry with old Cotter for alluding to me as a child I puzzled my head to extract meaning from his unfinished sentences. In the dark of my room I imagined that I saw again the heavy grey face of the paralytic. I drew the blankets over my head and tried to think of Christmas. But the grey face still followed me. It murmured; and I understood that it desired to confess something. I felt my soul receding into some pleasant and vicious region; and there again I found it waiting for me. It began to confess to me in a murmuring voice and I wondered why it smiled continually and why the lips were so moist with spittle. But then I remembered that it had died of paralysis and I felt that I too was smiling feebly as if to absolve the simoniac of his sin.[9]

The next morning after breakfast I went down to look at the little house in Great Britain Street.[10] It was an unassuming shop, registered under the vague name of *Drapery*.[11] The drapery consisted mainly of children's bootees and umbrellas; and on ordinary days a notice used to hang in the window, saying: *Umbrellas Recovered*. No notice was visible now for the shutters were up. A crape bouquet was tied to the door-knocker with ribbon. Two poor women and a telegram boy were reading the card pinned on the crape. I also approached and read:

July 1st, 1895 [12]
The Rev. James Flynn (formerly of
S. Catherine's Church,[13] Meath Street),
aged sixty-five years.
R.I.P.[14]

The reading of the card persuaded me that he was dead and I was disturbed to find myself at check. Had he not been dead I would have gone into the little dark room behind the shop to find him sitting in his arm-chair by the fire, nearly smothered in his great-coat. Perhaps my aunt would have given me a packet of High Toast[15] for him and this present would have roused him from his stupefied doze. It was always I who emptied the packet into his black snuff-box for his hands trembled too much to allow him to do this without spilling half the snuff about the floor. Even as he raised his large trembling hand to his nose little clouds of smoke dribbled through his fingers over the front of his coat. It may have been these constant showers of snuff which gave his ancient priestly garments their green faded look for the red handkerchief, blackened, as it always was, with the snuff-stains of a week, with which he tried to brush away the fallen grains, was quite inefficacious.

I wished to go in and look at him but I had not the courage to knock. I walked away slowly along the sunny side of the street, reading all the theatrical advertisements in the shopwindows as I went. I found it strange that neither I nor the day seemed in a mourning mood and I felt even annoyed at discovering in myself a sensation of freedom as if I had been freed from something by his death. I wondered at this for, as my uncle had said the night before, he had taught me a great deal. He had studied in the Irish college in Rome[16] and he had taught me to pronounce Latin properly.[17] He had told me stories about the catacombs[18] and about Napoleon Bonaparte,[19] and he had explained to me the meaning of the different ceremonies of the Mass[20] and of the different vestments worn by the priest.[21] Sometimes he had amused himself by putting difficult questions to me, asking me what one should do in certain circumstances or whether such and such sins were mortal or venial[22] or only imperfections. His questions showed me how complex and mysterious were certain institutions of the Church which I had always regarded as the simplest acts. The duties of the priest towards the Eucharist[23] and towards the secrecy of the confessional[24] seemed so grave to me that I wondered how anybody had ever found in himself the courage to undertake them; and I was not surprised when he told me that the fathers of the Church[25] had written books as thick as the *Post Office Directory*[26] and as closely printed as the law notices in the newspaper, elucidating all these intricate questions. Often when I thought of this I could make no answer or only a very foolish and halting one upon which he used to smile and nod his head twice or thrice. Sometimes he used to put me through the responses[27] of the Mass which he had made me learn by heart; and, as I pattered, he used to smile pensively and nod his head, now and then pushing huge pinches of snuff up each nostril alternately. When he smiled he used to uncover his big discoloured teeth and let his tongue lie upon his lower lip – a habit which had made me feel uneasy in the beginning of our acquaintance before I knew him well.

As I walked along in the sun I remembered old Cotter's words and tried to remember what had happened afterwards in the dream. I remembered that I had noticed long velvet curtains and a swinging lamp of antique fashion. I felt that I had been very far away, in some land where the customs were strange – in Persia,[28] I thought. . . . But I could not remember the end of the dream.

In the evening my aunt took me with her to visit the house of mourning. It was after sunset; but the window-panes of the houses that looked to the west reflected the tawny gold of a great bank of clouds. Nannie received us in the hall; and, as it would have been unseemly to have shouted at her, my aunt shook hands with her for all. The old woman pointed upwards interrogatively and, on my aunt's nodding, proceeded to toil up the narrow staircase before us, her bowed head being scarcely above the level of the banister-rail. At the first landing she stopped and beckoned us forward encouragingly towards the open door of the dead-room. My aunt went in and the old woman, seeing that I hesitated to enter, began to beckon to me again repeatedly with her hand.

I went in on tiptoe. The room through the lace end of the blind was suffused with dusky golden light amid which the candles looked like pale thin flames. He had been coffined. Nannie gave the lead and we three knelt down at the foot of the bed. I pretended to pray but I could not gather my thoughts because the old woman's mutterings distracted me. I noticed how clumsily her skirt was hooked at the back and how the heels of her cloth boots were trodden down all to one side. The fancy came to me that the old priest was smiling as he lay there in his coffin.

But no. When we rose and went up to the head of the bed I saw that he was not smiling. There he lay, solemn and copious, vested as for the altar,[29] his large hands loosely retaining a chalice.[30] His face was very truculent, grey and massive, with black cavernous nostrils and circled by a scanty white fur. There was a heavy odour in the room – the flowers.

We blessed ourselves[31] and came away. In the little
room downstairs we found Eliza seated in his arm-chair
in state. I groped my way towards my usual chair in the
corner while Nannie went to the sideboard and brought
out a decanter of sherry and some wine-glasses. She set
these on the table and invited us to take a little glass of
wine. Then, at her sister's bidding, she poured out the
sherry into the glasses and passed them to us. She pressed
me to take some cream crackers also but I declined
because I thought I would make too much noise eating
them. She seemed to be somewhat disappointed at my
refusal and went over quietly to the sofa where she sat
down behind her sister. No one spoke: we all gazed at
the empty fireplace.

My aunt waited until Eliza sighed and then said:

—Ah, well, he's gone to a better world.

Eliza sighed again and bowed her head in assent. My
aunt fingered the stem of her wine-glass before sipping a
little.

—Did he . . . peacefully? she asked.

—O, quite peacefully, ma'am, said Eliza. You couldn't
tell when the breath went out of him. He had a beautiful
death, God be praised.

—And everything . . .?[32]

—Father O'Rourke was in with him a Tuesday and
anointed him and prepared him and all.

—He knew then?

—He was quite resigned.

—He looks quite resigned, said my aunt.

—That's what the woman we had in to wash him said.
She said he just looked as if he was asleep, he looked that
peaceful and resigned. No one would think he'd make
such a beautiful corpse.

—Yes, indeed, said my aunt.

She sipped a little more from her glass and said:

—Well, Miss Flynn, at any rate it must be a great comfort for you to know that you did all you could for him. You were both very kind to him, I must say.

Eliza smoothed her dress over her knees.

—Ah, poor James! she said. God knows we done all we could, as poor as we are – we wouldn't see him want anything while he was in it.

Nannie had leaned her head against the sofa-pillow and seemed about to fall asleep.

—There's poor Nannie, said Eliza, looking at her, she's wore out. All the work we had, she and me, getting in the woman to wash him and then laying him out and then the coffin and then arranging about the Mass in the chapel. Only for Father O'Rourke I don't know what we'd have done at all. It was him brought us all them flowers and them two candlesticks out of the chapel and wrote out the notice for the *Freeman's General*[33] and took charge of all the papers for the cemetery and poor James's insurance.[34]

—Wasn't that good of him? said my aunt.

Eliza closed her eyes and shook her head slowly.

—Ah, there's no friends like the old friends, she said, when all is said and done, no friends that a body can trust.

—Indeed, that's true, said my aunt. And I'm sure now that he's gone to his eternal reward he won't forget you and all your kindness to him.

—Ah, poor James! said Eliza. He was no great trouble to us. You wouldn't hear him in the house any more than now. Still, I know he's gone and all to that. . . .

—It's when it's all over that you'll miss him, said my aunt.

—I know that, said Eliza. I won't be bringing him in his cup of beef-tea[35] any more, nor you, ma'am, sending him his snuff. Ah, poor James!

She stopped, as if she were communing with the past and then said shrewdly:

—Mind you, I noticed there was something queer coming over him latterly. Whenever I'd bring in his soup to him I'd find him with his breviary[36] fallen to the floor, lying back in the chair and his mouth open.

She laid a finger against her nose and frowned: then she continued:

—But still and all he kept on saying that before the summer was over he'd go out for a drive one fine day just to see the old house again where we were all born down in Irishtown[37] and take me and Nannie with him. If we could only get one of them new-fangled carriages that makes no noise that Father O'Rourke told him about – them with the rheumatic wheels[38] – for the day cheap, he said, at Johnny Rush's[39] over the way there and drive out the three of us together of a Sunday evening. He had his mind set on that. . . . Poor James!

—The Lord have mercy on his soul! said my aunt.

Eliza took out her handkerchief and wiped her eyes with it. Then she put it back again in her pocket and gazed into the empty grate for some time without speaking.

—He was too scrupulous always, she said. The duties of the priesthood was too much for him. And then his life was, you might say, crossed.

—Yes, said my aunt. He was a disappointed man. You could see that.

A silence took possession of the little room and, under cover of it, I approached the table and tasted my sherry and then returned quietly to my chair in the corner. Eliza seemed to have fallen into a deep revery. We waited respectfully for her to break the silence: and after a long pause she said slowly:

—It was that chalice he broke. . . . That was the

9

beginning of it. Of course, they say it was all right, that it contained nothing,[40] I mean. But still. . . . They say it was the boy's fault.[41] But poor James was so nervous, God be merciful to him!

—And was that it? said my aunt. I heard something. . . .

Eliza nodded.

—That affected his mind, she said. After that he began to mope by himself, talking to no one and wandering about by himself. So one night he was wanted for to go on a call and they couldn't find him anywhere. They looked high up and low down; and still they couldn't see a sight of him anywhere. So then the clerk suggested to try the chapel. So then they got the keys and opened the chapel and the clerk and Father O'Rourke and another priest that was there brought in a light for to look for him. . . . And what do you think but there he was, sitting up by himself in the dark in his confession-box, wide-awake and laughing-like softly to himself?

She stopped suddenly as if to listen. I too listened; but there was no sound in the house: and I knew that the old priest was lying still in his coffin as we had seen him, solemn and truculent in death, an idle chalice on his breast.

Eliza resumed:

—Wide-awake and laughing-like to himself. . . . So then, of course, when they saw that, that made them think that there was something gone wrong with him. . . .

AN ENCOUNTER

It was Joe Dillon who introduced the Wild West[1] to us. He had a little library made up of old numbers of *The Union Jack, Pluck* and *The Halfpenny Marvel*.[2] Every evening after school we met in his back garden and arranged Indian battles.[3] He and his fat young brother Leo the idler held the loft of the stable while we tried to carry it by storm; or we fought a pitched battle on the grass. But, however well we fought, we never won siege or battle and all our bouts ended with Joe Dillon's war dance of victory. His parents went to eight-o'clock mass every morning[4] in Gardiner Street[5] and the peaceful odour of Mrs Dillon was prevalent in the hall of the house. But he played too fiercely for us who were younger and more timid. He looked like some kind of an Indian when he capered round the garden, an old tea-cosy on his head, beating a tin with his fist and yelling:

—Ya! yaka, yaka, yaka![6]

Everyone was incredulous when it was reported that he had a vocation for the priesthood.[7] Nevertheless it was true.

A spirit of unruliness diffused itself among us and, under its influence, differences of culture and constitution were waived. We banded ourselves together, some boldly, some in jest and some almost in fear: and of the number of these latter, the reluctant Indians who were afraid to seem studious or lacking in robustness, I was one. The adventures related in the literature of the Wild West were remote from my nature but, at least, they opened doors of escape. I liked better some American detective stories which were traversed from time to time by unkempt fierce and beautiful girls. Though there was nothing wrong in these stories and though their intention was sometimes literary they were circulated secretly at school. One day when Father Butler was hearing the four pages of Roman History[8] clumsy Leo Dillon was discovered with a copy of *The Halfpenny Marvel*.

—This page or this page? This page? Now, Dillon, up! *Hardly had the day* . . . Go on! What day? *Hardly had the day dawned . . .*[9] Have you studied it? What have you there in your pocket?

Everyone's heart palpitated as Leo Dillon handed up the paper and everyone assumed an innocent face. Father Butler turned over the pages, frowning.

—What is this rubbish? he said. *The Apache Chief!*[10] Is this what you read instead of studying your Roman History? Let me not find any more of this wretched stuff in this college.[11] The man who wrote it, I suppose, was some wretched scribbler that writes these things for a drink. I'm surprised at boys like you, educated, reading such stuff. I could understand it if you were . . . National School[12] boys. Now, Dillon, I advise you strongly, get at your work or . . .

This rebuke during the sober hours of school paled much of the glory of the Wild West for me and the confused puffy face of Leo Dillon awakened one of my consciences. But when the restraining influence of the school was at a distance I began to hunger again for wild sensations, for the escape which those chronicles of disorder alone seemed to offer me. The mimic warfare of the evening became at last as wearisome to me as the routine of school in the morning because I wanted real adventures to happen to myself. But real adventures, I reflected, do not happen to people who remain at home: they must be sought abroad.

The summer holidays were near at hand[13] when I made up my mind to break out of the weariness of school-life for one day at least. With Leo Dillon and a boy named Mahony I planned a day's miching.[14] Each of us saved up sixpence.[15] We were to meet at ten in the morning on the Canal Bridge.[16] Mahony's big sister was to write an excuse for him and Leo Dillon was to tell his brother to say he was sick. We arranged to go along the Wharf Road[17] until we came to the ships, then to cross in the ferryboat[18] and walk out to see the Pigeon House.[19] Leo Dillon was afraid we might meet Father Butler or someone out of the college; but Mahony asked, very sensibly, what would Father Butler be doing out at the Pigeon House. We were reassured: and I brought the first stage of the plot to an end by collecting sixpence from the other two, at the same time showing them my own sixpence. When we were making the last arrangements on the eve we were all vaguely excited. We shook hands, laughing, and Mahony said:

—Till to-morrow, mates.

That night I slept badly. In the morning I was first-comer to the bridge as I lived nearest. I hid my books in the long grass near the ashpit at the end of the garden where nobody ever came and hurried along the canal bank. It was a mild sunny morning in the first week of June. I sat up on the coping of the bridge admiring my frail canvas shoes which I had diligently pipeclayed[20] overnight and watching the docile horses pulling a tram-load of business people up the hill. All the branches of the tall trees which lined the mall[21] were gay with little light green leaves and the sunlight slanted through them on to the water. The granite stone of the bridge was beginning to be warm and I began to pat it with my hands in time to an air in my head. I was very happy.

When I had been sitting there for five or ten minutes I

saw Mahony's grey suit approaching. He came up the hill, smiling, and clambered up beside me on the bridge. While we were waiting he brought out the catapult which bulged from his inner pocket and explained some improvements which he had made in it. I asked him why he had brought it and he told me he had brought it to have some gas[22] with the birds. Mahony used slang freely, and spoke of Father Butler as Bunsen Burner.[23] We waited on for a quarter of an hour more but still there was no sign of Leo Dillon. Mahony, at last, jumped down and said:

—Come along. I knew Fatty'd funk it.

—And his sixpence . . .? I said.

—That's forfeit, said Mahony. And so much the better for us – a bob[24] and a tanner[25] instead of a bob.

We walked along the North Strand Road[26] till we came to the Vitriol Works[27] and then turned to the right along the Wharf Road.[28] Mahony began to play the Indian as soon as we were out of public sight. He chased a crowd of ragged girls, brandishing his unloaded catapult and, when two ragged boys[29] began, out of chivalry, to fling stones at us, he proposed that we should charge them. I objected that the boys were too small, and so we walked on, the ragged troop screaming after us: *Swaddlers! Swaddlers!*[30] thinking that we were Protestants because Mahony, who was dark-complexioned, wore the silver badge of a cricket[31] club in his cap. When we came to the Smoothing Iron[32] we arranged a siege; but it was a failure because you must have at least three. We revenged ourselves on Leo Dillon by saying what a funk he was and guessing how many he would get at three o'clock from Mr Ryan.

We came then near the river. We spent a long time walking about the noisy streets flanked by high stone walls, watching the working of cranes and engines and often being shouted at for our immobility by the drivers of groaning carts. It was noon when we reached the quays and, as all the labourers seemed to be eating their lunches, we bought two big currant buns and sat down to eat them on some metal piping beside the river. We pleased ourselves with the spectacle of Dublin's commerce – the barges signalled from far away by their curls of woolly smoke, the brown fishing fleet beyond Ringsend,[33] the big white sailing-vessel which was being discharged on the opposite quay. Mahony said it would be right skit[34] to run away to sea on one of those big ships and even I, looking at the high masts, saw, or imagined, the geography which had been scantily dosed to me at school gradually taking substance under my eyes. School and home seemed to recede from us and their influences upon us seemed to wane.

We crossed the Liffey[35] in the ferryboat, paying our toll to be transported in the company of two labourers and a little Jew with a bag. We were serious to the point of solemnity, but once during the short voyage our eyes met and we laughed. When we landed we watched the discharging of the graceful threemaster which we had observed from the other quay. Some bystander said that she was a Norwegian vessel. I went to the stern and tried to decipher the legend upon it but, failing to do so, I came back and examined the foreign sailors to see had any of them green eyes[36] for I had some confused notion. . . . The sailors' eyes were blue and grey and even black. The only sailor whose eyes could have been called green was a tall man who amused the crowd on the quay by calling out cheerfully every time the planks fell:

—All right! All right!

When we were tired of this sight we wandered slowly into Ringsend. The day had grown sultry, and in the windows of the grocers' shops musty biscuits lay bleaching. We bought some biscuits and chocolate which we ate sedulously as we wandered through the squalid streets where the families of the fishermen live. We could find no dairy and so we went into a huckster's shop and bought a bottle of raspberry lemonade each. Refreshed by this, Mahony chased a cat down a lane, but the cat escaped into a wide field. We both felt rather tired and when we reached the field we made at once for a sloping bank over the ridge of which we could see the Dodder.[37]

It was too late and we were too tired to carry out our project of visiting the Pigeon House. We had to be home before four o'clock lest our adventure should be discovered. Mahony looked regretfully at his catapult and I had to suggest going home by train before he regained any cheerfulness. The sun went in behind some clouds and left us to our jaded thoughts and the crumbs of our provisions.

There was nobody but ourselves in the field. When we had lain on the bank for some time without speaking I saw a man approaching from the far end of the field. I watched him lazily as I chewed one of those green stems on which girls tell fortunes. He came along by the bank slowly. He walked with one hand upon his hip and in the other hand he held a stick with which he tapped the turf lightly. He was shabbily dressed in a suit of greenish-black and wore what we used to call a jerry hat[38] with a high crown. He seemed to be fairly old for his moustache was ashen-grey. When he passed at our feet he glanced up at us quickly and then continued his way. We followed him with our eyes and saw that when he had gone on for perhaps fifty paces he turned about and began to retrace his steps. He walked towards us very slowly, always tapping the ground with his stick, so slowly that I thought he was looking for something in the grass.

He stopped when he came level with us and bade us good-day. We answered him and he sat down beside us on the slope slowly and with great care. He began to talk of the weather, saying that it would be a very hot summer and adding that the seasons had changed greatly since he was a boy – a long time ago. He said that the happiest time of one's life was undoubtedly one's school-boy days and that he would give anything to be young again. While he expressed these sentiments which bored us a little we kept silent. Then he began to talk of school and of books. He asked us whether we had read the poetry of Thomas Moore[39] or the works of Sir Walter Scott[40] and Lord Lytton.[41] I pretended that I had read every book he mentioned so that in the end he said:

—Ah, I can see you are a bookworm like myself. Now, he added, pointing to Mahony who was regarding us with open eyes, he is different; he goes in for games.

He said he had all Sir Walter Scott's works and all Lord Lytton's works at home and never tired of reading them. Of course, he said, there were some of Lord Lytton's works which boys couldn't read. Mahony asked why couldn't boys read them – a question which agitated and pained me because I was afraid the man would think I was as stupid as Mahony. The man, however, only smiled. I saw that he had great gaps in his mouth between his yellow teeth. Then he asked us which of us had the most sweethearts. Mahony mentioned lightly that he had three totties.[42] The man asked me how many had I. I answered that I had none. He did not believe me and said he was sure I must have one. I was silent.

—Tell us, said Mahony pertly to the man, how many have you yourself?

The man smiled as before and said that when he was our age he had lots of sweethearts.

—Every boy, he said, has a little sweetheart.

His attitude on this point struck me as strangely liberal in a man of his age. In my heart I thought that what he said about boys and sweethearts was reasonable. But I disliked the words in his mouth and I wondered why he shivered once or twice as if he feared something or felt a sudden chill. As he proceeded I noticed that his accent was good. He began to speak to us about girls, saying what nice soft hair they had and how soft their hands were and how all girls were not so good as they seemed to be if one only knew. There was nothing he liked, he said, so much as looking at a nice young girl, at her nice white hands and her beautiful soft hair. He gave me the impression that he was repeating something which he had learned by heart or that, magnetised by some words of his own speech, his mind was slowly circling round and round in the same orbit. At times he spoke as if he were simply alluding to some fact that everybody knew, and at times he lowered his voice and spoke mysteriously as if he were telling us something secret which he did not wish others to overhear. He repeated his phrases over and over again, varying them and surrounding them with his monotonous voice. I continued to gaze towards the foot of the slope, listening to him.

After a long while his monologue paused. He stood up slowly, saying that he had to leave us for a minute or so, a few minutes, and, without changing the direction of my gaze, I saw him walking slowly away from us towards the near end of the field. We remained silent when he had gone. After a silence of a few minutes I heard Mahony exclaim:

—I say! Look what he's doing!

As I neither answered nor raised my eyes Mahony exclaimed again:

—I say . . . He's a queer old josser![43]

—In case he asks us for our names, I said, let you be Murphy and I'll be Smith.

We said nothing further to each other. I was still

considering whether I would go away or not when the man came back and sat down beside us again. Hardly had he sat down when Mahony, catching sight of the cat which had escaped him, sprang up and pursued her across the field. The man and I watched the chase. The cat escaped once more and Mahony began to throw stones at the wall she had escaladed. Desisting from this, he began to wander about the far end of the field, aimlessly.

After an interval the man spoke to me. He said that my friend was a very rough boy and asked did he get whipped often at school. I was going to reply indignantly that we were not National School boys to be *whipped*, as he called it; but I remained silent. He began to speak on the subject of chastising boys. His mind, as if magnetised again by his speech, seemed to circle slowly round and round its new centre. He said that when boys were that kind they ought to be whipped and well whipped. When a boy was rough and unruly there was nothing would do him any good but a good sound whipping. A slap on the hand or a box on the ear was no good: what he wanted was to get a nice warm whipping. I was surprised at this sentiment and involuntarily glanced up at his face. As I did so I met the gaze of a pair of bottle-green eyes peering at me from under a twitching forehead. I turned my eyes away again.

The man continued his monologue. He seemed to have forgotten his recent liberalism. He said that if ever he found a boy talking to girls or having a girl for a sweetheart he would whip him and whip him; and that would teach him not to be talking to girls. And if a boy had a girl for a sweetheart and told lies about it then he would give him such a whipping as no boy ever got in this world. He said that there was nothing in this world he would like so well as that. He described to me how he would whip such a boy as if he were unfolding some elaborate mystery. He would love that, he said, better than anything in this world; and his voice, as he led me monotonously through the mystery, grew almost affectionate and seemed to plead with me that I should understand him.

I waited till his monologue paused again. Then I stood up abruptly. Lest I should betray my agitation I delayed a few moments pretending to fix my shoe properly and then, saying that I was obliged to go, I bade him good-day. I went up the slope calmly but my heart was beating quickly with fear that he would seize me by the ankles. When I reached the top of the slope I turned round and, without looking at him, called loudly across the field:

—Murphy!

My voice had an accent of forced bravery in it and I was ashamed of my paltry stratagem. I had to call the name again before Mahony saw me and hallooed in answer. How my heart beat as he came running across the field to me! He ran as if to bring me aid. And I was penitent; for in my heart I had always despised him a little.[44]

ARABY [1]

North Richmond Street,[2] being blind,[3] was a quiet street except at the hour when the Christian Brothers' School [4] set the boys free. An uninhabited house of two storeys stood at the blind end, detached from its neighbours in a square ground. The other houses of the street, conscious of decent lives within them, gazed at one another with brown [5] imperturbable faces.

The former tenant of our house, a priest, had died in the back drawing-room. Air, musty from having been long enclosed, hung in all the rooms, and the waste room behind the kitchen was littered with old useless papers. Among these I found a few paper-covered books, the pages of which were curled and damp: *The Abbot*, by Walter Scott,[6] *The Devout Communicant* [7] and *The Memoirs of Vidocq*.[8] I liked the last best because its leaves were yellow. The wild garden behind the house contained a central apple-tree and a few straggling bushes under one of which I found the late tenant's rusty bicycle-pump. He had been a very charitable priest; in his will he had left all his money to institutions and the furniture of his house to his sister.

When the short days of winter came dusk fell before we had well eaten our dinners. When we met in the street the houses had grown sombre. The space of sky above us was the colour of ever-changing violet and towards it the lamps of the street lifted their feeble lanterns. The cold air stung us and we played till our bodies glowed. Our shouts echoed in the silent street. The career of our play brought us through the dark muddy lanes behind the houses where we ran the gantlet of the rough tribes from the cottages, to the back doors of the dark dripping gardens where odours arose from the ashpits, to the dark odorous stables where a coachman smoothed and combed the horse or shook music from the buckled harness. When we returned to the street light from the kitchen windows had filled the areas.⁹ If my uncle was seen turning the corner we hid in the shadow until we had seen him safely housed. Or if Mangan's sister ¹⁰ came out on the doorstep to call her brother in to his tea we watched her from our shadow peer up and down the street. We waited to see whether she would remain or go in and, if she remained, we left our shadow and walked up to Mangan's steps resignedly. She was waiting for us, her figure defined by the light from the half-opened door. Her brother always teased her before he obeyed and I stood by the railings looking at her. Her dress swung as she moved her body and the soft rope of her hair tossed from side to side.

Every morning I lay on the floor in the front parlour watching her door. The blind was pulled down to within an inch of the sash so that I could not be seen. When she came out on the doorstep my heart leaped. I ran to the hall, seized my books and followed her. I kept her brown figure always in my eye and, when we came near the point at which our ways diverged, I quickened my pace and passed her. This happened morning after morning. I had never spoken to her, except for a few casual words, and yet her name was like a summons to all my foolish blood.

Her image accompanied me even in places the most hostile to romance. On Saturday evenings when my aunt went marketing I had to go to carry some of the parcels. We walked through the flaring streets, jostled by drunken men and bargaining women, amid the curses of labourers, the shrill litanies of shop-boys who stood on guard by the barrels of pigs' cheeks, the nasal chanting of street-singers, who sang a *come-all-you*[11] about O'Donovan Rossa,[12] or a ballad about the troubles in our native land.[13] These noises converged in a single sensation of life for me: I imagined that I bore my chalice[14] safely through a throng of foes. Her name sprang to my lips at moments in strange prayers and praises which I myself did not understand. My eyes were often full of tears (I could not tell why) and at times a flood from my heart seemed to pour itself out into my bosom. I thought little of the future. I did not know whether I would ever speak to her or not or, if I spoke to her, how I could tell her of my confused adoration. But my body was like a harp and her words and gestures were like fingers running upon the wires.

One evening I went into the back drawing-room in which the priest had died. It was a dark rainy evening and there was no sound in the house. Through one of the broken panes I heard the rain impinge upon the earth, the fine incessant needles of water playing in the sodden beds. Some distant lamp or lighted window gleamed below me. I was thankful that I could see so little. All my senses seemed to desire to veil themselves and, feeling that I was about to slip from them, I pressed the palms of my hands together until they trembled, murmuring: *O love! O love!* many times.

At last she spoke to me. When she addressed the first words to me I was so confused that I did not know what to answer. She asked me was I going to *Araby*. I forget whether I answered yes or no. It would be a splendid bazaar, she said; she would love to go.

—And why can't you? I asked.

While she spoke she turned a silver bracelet round and round her wrist. She could not go, she said, because there would be a retreat[15] that week in her convent. Her brother and two other boys were fighting for their caps and I was alone at the railings. She held one of the spikes, bowing her head towards me. The light from the lamp opposite our door caught the white curve of her neck, lit up her hair that rested there and, falling, lit up the hand upon the railing. It fell over one side of her dress and caught the white border of a petticoat, just visible as she stood at ease.

—It's well for you, she said.

—If I go, I said, I will bring you something.

What innumerable follies laid waste my waking and sleeping thoughts after that evening! I wished to annihilate the tedious intervening days. I chafed against the work of school. At night in my bedroom and by day in the classroom her image came between me and the page I strove to read. The syllables of the word *Araby* were called to me through the silence in which my soul luxuriated and cast an Eastern enchantment over me. I asked for leave to go to the bazaar on Saturday night. My aunt was surprised and hoped it was not some Freemason affair.[16] I answered few questions in class. I watched my master's face pass from amiability to sternness; he hoped I was not beginning to idle. I could not call my wandering thoughts together. I had hardly any patience with the serious work of life which, now that it stood between me and my desire, seemed to me child's play, ugly monotonous child's play.

On Saturday morning I reminded my uncle that I wished to go to the bazaar in the evening. He was fussing at the hallstand, looking for the hat-brush, and answered me curtly:

—Yes, boy, I know.

As he was in the hall I could not go into the front parlour and lie at the window. I left the house in bad humour and walked slowly towards the school. The air was pitilessly raw and already my heart misgave me.

When I came home to dinner my uncle had not yet been home. Still it was early. I sat staring at the clock for some time and, when its ticking began to irritate me, I left the room. I mounted the staircase and gained the upper part of the house. The high cold empty gloomy rooms liberated me and I went from room to room singing. From the front window I saw my companions playing below in the street. Their cries reached me weakened and indistinct and, leaning my forehead against the cool glass, I looked over at the dark house where she lived. I may have stood there for an hour, seeing nothing but the brown-clad figure cast by my imagination, touched discreetly by the lamplight at the curved neck, at the hand upon the railings and at the border below the dress.

When I came downstairs again I found Mrs Mercer sitting at the fire. She was an old garrulous woman, a pawnbroker's widow, who collected used stamps for some pious purpose.[17] I had to endure the gossip of the tea-table. The meal was prolonged beyond an hour and still my uncle did not come. Mrs Mercer stood up to go: she was sorry she couldn't wait any longer, but it was after eight o'clock and she did not like to be out late, as the night air was bad for her. When she had gone I began to walk up and down the room, clenching my fists. My aunt said:

—I'm afraid you may put off your bazaar for this night of Our Lord.[18]

At nine o'clock I heard my uncle's latchkey in the halldoor. I heard him talking to himself and heard the hallstand rocking when it had received the weight of his overcoat. I could interpret these signs. When he was midway through his dinner I asked him to give me the money to go to the bazaar. He had forgotten.

—The people are in bed and after their first sleep now, he said.

I did not smile. My aunt said to him energetically:

—Can't you give him the money and let him go? You've kept him late enough as it is.

My uncle said he was very sorry he had forgotten. He said he believed in the old saying: *All work and no play makes Jack a dull boy*. He asked me where I was going and, when I had told him a second time he asked me did I know *The Arab's Farewell to his Steed*.[19] When I left the kitchen he was about to recite the opening lines of the piece to my aunt.

I held a florin[20] tightly in my hand as I strode down Buckingham Street[21] towards the station. The sight of the streets thronged with buyers and glaring with gas recalled to me the purpose of my journey. I took my seat in a third-class carriage of a deserted train. After an intolerable delay the train moved out of the station slowly. It crept onward among ruinous houses and over the twinkling river. At Westland Row Station[22] a crowd of people pressed to the carriage doors; but the porters moved them back, saying that it was a special train for the bazaar. I remained alone in the bare carriage. In a few minutes the train drew up beside an improvised wooden platform. I passed out on to the road and saw by the lighted dial of a clock that it was ten minutes to ten. In front of me was a large building which displayed the magical name.

I could not find any sixpenny entrance and, fearing that the bazaar would be closed, I passed in quickly through a turnstile, handing a shilling to a weary-looking man. I found myself in a big hall girdled at half its height by a gallery. Nearly all the stalls were closed and the greater part of the hall was in darkness. I recognised a silence like that which pervades a church after a service. I walked into the centre of the bazaar timidly. A few people were gathered about the stalls which were still open. Before a curtain, over which the words *Café Chant-ant* [23] were written in coloured lamps, two men were counting money on a salver. [24] I listened to the fall of the coins.

Remembering with difficulty why I had come I went over to one of the stalls and examined porcelain vases and flowered tea-sets. At the door of the stall a young lady was talking and laughing with two young gentlemen. I remarked their English accents and listened vaguely to their conversation.

—O, I never said such a thing!

—O, but you did!

—O, but I didn't!

—Didn't she say that?

—Yes. I heard her.

—O, there's a . . . fib!

Observing me the young lady came over and asked me did I wish to buy anything. The tone of her voice was not encouraging; she seemed to have spoken to me out of a sense of duty. I looked humbly at the great jars that stood like eastern guards at either side of the dark entrance to the stall and murmured:

—No, thank you.

The young lady changed the position of one of the vases and went back to the two young men. They began to talk of the same subject. Once or twice the young lady glanced at me over her shoulder.

I lingered before her stall, though I knew my stay was useless, to make my interest in her wares seem the more real. Then I turned away slowly and walked down the middle of the bazaar. I allowed the two pennies to fall against the sixpence in my pocket. I heard a voice call from one end of the gallery that the light was out. The upper part of the hall was now completely dark.

Gazing up into the darkness I saw myself as a creature driven and derided by vanity; and my eyes burned with anguish and anger.

EVELINE [1]

She sat at the window watching the evening invade the avenue. Her head was leaned against the window curtains and in her nostrils was the odour of dusty cretonne. She was tired.

Few people passed. The man out of the last house passed on his way home; she heard his footsteps clacking along the concrete pavement and afterwards crunching on the cinder path before the new red houses. One time there used to be a field there in which they used to play every evening with other people's children. Then a man from Belfast [2] bought the field and built houses in it – not like their little brown houses but bright brick houses with shining roofs. The children of the avenue used to play together in that field – the Devines, the Waters, the Dunns, little Keogh the cripple, she and her brothers and sisters. Ernest, however, never played: he was too grown up. Her father used often to hunt them in out of the field with his blackthorn stick; but usually little Keogh used to keep *nix* [3] and call out when he saw her father coming. Still they seemed to have been rather happy then. Her father was not so bad then; and besides, her mother was alive. That was a long time ago; she and her brothers and sisters were all grown up; her mother was dead. Tizzie Dunn was dead, too, and the Waters had gone back to England. Everything changes. Now she was going to go away like the others, to leave her home.

Home! She looked round the room, reviewing all its familiar objects which she had dusted once a week for so many years, wondering where on earth all the dust came from. Perhaps she would never see again those familiar objects from which she had never dreamed of being divided. And yet during all those years she had never found out the name of the priest whose yellowing photograph hung on the wall above the broken harmonium beside the coloured print of the promises made to Blessed Margaret Mary Alacoque.[4] He had been a school friend of her father. Whenever he showed the photograph to a visitor her father used to pass it with a casual word:

—He is in Melbourne[5] now.

She had consented to go away, to leave her home. Was that wise? She tried to weigh each side of the question. In her home anyway she had shelter and food; she had those whom she had known all her life about her. Of course she had to work hard both in the house and at business. What would they say of her in the Stores[6] when they found out that she had run away with a fellow? Say she was a fool, perhaps; and her place would be filled up by advertisement. Miss Gavan would be glad. She had always had an edge on her, especially whenever there were people listening.

—Miss Hill, don't you see these ladies are waiting?

—Look lively, Miss Hill, please.

She would not cry many tears at leaving the Stores.

But in her new home, in a distant unknown country, it would not be like that. Then she would be married – she, Eveline. People would treat her with respect then. She would not be treated as her mother had been. Even now, though she was over nineteen, she sometimes felt herself in danger of her father's violence. She knew it was that that had given her the palpitations. When they were growing up he had never gone for her, like he used to go for Harry and Ernest, because she was a girl; but latterly he had begun to threaten her and say what he would do to her only for her dead mother's sake. And now she had nobody to protect her. Ernest was dead and Harry, who was in the church decorating business, was nearly always down somewhere in the country.[7] Besides, the invariable squabble for money on Saturday nights had begun to weary her unspeakably. She always gave her entire wages – seven shillings – and Harry always sent up what he could but the trouble was to get any money from her father. He said she used to squander the money, that she had no head, that he wasn't going to give her his hard-earned money to throw about the streets, and much more, for he was usually fairly bad of a Saturday night. In the end he would give her the money and ask her had she any intention of buying Sunday's dinner. Then she had to rush out as quickly as she could and do her marketing, holding her black leather purse tightly in her hand as she elbowed her way through the crowds and returning home late under her load of provisions. She had hard work to keep the house together and to see that the two young children who had been left to her charge went to school regularly and got their meals regularly. It was hard work – a hard life – but now that she was about to leave it she did not find it a wholly undesirable life.

She was about to explore another life with Frank. Frank was very kind, manly, open-hearted. She was to go away with him by the night-boat[8] to be his wife and to live with him in Buenos Ayres[9] where he had a home waiting for her. How well she remembered the first time she had seen him; he was lodging in a house on the main road where she used to visit. It seemed a few weeks ago. He was standing at the gate, his peaked cap pushed back on his head and his hair tumbled forward over a face of bronze. Then they had come to know each other. He used to meet her outside the Stores every evening and see her home. He took her to see *The Bohemian Girl*[10] and she felt elated as she sat in an unaccustomed part of the theatre with him. He was awfully fond of music and sang a little. People knew that they were courting and, when he sang about the lass that loves a sailor,[11] she always felt pleasantly confused. He used to call her Poppens out of fun. First of all it had been an excitement for her to have a fellow and then she had begun to like him. He had tales of distant countries. He had started as a deck boy at a pound a month on a ship of the Allan Line[12] going out to Canada. He told her the names of the ships he had been on and the names of the different services. He had sailed through the Straits of Magellan and he told her stories of the terrible Patagonians.[13] He had fallen on his feet in Buenos Ayres, he said, and had come over to the old country just for a holiday. Of course, her father had found out the affair and had forbidden her to have anything to say to him.

—I know these sailor chaps, he said.

One day he had quarrelled with Frank and after that she had to meet her lover secretly.

The evening deepened in the avenue. The white of two letters in her lap grew indistinct. One was to Harry; the other was to her father. Ernest had been her favourite but she liked Harry too. Her father was becoming old lately, she noticed; he would miss her. Sometimes he could be very nice. Not long before, when she had been laid up for a day, he had read her out a ghost story and made toast for her at the fire. Another day, when their mother was alive, they had all gone for a picnic to the Hill of Howth.[14] She remembered her father putting on her mother's bonnet to make the children laugh.

Her time was running out but she continued to sit by the window, leaning her head against the window curtain, inhaling the odour of dusty cretonne. Down far in the avenue she could hear a street organ playing. She knew the air. Strange that it should come that very night to remind her of the promise to her mother, her promise to keep the home together as long as she could. She remembered the last night of her mother's illness; she was again in the close dark room at the other side of the hall and outside she heard a melancholy air of Italy. The organ-player had been ordered to go away and given sixpence. She remembered her father strutting back into the sick-room saying:

—Damned Italians! coming over here![15]

As she mused the pitiful vision of her mother's life laid its spell on the very quick of her being – that life of commonplace sacrifices closing in final craziness. She trembled as she heard again her mother's voice saying constantly with foolish insistence:

—Derevaun Seraun! Derevaun Seraun![16]

She stood up in a sudden impulse of terror. Escape! She must escape! Frank would save her. He would give her life, perhaps love, too. But she wanted to live. Why should she be unhappy? She had a right to happiness. Frank would take her in his arms, fold her in his arms. He would save her.

She stood among the swaying crowd in the station at the North Wall.[17] He held her hand and she knew that he was speaking to her, saying something about the passage over and over again. The station was full of soldiers with brown baggages. Through the wide doors of the sheds she caught a glimpse of the black mass of the boat, lying in beside the quay wall, with illumined portholes. She answered nothing. She felt her cheek pale and cold and, out of a maze of distress, she prayed to God to direct her, to show her what was her duty. The boat blew a long mournful whistle into the mist. If she went, to-morrow she would be on the sea with Frank, steaming towards Buenos Ayres. Their passage had been booked. Could she still draw back after all he had done for her? Her distress awoke a nausea in her body and she kept moving her lips in silent fervent prayer.

A bell clanged upon her heart. She felt him seize her hand:

—Come!

All the seas of the world tumbled about her heart. He was drawing her into them: he would drown her. She gripped with both hands at the iron railing.

—Come!

No! No! No! It was impossible. Her hands clutched the iron in frenzy. Amid the seas she sent a cry of anguish!

—Eveline! Evvy!

He rushed beyond the barrier and called to her to follow. He was shouted at to go on but he still called to her. She set her white face to him, passive, like a helpless animal. Her eyes gave him no sign of love or farewell or recognition.

AFTER THE RACE [1]

The cars came scudding in towards Dublin, running evenly like pellets in the groove of the Naas Road.[2] At the crest of the hill at Inchicore[3] sightseers had gathered in clumps to watch the cars careering homeward and through this channel of poverty and inaction the Continent sped its wealth and industry. Now and again the clumps of people raised the cheer of the gratefully oppressed. Their sympathy, however, was for the blue cars – the cars of their friends, the French.[4]

The French, moreover, were virtual victors. Their team had finished solidly; they had been placed second and third and the driver of the winning German car was reported a Belgian. Each blue car, therefore, received a double round of welcome as it topped the crest of the hill and each cheer of welcome was acknowledged with smiles and nods by those in the car. In one of these trimly built cars was a party of four young men whose spirits seemed to be at present well above the level of successful Gallicism:[5] in fact, these four young men were almost hilarious. They were Charles Ségouin, the owner of the car; André Rivière, a young electrician of Canadian birth; a huge Hungarian named Villona and a neatly groomed young man named Doyle. Ségouin was in good humour because he had unexpectedly received some orders in advance (he was about to start a motor establishment in Paris) and Rivière was in good humour because he was to be appointed manager of the establishment; these two young men (who were cousins) were also in good humour because of the success of the French cars. Villona was in good humour because he had had a very satisfactory luncheon; and besides he was an optimist by nature. The fourth member of the party, however, was too excited to be genuinely happy.

He was about twenty-six years of age, with a soft, light brown moustache and rather innocent-looking grey eyes. His father, who had begun life as an advanced Nationalist,[6] had modified his views early. He had made his money as a butcher in Kingstown[7] and by opening shops in Dublin and in the suburbs he had made his money many times over. He had also been fortunate enough to secure some of the police contracts[8] and in the end he had become rich enough to be alluded to in the Dublin newspapers as a merchant prince. He had sent his son to England to be educated in a big Catholic college[9] and had afterwards sent him to Dublin University[10] to study law. Jimmy did not study very earnestly and took to bad courses for a while. He had money and he was popular; and he divided his time curiously between musical and motoring circles. Then he had been sent for a term to Cambridge[11] to see a little life. His father, remonstrative, but covertly proud of the excess, had paid his bills and brought him home. It was at Cambridge that he had met Ségouin. They were not much more than acquaintances as yet but Jimmy found great pleasure in the society of one who had seen so much of the world and was reputed to own some of the biggest hotels in France. Such a person (as his father agreed) was well worth knowing, even if he had not been the charming companion he was. Villona was entertaining also – a brilliant pianist – but, unfortunately, very poor.

The car ran on merrily with its cargo of hilarious youth. The two cousins sat on the front seat; Jimmy and his Hungarian friend sat behind. Decidedly Villona was in excellent spirits; he kept up a deep bass hum of melody for miles of the road. The Frenchmen flung their laughter and light words over their shoulders and often Jimmy had to strain forward to catch the quick phrase. This was not altogether pleasant for him, as he had nearly always to make a deft guess at the meaning and shout back a suitable answer in the teeth of a high wind. Besides Villona's humming would confuse anybody; the noise of the car, too.

Rapid motion through space elates one; so does notoriety; so does the possession of money. These were three good reasons for Jimmy's excitement. He had been seen by many of his friends that day in the company of these Continentals. At the control Ségouin had presented him to one of the French competitors and, in answer to his confused murmur of compliment, the swarthy face of the driver had disclosed a line of shining white teeth. It was pleasant after that honour to return to the profane world of spectators amid nudges and significant looks. Then as to money – he really had a great sum under his control. Ségouin, perhaps, would not think it a great sum but Jimmy who, in spite of temporary errors, was at heart the inheritor of solid instincts knew well with what difficulty it had been got together. This knowledge had previously kept his bills within the limits of reasonable recklessness and, if he had been so conscious of the labour latent in money when there had been question merely of some freak of the higher intelligence, how much more so now when he was about to stake the greater part of his substance! It was a serious thing for him.

Of course, the investment was a good one and Ségouin had managed to give the impression that it was by a favour of friendship the mite of Irish money was to be included in the capital of the concern. Jimmy had a respect for his father's shrewdness in business matters and in this case it had been his father who had first suggested the investment; money to be made in the motor business, pots of money. Moreover Ségouin had the unmistakable air of wealth. Jimmy set out to translate into days' work that lordly car in which he sat. How smoothly it ran. In what style they had come careering along the country roads! The journey laid a magical finger on the genuine pulse of life and gallantly the machinery of human nerves strove to answer the bounding courses of the swift blue animal.

They drove down Dame Street.[12] The street was busy with unusual traffic, loud with the horns of motorists and the gongs of impatient tram-drivers. Near the Bank[13] Ségouin drew up and Jimmy and his friend alighted. A little knot of people collected on the footpath to pay homage to the snorting motor. The party was to dine together that evening in Ségouin's hotel and, meanwhile, Jimmy and his friend, who was staying with him, were to go home to dress. The car steered out slowly for Grafton Street[14] while the two young men pushed their way through the knot of gazers. They walked northward[15] with a curious feeling of disappointment in the exercise, while the city hung its pale globes of light above them in a haze of summer evening.

In Jimmy's house this dinner had been pronounced an occasion. A certain pride mingled with his parents' trepidation, a certain eagerness, also, to play fast and loose for the names of great foreign cities have at least this virtue. Jimmy, too, looked very well when he was dressed and, as he stood in the hall giving a last equation to the bows of his dress tie, his father may have felt even commercially satisfied at having secured for his son qualities often unpurchasable. His father, therefore, was unusually friendly with Villona and his manner expressed a real respect for foreign accomplishments; but this subtlety of his host was probably lost upon the Hungarian, who was beginning to have a sharp desire for his dinner.

The dinner was excellent, exquisite. Ségouin, Jimmy decided, had a very refined taste. The party was increased by a young Englishman named Routh whom Jimmy had seen with Ségouin at Cambridge. The young men supped in a snug room lit by electric candle-lamps.[16] They talked volubly and with little reserve. Jimmy, whose imagination was kindling, conceived the lively youth of the Frenchmen twined elegantly upon the firm framework of the Englishman's manner. A graceful image of his, he thought, and a just one. He admired the dexterity with which their host directed the conversation. The five young men had various tastes and their tongues had been loosened. Villona, with immense respect, began to discover to the mildly surprised Englishman the beauties of the English madrigal,[17] deploring the loss of old instruments.[18] Rivière, not wholly ingenuously, undertook to explain to Jimmy the triumph of the French mechanicians. The resonant voice of the Hungarian was about to prevail in ridicule of the spurious lutes of the romantic painters when Ségouin shepherded his party into politics. Here was congenial ground for all. Jimmy, under generous influences, felt the buried zeal of his father wake to life within him: he aroused the torpid Routh at last. The room grew doubly hot and Ségouin's task grew harder each moment: there was even danger of personal spite. The alert host at an opportunity lifted his glass to Humanity and, when the toast had been drunk, he threw open a window significantly.

That night the city wore the mask of a capital.[19] The five young men strolled along Stephen's Green[20] in a faint cloud of aromatic smoke. They talked loudly and gaily and their cloaks dangled from their shoulders. The people made way for them. At the corner of Grafton

Street a short fat man was putting two handsome ladies on a car in charge of another fat man. The car drove off and the short fat man caught sight of the party.

—André.

—It's Farley!

A torrent of talk followed. Farley was an American. No one knew very well what the talk was about. Villona and Rivière were the noisiest, but all the men were excited. They got up on a car, squeezing themselves together amid much laughter. They drove by the crowd, blended now into soft colours, to a music of merry bells. They took the train at Westland Row[21] and in a few seconds, as it seemed to Jimmy, they were walking out of Kingstown Station.[22] The ticket-collector saluted Jimmy; he was an old man:

—Fine night, sir!

It was a serene summer night; the harbour lay like a darkened mirror at their feet. They proceeded towards it with linked arms, singing *Cadet Roussel*[23] in chorus, stamping their feet at every:

—*Ho! Ho! Hohé, vraiment!*[24]

They got into a rowboat at the slip and made out for the American's yacht. There was to be supper, music, cards. Villona said with conviction:

—It is beautiful!

There was a yacht piano in the cabin. Villona played a waltz for Farley and Rivière, Farley acting as cavalier and Rivière as lady. Then an impromptu square dance, the men devising original figures. What merriment! Jimmy took his part with a will; this was seeing life, at least. Then Farley got out of breath and cried *Stop!* A man brought in a light supper, and the young men sat down to it for form's sake. They drank, however: it was Bohemian.[25] They drank Ireland, England, France, Hungary, the United States of America. Jimmy made a speech, a

long speech, Villona saying *Hear! hear!* whenever there
was a pause. There was a great clapping of hands when
he sat down. It must have been a good speech. Farley
clapped him on the back and laughed loudly. What jovial
fellows! What good company they were!

Cards! cards! The table was cleared. Villona returned
quietly to his piano and played voluntaries for them.
The other men played game after game, flinging themselves boldly into the adventure. They drank the health
of the Queen of Hearts and of the Queen of Diamonds.[26]
Jimmy felt obscurely the lack of an audience: the wit
was flashing. Play ran very high and paper began to
pass. Jimmy did not know exactly who was winning but
he knew that he was losing. But it was his own fault for
he frequently mistook his cards and the other men had
to calculate his I.O.U.'s for him. They were devils of
fellows but he wished they would stop: it was getting
late. Someone gave the toast of the yacht *The Belle of
Newport*[27] and then someone proposed one great game
for a finish.

The piano had stopped; Villona must have gone up on
deck. It was a terrible game. They stopped just before the
end of it to drink for luck. Jimmy understood that the
game lay between Routh and Ségouin. What excitement!
Jimmy was excited too; he would lose, of course. How
much had he written away? The men rose to their feet to
play the last tricks, talking and gesticulating. Routh won.
The cabin shook with the young men's cheering and the
cards were bundled together. They began then to gather
in what they had won. Farley and Jimmy were the
heaviest losers.

He knew that he would regret in the morning but at
present he was glad of the rest, glad of the dark stupor
that would cover up his folly. He leaned his elbows on
the table and rested his head between his hands, counting

the beats of his temples. The cabin door opened and he saw the Hungarian standing in a shaft of grey light:

—Daybreak, gentlemen!

TWO GALLANTS

The grey warm evening of August had descended upon the city and a mild warm air, a memory of summer, circulated in the streets. The streets, shuttered for the repose of Sunday, swarmed with a gaily coloured crowd. Like illumined pearls the lamps shone from the summits of their tall poles upon the living texture below which, changing shape and hue unceasingly, sent up into the warm grey evening air an unchanging unceasing murmur.

Two young men came down the hill of Rutland Square.[1] One of them was just bringing a long monologue to a close. The other, who walked on the verge of the path and was at times obliged to step on to the road, owing to his companion's rudeness, wore an amused listening face. He was squat and ruddy. A yachting cap was shoved far back from his forehead and the narrative to which he listened made constant waves of expression break forth over his face from the corners of his nose and eyes and mouth. Little jets of wheezing laughter followed one another out of his convulsed body. His eyes, twinkling with cunning enjoyment, glanced at every moment towards his companion's face. Once or twice he rearranged the light waterproof which he had slung over one shoulder in toreador fashion. His breeches, his white rubber shoes and his jauntily slung waterproof expressed youth. But his figure fell into rotundity[2] at the waist, his hair was scant and grey and his face, when the waves of expression had passed over it, had a ravaged look.

When he was quite sure that the narrative had ended he laughed noiselessly for fully half a minute. Then he said:

—Well! . . . That takes the biscuit!

His voice seemed winnowed of vigour; and to enforce his words he added with humour:

—That takes the solitary, unique, and, if I may so call it, *recherché*[3] biscuit!

He became serious and silent when he had said this. His tongue was tired for he had been talking all the afternoon in a public-house in Dorset Street.[4] Most people considered Lenehan a leech but, in spite of this reputation, his adroitness and eloquence had always prevented his friends from forming any general policy against him. He had a brave manner of coming up to a party of them in a bar and of holding himself nimbly at the borders of the company until he was included in a round. He was a sporting vagrant armed with a vast stock of stories, limericks and riddles. He was insensitive to all kinds of discourtesy. No one knew how he achieved the stern task of living, but his name was vaguely associated with racing tissues.[5]

—And where did you pick her up, Corley? he asked.

Corley ran his tongue swiftly along his upper lip.

—One night, man, he said, I was going along Dame Street[6] and I spotted a fine tart under Waterhouse's clock[7] and said good-night, you know. So we went for a walk round by the canal[8] and she told me she was a slavey[9] in a house in Baggot Street.[10] I put my arm round her and squeezed her a bit that night. Then next Sunday, man, I met her by appointment. We went out to Donnybrook[11] and I brought her into a field there. She told me she used to go with a dairyman. . . . It was fine, man. Cigarettes every night she'd bring me and paying the tram out and back. And one night she brought me two bloody fine cigars – O, the real cheese,[12] you know, that the old fellow used to smoke. . . . I was afraid, man, she'd get in the family way. But she's up to the dodge.[13]

—Maybe she thinks you'll marry her, said Lenehan.

—I told her I was out of a job, said Corley. I told her I was in Pim's.[14] She doesn't know my name. I was too hairy[15] to tell her that. But she thinks I'm a bit of class, you know.

Lenehan laughed again, noiselessly.

—Of all the good ones ever I heard, he said, that emphatically takes the biscuit.

Corley's stride acknowledged the compliment. The swing of his burly body made his friend execute a few light skips from the path to the roadway and back again. Corley was the son of an inspector of police[16] and he had inherited his father's frame and gait. He walked with his hands by his sides, holding himself erect and swaying his head from side to side. His head was large, globular and oily; it sweated in all weathers; and his large round hat, set upon it sideways, looked like a bulb which had grown out of another. He always stared straight before him as if he were on parade and, when he wished to gaze after someone in the street, it was necessary for him to move his body from the hips. At present he was about town.[17] Whenever any job was vacant a friend was always ready to give him the hard word.[18] He was often to be seen walking with policemen in plain clothes, talking earnestly.[19] He knew the inner side of all affairs and was fond of delivering final judgments. He spoke without listening to the speech of his companions. His conversation was mainly about himself: what he had said to such a person and what such a person had said to him and what he had said to settle the matter. When he reported these dialogues he aspirated the first letter of his name after the manner of Florentines.[20]

Lenehan offered his friend a cigarette. As the two young men walked on through the crowd Corley occasionally turned to smile at some of the passing girls but

Lenehan's gaze was fixed on the large faint moon circled with a double halo. He watched earnestly the passing of the grey web of twilight across its face. At length he said:

—Well . . . tell me, Corley, I suppose you'll be able to pull it off all right, eh?

Corley closed one eye expressively as an answer.

—Is she game for that? asked Lenehan dubiously. You can never know women.

—She's all right, said Corley. I know the way to get around her, man. She's a bit gone on me.

—You're what I call a gay Lothario,[21] said Lenehan. And the proper kind of a Lothario, too!

A shade of mockery relieved the servility of his manner. To save himself he had the habit of leaving his flattery open to the interpretation of raillery. But Corley had not a subtle mind.

—There's nothing to touch a good slavey, he affirmed. Take my tip for it.

—By one who has tried them all, said Lenehan.

—First I used to go with girls, you know, said Corley, unbosoming; girls off the South Circular.[22] I used to take them out, man, on the tram somewhere and pay the tram or take them to a band or a play at the theatre or buy them chocolate and sweets or something that way. I used to spend money on them right enough, he added, in a convincing tone, as if he were conscious of being disbelieved.

But Lenehan could well believe it; he nodded gravely.

—I know that game, he said, and it's a mug's game.

—And damn the thing I ever got out of it, said Corley.

—Ditto here, said Lenehan.

—Only off of one of them, said Corley.

He moistened his upper lip by running his tongue along it. The recollection brightened his eyes. He too gazed at the pale disc of the moon, now nearly veiled, and seemed to meditate.

—She was . . . a bit of all right, he said regretfully.

He was silent again. Then he added:

—She's on the turf[23] now. I saw her driving down Earl Street[24] one night with two fellows with her on a car.[25]

—I suppose that's your doing, said Lenehan.

—There was others at her before me, said Corley philosophically.

This time Lenehan was inclined to disbelieve. He shook his head to and fro and smiled.

—You know you can't kid me, Corley, he said.

—Honest to God! said Corley. Didn't she tell me herself? Lenehan made a tragic gesture.

—Base betrayer! he said.

As they passed along the railings of Trinity College,[26] Lenehan skipped out into the road and peered up at the clock.

—Twenty after, he said.

—Time enough, said Corley. She'll be there all right. I always let her wait a bit.

Lenehan laughed quietly.

—Ecod! Corley, you know how to take them, he said.

—I'm up to all their little tricks, Corley confessed.

—But tell me, said Lenehan again, are you sure you can bring it off all right? You know it's a ticklish job. They're damn close on that point. Eh? . . . What?

His bright, small eyes searched his companion's face for reassurance. Corley swung his head to and fro as if to toss aside an insistent insect, and his brows gathered.

—I'll pull it off, he said. Leave it to me, can't you?

Lenehan said no more. He did not wish to ruffle his friend's temper, to be sent to the devil and told that his advice was not wanted. A little tact was necessary. But Corley's brow was soon smooth again. His thoughts were running another way.

She's a fine decent tart, he said, with appreciation; that's what she is.

They walked along Nassau Street[27] and then turned into Kildare Street.[28] Not far from the porch of the club[29] a harpist stood in the roadway, playing to a little ring of listeners. He plucked at the wires heedlessly, glancing quickly from time to time at the face of each new-comer and from time to time, wearily also, at the sky. His harp[30] too, heedless that her coverings had fallen about her knees,[31] seemed weary alike of the eyes of strangers[32] and of her master's hands. One hand played in the bass the melody of *Silent, O Moyle,*[33] while the other hand careered in the treble after each group of notes. The notes of the air throbbed deep and full.

The two young men walked up the street without speaking, the mournful music following them. When they reached Stephen's Green[34] they crossed the road. Here the noise of trams, the lights and the crowd released them from their silence.

—There she is! said Corley.

At the corner of Hume Street[35] a young woman was standing. She wore a blue dress and a white sailor hat.[36] She stood on the curbstone, swinging a sunshade in one hand. Lenehan grew lively.

—Let's have a squint at her, Corley, he said.

Corley glanced sideways at his friend and an unpleasant grin appeared on his face.

—Are you trying to get inside me?[37] he asked.

—Damn it! said Lenehan boldly, I don't want an introduction. All I want is to have a look at her. I'm not going to eat her.

—O . . . A look at her? said Corley, more amiably. Well . . . I'll tell you what. I'll go over and talk to her and you can pass by.

—Right! said Lenehan.

Corley had already thrown one leg over the chains[38] when Lenehan called out:

—And after? Where will we meet?

—Half ten, answered Corley, bringing over his other leg.

—Where?

—Corner of Merrion Street.[39] We'll be coming back.

—Work it all right now, said Lenehan in farewell.

Corley did not answer. He sauntered across the road[40] swaying his head from side to side. His bulk, his easy pace and the solid sound of his boots had something of the conqueror in them. He approached the young woman and, without saluting, began at once to converse with her. She swung her sunshade more quickly and executed half turns on her heels. Once or twice when he spoke to her at close quarters she laughed and bent her head.

Lenehan observed them for a few minutes. Then he walked rapidly along beside the chains to some distance and crossed the road obliquely. As he approached Hume Street corner[41] he found the air heavily scented and his eyes made a swift anxious scrutiny of the young woman's appearance. She had her Sunday finery on. Her blue serge skirt was held at the waist by a belt of black leather. The great silver buckle of her belt seemed to depress the centre of her body, catching the light stuff of her white blouse like a clip. She wore a short black jacket with mother-of-pearl buttons and a ragged black boa. The ends of her tulle collarette had been carefully disordered and a big bunch of red flowers was pinned in her bosom, stems upwards.[42] Lenehan's eyes noted approvingly her stout short muscular body. Frank rude health glowed in her face, on her fat red cheeks and in her unabashed blue eyes. Her features were blunt. She had broad nostrils, a straggling mouth which lay open in a contented leer, and two projecting front teeth. As he passed Lenehan took off his cap and, after about ten seconds, Corley returned a salute to the air. This he did by raising his hand vaguely and pensively changing the angle of position of his hat.

Lenehan walked as far as the Shelbourne Hotel[43] where he halted and waited. After waiting for a little time he saw them coming towards him and, when they turned to the right,[44] he followed them,[45] stepping lightly in his white shoes, down one side of Merrion Square.[46] As he walked on slowly, timing his pace to theirs, he watched Corley's head which turned at every moment towards the young woman's face like a big ball revolving on a pivot. He kept the pair in view until he had seen them climbing the stairs of the Donnybrook tram;[47] then he turned about and went back the way he had come.

Now that he was alone his face looked older. His gaiety seemed to forsake him and, as he came by the railings of the Duke's Lawn,[48] he allowed his hand to run along them. The air which the harpist had played began to control his movements. His softly padded feet played the melody while his fingers swept a scale of variations idly along the railings after each group of notes.

He walked listlessly round Stephen's Green and then down Grafton Street.[49] Though his eyes took note of many elements of the crowd through which he passed they did so morosely. He found trivial all that was meant to charm him and did not answer the glances which invited him to be bold. He knew that he would have to speak a great deal, to invent and to amuse, and his brain and throat were too dry for such a task. The problem of how he could pass the hours till he met Corley again troubled him a little. He could think of no way of passing them but to keep on walking. He turned to the left[50] when he came to the corner of Rutland Square and felt more at ease in the dark quiet street, the sombre look of which suited his mood. He paused at last before the window of a poor-looking shop over which the words *Refreshment Bar* were printed in white letters. On the glass of the window were two flying inscriptions: *Ginger Beer* and *Ginger Ale*. A cut ham was exposed on a great blue dish while near it on a plate lay a segment of very light plum-pudding. He eyed this food earnestly for some time and then, after glancing warily up and down the street, went into the shop quickly.

He was hungry for, except some biscuits which he had asked two grudging curates[51] to bring him, he had eaten nothing since breakfast-time. He sat down at an uncovered wooden table opposite two work-girls and a mechanic. A slatternly girl waited on him.

—How much is a plate of peas? he asked.

—Three halfpence,[52] sir, said the girl.

—Bring me a plate of peas, he said, and a bottle of ginger beer.[53]

He spoke roughly in order to belie his air of gentility for his entry had been followed by a pause of talk. His face was heated. To appear natural he pushed his cap back on his head and planted his elbows on the table. The mechanic and the two work-girls examined him point by point before resuming their conversation in a subdued voice. The girl brought him a plate of hot grocer's peas, seasoned with pepper and vinegar, a fork and his ginger beer. He ate his food greedily and found it so good that he made a note of the shop mentally. When he had eaten all the peas he sipped his ginger beer and sat for some time thinking of Corley's adventure. In his imagination he beheld the pair of lovers walking along some dark road; he heard Corley's voice in deep energetic gallantries and saw again the leer of the young woman's mouth. This vision made him feel keenly his own poverty of purse and spirit. He was tired of knocking about, of pulling the devil by the tail,[54] of shifts and intrigues. He would be thirty-one in November. Would he never get a good job? Would he never have a home of his own? He thought how pleasant it would be to have a warm fire to sit by and a good dinner to sit down to. He had walked the streets long enough with friends and with girls. He knew what those friends were worth: he knew the girls too. Experience had embittered his heart against the world. But all hope had not left him. He felt better after having eaten than he had felt before, less weary of his life, less vanquished in spirit. He might yet be able to settle down in some snug corner and live happily if he could only come across some good simple-minded girl with a little of the ready.[55]

He paid twopence halfpenny to the slatternly girl and went out of the shop to begin his wandering again. He went into Capel Street[56] and walked along towards the City Hall.[57] Then he turned into Dame Street.[58] At the corner of George's Street[59] he met two friends of his and stopped to converse with them. He was glad that he could rest from all his walking. His friends asked him had he seen Corley and what was the latest. He replied that he had spent the day with Corley. His friends talked very little. They looked vacantly after some figures in the crowd and sometimes made a critical remark. One said that he had seen Mac an hour before in Westmoreland Street.[60] At this Lenehan said that he had been with Mac the night before in Egan's.[61] The young man who had seen Mac in Westmoreland Street asked was it true that Mac had won a bit over a billiard match. Lenehan did not know: he said that Holohan[62] had stood them drinks in Egan's.

He left his friends at a quarter to ten and went up George's Street. He turned to the left at the City Markets[63] and walked on into Grafton Street. The crowd of girls and young men had thinned and on his way up the street he heard many groups and couples bidding one another good-night. He went as far as the clock of the College of Surgeons:[64] it was on the stroke of ten. He set off briskly along the northern side of the Green, hurrying for fear Corley should return too soon. When he reached the corner of Merrion Street[65] he took his stand in the shadow of a lamp and brought out one of the cigarettes which he had reserved and lit it. He leaned against the lamp-post and kept his gaze fixed on the part from which he expected to see Corley and the young woman return.

His mind became active again. He wondered had Corley managed it successfully. He wondered if he had asked her yet or if he would leave it to the last. He suffered all the pangs and thrills of his friend's situation as well as those of his own. But the memory of Corley's slowly revolving head calmed him somewhat: he was sure Corley would pull it off all right. All at once the idea struck him that perhaps Corley had seen her home by another way and given him the slip. His eyes searched the street: there was no sign of them. Yet it was surely half-an-hour since he had seen the clock of the College of Surgeons. Would Corley do a thing like that? He lit his last cigarette and began to smoke it nervously. He strained his eyes as each tram stopped at the far corner of the square. They must have gone home by another way. The paper of his cigarette broke and he flung it into the road with a curse.

Suddenly he saw them coming towards him. He started with delight and, keeping close to his lamp-post, tried to read the result in their walk. They were walking quickly, the young woman taking quick short steps, while Corley kept beside her with his long stride. They did not seem to be speaking. An intimation of the result pricked him like the point of a sharp instrument. He knew Corley would fail; he knew it was no go.

They turned down Baggot Street[66] and he followed them at once, taking the other footpath. When they stopped he stopped too. They talked for a few moments and then the young woman went down the steps into the area of a house.[67] Corley remained standing at the edge of the path, a little distance from the front steps. Some minutes passed. Then the hall-door was opened slowly and cautiously. A woman came running down the front steps and coughed.[68] Corley turned and went towards her. His broad figure hid hers from view for a few seconds and then she reappeared running up the steps. The door closed on her and Corley began to walk swiftly towards Stephen's Green.

Lenehan hurried on in the same direction. Some drops of light rain fell. He took them as a warning and, glancing back towards the house which the young woman had entered to see that he was not observed, he ran eagerly across the road. Anxiety and his swift run made him pant. He called out:

—Hallo, Corley!

Corley turned his head to see who had called him, and then continued walking as before. Lenehan ran after him, settling the waterproof on his shoulders with one hand.

—Hallo, Corley! he cried again.

He came level with his friend and looked keenly in his face. He could see nothing there.

—Well? he said. Did it come off?

They had reached the corner of Ely Place.[69] Still without answering Corley swerved to the left and went up the side street. His features were composed in stern calm. Lenehan kept up with his friend, breathing uneasily. He was baffled and a note of menace pierced through his voice.

—Can't you tell us? he said. Did you try her?

Corley halted at the first lamp and stared grimly before

him. Then with a grave gesture he extended a hand towards the light and, smiling, opened it slowly to the gaze of his disciple. A small gold coin shone in the palm.[70]

THE BOARDING HOUSE

Mrs Mooney was a butcher's daughter. She was a woman who was quite able to keep things to herself: a determined woman. She had married her father's foreman[1] and opened a butcher's shop near Spring Gardens.[2] But as soon as his father-in-law was dead Mr Mooney began to go to the devil. He drank, plundered the till, ran headlong into debt. It was no use making him take the pledge:[3] he was sure to break out again a few days after. By fighting his wife in the presence of customers and by buying bad meat he ruined his business. One night he went for his wife with the cleaver and she had to sleep in a neighbour's house.

After that they lived apart. She went to the priest and got a separation[4] from him with care of the children. She would give him neither money nor food nor house-room; and so he was obliged to enlist himself as a sheriff's man.[5] He was a shabby stooped little drunkard with a white face and a white moustache and white eyebrows, pencilled above his little eyes, which were pink-veined and raw; and all day long he sat in the bailiff's room, waiting to be put on a job. Mrs Mooney, who had taken what remained of her money out of the butcher business and set up a boarding house in Hardwicke Street,[6] was a big imposing woman. Her house had a floating population made up of tourists from Liverpool[7] and the Isle of Man[8] and, occasionally, *artistes* from the music halls.[9] Its resident population was made up of clerks from the city. She governed her house cunningly and firmly, knew when to give credit, when to be stern and when to let things pass. All the resident young men spoke of her as *The Madam*.[10]

Mrs Mooney's young men paid fifteen shillings a week for board and lodgings (beer or stout at dinner excluded). They shared in common tastes and occupations and for this reason they were very chummy with one another. They discussed with one another the chances of favourites and outsiders.[11] Jack Mooney, the Madam's son, who was clerk to a commission agent[12] in Fleet Street,[13] had the reputation of being a hard case. He was fond of using soldiers' obscenities: usually he came home in the small hours. When he met his friends he had always a good one to tell them and he was always sure to be on to a good thing – that is to say, a likely horse or a likely *artiste*. He was also handy with the mits[14] and sang comic songs. On Sunday nights there would often be a reunion in Mrs Mooney's front drawing-room. The music-hall *artistes* would oblige; and Sheridan played waltzes and polkas and vamped accompaniments. Polly Mooney, the Madam's daughter would also sing. She sang:

> *I'm a . . . naughty girl.*[15]
> *You needn't sham:*
> *You know I am.*

Polly was a slim girl of nineteen; she had light soft hair and a small full mouth. Her eyes, which were grey with a shade of green through them, had a habit of glancing upwards when she spoke with anyone, which made her look like a little perverse madonna. Mrs Mooney had first sent her daughter to be a typist in a corn-factor's[16] office but, as a disreputable sheriff's man used to come every other day to the office, asking to be allowed to say a word to his daughter, she had taken her daughter home again and set her to do housework. As Polly was very lively the intention was to give her the run of the young men. Besides, young men like to feel that there is a young woman not very far away. Polly, of course, flirted with the young men but Mrs Mooney, who was a shrewd judge, knew that the young men were only passing the time away: none of them meant business. Things went on so for a long time and Mrs Mooney began to think of sending Polly back to typewriting when she noticed that something was going on between Polly and one of the young men. She watched the pair and kept her own counsel.

Polly knew that she was being watched, but still her mother's persistent silence could not be misunderstood. There had been no open complicity between mother and daughter, no open understanding but, though people in the house began to talk of the affair, still Mrs Mooney did not intervene. Polly began to grow a little strange in her manner and the young man was evidently perturbed. At last, when she judged it to be the right moment, Mrs Mooney intervened. She dealt with moral problems as a cleaver deals with meat: and in this case she had made up her mind.

It was a bright Sunday morning of early summer, promising heat, but with a fresh breeze blowing. All the windows of the boarding house were open and the lace curtains ballooned gently towards the street beneath the raised sashes. The belfry of George's Church[17] sent out constant peals and worshippers, singly or in groups, traversed the little circus before the church, revealing their purpose by their self-contained demeanour no less than by the little volumes in their gloved hands.[18] Breakfast was over in the boarding house and the table of the breakfast-room was covered with plates on which lay yellow streaks of eggs with morsels of bacon-fat and bacon-rind. Mrs Mooney sat in the straw arm-chair and watched the servant Mary remove the breakfast things.

She made Mary collect the crusts and pieces of broken bread to help to make Tuesday's bread-pudding. When the table was cleared, the broken bread collected, the sugar and butter safe under lock and key, she began to reconstruct the interview which she had had the night before with Polly. Things were as she had suspected: she had been frank in her questions and Polly had been frank in her answers. Both had been somewhat awkward, of course. She had been made awkward by her not wishing to receive the news in too cavalier a fashion or to seem to have connived and Polly had been made awkward not merely because allusions of that kind always made her awkward but also because she did not wish it to be thought that in her wise innocence she had divined the intention behind her mother's tolerance.

Mrs Mooney glanced instinctively at the little gilt clock on the mantelpiece as soon as she had become aware through her revery that the bells of George's Church had stopped ringing. It was seventeen minutes past eleven: she would have lots of time to have the matter out with Mr Doran[19] and then catch short twelve at Marlborough Street.[20] She was sure she would win. To begin with she had all the weight of social opinion on her side: she was an outraged mother. She had allowed him to live beneath her roof, assuming that he was a man of honour, and he had simply abused her hospitality. He was thirty-four or thirty-five years of age, so that youth could not be pleaded as his excuse; nor could ignorance be his excuse since he was a man who had seen something of the world. He had simply taken advantage of Polly's youth and inexperience: that was evident. The question was: What reparation would he make?

There must be reparation made in such cases. It is all very well for the man: he can go his ways as if nothing had happened, having had his moment of pleasure, but the girl has to bear the brunt. Some mothers would be content to patch up such an affair for a sum of money; she had known cases of it. But she would not do so. For her only one reparation could make up for the loss of her daughter's honour: marriage.

She counted all her cards again before sending Mary up to Mr Doran's room to say that she wished to speak with him. She felt sure she would win. He was a serious young man, not rakish or loud-voiced like the others. If it had been Mr Sheridan or Mr Meade or Bantam Lyons her task would have been much harder. She did not think he would face publicity. All the lodgers in the house knew something of the affair; details had been invented by some. Besides, he had been employed for thirteen years in a great Catholic wine-merchant's office and publicity would mean for him, perhaps, the loss of his sit.[21] Whereas if he agreed all might be well. She knew he had a good screw[22] for one thing and she suspected he had a bit of stuff put by.[23]

Nearly the half-hour! She stood up and surveyed herself in the pier-glass.[24] The decisive expression of her great florid face satisfied her and she thought of some mothers she knew who could not get their daughters off their hands.

Mr Doran was very anxious indeed this Sunday morning. He had made two attempts to shave but his hand had been so unsteady that he had been obliged to desist. Three days' reddish beard fringed his jaws and every two or three minutes a mist gathered on his glasses so that he had to take them off and polish them with his pocket-handkerchief. The recollection of his confession of the night before was a cause of acute pain to him; the priest had drawn out every ridiculous detail of the affair and in the end had so magnified his sin that he was almost thankful at being afforded a loophole of reparation.[25]

The harm was done. What could he do now but marry her or run away? He could not brazen it out. The affair would be sure to be talked of and his employer would be certain to hear of it. Dublin is such a small city: everyone knows everyone else's business. He felt his heart leap warmly in his throat as he heard in his excited imagination old Mr Leonard calling out in his rasping voice: *Send Mr Doran here, please.*

All his long years of service gone for nothing! All his industry and diligence thrown away! As a young man he had sown his wild oats, of course; he had boasted of his free-thinking and denied the existence of God to his companions in public-houses. But that was all passed and done with . . . nearly. He still bought a copy of *Reynolds's Newspaper* [26] every week but he attended to his religious duties [27] and for nine-tenths of the year lived a regular life. He had money enough to settle down on; it was not that. But the family would look down on her. First of all there was her disreputable father and then her mother's boarding house was beginning to get a certain fame. [28] He had a notion that he was being had. He could imagine his friends talking of the affair and laughing. She *was* a little vulgar; sometimes she said *I seen* and *If I had've known.* But what would grammar matter if he really loved her? He could not make up his mind whether to like her or despise her for what she had done. Of course, he had done it too. His instinct urged him to remain free, not to marry. Once you are married you are done for, it said.

While he was sitting helplessly on the side of the bed in shirt and trousers she tapped lightly at his door and entered. She told him all, that she had made a clean breast of it to her mother and that her mother would speak with him that morning. She cried and threw her arms round his neck, saying:

—O, Bob! Bob! What am I to do? What am I to do at all?

She would put an end to herself, she said.

He comforted her feebly, telling her not to cry, that it would be all right, never fear. He felt against his shirt the agitation of her bosom.

It was not altogether his fault that it had happened. He remembered well, with the curious patient memory of the celibate, the first casual caresses her dress, her breath, her fingers had given him. Then late one night as he was undressing for bed she had tapped at his door, timidly. She wanted to relight her candle at his for hers had been blown out by a gust. It was her bath night. She wore a loose open combing-jacket[29] of printed flannel. Her white instep shone in the opening of her furry slippers and the blood glowed warmly behind her perfumed skin. From her hands and wrists too as she lit and steadied her candle a faint perfume arose.

On nights when he came in very late it was she who warmed up his dinner. He scarcely knew what he was eating, feeling her beside him alone, at night, in the sleeping house. And her thoughtfulness! If the night was anyway cold or wet or windy there was sure to be a little tumbler of punch ready for him. Perhaps they could be happy together . . .

They used to go upstairs together on tiptoe, each with a candle, and on the third landing exchange reluctant good-nights. They used to kiss. He remembered well her eyes, the touch of her hand and his delirium . . .

But delirium passes. He echoed her phrase, applying it to himself: *What am I to do?* The instinct of the celibate warned him to hold back. But the sin was there; even his sense of honour told him that reparation must be made for such a sin.

While he was sitting with her on the side of the bed Mary came to the door and said that the missus wanted to see him in the parlour. He stood up to put on his coat and waistcoat, more helpless than ever. When he was dressed he went over to her to comfort her. It would be all right, never fear. He left her crying on the bed and moaning softly: *O my God!*

Going down the stairs his glasses became so dimmed with moisture that he had to take them off and polish them. He longed to ascend through the roof and fly away to another country where he would never hear again of his trouble, and yet a force pushed him downstairs step by step. The implacable faces of his employer and of the Madam stared upon his discomfiture. On the last flight of stairs he passed Jack Mooney who was coming up from the pantry nursing two bottles of *Bass*.[30] They saluted coldly; and the lover's eyes rested for a second or two on a thick bulldog face and a pair of thick short arms. When he reached the foot of the staircase he glanced up and saw Jack regarding him from the door of the return-room.[31]

Suddenly he remembered the night when one of the music-hall *artistes*, a little blond Londoner, had made a rather free allusion to Polly. The reunion had been almost broken up on account of Jack's violence. Everyone tried to quiet him. The music-hall *artiste*, a little paler than usual, kept smiling and saying that there was no harm meant: but Jack kept shouting at him that if any fellow tried that sort of a game on with *his* sister he'd bloody well put his teeth down his throat, so he would.

Polly sat for a little time on the side of the bed, crying. Then she dried her eyes and went over to the looking-glass. She dipped the end of the towel in the water-jug and refreshed her eyes with the cool water. She looked at herself in profile and readjusted a hairpin above her ear. Then she went back to the bed again and sat at the foot. She regarded the pillows for a long time and the sight of them awakened in her mind secret amiable memories. She rested the nape of her neck against the cool iron bed-rail and fell into a revery. There was no longer any perturbation visible on her face.

She waited on patiently, almost cheerfully, without alarm, her memories gradually giving place to hopes and visions of the future. Her hopes and visions were so intricate that she no longer saw the white pillows on which her gaze was fixed or remembered that she was waiting for anything.

At last she heard her mother calling. She started to her feet and ran to the banisters.

—Polly! Polly!

—Yes, mamma?

—Come down, dear. Mr Doran wants to speak to you.

Then she remembered what she had been waiting for.

A LITTLE CLOUD[1]

Eight years before he had seen his friend off at the North Wall[2] and wished him godspeed. Gallaher had got on. You could tell that at once by his travelled air, his well-cut tweed suit and fearless accent. Few fellows had talents like his and fewer still could remain unspoiled by such success. Gallaher's heart was in the right place and he had deserved to win. It was something to have a friend like that.

Little Chandler's thoughts ever since lunch-time had been of his meeting with Gallaher, of Gallaher's invitation and of the great city London where Gallaher lived. He was called Little Chandler because, though he was but slightly under the average stature, he gave one the idea of being a little man. His hands were white and small, his frame was fragile, his voice was quiet and his manners were refined. He took the greatest care of his fair silken hair and moustache and used perfume discreetly on his handkerchief. The half-moons of his nails were perfect and when he smiled you caught a glimpse of a row of childish white teeth.

As he sat at his desk in the King's Inns[3] he thought what changes those eight years had brought. The friend whom he had known under a shabby and necessitous guise had become a brilliant figure on the London Press.[4] He turned often from his tiresome writing to gaze out of the office window. The glow of a late autumn sunset covered the grass plots and walks. It cast a shower of kindly golden dust on the untidy nurses and decrepit old men who drowsed on the benches; it flickered upon all the moving figures – on the children who ran screaming along the gravel paths and on everyone who passed through the gardens. He watched the scene and thought of life; and (as always happened when he thought of life) he became sad. A gentle melancholy took possession of him. He felt how useless it was to struggle against fortune, this being the burden of wisdom which the ages had bequeathed to him.

He remembered the books of poetry upon his shelves at home. He had bought them in his bachelor days and many an evening, as he sat in the little room off the hall, he had been tempted to take one down from the bookshelf and read out something to his wife. But shyness had always held him back; and so the books had remained on their shelves. At times he repeated lines to himself and this consoled him.

When his hour had struck[5] he stood up and took leave of his desk and of his fellow-clerks punctiliously. He emerged from under the feudal arch of the King's Inns, a neat modest figure, and walked swiftly down Henrietta Street.[6] The golden sunset was waning and the air had grown sharp. A horde of grimy children populated the street. They stood or ran in the roadway or crawled up the steps before the gaping doors or squatted like mice upon the thresholds. Little Chandler gave them no thought. He picked his way deftly through all that minute vermin-like life and under the shadow of the gaunt spectral mansions in which the old nobility of Dublin had roistered.[7] No memory of the past[8] touched him, for his mind was full of a present joy.

He had never been in Corless's[9] but he knew the value of the name. He knew that people went there after the theatre to eat oysters and drink liqueurs; and he had heard that the waiters there spoke French and German. Walking swiftly by at night he had seen cabs drawn up before the door and richly dressed ladies, escorted by cavaliers, alight and enter quickly. They wore noisy dresses and many wraps. Their faces were powdered and they caught up their dresses, when they touched earth, like alarmed Atalantas.[10] He had always passed without turning his head to look. It was his habit to walk swiftly in the street even by day and whenever he found himself in the city late at night he hurried on his way apprehensively and excitedly. Sometimes, however, he courted the causes of his fear. He chose the darkest and narrowest streets and, as he walked boldly forward, the silence that was spread about his footsteps troubled him, the wandering silent figures troubled him; and at times a sound of low fugitive laughter made him tremble like a leaf.

He turned to the right towards Capel Street.[11] Ignatius Gallaher on the London Press! Who would have thought it possible eight years before? Still, now that he reviewed the past, Little Chandler could remember many signs of future greatness in his friend. People used to say that Ignatius Gallaher was wild. Of course, he did mix with a rakish set of fellows at that time, drank freely and borrowed money on all sides. In the end he had got mixed up in some shady affair, some money transaction: at least, that was one version of his flight. But nobody denied him talent. There was always a certain . . . something in Ignatius Gallaher that impressed you in spite of yourself. Even when he was out at elbows and at his wits' end for money he kept up a bold face. Little Chandler remembered (and the remembrance brought a slight flush of pride to his cheek) one of Ignatius Gallaher's sayings when he was in a tight corner:

—Half time,[12] now, boys, he used to say lightheartedly. Where's my considering cap?[13]

That was Ignatius Gallaher all out;[14] and, damn it, you couldn't but admire him for it.

Little Chandler quickened his pace. For the first time in his life he felt himself superior to the people he passed. For the first time his soul revolted against the dull inelegance of Capel Street. There was no doubt about it: if you wanted to succeed you had to go away. You could do nothing in Dublin. As he crossed Grattan Bridge[15] he looked down the river towards the lower quays and pitied the poor stunted houses. They seemed to him a band of tramps, huddled together along the river-banks, their old coats covered with dust and soot, stupefied by the panorama of sunset and waiting for the first chill of night to bid them arise, shake themselves and begone. He wondered whether he could write a poem to express his idea. Perhaps Gallaher might be able to get it into some London paper for him. Could he write something original? He was not sure what idea he wished to express but the thought that a poetic moment had touched him took life within him like an infant hope. He stepped onward bravely.

Every step brought him nearer to London,[16] farther from his own sober inartistic life. A light began to tremble on the horizon of his mind. He was not so old – thirty-two. His temperament might be said to be just at the point of maturity. There were so many different moods and impressions that he wished to express in verse. He felt them within him. He tried to weigh his soul to see if it was a poet's soul. Melancholy was the dominant note of his temperament, he thought, but it was a melancholy tempered by recurrences of faith and resignation and simple joy. If he could give expression to it in a book of poems perhaps men would listen. He would never be popular: he saw that. He could not sway the crowd but he might appeal to a little circle of kindred minds. The English critics, perhaps, would recognise him as one of the Celtic school by reason of the melancholy tone of his poems; besides that, he would put in allusions. He began to invent sentences and phrases from the notices which his book would get. *Mr Chandler has the gift of easy and graceful verse. . . . A wistful sadness pervades these poems . . . The Celtic note.*[17] It was a pity his name was not more Irish-looking.[18] Perhaps it would be better to insert his mother's name before the surname: Thomas Malone[19] Chandler, or better still: T. Malone Chandler. He would speak to Gallaher about it.

He pursued his revery so ardently that he passed his street and had to turn back. As he came near Corless's his former agitation began to overmaster him and he halted before the door in indecision. Finally he opened the door and entered.

The light and noise of the bar held him at the doorway for a few moments. He looked about him, but his sight was confused by the shining of many red and green wine-glasses. The bar seemed to him to be full of people and he felt that the people were observing him curiously. He glanced quickly to right and left (frowning slightly to make his errand appear serious), but when his sight cleared a little he saw that nobody had turned to look at him: and there, sure enough, was Ignatius Gallaher leaning with his back against the counter and his feet planted far apart.

—Hallo, Tommy, old hero, here you are! What is it to be? What will you have? I'm taking whisky: better stuff than we get across the water.[20] Soda? Lithia?[21] No mineral? I'm the same. Spoils the flavour. . . . Here, *garçon*,[22] bring us two halves of malt whisky, like a good fellow. . . . Well, and how have you been pulling along since I saw you last? Dear God, how old we're getting! Do you see any signs of aging in me – eh, what? A little grey and thin on the top – what?

Ignatius Gallaher took off his hat and displayed a large

closely cropped head. His face was heavy, pale and clean-shaven. His eyes, which were of bluish slate-colour, relieved his unhealthy pallor and shone out plainly above the vivid orange tie he wore. Between these rival features the lips appeared very long and shapeless and colourless. He bent his head and felt with two sympathetic fingers the thin hair at the crown. Little Chandler shook his head as a denial. Ignatius Gallaher put on his hat again.

—It pulls you down, he said, Press life. Always hurry and scurry, looking for copy and sometimes not finding it: and then, always to have something new in your stuff. Damn proofs and printers, I say, for a few days. I'm deuced glad, I can tell you, to get back to the old country. Does a fellow good, a bit of a holiday. I feel a ton better since I landed again in dear dirty Dublin.[23] . . . Here you are, Tommy. Water? Say when.

Little Chandler allowed his whisky to be very much diluted.

—You don't know what's good for you, my boy, said Ignatius Gallaher. I drink mine neat.

—I drink very little as a rule, said Little Chandler modestly. An odd half-one or so when I meet any of the old crowd: that's all.

—Ah, well, said Ignatius Gallaher, cheerfully, here's to us and to old times and old acquaintance.

They clinked glasses and drank the toast.

—I met some of the old gang to-day, said Ignatius Gallaher. O'Hara seems to be in a bad way. What's he doing?

—Nothing, said Little Chandler. He's gone to the dogs.[24]

—But Hogan has a good sit,[25] hasn't he?

—Yes; he's in the Land Commission.[26]

—I met him one night in London and he seemed to be very flush.[27] . . . Poor O'Hara! Boose,[28] I suppose?

—Other things, too, said Little Chandler shortly.

Ignatius Gallaher laughed.

—Tommy, he said, I see you haven't changed an atom. You're the very same serious person that used to lecture me on Sunday mornings when I had a sore head and a fur on my tongue. You'd want to knock about a bit in the world. Have you never been anywhere, even for a trip?

—I've been to the Isle of Man,[29] said Little Chandler.

Ignatius Gallaher laughed.

—The Isle of Man! he said. Go to London or Paris: Paris, for choice. That'd do you good.

—Have you seen Paris?

—I should think I have! I've knocked about there a little.

—And is it really so beautiful as they say? asked Little Chandler.

He sipped a little of his drink while Ignatius Gallaher finished his boldly.

—Beautiful? said Ignatius Gallaher, pausing on the word and on the flavour of his drink. It's not so beautiful, you know. Of course, it is beautiful. . . . But it's the life of Paris; that's the thing. Ah, there's no city like Paris for gaiety, movement, excitement. . . .

Little Chandler finished his whisky and, after some trouble, succeeded in catching the barman's eye. He ordered the same again.

—I've been to the Moulin Rouge,[30] Ignatius Gallaher continued when the barman had removed their glasses, and I've been to all the Bohemian cafés.[31] Hot stuff! Not for a pious chap like you, Tommy.

Little Chandler said nothing until the barman returned with the two glasses: then he touched his friend's glass lightly and reciprocated the former toast. He was beginning to feel somewhat disillusioned. Gallaher's accent and way of expressing himself did not please him. There was something vulgar in his friend which he had not observed before. But perhaps it was only the result of living in London amid the bustle and competition of the Press. The old personal charm was still there under this new gaudy manner. And, after all, Gallaher had lived, he had seen the world. Little Chandler looked at his friend enviously.

—Everything in Paris is gay,[32] said Ignatius Gallaher. They believe in enjoying life – and don't you think they're right? If you want to enjoy yourself properly you must go to Paris. And, mind you, they've a great feeling for the Irish there. When they heard I was from Ireland they were ready to eat me, man.

Little Chandler took four or five sips from his glass.

—Tell me, he said, is it true that Paris is so . . . immoral as they say?

Ignatius Gallaher made a catholic gesture[33] with his right arm.

—Every place is immoral, he said. Of course you do find spicy bits in Paris. Go to one of the students' balls[34] for instance. That's lively, if you like, when the *cocottes*[35] begin to let themselves loose. You know what they are, I suppose?

—I've heard of them, said Little Chandler.

Ignatius Gallaher drank off his whisky and shook his head.

—Ah, he said, you may say what you like. There's no woman like the Parisienne – for style, for go.

—Then it is an immoral city, said Little Chandler, with timid insistence – I mean, compared with London or Dublin?

—London! said Ignatius Gallaher. It's six of one and half-a-dozen of the other. You ask Hogan, my boy. I showed him a bit about London when he was over there. He'd open your eye. . . . I say, Tommy, don't make punch of that whisky: liquor up.

—No, really. . . .

—O, come on, another one won't do you any harm. What is it? The same again, I suppose?

—Well . . . all right.

—*François*, the same again. . . . Will you smoke, Tommy?

Ignatius Gallaher produced his cigar-case. The two friends lit their cigars and puffed at them in silence until their drinks were served.

—I'll tell you my opinion, said Ignatius Gallaher, emerging after some time from the clouds of smoke in which he had taken refuge, it's a rum world. Talk of immorality! I've heard of cases – what am I saying? – I've known them: cases of . . . immorality. . . .

Ignatius Gallaher puffed thoughtfully at his cigar and then, in a calm historian's tone, he proceeded to sketch for his friend some pictures of the corruption which was rife abroad. He summarised the vices of many capitals and seemed inclined to award the palm to Berlin. Some things he could not vouch for (his friends had told him), but of others he had had personal experience. He spared neither rank nor caste. He revealed many of the secrets of religious houses on the Continent [36] and described some of the practices which were fashionable in high society and ended by telling, with details, a story about an English duchess [37] – a story which he knew to be true. Little Chandler was astonished.

—Ah, well, said Ignatius Gallaher, here we are in old jog-along Dublin where nothing is known of such things.

—How dull you must find it, said Little Chandler, after all the other places you've seen!

—Well, said Ignatius Gallaher, it's a relaxation to come over here, you know. And, after all, it's the old country, as they say, isn't it? You can't help having a certain feeling for it. That's human nature. . . . But tell me

something about yourself. Hogan told me you had . . .
tasted the joys of connubial bliss. Two years ago, wasn't
it?

Little Chandler blushed and smiled.

—Yes, he said. I was married last May twelve months.

—I hope it's not too late in the day to offer my best
wishes, said Ignatius Gallaher. I didn't know your address
or I'd have done so at the time.

He extended his hand, which Little Chandler took.

—Well, Tommy, he said, I wish you and yours every
joy in life, old chap, and tons of money, and may you
never die till I shoot you. And that's the wish of a sincere
friend, an old friend. You know that?

—I know that, said Little Chandler.

—Any youngsters? said Ignatius Gallaher.

Little Chandler blushed again.

—We have one child, he said.

—Son or daughter?

—A little boy.

Ignatius Gallaher slapped his friend sonorously on the
back.

—Bravo, he said, I wouldn't doubt you, Tommy.

Little Chandler smiled, looked confusedly at his glass
and bit his lower lip with three childishly white front
teeth.

—I hope you'll spend an evening with us, he said,
before you go back. My wife will be delighted to meet
you. We can have a little music and –

—Thanks awfully, old chap, said Ignatius Gallaher,
I'm sorry we didn't meet earlier. But I must leave to-
morrow night.

—To-night, perhaps . . .?

—I'm awfully sorry, old man. You see I'm over here
with another fellow, clever young chap he is too, and we
arranged to go to a little card-party. Only for that . . .

—O, in that case. . . .

—But who knows? said Ignatius Gallaher considerately. Next year I may take a little skip over here now that I've broken the ice. It's only a pleasure deferred.

—Very well, said Little Chandler, the next time you come we must have an evening together. That's agreed now, isn't it?

—Yes, that's agreed, said Ignatius Gallaher. Next year if I come, *parole d'honneur*.[38]

—And to clinch the bargain, said Little Chandler, we'll just have one more now.

Ignatius Gallaher took out a large gold watch and looked at it.

—Is it to be the last? he said. Because you know, I have an a. p.[39]

—O, yes, positively, said Little Chandler.

—Very well, then, said Ignatius Gallaher, let us have another one as a *deoc an doruis*[40] – that's good vernacular for a small whisky, I believe.

Little Chandler ordered the drinks. The blush which had risen to his face a few moments before was establishing itself. A trifle made him blush at any time: and now he felt warm and excited. Three small whiskies had gone to his head and Gallaher's strong cigar had confused his mind, for he was a delicate and abstinent person. The adventure of meeting Gallaher after eight years, of finding himself with Gallaher in Corless's surrounded by lights and noise, of listening to Gallaher's stories and of sharing for a brief space Gallaher's vagrant and triumphant life, upset the equipoise of his sensitive nature. He felt acutely the contrast between his own life and his friend's, and it seemed to him unjust. Gallaher was his inferior in birth and education. He was sure that he could do something better than his friend had ever done, or could ever do, something higher than mere tawdry journalism if he only got the chance. What was it that stood in his way? His unfortunate timidity! He wished to vindicate himself in some way, to assert his manhood. He saw behind Galla-her's refusal of his invitation. Gallaher was only patronis-ing him by his friendliness just as he was patronising Ireland by his visit.

The barman brought their drinks. Little Chandler pushed one glass towards his friend and took up the other boldly.

—Who knows? he said, as they lifted their glasses. When you come next year I may have the pleasure of wishing long life and happiness to Mr and Mrs Ignatius Gallaher.

Ignatius Gallaher in the act of drinking closed one eye expressively over the rim of his glass. When he had drunk he smacked his lips decisively, set down his glass and said:

—No blooming fear of that, my boy. I'm going to have my fling first and see a bit of life and the world before I put my head in the sack – if I ever do.

—Some day you will, said Little Chandler calmly.

Ignatius Gallaher turned his orange tie and slate-blue eyes full upon his friend.

—You think so? he said.

—You'll put your head in the sack, repeated Little Chandler stoutly, like everyone else if you can find the girl.

He had slightly emphasised his tone and he was aware that he had betrayed himself; but, though the colour had heightened in his cheek, he did not flinch from his friend's gaze. Ignatius Gallaher watched him for a few moments and then said:

—If ever it occurs, you may bet your bottom dollar there'll be no mooning and spooning about it. I mean to marry money. She'll have a good fat account at the bank or she won't do for me.

Little Chandler shook his head.

—Why, man alive, said Ignatius Gallaher, vehemently, do you know what it is? I've only to say the word and to-morrow I can have the woman and the cash. You don't believe it? Well, I know it. There are hundreds – what am I saying? – thousands of rich Germans and Jews, rotten with money, that'd only be too glad. . . . You wait a while, my boy. See if I don't play my cards properly. When I go about a thing I mean business, I tell you. You just wait.

He tossed his glass to his mouth, finished his drink and laughed loudly. Then he looked thoughtfully before him and said in a calmer tone:

—But I'm in no hurry. They can wait. I don't fancy tying myself up to one woman, you know.

He imitated with his mouth the act of tasting and made a wry face.

—Must get a bit stale, I should think, he said.

. . . .

Little Chandler sat in the room off the hall, holding a child in his arms. To save money they kept no servant but Annie's young sister Monica came for an hour or so in the morning and an hour or so in the evening to help. But Monica had gone home long ago. It was a quarter to nine. Little Chandler had come home late for tea and, moreover, he had forgotten to bring Annie home the parcel of coffee from Bewley's.[41] Of course she was in a bad humour and gave him short answers. She said she would do without any tea but when it came near the time at which the shop at the corner closed she decided to go out herself for a quarter of a pound of tea and two pounds of sugar. She put the sleeping child deftly in his arms and said:

—Here. Don't waken him.

A little lamp with a white china shade stood upon the

table and its light fell over a photograph which was
enclosed in a frame of crumpled horn. It was Annie's
photograph. Little Chandler looked at it, pausing at the
thin tight lips. She wore the pale blue summer blouse
which he had brought her home as a present one Saturday.
It had cost him ten and elevenpence;[42] but what an agony
of nervousness it had cost him! How he had suffered that
day, waiting at the shop door until the shop was empty,
standing at the counter and trying to appear at his ease
while the girl piled ladies' blouses before him, paying at
the desk and forgetting to take up the odd penny of his
change, being called back by the cashier, and, finally,
striving to hide his blushes as he left the shop by examining the parcel to see if it was securely tied. When he
brought the blouse home Annie kissed him and said it
was very pretty and stylish; but when she heard the price
she threw the blouse on the table and said it was a
regular swindle to charge ten and elevenpence for that.
At first she wanted to take it back but when she tried it
on she was delighted with it, especially with the make of
the sleeves, and kissed him and said he was very good to
think of her.

Hm! . . .

He looked coldly into the eyes of the photograph and
they answered coldly. Certainly they were pretty and the
face itself was pretty. But he found something mean in it.
Why was it so unconscious and lady-like? The composure
of the eyes irritated him. They repelled him and defied
him: there was no passion in them, no rapture. He
thought of what Gallaher had said about rich Jewesses.
Those dark Oriental eyes, he thought, how full they are
of passion, of voluptuous longing! . . . Why had he married the eyes in the photograph?

He caught himself up at the question and glanced
nervously round the room. He found something mean in

the pretty furniture which he had bought for his house on the hire system.[43] Annie had chosen it herself and it reminded him of her. It too was prim and pretty. A dull resentment against his life awoke within him. Could he not escape from his little house? Was it too late for him to try to live bravely like Gallaher? Could he go to London? There was the furniture still to be paid for. If he could only write a book and get it published, that might open the way for him.

A volume of Byron's poems[44] lay before him on the table. He opened it cautiously with his left hand lest he should waken the child and began to read the first poem in the book:

> Hushed are the winds and still the evening gloom,
>   Not e'en a Zephyr wanders through the grove,
> Whilst I return to view my Margaret's tomb
>   And scatter flowers on the dust I love.[45]

He paused. He felt the rhythm of the verse about him in the room. How melancholy it was! Could he, too, write like that, express the melancholy of his soul in verse? There were so many things he wanted to describe: his sensation of a few hours before on Grattan Bridge, for example. If he could get back again into that mood. . . .

The child awoke and began to cry. He turned from the page and tried to hush it: but it would not be hushed. He began to rock it to and fro in his arms but its wailing cry grew keener. He rocked it faster while his eyes began to read the second stanza:

> Within this narrow cell reclines her clay,
>   That clay where once . . .

It was useless. He couldn't read. He couldn't do anything. The wailing of the child pierced the drum of his ear. It was useless, useless! He was a prisoner for life. His arms trembled with anger and suddenly bending to the child's face he shouted:

—Stop!

The child stopped for an instant, had a spasm of fright and began to scream. He jumped up from his chair and walked hastily up and down the room with the child in his arms. It began to sob piteously, losing its breath for four or five seconds, and then bursting out anew. The thin walls of the room echoed the sound. He tried to soothe it but it sobbed more convulsively. He looked at the contracted and quivering face of the child and began to be alarmed. He counted seven sobs without a break between them and caught the child to his breast in fright. If it died! . . .

The door was burst open and a young woman ran in, panting.

—What is it? What is it? she cried.

The child, hearing its mother's voice, broke out into a paroxysm of sobbing.

—It's nothing, Annie . . . it's nothing. . . . He began to cry . . .

She flung her parcels on the floor and snatched the child from him.

—What have you done to him? she cried, glaring into his face.

Little Chandler sustained for one moment the gaze of her eyes and his heart closed together as he met the hatred in them. He began to stammer:

—It's nothing. . . . He . . . he began to cry. . . . I couldn't . . . I didn't do anything. . . . What?

Giving no heed to him she began to walk up and down the room, clasping the child tightly in her arms and murmuring:

—My little man! My little mannie! Was 'ou frightened,

love? . . . There now, love! There now! . . . Lambabaun![46] Mamma's little lamb of the world![47] . . . There now!

Little Chandler felt his cheeks suffused with shame and he stood back out of the lamplight. He listened while the paroxysm of the child's sobbing grew less and less; and tears of remorse started to his eyes.

COUNTERPARTS

The bell rang furiously and, when Miss Parker[1] went to the tube,[2] a furious voice called out in a piercing North of Ireland accent:[3]

—Send Farrington here!

Miss Parker returned to her machine, saying to a man who was writing at a desk:

—Mr Alleyne[4] wants you upstairs.

The man muttered *Blast him!* under his breath and pushed back his chair to stand up. When he stood up he was tall and of great bulk. He had a hanging face, dark wine-coloured, with fair eyebrows and moustache: his eyes bulged forward slightly and the whites of them were dirty. He lifted up the counter and, passing by the clients, went out of the office with a heavy step.

He went heavily upstairs until he came to the second landing, where a door bore a brass plate with the inscription *Mr Alleyne*. Here he halted, puffing with labour and vexation, and knocked. The shrill voice cried:

—Come in!

The man entered Mr Alleyne's room. Simultaneously Mr Alleyne, a little man wearing gold-rimmed glasses on a clean-shaven face, shot his head up over a pile of documents. The head itself was so pink and hairless that it seemed like a large egg reposing on the papers. Mr Alleyne did not lose a moment:

—Farrington? What is the meaning of this? Why have I always to complain of you? May I ask you why you haven't made a copy of that contract between Bodley and Kirwan?[5] I told you it must be ready by four o'clock.

—But Mr Shelley[6] said, sir –

—*Mr Shelley said, sir*. . . . Kindly attend to what I say and not to what *Mr Shelley says, sir*. You have always some excuse or another for shirking work. Let me tell you that if the contract is not copied before this evening I'll lay the matter before Mr Crosbie[7]. . . . Do you hear me now?

—Yes, sir.

—Do you hear me now? . . . Ay and another little matter! I might as well be talking to the wall as talking to you. Understand once for all that you get a half an hour for your lunch and not an hour and a half. How many courses do you want, I'd like to know. . . . Do you mind me, now?

—Yes, sir.

Mr Alleyne bent his head again upon his pile of papers. The man stared fixedly at the polished skull which directed the affairs of Crosbie & Alleyne, gauging its fragility. A spasm of rage gripped his throat for a few moments and then passed, leaving after it a sharp sensation of thirst. The man recognised the sensation and felt that he must have a good night's drinking. The middle of the month was passed and, if he could get the copy done in time, Mr Alleyne might give him an order on the cashier.[8] He stood still, gazing fixedly at the head upon the pile of papers. Suddenly Mr Alleyne began to upset all the papers, searching for something. Then, as if he had been unaware of the man's presence till that moment, he shot up his head again, saying:

—Eh? Are you going to stand there all day? Upon my word, Farrington, you take things easy!

—I was waiting to see . . .

—Very good, you needn't wait to see. Go downstairs and do your work.

The man walked heavily towards the door and, as he

went out of the room, he heard Mr Alleyne cry after him that if the contract was not copied by evening Mr Crosbie would hear of the matter.

He returned to his desk in the lower office and counted the sheets which remained to be copied. He took up his pen and dipped it in the ink but he continued to stare stupidly at the last words he had written: *In no case shall the said Bernard Bodley be* ... The evening was falling and in a few minutes they would be lighting the gas: then he could write. He felt that he must slake the thirst in his throat. He stood up from his desk and, lifting the counter as before, passed out of the office. As he was passing out the chief clerk looked at him inquiringly.

—It's all right, Mr Shelley, said the man, pointing with his finger to indicate the objective of his journey.[9]

The chief clerk glanced at the hat-rack but, seeing the row complete, offered no remark. As soon as he was on the landing the man pulled a shepherd's plaid cap out of his pocket, put it on his head and ran quickly down the rickety stairs. From the street door he walked on furtively on the inner side of the path towards the corner and all at once dived into a doorway. He was now safe in the dark snug of O'Neill's shop,[10] and, filling up the little window that looked into the bar with his inflamed face, the colour of dark wine or dark meat, he called out:

—Here, Pat, give us a g.p.,[11] like a good fellow.

The curate[12] brought him a glass of plain porter. The man drank it at a gulp and asked for a caraway seed.[13] He put his penny on the counter and, leaving the curate to grope for it in the gloom, retreated out of the snug as furtively as he had entered it.

Darkness, accompanied by a thick fog, was gaining upon the dusk of February and the lamps in Eustace Street had been lit. The man went up by the houses until he reached the door of the office, wondering whether he could finish his copy in time. On the stairs a moist pungent odour of perfumes saluted his nose: evidently Miss Delacour[14] had come while he was out in O'Neill's. He crammed his cap back again into his pocket and re-entered the office, assuming an air of absent-mindedness.

—Mr Alleyne has been calling for you, said the chief clerk severely. Where were you?

The man glanced at the two clients who were standing at the counter as if to intimate that their presence prevented him from answering. As the clients were both male the chief clerk allowed himself a laugh.

—I know that game, he said. Five times in one day is a little bit. . . . Well, you better look sharp and get a copy of our correspondence in the Delacour case for Mr Alleyne.

This address in the presence of the public, his run upstairs and the porter he had gulped down so hastily confused the man and, as he sat down at his desk to get what was required, he realised how hopeless was the task of finishing his copy of the contract before half past five. The dark damp night was coming and he longed to spend it in the bars, drinking with his friends amid the glare of gas and the clatter of glasses. He got out the Delacour correspondence and passed out of the office. He hoped Mr Alleyne would not discover that the last two letters were missing.

The moist pungent perfume lay all the way up to Mr Alleyne's room. Miss Delacour was a middle-aged woman of Jewish appearance. Mr Alleyne was said to be sweet on her or on her money. She came to the office often and stayed a long time when she came. She was sitting beside his desk now in an aroma of perfumes, smoothing the handle of her umbrella and nodding the great black feather in her hat. Mr Alleyne had swivelled his chair round to face her and thrown his right foot jauntily upon his left knee. The man put the correspondence on the desk and bowed respectfully but neither Mr Alleyne nor Miss Delacour took any notice of his bow. Mr Alleyne tapped a finger on the correspondence and then flicked it towards him as if to say: *That's all right: you can go.*

The man returned to the lower office and sat down again at his desk. He stared intently at the incomplete phrase: *In no case shall the said Bernard Bodley be . . .* and thought how strange it was that the last three words began with the same letter. The chief clerk began to hurry Miss Parker, saying she would never have the letters typed in time for post. The man listened to the clicking of the machine for a few minutes and then set to work to finish his copy. But his head was not clear and his mind wandered away to the glare and rattle of the public-house. It was a night for hot punches.[15] He struggled on with his copy, but when the clock struck five he had still fourteen pages to write. Blast it! He couldn't finish it in time. He longed to execrate aloud, to bring his fist down on something violently. He was so enraged that he wrote *Bernard Bernard* instead of *Bernard Bodley* and had to begin again on a clean sheet.

He felt strong enough to clear out the whole office single-handed. His body ached to do something, to rush out and revel in violence. All the indignities of his life enraged him. . . . Could he ask the cashier privately for an advance? No, the cashier was no good, no damn good: he wouldn't give an advance. . . . He knew where he would meet the boys: Leonard and O'Halloran and Nosey Flynn. The barometer of his emotional nature was set for a spell of riot.

His imagination had so abstracted him that his name was called twice before he answered. Mr Alleyne and Miss Delacour were standing outside the counter and all the clerks had turned round in anticipation of something. The man got up from his desk. Mr Alleyne began a tirade of abuse, saying that two letters were missing. The man answered that he knew nothing about them, that he had made a faithful copy. The tirade continued: it was so bitter and violent that the man could hardly restrain his fist from descending upon the head of the manikin[16] before him.

—I know nothing about any other two letters, he said stupidly.

—*You – know – nothing.* Of course you know nothing, said Mr Alleyne. Tell me, he added, glancing first for approval to the lady beside him, do you take me for a fool? Do you think me an utter fool?

The man glanced from the lady's face to the little egg-shaped head and back again; and, almost before he was aware of it, his tongue had found a felicitous moment:

—I don't think, sir, he said, that that's a fair question to put to me.

There was a pause in the very breathing of the clerks. Everyone was astounded (the author of the witticism no less than his neighbours) and Miss Delacour, who was a stout amiable person, began to smile broadly. Mr Alleyne flushed to the hue of a wild rose and his mouth twitched with a dwarf's passion. He shook his fist in the man's face till it seemed to vibrate like the knob of some electric machine:

—You impertinent ruffian! You impertinent ruffian! I'll make short work of you! Wait till you see! You'll apologise to me for your impertinence or you'll quit the office instanter! You'll quit this, I'm telling you, or you'll apologise to me!

       .   .   .   .

He stood in a doorway opposite the office watching to see if the cashier would come out alone. All the clerks passed out and finally the cashier came out with the chief clerk. It was no use trying to say a word to him when he was with the chief clerk. The man felt that his position was bad enough. He had been obliged to offer an abject apology to Mr Alleyne for his impertinence but he knew what a hornet's nest the office would be for him. He could remember the way in which Mr Alleyne had hounded little Peake out of the office in order to make room for his own nephew. He felt savage and thirsty and revengeful, annoyed with himself and with everyone else. Mr Alleyne would never give him an hour's rest; his life would be a hell to him. He had made a proper fool of himself this time. Could he not keep his tongue in his cheek? But they had never pulled together from the first, he and Mr Alleyne, ever since the day Mr Alleyne had overheard him mimicking his North of Ireland accent to amuse Higgins and Miss Parker: that had been the beginning of it. He might have tried Higgins for the money, but sure Higgins never had anything for himself. A man with two establishments to keep up, of course he couldn't. . . .

He felt his great body again aching for the comfort of the public-house. The fog had begun to chill him and he wondered could he touch Pat in O'Neill's. He could not touch him for more than a bob[17] – and a bob was no use. Yet he must get money somewhere or other: he had spent his last penny for the g.p. and soon it would be too late for getting money anywhere. Suddenly, as he was fingering his watch-chain, he thought of Terry Kelly's pawn-office in Fleet Street.[18] That was the dart![19] Why didn't he think of it sooner?

He went through the narrow alley of Temple Bar[20] quickly, muttering to himself that they could all go to hell because he was going to have a good night of it. The clerk in Terry Kelly's said A crown![21] but the consignor held out for six shillings;[22] and in the end the six shillings was allowed him literally. He came out of the pawn-

office joyfully, making a little cylinder of the coins between his thumb and fingers. In Westmoreland Street[23]
the footpaths were crowded with young men and women
returning from business and ragged urchins ran here and
there yelling out the names of the evening editions.[24] The
man passed through the crowd, looking on the spectacle
generally with proud satisfaction and staring masterfully
at the office-girls. His head was full of the noises of tram-
gongs and swishing trolleys and his nose already sniffed
the curling fumes of punch. As he walked on he preconsid-
ered the terms in which he would narrate the incident to
the boys:

—So, I just looked at him – coolly, you know, and
looked at her. Then I looked back at him again – taking
my time, you know. *I don't think that that's a fair
question to put to me*, says I.

Nosey Flynn was sitting up in his usual corner of Davy
Byrne's[25] and, when he heard the story, he stood Farrington a half-one,[26] saying it was as smart a thing as
ever he heard. Farrington stood a drink in his turn. After
a while O'Halloran and Paddy Leonard came in and the
story was repeated to them. O'Halloran stood tailors of
malt,[27] hot, all round and told the story of the retort he
had made to the chief clerk when he was in Callan's of
Fownes's Street;[28] but, as the retort was after the manner
of the liberal shepherds in the eclogues,[29] he had to admit
that it was not so clever as Farrington's retort. At this
Farrington told the boys to polish off that and have another.

Just as they were naming their poisons[30] who should
come in but Higgins! Of course he had to join in with the
others. The men asked him to give his version of it, and
he did so with great vivacity for the sight of five small
hot whiskies was very exhilarating. Everyone roared laughing when he showed the way in which Mr Alleyne shook

his fist in Farrington's face. Then he imitated Farrington, saying, *And here was my nabs,*[31] *as cool as you please,* while Farrington looked at the company out of his heavy dirty eyes, smiling and at times drawing forth stray drops of liquor from his moustache with the aid of his lower lip.

When that round was over there was a pause. O'Halloran had money but neither of the other two seemed to have any; so the whole party left the shop somewhat regretfully. At the corner of Duke Street[32] Higgins and Nosey Flynn bevelled[33] off to the left while the other three turned back towards the city. Rain was drizzling down on the cold streets and, when they reached the Ballast Office,[34] Farrington suggested the Scotch House.[35] The bar was full of men and loud with the noise of tongues and glasses. The three men pushed past the whining match-sellers at the door and formed a little party at the corner of the counter. They began to exchange stories. Leonard introduced them to a young fellow named Weathers who was performing at the Tivoli[36] as an acrobat and knock-about *artiste.* Farrington stood a drink all round. Weathers said he would take a small Irish and Apollinaris.[37] Farrington, who had definite notions of what was what, asked the boys would they have an Apollinaris too; but the boys told Tim to make theirs hot. The talk became theatrical. O'Halloran stood a round and then Farrington stood another round, Weathers protesting that the hospitality was too Irish.[38] He promised to get them in behind the scenes and introduce them to some nice girls.[39] O'Halloran said that he and Leonard would go but that Farrington wouldn't go because he was a married man; and Farrington's heavy dirty eyes leered at the company in token that he understood he was being chaffed. Weathers made them all have just one little tincture[40] at his expense and promised to meet them later on at Mulligan's in Poolbeg Street.[41]

When the Scotch House closed [42] they went round to Mulligan's. They went into the parlour at the back and O'Halloran ordered small hot specials [43] all round. They were all beginning to feel mellow. Farrington was just standing another round when Weathers came back. Much to Farrington's relief he drank a glass of bitter [44] this time. Funds were running low but they had enough to keep them going. Presently two young women with big hats and a young man in a check suit came in and sat at a table close by. Weathers saluted them and told the company that they were out of the Tivoli. Farrington's eyes wandered at every moment in the direction of one of the young women. There was something striking in her appearance. An immense scarf of peacock-blue muslin was wound round her hat and knotted in a great bow under her chin; and she wore bright yellow gloves, reaching to the elbow. Farrington gazed admiringly at the plump arm which she moved very often and with much grace; and when, after a little time, she answered his gaze he admired still more her large dark brown eyes. The oblique staring expression in them fascinated him. She glanced at him once or twice and, when the party was leaving the room, she brushed against his chair and said *O, pardon!* in a London accent. He watched her leave the room in the hope that she would look back at him, but he was disappointed. He cursed his want of money and cursed all the rounds he had stood, particularly all the whiskies and Apollinaris which he had stood to Weathers. If there was one thing that he hated it was a sponge. [45] He was so angry that he lost count of the conversation of his friends.

When Paddy Leonard called him he found that they were talking about feats of strength. Weathers was showing his biceps muscle to the company and boasting so much that the other two had called on Farrington to uphold the national honour. Farrington pulled up his sleeve accordingly and showed his biceps muscle to the company. The two arms were examined and compared and finally it was agreed to have a trial of strength. The table was cleared and the two men rested their elbows on it, clasping hands. When Paddy Leonard said *Go!* each was to try to bring down the other's hand on to the table. Farrington looked very serious and determined.

The trial began. After about thirty seconds Weathers brought his opponent's hand slowly down on to the table. Farrington's dark wine-coloured face flushed darker still with anger and humiliation at having been defeated by such a stripling.

—You're not to put the weight of your body behind it. Play fair, he said.

—Who's not playing fair? said the other.

—Come on again. The two best out of three.

The trial began again. The veins stood out on Farrington's forehead, and the pallor of Weathers' complexion changed to peony. Their hands and arms trembled under the stress. After a long struggle Weathers again brought his opponent's hand slowly on to the table. There was a murmur of applause from the spectators. The curate, who was standing beside the table, nodded his red head towards the victor and said with loutish familiarity:

—Ah! that's the knack!

—What the hell do you know about it? said Farrington fiercely, turning on the man. What do you put in your gab[46] for?

—Sh, sh! said O'Halloran, observing the violent expression of Farrington's face. Pony up,[47] boys. We'll have just one little smahan[48] more and then we'll be off.

A very sullen-faced man stood at the corner of O'Connell

Bridge[49] waiting for the little Sandymount tram[50] to take him home. He was full of smouldering anger and revenge-fulness. He felt humiliated and discontented; he did not even feel drunk; and he had only twopence in his pocket. He cursed everything. He had done for himself in the office, pawned his watch, spent all his money; and he had not even got drunk. He began to feel thirsty again and he longed to be back again in the hot reeking public-house. He had lost his reputation as a strong man, having been defeated twice by a mere boy. His heart swelled with fury and, when he thought of the woman in the big hat who had brushed against him and said *Pardon!* his fury nearly choked him.

His tram let him down at Shelbourne Road[51] and he steered his great body along in the shadow of the wall of the barracks.[52] He loathed returning to his home. When he went in by the side-door he found the kitchen empty and the kitchen fire nearly out. He bawled upstairs:

—Ada! Ada!

His wife was a little sharp-faced woman who bullied her husband when he was sober and was bullied by him when he was drunk. They had five children. A little boy came running down the stairs.

—Who is that? said the man, peering through the dark-ness.

—Me, pa.

—Who are you? Charlie?

—No, pa. Tom.

—Where's your mother?

—She's out at the chapel.[53]

—That's right. . . . Did she think of leaving any dinner for me?

—Yes, pa. I –

—Light the lamp. What do you mean by having the place in darkness? Are the other children in bed?

The man sat down heavily on one of the chairs while the little boy lit the lamp. He began to mimic his son's flat accent, saying half to himself: *At the chapel. At the chapel, if you please!* When the lamp was lit he banged his fist on the table and shouted:

—What's for my dinner?

—I'm going . . . to cook it, pa, said the little boy.

The man jumped up furiously and pointed to the fire.

—On that fire! You let the fire out! By God, I'll teach you to do that again!

He took a step to the door and seized the walking-stick which was standing behind it.

—I'll teach you to let the fire out! he said, rolling up his sleeve in order to give his arm free play.

The little boy cried O, *pa!* and ran whimpering round the table, but the man followed him and caught him by the coat. The little boy looked about him wildly but, seeing no way of escape, fell upon his knees.

—Now, you'll let the fire out the next time! said the man, striking at him viciously with the stick. Take that, you little whelp!

The boy uttered a squeal of pain as the stick cut his thigh. He clasped his hands together in the air and his voice shook with fright.

—O, pa! he cried. Don't beat me, pa! And I'll . . . I'll say a *Hail Mary*[54] for you. . . . I'll say a *Hail Mary* for you, pa, if you don't beat me. . . . I'll say a *Hail Mary* . . .

CLAY

The matron had given her leave to go out as soon as the women's tea was over and Maria looked forward to her evening out. The kitchen was spick and span: the cook said you could see yourself in the big copper boilers. The fire was nice and bright and on one of the side-tables were four very big barmbracks.[1] These barmbracks seemed uncut; but if you went closer you would see that they had been cut into long thick even slices and were ready to be handed round at tea. Maria had cut them herself.

Maria was a very, very small person indeed but she had a very long nose and a very long chin. She talked a little through her nose, always soothingly: *Yes, my dear,* and *No, my dear.* She was always sent for when the women quarrelled over their tubs and always succeeded in making peace. One day the matron had said to her:

—Maria, you are a veritable peace-maker![2]

And the sub-matron and two of the Board ladies[3] had heard the compliment. And Ginger Mooney was always saying what she wouldn't do to the dummy who had charge of the irons if it wasn't for Maria. Everyone was so fond of Maria.

The women would have their tea at six o'clock and she would be able to get away before seven. From Ballsbridge[4] to the Pillar,[5] twenty minutes; from the Pillar to Drumcondra,[6] twenty minutes; and twenty minutes to buy the things. She would be there before eight. She took out her purse with the silver clasps and read again the words *A Present from Belfast.* She was very

95

fond of that purse because Joe had brought it to her five years before when he and Alphy had gone to Belfast on a Whit-Monday[7] trip. In the purse were two half-crowns[8] and some coppers.[9] She would have five shillings clear after paying tram fare. What a nice evening they would have, all the children singing! Only she hoped that Joe wouldn't come in drunk. He was so different when he took any drink.

Often he had wanted her to go and live with them; but she would have felt herself in the way (though Joe's wife was ever so nice with her) and she had become accustomed to the life of the laundry. Joe was a good fellow. She had nursed him and Alphy too; and Joe used often say:

—Mamma is mamma but Maria is my proper mother.

After the break-up at home the boys had got her that position in the *Dublin by Lamplight* laundry, and she liked it. She used to have such a bad opinion of Protestants but now she thought they were very nice people, a little quiet and serious, but still very nice people to live with. Then she had her plants in the conservatory and she liked looking after them. She had lovely ferns and wax-plants and, whenever anyone came to visit her, she always gave the visitor one or two slips from her conservatory. There was one thing she didn't like and that was the tracts on the walls;[10] but the matron was such a nice person to deal with, so genteel.

When the cook told her everything was ready she went into the women's room and began to pull the big bell. In a few minutes the women began to come in by twos and threes, wiping their steaming hands in their petticoats and pulling down the sleeves of their blouses over their red steaming arms. They settled down before their huge mugs which the cook and the dummy filled up with hot tea, already mixed with milk and sugar[11] in huge tin cans. Maria superintended the distribution of the barm-brack and saw that every woman got her four slices. There was a great deal of laughing and joking during the meal. Lizzie Fleming said Maria was sure to get the ring[12] and, though Fleming had said that for so many Hallow Eves,[13] Maria had to laugh and say she didn't want any ring or man either; and when she laughed her grey-green eyes sparkled with disappointed shyness and the tip of her nose nearly met the tip of her chin. Then Ginger Mooney lifted up her mug of tea and proposed Maria's health while all the other women clattered with their mugs on the table, and said she was sorry she hadn't a sup of porter to drink it in. And Maria laughed again till the tip of her nose nearly met the tip of her chin and till her minute body nearly shook itself asunder because she knew that Mooney meant well though, of course, she had the notions of a common woman.

But wasn't Maria glad when the women had finished their tea and the cook and the dummy had begun to clear away the tea-things! She went into her little bedroom and, remembering that the next morning was a mass morning,[14] changed the hand of the alarm from seven to six.[15] Then she took off her working skirt and her house-boots and laid her best skirt out on the bed and her tiny dress-boots beside the foot of the bed. She changed her blouse too and, as she stood before the mirror, she thought of how she used to dress for mass on Sunday morning when she was a young girl; and she looked with quaint affection at the diminutive body which she had so often adorned. In spite of its years she found it a nice tidy little body.

When she got outside the streets were shining with rain and she was glad of her old brown raincloak. The tram was full and she had to sit on the little stool at the end of the car, facing all the people, with her toes barely touching the floor. She arranged in her mind all she was going to do and thought how much better it was to be independent and to have your own money in your pocket. She hoped they would have a nice evening. She was sure they would but she could not help thinking what a pity it was Alphy and Joe were not speaking. They were always falling out now but when they were boys together they used to be the best of friends: but such was life.

She got out of her tram at the Pillar and ferreted her way quickly among the crowds. She went into Downes's cake-shop [16] but the shop was so full of people that it was a long time before she could get herself attended to. She bought a dozen of mixed penny cakes, and at last came out of the shop laden with a big bag. Then she thought what else would she buy: she wanted to buy something really nice. They would be sure to have plenty of apples and nuts. [17] It was hard to know what to buy and all she could think of was cake. She decided to buy some plum-cake but Downes's plumcake had not enough almond icing on top of it so she went over to a shop in Henry Street. [18] Here she was a long time in suiting herself and the stylish young lady behind the counter, who was evidently a little annoyed by her, asked her was it wedding-cake she wanted to buy. That made Maria blush and smile at the young lady; but the young lady took it all very seriously and finally cut a thick slice of plumcake, parcelled it up and said:

—Two-and-four, [19] please.

She thought she would have to stand in the Drumcondra tram because none of the young men seemed to notice her but an elderly gentleman made room for her. He was a stout gentleman and he wore a brown hard hat; he had a square red face and a greyish moustache. Maria thought he was a colonel-looking gentleman [20] and she reflected how much more polite he was than the young men who simply stared straight before them. The gentleman began to chat with her about Hallow Eve and the rainy weather. He supposed the bag was full of good things for the little ones and said it was only right that the youngsters should enjoy themselves while they were young. Maria agreed with him and favoured him with demure nods and hems. He was very nice with her, and when she was getting out at the Canal Bridge[21] she thanked him and bowed, and he bowed to her and raised his hat and smiled agreeably; and while she was going up along the terrace,[22] bending her tiny head under the rain, she thought how easy it was to know a gentleman even when he has a drop taken.[23]

Everybody said: *O, here's Maria!* when she came to Joe's house. Joe was there, having come home from business, and all the children had their Sunday dresses on. There were two big girls in from next door and games were going on. Maria gave the bag of cakes to the eldest boy, Alphy, to divide and Mrs Donnelly said it was too good of her to bring such a big bag of cakes and made all the children say:

—Thanks, Maria.

But Maria said she had brought something special for papa and mamma, something they would be sure to like, and she began to look for her plumcake. She tried in Downes's bag and then in the pockets of her raincloak and then on the hall-stand but nowhere could she find it. Then she asked all the children had any of them eaten it – by mistake, of course – but the children all said no and looked as if they did not like to eat cakes if they were to be accused of stealing. Everybody had a solution for the mystery and Mrs Donnelly said it was plain that Maria had left it behind her in the tram. Maria, remembering how confused the gentleman with the greyish moustache had made her, coloured with shame and vexation and disappointment. At the thought of the failure of her little surprise and of the two and fourpence she had thrown away for nothing she nearly cried outright.

But Joe said it didn't matter and made her sit down by the fire. He was very nice with her. He told her all that went on in his office, repeating for her a smart answer which he had made to the manager. Maria did not understand why Joe laughed so much over the answer he had made but she said that the manager must have been a very overbearing person to deal with. Joe said he wasn't so bad when you knew how to take him, that he was a decent sort so long as you didn't rub him the wrong way. Mrs Donnelly played the piano for the children and they danced and sang. Then the two next-door girls handed round the nuts. Nobody could find the nut-crackers and Joe was nearly getting cross over it and asked how did they expect Maria to crack nuts without a nutcracker. But Maria said she didn't like nuts and that they weren't to bother about her. Then Joe asked would she take a bottle of stout and Mrs Donnelly said there was port wine too in the house if she would prefer that. Maria said she would rather they didn't ask her to take anything: but Joe insisted.

So Maria let him have his way and they sat by the fire talking over old times and Maria thought she would put in a good word for Alphy. But Joe cried that God might strike him stone dead if ever he spoke a word to his brother again and Maria said she was sorry she had mentioned the matter. Mrs Donnelly told her husband it was a great shame for him to speak that way of his own flesh and blood but Joe said that Alphy was no brother of his and there was nearly being a row on the head of it. But Joe said he would not lose his temper on account of the night it was and asked his wife to open some more stout. The two next-door girls had arranged some Hallow

Eve games [24] and soon everything was merry again. Maria was delighted to see the children so merry and Joe and his wife in such good spirits. The next-door girls put some saucers on the table and then led the children up to the table, blindfold. One got the prayer-book and the other three got the water; and when one of the next-door girls got the ring Mrs Donnelly shook her finger at the blushing girl as much as to say: *O, I know all about it!* They insisted then on blindfolding Maria and leading her up to the table to see what she would get; and, while they were putting on the bandage, Maria laughed and laughed again till the tip of her nose nearly met the tip of her chin.

They led her up to the table amid laughing and joking and she put her hand out in the air as she was told to do. She moved her hand about here and there in the air and descended on one of the saucers. She felt a soft wet substance with her fingers and was surprised that nobody spoke or took off her bandage. There was a pause for a few seconds; and then a great deal of scuffling and whispering. Somebody said something about the garden, and at last Mrs Donnelly said something very cross to one of the next-door girls and told her to throw it out at once: that was no play. Maria understood that it was wrong that time and so she had to do it over again: and this time she got the prayer-book.

After that Mrs Donnelly played Miss McCloud's Reel [25] for the children and Joe made Maria take a glass of wine. Soon they were all quite merry again and Mrs Donnelly said Maria would enter a convent before the year was out because she had got the prayer-book. Maria had never seen Joe so nice to her as he was that night, so full of pleasant talk and reminiscences. She said they were all very good to her.

At last the children grew tired and sleepy and Joe

asked Maria would she not sing some little song before she went, one of the old songs. Mrs Donnelly said *Do, please, Maria!* and so Maria had to get up and stand beside the piano. Mrs Donnelly bade the children be quiet and listen to Maria's song. Then she played the prelude and said *Now, Maria!* and Maria, blushing very much, began to sing in a tiny quavering voice. She sang *I Dreamt that I Dwelt*,[26] and when she came to the second verse she sang again:

> *I dreamt that I dwelt in marble halls*
> *With vassals and serfs at my side*
> *And of all who assembled within those walls*
> *That I was the hope and the pride.*
> *I had riches too great to count, could boast*
> *Of a high ancestral name,*
> *But I also dreamt, which pleased me most,*
> *That you loved me still the same.*

But no one tried to show her her mistake;[27] and when she had ended her song Joe was very much moved. He said that there was no time like the long ago and no music for him like poor old Balfe,[28] whatever other people might say; and his eyes filled up so much with tears that he could not find what he was looking for and in the end he had to ask his wife to tell him where the corkscrew was.

A PAINFUL CASE

Mr James Duffy[1] lived in Chapelizod[2] because he wished to live as far as possible from the city of which he was a citizen and because he found all the other suburbs of Dublin mean, modern and pretentious. He lived in an old sombre house and from his windows he could look into the disused distillery[3] or upwards along the shallow river on which Dublin is built. The lofty walls of his uncarpeted room were free from pictures. He had himself bought every article of furniture in the room: a black iron bed-stead, an iron washstand, four cane chairs, a clothes-rack, a coal-scuttle, a fender and irons and a square table on which lay a double desk.[4] A bookcase had been made in an alcove by means of shelves of white wood. The bed was clothed with white bed-clothes and a black and scarlet rug covered the foot. A little hand-mirror hung above the washstand and during the day a white-shaded lamp stood as the sole ornament of the mantelpiece. The books on the white wooden shelves were arranged from below upwards according to bulk. A complete Words-worth[5] stood at one end of the lowest shelf and a copy of the *Maynooth Catechism*,[6] sewn into the cloth cover of a notebook, stood at one end of the top shelf. Writing materials were always on the desk. In the desk lay a manuscript translation of Hauptmann's *Michael Kramer*,[7] the stage directions of which were written in purple ink, and a little sheaf of papers held together by a brass pin. In these sheets a sentence was inscribed from time to time and, in an ironical moment, the headline of an advertise-ment for *Bile Beans*[8] had been pasted on to the first sheet. On lifting the lid of the desk a faint fragrance escaped – the fragrance of new cedarwood pencils or of a bottle of gum or of an over-ripe apple which might have been left there and forgotten.

Mr Duffy abhorred anything which betokened physical or mental disorder. A mediæval doctor would have called him saturnine.[9] His face, which carried the entire tale of his years, was of the brown tint of Dublin streets. On his long and rather large head grew dry black hair and a tawny moustache did not quite cover an unamiable mouth. His cheekbones also gave his face a harsh character; but there was no harshness in the eyes which, looking at the world from under their tawny eyebrows, gave the impression of a man ever alert to greet a redeeming instinct in others but often disappointed. He lived at a little distance from his body, regarding his own acts with doubtful side-glances. He had an odd autobiographical habit which led him to compose in his mind from time to time a short sentence about himself containing a subject in the third person and a predicate in the past tense. He never gave alms to beggars and walked firmly, carrying a stout hazel.[10]

He had been for many years cashier of a private bank in Baggot Street.[11] Every morning he came in from Chapelizod by tram. At midday he went to Dan Burke's [12] and took his lunch – a bottle of lager beer and a small trayful of arrowroot biscuits. At four o'clock he was set free. He dined in an eating-house in George's Street [13] where he felt himself safe from the society of Dublin's gilded youth and where there was a certain plain honesty in the bill of fare. His evenings were spent either before his landlady's piano or roaming about the outskirts of the city. His liking for Mozart's music [14] brought him sometimes to an opera or a concert: these were the only dissipations of his life.

He had neither companions nor friends, church nor creed. He lived his spiritual life without any communion with others, visiting his relatives at Christmas and escorting them to the cemetery when they died. He performed these two social duties for old dignity' sake but conceded nothing further to the conventions which regulate the civic life. He allowed himself to think that in certain circumstances he would rob his bank but, as these circumstances never arose, his life rolled out evenly – an adventureless tale.

One evening he found himself sitting beside two ladies in the Rotunda.[15] The house, thinly peopled and silent, gave distressing prophecy of failure. The lady who sat next him looked round at the deserted house once or twice and then said:

—What a pity there is such a poor house to-night! It's so hard on people to have to sing to empty benches.

He took the remark as an invitation to talk. He was surprised that she seemed so little awkward. While they talked he tried to fix her permanently in his memory. When he learned that the young girl beside her was her daughter he judged her to be a year or so younger than himself. Her face, which must have been handsome, had remained intelligent. It was an oval face with strongly marked features. The eyes were very dark blue and steady. Their gaze began with a defiant note but was confused by what seemed a deliberate swoon of the pupil into the iris, revealing for an instant a temperament of great sensibility. The pupil reasserted itself quickly, this half-disclosed nature fell again under the reign of prudence, and her astrakhan jacket, moulding a bosom of a certain fulness, struck the note of defiance more definitely.

He met her again a few weeks afterwards at a concert in Earlsfort Terrace[16] and seized the moments when her daughter's attention was diverted to become intimate. She alluded once or twice to her husband but her tone was not such as to make the allusion a warning. Her name was Mrs Sinico. Her husband's great-great-grandfather had come from Leghorn.[17] Her husband was captain of a mercantile boat plying between Dublin and Holland; and they had one child.

Meeting her a third time by accident he found courage to make an appointment. She came. This was the first of many meetings; they met always in the evening and chose the most quiet quarters for their walks together. Mr Duffy, however, had a distaste for underhand ways and, finding that they were compelled to meet stealthily, he forced her to ask him to her house. Captain Sinico encouraged his visits, thinking that his daughter's hand was in question. He had dismissed his wife so sincerely from his gallery of pleasures that he did not suspect that anyone else would take an interest in her. As the husband was often away and the daughter out giving music lessons Mr Duffy had many opportunities of enjoying the lady's society. Neither he nor she had had any such adventure before and neither was conscious of any incongruity. Little by little he entangled his thoughts with hers. He lent her books, provided her with ideas, shared his intellectual life with her. She listened to all.

Sometimes in return for his theories she gave out some fact of her own life. With almost maternal solicitude she urged him to let his nature open to the full; she became his confessor. He told her that for some time he had assisted at the meetings of an Irish Socialist Party[18] where he had felt himself a unique figure amidst a score of sober workmen in a garret lit by an inefficient oil-lamp. When the party had divided into three sections, each under its own leader and in its own garret, he had discontinued his attendances. The workmen's discussions, he said, were too timorous; the interest they took in the question of wages was inordinate. He felt that they were hard-featured realists and that they resented an exactitude which was the product of a leisure not within their reach. No social revolution, he told her, would be likely to strike Dublin for some centuries.

She asked him why did he not write out his thoughts. For what, he asked her, with careful scorn. To compete with phrasemongers, incapable of thinking consecutively for sixty seconds? To submit himself to the criticisms of an obtuse middle class which entrusted its morality to policemen and its fine arts to impresarios?

He went often to her little cottage outside Dublin; often they spent their evenings alone. Little by little, as their thoughts entangled, they spoke of subjects less remote. Her companionship was like a warm soil about an exotic. Many times she allowed the dark to fall upon them, refraining from lighting the lamp. The dark discreet room, their isolation, the music that still vibrated in their ears united them. This union exalted him, wore away the rough edges of his character, emotionalised his mental life. Sometimes he caught himself listening to the sound of his own voice. He thought that in her eyes he would ascend to an angelical stature; and, as he attached the fervent nature of his companion more and more closely to him, he heard the strange impersonal voice which he recognised as his own, insisting on the soul's incurable loneliness. We cannot give ourselves, it said: we are our own. The end of these discourses was that one night during which she had shown every sign of unusual excitement, Mrs Sinico caught up his hand passionately and pressed it to her cheek.

Mr Duffy was very much surprised. Her interpretation of his words disillusioned him. He did not visit her for a week; then he wrote to her asking her to meet him. As he did not wish their last interview to be troubled by the influence of their ruined confessional they met in a little cakeshop near the Parkgate.[19] It was cold autumn weather but in spite of the cold they wandered up and down the roads of the Park for nearly three hours. They agreed to break off their intercourse: every bond, he said, is a bond to sorrow. When they came out of the Park they walked in silence towards the tram; but here she began to tremble so violently that, fearing another collapse on her part, he bade her good-bye quickly and left her. A few days later he received a parcel containing his books and music.

Four years passed. Mr Duffy returned to his even way of life. His room still bore witness of the orderliness of his mind. Some new pieces of music encumbered the music-stand in the lower room and on his shelves stood two volumes by Nietzsche: *Thus Spake Zarathustra* and *The Gay Science*.[20] He wrote seldom in the sheaf of papers which lay in his desk. One of his sentences, written two months after his last interview with Mrs Sinico, read: Love between man and man is impossible because there must not be sexual intercourse and friendship between man and woman is impossible because there must be sexual intercourse. He kept away from concerts lest he should meet her. His father died; the junior partner of the bank retired. And still every morning he went into the city by tram and every evening walked home from the city after having dined moderately in George's Street and read the evening paper for dessert.

One evening as he was about to put a morsel of corned beef and cabbage into his mouth his hand stopped. His eyes fixed themselves on a paragraph in the evening paper which he had propped against the water-carafe. He replaced the morsel of food on his plate and read the paragraph attentively. Then he drank a glass of water, pushed his plate to one side, doubled the paper down before him between his elbows and read the paragraph over and over again. The cabbage began to deposit a cold white grease on his plate. The girl came over to him to ask was his dinner not properly cooked. He said it was very good and ate a few mouthfuls of it with difficulty. Then he paid his bill and went out.

He walked along quickly through the November twilight, his stout hazel stick striking the ground regularly, the fringe of the buff *Mail*[21] peeping out of a side-pocket of his tight reefer over-coat.[22] On the lonely road which leads from the Parkgate to Chapelizod he slackened his pace. His stick struck the ground less emphatically and his breath, issuing irregularly, almost with a sighing sound, condensed in the wintry air. When he reached his house he went up at once to his bedroom and, taking the paper from his pocket, read the paragraph again by the failing light of the window. He read it not aloud, but moving his lips as a priest does when he reads the prayers *Secreto*.[23] This was the paragraph:

DEATH OF A LADY AT SYDNEY PARADE

A PAINFUL CASE

To-day at the City of Dublin Hospital[24] the Deputy Coroner[25] (in the absence of Mr Leverett) held an inquest on the body of Mrs Emily Sinico, aged forty-three years, who was killed at Sydney Parade Station[26] yesterday evening. The evidence showed that the deceased lady, while attempting to cross the line, was knocked down by the engine of the ten o'clock slow train from Kingstown,[27] thereby sustaining injuries of the head and right side which led to her death.

James Lennon, driver of the engine, stated that he had been in the employment of the railway company for fifteen years. On hearing the guard's whistle he set the train in motion and a second or two afterwards brought it to rest in response to loud cries. The train was going slowly.

P. Dunne, railway porter, stated that as the train was about to start he observed a woman attempting to cross the lines. He ran towards her and shouted but, before he could reach her, she was caught by the buffer of the engine and fell to the ground.

A juror – You saw the lady fall?

Witness – Yes.

Police Sergeant Croly deposed that when he arrived he found the deceased lying on the platform apparently dead. He had the body taken to the waiting-room pending the arrival of the ambulance.

Constable 57E corroborated.

Dr Halpin, assistant house surgeon of the City of Dublin Hospital, stated that the deceased had two lower ribs fractured and had sustained severe contusions of the right shoulder. The right side of the head had been injured in the fall. The injuries were not sufficient to have caused death in a normal person. Death, in his opinion, had been probably due to shock and sudden failure of the heart's action.

Mr H. B. Patterson Finlay, on behalf of the railway company, expressed his deep regret at the accident. The company had always taken every precaution to prevent people crossing the lines except by the bridges, both by placing notices in every station and by the use of patent spring gates at level crossings. The deceased had been in the habit of crossing the lines late at night from platform to platform and, in view of certain other circumstances of the case, he did not think the railway officials were to blame.

Captain Sinico, of Leoville,[28] Sydney Parade, husband of the deceased, also gave evidence. He stated that the deceased was his wife. He was not in Dublin at the time of the accident as he had arrived only that morning from Rotterdam.[29] They had been married for twenty-two years and had lived happily until about two years ago when his wife began to be rather intemperate in her habits.

Miss Mary Sinico said that of late her mother had been in the habit of going out at night to buy spirits. She, witness, had often tried to reason with her mother and had induced her to join a league.[30] She was not at home until an hour after the accident.

The jury returned a verdict in accordance with the medical evidence and exonerated Lennon from all blame.

The Deputy Coroner said it was a most painful case, and expressed great sympathy with Captain Sinico and his daughter. He urged on the railway company to take strong measures to prevent the possibility of similar accidents in the future. No blame attached to anyone.

Mr Duffy raised his eyes from the paper and gazed out of his window on the cheerless evening landscape. The river lay quiet beside the empty distillery and from time to time a light appeared in some house on the Lucan road.[31] What an end! The whole narrative of her death revolted him and it revolted him to think that he had ever spoken to her of what he held sacred. The threadbare phrases, the inane expressions of sympathy, the cautious words of a reporter won over to conceal the details of a commonplace vulgar death attacked his stomach. Not merely had she degraded herself; she had degraded him. He saw the squalid tract of her vice, miserable and malodorous. His soul's companion! He thought of the hobbling wretches whom he had seen carrying cans and bottles to be filled by the barman. Just God, what an end! Evidently she had been unfit to live, without any strength of purpose, an easy prey to habits, one of the wrecks on which civilisation has been reared. But that she could have sunk so low! Was it possible he had deceived himself so utterly about her? He remembered her outburst of that night and interpreted it in a harsher sense than he had ever done. He had no difficulty now in approving of the course he had taken.

As the light failed and his memory began to wander he thought her hand touched his. The shock which had first attacked his stomach was now attacking his nerves. He put on his overcoat and hat quickly and went out. The cold air met him on the threshold; it crept into the sleeves of his coat. When he came to the public-house at Chapel-izod Bridge [32] he went in and ordered a hot punch.

The proprietor served him obsequiously but did not venture to talk. There were five or six working-men in the shop discussing the value of a gentleman's estate in County Kildare. [33] They drank at intervals from their huge pint tumblers and smoked, spitting often on the floor and sometimes dragging the sawdust over their spits with their heavy boots. Mr Duffy sat on his stool and gazed at them, without seeing or hearing them. After a while they went out and he called for another punch. He sat a long time over it. The shop was very quiet. The proprietor sprawled on the counter reading the *Herald* [34] and yawning. Now and again a tram was heard swishing along the lonely road outside.

As he sat there, living over his life with her and evoking alternately the two images in which he now conceived her, he realised that she was dead, that she had ceased to exist, that she had become a memory. He began to feel ill at ease. He asked himself what else could he have done. He could not have carried on a comedy of deception with her; he could not have lived with her openly. He had done what seemed to him best. How was he to blame? Now that she was gone he understood how lonely her life must have been, sitting night after night alone in that room. His life would be lonely too until he, too, died, ceased to exist, became a memory – if anyone remembered him.

It was after nine o'clock when he left the shop. The night was cold and gloomy. He entered the Park by the first gate and walked along under the gaunt trees. He walked through the bleak alleys where they had walked four years before. She seemed to be near him in the darkness. At moments he seemed to feel her voice touch his ear, her hand touch his. He stood still to listen. Why had he withheld life from her? Why had he sentenced her to death? He felt his moral nature falling to pieces.

When he gained the crest of the Magazine Hill[35] he halted and looked along the river towards Dublin, the lights of which burned redly and hospitably in the cold night. He looked down the slope and, at the base, in the shadow of the wall of the Park, he saw some human figures lying. Those venal and furtive loves filled him with despair. He gnawed the rectitude of his life; he felt that he had been outcast from life's feast. One human being had seemed to love him and he had denied her life and happiness: he had sentenced her to ignominy, a death of shame. He knew that the prostrate creatures down by the wall were watching him and wished him gone. No one wanted him; he was outcast from life's feast. He turned his eyes to the grey gleaming river, winding along towards Dublin. Beyond the river he saw a goods train winding out of Kingsbridge Station,[36] like a worm with a fiery head winding through the darkness, obstinately and laboriously. It passed slowly out of sight; but still he heard in his ears the laborious drone of the engine reiterating the syllables of her name.

He turned back the way he had come, the rhythm of the engine pounding in his ears. He began to doubt the

DUBLINERS

reality of what memory told him. He halted under a tree
and allowed the rhythm to die away. He could not feel
her near him in the darkness nor her voice touch his ear.
He waited for some minutes listening. He could hear
nothing: the night was perfectly silent. He listened again:
perfectly silent. He felt that he was alone.

IVY DAY[1] IN
THE COMMITTEE ROOM[2]

Old Jack raked the cinders together with a piece of cardboard and spread them judiciously over the whitening dome of coals. When the dome was thinly covered his face lapsed into darkness but, as he set himself to fan the fire again, his crouching shadow ascended the opposite wall and his face slowly re-emerged into light. It was an old man's face, very bony and hairy. The moist blue eyes blinked at the fire and the moist mouth fell open at times, munching once or twice mechanically when it closed. When the cinders had caught he laid the piece of cardboard against the wall, sighed and said:

—That's better now, Mr O'Connor.

Mr O'Connor, a grey-haired young man, whose face was disfigured by many blotches and pimples, had just brought the tobacco for a cigarette into a shapely cylinder but when spoken to he undid his handiwork meditatively. Then he began to roll the tobacco again meditatively and after a moment's thought decided to lick the paper.

—Did Mr Tierney say when he'd be back? he asked in a husky falsetto.

—He didn't say.

Mr O'Connor put his cigarette into his mouth and began to search his pockets. He took out a pack of thin pasteboard cards.

—I'll get you a match, said the old man.

—Never mind, this'll do, said Mr O'Connor.

He selected one of the cards and read what was printed on it:

MUNICIPAL ELECTIONS[3]

ROYAL EXCHANGE WARD[4]

Mr Richard J. Tierney, P.L.G.,[5] respectfully solicits the favour of your vote and influence at the coming election in the Royal Exchange Ward

Mr O'Connor had been engaged by Mr Tierney's agent to canvass one part of the ward but, as the weather was inclement and his boots let in the wet, he spent a great part of the day sitting by the fire in the Committee Room in Wicklow Street[6] with Jack, the old caretaker. They had been sitting thus since the short day had grown dark. It was the sixth of October, dismal and cold out of doors.

Mr O'Connor tore a strip off the card and, lighting it, lit his cigarette. As he did so the flame lit up a leaf of dark glossy ivy in the lapel of his coat. The old man watched him attentively and then, taking up the piece of cardboard again, began to fan the fire slowly while his companion smoked.

—Ah, yes, he said, continuing, it's hard to know what way to bring up children. Now who'd think he'd turn out like that! I sent him to the Christian Brothers[7] and I done what I could for him, and there he goes boosing about. I tried to make him someway decent.

He replaced the cardboard wearily.

—Only I'm an old man now I'd change his tune for him. I'd take the stick to his back and beat him while I could stand over him – as I done many a time before. The mother, you know, she cocks him up[8] with this and that. . . .

—That's what ruins children, said Mr O'Connor.

—To be sure it is, said the old man. And little thanks you get for it, only impudence. He takes th'upper hand of me whenever he sees I've a sup taken.[9] What's the world coming to when sons speaks that way to their father?

—What age is he? said Mr O'Connor.

—Nineteen, said the old man.

—Why don't you put him to something?

—Sure, amn't I never done at the drunken bowsy [10] ever since he left school? *I won't keep you*, I says. *You must get a job for yourself*. But, sure, it's worse whenever he gets a job; he drinks it all.

Mr O'Connor shook his head in sympathy, and the old man fell silent, gazing into the fire. Someone opened the door of the room and called out:

—Hello! Is this a Freemasons' meeting? [11]

—Who's that? said the old man.

—What are you doing in the dark? asked a voice.

—Is that you, Hynes? asked Mr O'Connor.

—Yes. What are you doing in the dark? said Mr Hynes, advancing into the light of the fire.

He was a tall slender young man with a light brown moustache. Imminent little drops of rain hung at the brim of his hat and the collar of his jacket-coat was turned up.

—Well, Mat, he said to Mr O'Connor, how goes it?

Mr O'Connor shook his head. The old man left the hearth and, after stumbling about the room returned with two candlesticks which he thrust one after the other into the fire and carried to the table. A denuded room came into view and the fire lost all its cheerful colour. The walls of the room were bare except for a copy of an election address. In the middle of the room was a small table on which papers were heaped.

Mr Hynes leaned against the mantelpiece and asked:

—Has he paid you yet? [12]

—Not yet, said Mr O'Connor. I hope to God he'll not leave us in the lurch to-night.

Mr Hynes laughed.

—O, he'll pay you. Never fear, he said.

—I hope he'll look smart about it if he means business, said Mr O'Connor.

—What do you think, Jack? said Mr Hynes satirically to the old man.

The old man returned to his seat by the fire, saying:

—It isn't but he has it, anyway. Not like the other tinker.[13]

—What other tinker? said Mr Hynes.

—Colgan, said the old man scornfully.

—Is it because Colgan's a working-man you say that? What's the difference between a good honest bricklayer and a publican – eh? Hasn't the working-man as good a right to be in the Corporation as anyone else – ay, and a better right than those shoneens[14] that are always hat in hand before any fellow with a handle to his name?[15] Isn't that so, Mat? said Mr Hynes, addressing Mr O'Connor.

—I think you're right, said Mr O'Connor.

—One man is a plain honest man with no hunker-sliding[16] about him. He goes in to represent the labour classes. This fellow you're working for only wants to get some job or other.

—Of course, the working-classes should be represented, said the old man.

—The working-man, said Mr Hynes, gets all kicks and no halfpence. But it's labour produces everything. The working-man is not looking for fat jobs for his sons and nephews and cousins. The working-man is not going to drag the honour of Dublin in the mud to please a German monarch.[17]

—How's that? said the old man.

—Don't you know they want to present an address of welcome[18] to Edward Rex if he comes here next year? What do we want kowtowing to a foreign king?

—Our man won't vote for the address, said Mr O'Connor. He goes in on the Nationalist ticket.[19]

—Won't he? said Mr Hynes. Wait till you see whether he will or not. I know him. Is it Tricky Dicky Tierney?

—By God! perhaps you're right, Joe, said Mr O'Connor. Anyway, I wish he'd turn up with the spondulics.[20]

The three men fell silent. The old man began to rake more cinders together. Mr Hynes took off his hat, shook it and then turned down the collar of his coat, displaying, as he did so, an ivy leaf in the lapel.

—If this man was alive, he said, pointing to the leaf, we'd have no talk of an address of welcome.

—That's true, said Mr O'Connor.

—Musha,[21] God be with them times! said the old man. There was some life in it then.

The room was silent again. Then a bustling little man with a snuffling nose and very cold ears pushed in the door. He walked over quickly to the fire, rubbing his hands as if he intended to produce a spark from them.

—No money, boys, he said.

—Sit down here, Mr Henchy, said the old man, offering him his chair.

—O, don't stir, Jack, don't stir, said Mr Henchy.

He nodded curtly to Mr Hynes and sat down on the chair which the old man vacated.

—Did you serve Aungier Street?[22] he asked Mr O'Connor.

—Yes, said Mr O'Connor, beginning to search his pockets for memoranda.

—Did you call on Grimes?

—I did.

—Well? How does he stand?

—He wouldn't promise. He said: *I won't tell anyone what way I'm going to vote.* But I think he'll be all right.

—Why so?

—He asked me who the nominators were; and I told him. I mentioned Father Burke's name. I think it'll be all right.

Mr Henchy began to snuffle and to rub his hands over the fire at a terrific speed. Then he said:

—For the love of God, Jack, bring us a bit of coal. There must be some left.

The old man went out of the room.

—It's no go, said Mr Henchy, shaking his head. I asked the little shoeboy, but he said: *O, now, Mr Henchy, when I see the work going on properly I won't forget you, you may be sure.* Mean little tinker! 'Usha,[23] how could he be anything else?

—What did I tell you, Mat? said Mr Hynes. Tricky Dicky Tierney.

—O, he's as tricky as they make 'em, said Mr Henchy. He hasn't got those little pigs' eyes for nothing. Blast his soul! Couldn't he pay up like a man instead of: *O, now, Mr Henchy, I must speak to Mr Fanning. . . .*[24] *I've spent a lot of money?* Mean little shoeboy[25] of hell! I suppose he forgets the time his little old father kept the hand-me-down shop[26] in Mary's Lane.[27]

—But is that a fact? asked Mr O'Connor.

—God, yes, said Mr Henchy. Did you never hear that? And the men used to go in on Sunday morning before the houses[28] were open to buy a waistcoat or a trousers – moya![29] But Tricky Dicky's little old father always had a tricky little black bottle up in a corner.[30] Do you mind now? That's that. That's where he first saw the light.

The old man returned with a few lumps of coal which he placed here and there on the fire.

—That's a nice how-do-you-do, said Mr O'Connor. How does he expect us to work for him if he won't stump up?

—I can't help it, said Mr Henchy. I expect to find the bailiffs in the hall when I go home.

Mr Hynes laughed and, shoving himself away from the mantelpiece with the aid of his shoulders, made ready to leave.

—It'll be all right when King Eddie comes, he said. Well, boys, I'm off for the present. See you later. 'Bye, 'bye.

He went out of the room slowly. Neither Mr Henchy nor the old man said anything but, just as the door was closing, Mr O'Connor, who had been staring moodily into the fire, called out suddenly:

—'Bye, Joe.

Mr Henchy waited a few moments and then nodded in the direction of the door.

—Tell me, he said across the fire, what brings our friend in here? What does he want?

—'Usha, poor Joe! said Mr O'Connor, throwing the end of his cigarette into the fire, he's hard up like the rest of us.

Mr Henchy snuffled vigorously and spat so copiously that he nearly put out the fire which uttered a hissing protest.

—To tell you my private and candid opinion, he said, I think he's a man from the other camp. He's a spy of Colgan's if you ask me. *Just go round and try and find out how they're getting on. They won't suspect you.* Do you twig?

—Ah, poor Joe is a decent skin,[31] said Mr O'Connor.

—His father was a decent respectable man, Mr Henchy admitted. Poor old Larry Hynes! Many a good turn he did in his day! But I'm greatly afraid our friend is not nineteen carat. Damn it, I can understand a fellow being hard up but what I can't understand is a fellow sponging. Couldn't he have some spark of manhood about him?

—He doesn't get a warm welcome from me when he comes, said the old man. Let him work for his own side and not come spying around here.

—I don't know, said Mr O'Connor dubiously, as he took out cigarette-papers and tobacco. I think Joe Hynes is a straight man. He's a clever chap, too, with the pen. Do you remember that thing he wrote . . .?

—Some of these hillsiders and fenians [32] are a bit too clever if you ask me, said Mr Henchy. Do you know what my private and candid opinion is about some of those little jokers? I believe half of them are in the pay of the Castle.

—There's no knowing, said the old man.

—O, but I know it for a fact, said Mr Henchy. They're Castle hacks [33] . . . I don't say Hynes . . . No, damn it, I think he's a stroke above that . . . But there's a certain little nobleman with a cock-eye – you know the patriot I'm alluding to?

Mr O'Connor nodded.

—There's a lineal descendant of Major Sirr [34] for you if you like! O, the heart's blood of a patriot! That's a fellow now that'd sell his country for fourpence – ay – and go down on his bended knees and thank the Almighty Christ he had a country to sell.

There was a knock at the door.

—Come in! said Mr Henchy.

A person resembling a poor clergyman or a poor actor appeared in the doorway. His black clothes were tightly buttoned on his short body and it was impossible to say whether he wore a clergyman's collar or a layman's because the collar of his shabby frock-coat, the uncovered buttons of which reflected the candlelight, was turned up about his neck. He wore a round hat of hard black felt. His face, shining with raindrops, had the appearance of damp yellow cheese save where two rosy spots indicated the cheekbones. He opened his very long mouth suddenly to express disappointment and at the same time opened wide his very bright blue eyes to express pleasure and surprise.

—O, Father Keon! said Mr Henchy, jumping up from his chair. Is that you? Come in!

—O, no, no, no! said Father Keon quickly, pursing his lips as if he were addressing a child.

—Won't you come in and sit down?

—No, no, no! said Father Keon, speaking in a discreet indulgent velvety voice. Don't let me disturb you now! I'm just looking for Mr Fanning. . . .

—He's round at the *Black Eagle*,[35] said Mr Henchy. But won't you come in and sit down a minute?

—No, no, thank you. It was just a little business matter, said Father Keon. Thank you, indeed.

He retreated from the doorway and Mr Henchy, seizing one of the candlesticks, went to the door to light him downstairs.

—O, don't trouble, I beg!

—No, but the stairs is so dark.

—No, no, I can see. . . . Thank you, indeed.

—Are you right now?

—All right, thanks. . . . Thanks.

Mr Henchy returned with the candlestick and put it on the table. He sat down again at the fire. There was silence for a few moments.

—Tell me, John, said Mr O'Connor, lighting his cigarette with another pasteboard card.

—Hm?

—What is he exactly?

—Ask me an easier one, said Mr Henchy.

—Fanning and himself seem to me very thick. They're often in Kavanagh's[36] together. Is he a priest at all?

—'Mmmyes, I believe so. . . . I think he's what you call a black sheep.[37] We haven't many of them, thank God! but we have a few. . . . He's an unfortunate man of some kind. . . .

—And how does he knock it out?[38] asked Mr O'Connor.

—That's another mystery.

—Is he attached to any chapel or church or institution or –

—No, said Mr Henchy. I think he's travelling on his own account.[39] . . . God forgive me, he added, I thought he was the dozen of stout.

—Is there any chance of a drink itself? asked Mr O'Connor.

—I'm dry too, said the old man.

—I asked that little shoeboy three times, said Mr Henchy, would he send up a dozen of stout. I asked him again now but he was leaning on the counter in his shirt-sleeves having a deep goster[40] with Alderman Cowley.

—Why didn't you remind him? said Mr O'Connor.

—Well, I couldn't go over while he was talking to Alderman Cowley. I just waited till I caught his eye, and said: *About that little matter I was speaking to you about. . . . That'll be all right, Mr H.,* he said. Yerra,[41] sure the little hop-o'-my-thumb[42] has forgotten all about it.

—There's some deal on in that quarter, said Mr O'Connor thoughtfully. I saw the three of them hard at it yesterday at Suffolk Street corner.[43]

—I think I know the little game they're at, said Mr Henchy. You must owe the City Fathers money nowadays if you want to be made Lord Mayor. Then they'll make you Lord Mayor. By God! I'm thinking seriously of becoming a City Father myself. What do you think? Would I do for the job?

Mr O'Connor laughed.

—So far as owing money goes. . . .

—Driving out of the Mansion House,[44] said Mr Henchy, in all my vermin,[45] with Jack here standing up behind me in a powdered wig – eh?

—And make me your private secretary, John.

—Yes. And I'll make Father Keon my private chaplain. We'll have a family party.

—Faith, Mr Henchy, said the old man, you'd keep up better style than some of them. I was talking one day to old Keegan, the porter. *And how do you like your new master, Pat?* says I to him. *You haven't much entertaining now*, says I. *Entertaining!* says he. *He'd live on the smell of an oil-rag*. And do you know what he told me? Now, I declare to God, I didn't believe him.

—What? said Mr Henchy and Mr O'Connor.

—He told me: *What do you think of a Lord Mayor of Dublin sending out for a pound of chops*[46] *for his dinner? How's that for high living?* says he. *Wisha!*[47] *wisha*, says I. *A pound of chops*, says he, *coming into the Mansion House. Wisha!* says I, *what kind of people is going at all now?*

At this point there was a knock at the door, and a boy put in his head.

—What is it? said the old man.

—From the *Black Eagle*, said the boy, walking in sideways and depositing a basket on the floor with a noise of shaken bottles.

The old man helped the boy to transfer the bottles from the basket to the table and counted the full tally. After the transfer the boy put his basket on his arm and asked:

—Any bottles?[48]

—What bottles? said the old man.

—Won't you let us drink them first? said Mr Henchy.

—I was told to ask for bottles.

—Come back to-morrow, said the old man.

—Here, boy! said Mr Henchy, will you run over to O'Farrell's and ask him to lend us a corkscrew – for Mr Henchy, say. Tell him we won't keep it a minute. Leave the basket there.

The boy went out and Mr Henchy began to rub his hands cheerfully, saying:

—Ah, well, he's not so bad after all. He's as good as his word, anyhow.

—There's no tumblers, said the old man.

—O, don't let that trouble you, Jack, said Mr Henchy. Many's the good man before now drank out of the bottle.

—Anyway, it's better than nothing, said Mr O'Connor.

—He's not a bad sort, said Mr Henchy, only Fanning has such a loan of him.[49] He means well, you know, in his own tinpot way.[50]

The boy came back with the corkscrew. The old man opened three bottles and was handing back the corkscrew when Mr Henchy said to the boy:

—Would you like a drink, boy?

—If you please, sir, said the boy.

The old man opened another bottle grudgingly, and handed it to the boy.

—What age are you? he asked.

—Seventeen, said the boy.

As the old man said nothing further the boy took the bottle, said: *Here's my best respects, sir* to Mr Henchy, drank the contents, put the bottle back on the table and wiped his mouth with his sleeve. Then he took up the corkscrew and went out of the door sideways, muttering some form of salutation.

—That's the way it begins, said the old man.

—The thin end of the wedge,[51] said Mr Henchy.

The old man distributed the three bottles which he had opened and the men drank from them simultaneously. After having drunk each placed his bottle on the mantelpiece within hand's reach and drew in a long breath of satisfaction.

—Well, I did a good day's work to-day, said Mr Henchy, after a pause.

—That so, John?

—Yes. I got him one or two sure things in Dawson Street,[52] Crofton[53] and myself. Between ourselves, you know, Crofton (he's a decent chap, of course), but he's not worth a damn as a canvasser. He hasn't a word to throw to a dog. He stands and looks at the people while I do the talking.

Here two men entered the room. One of them was a very fat man, whose blue serge clothes seemed to be in danger of falling from his sloping figure. He had a big face which resembled a young ox's face in expression, staring blue eyes and a grizzled moustache. The other man, who was much younger and frailer, had a thin clean-shaven face. He wore a very high double collar and a wide-brimmed bowler hat.

—Hello, Crofton! said Mr Henchy to the fat man. Talk of the devil. . . .

—Where did the boose[54] come from? asked the young man. Did the cow calve?[55]

—O, of course, Lyons[56] spots the drink first thing! said Mr O'Connor, laughing.

—Is that the way you chaps canvass, said Mr Lyons, and Crofton and I out in the cold and rain looking for votes?

—Why, blast your soul, said Mr Henchy, I'd get more votes in five minutes than you two'd get in a week.

—Open two bottles of stout, Jack, said Mr O'Connor.

—How can I? said the old man, when there's no corkscrew?

—Wait now, wait now! said Mr Henchy, getting up quickly. Did you ever see this little trick?

He took two bottles from the table and, carrying them to the fire, put them on the hob. Then he sat down again by the fire and took another drink from his bottle. Mr Lyons sat on the edge of the table, pushed his hat towards the nape of his neck and began to swing his legs.

—Which is my bottle? he asked.

—This lad, said Mr Henchy.

Mr Crofton sat down on a box and looked fixedly at
the other bottle on the hob. He was silent for two
reasons. The first reason, sufficient in itself, was that he
had nothing to say; the second reason was that he considered his companions beneath him. He had been a
canvasser for Wilkins, the Conservative, but when the Conservatives[57] had withdrawn their man and, choosing the
lesser of two evils, given their support to the Nationalist
candidate, he had been engaged to work for Mr Tierney.

In a few minutes an apologetic *Pok!* was heard as the
cork flew out of Mr Lyons' bottle. Mr Lyons jumped off
the table, went to the fire, took his bottle and carried it
back to the table.

—I was just telling them, Crofton, said Mr Henchy,
that we got a good few votes to-day.

—Who did you get? asked Mr Lyons.

—Well, I got Parkes for one, and I got Atkinson for
two, and I got Ward[58] of Dawson Street. Fine old chap
he is, too – regular old toff, old Conservative! *But isn't
your candidate a Nationalist?* said he. *He's a respectable
man*, said I. *He's in favour of whatever will benefit this
country. He's a big rate-payer,*[59] I said. *He has extensive
house property in the city and three places of business
and isn't it to his own advantage to keep down the rates?
He's a prominent and respected citizen*, said I, *and a Poor
Law Guardian, and he doesn't belong to any party, good,
bad, or indifferent*. That's the way to talk to 'em.

—And what about the address to the King? said Mr
Lyons, after drinking and smacking his lips.

—Listen to me, said Mr Henchy. What we want in this
country, as I said to old Ward, is capital. The King's
coming here will mean an influx of money into this
country. The citizens of Dublin will benefit by it. Look at

all the factories down by the quays there, idle! Look at all the money there is in the country if we only worked the old industries, the mills, the shipbuilding yards and factories. It's capital we want.

—But look here, John, said Mr O'Connor. Why should we welcome the King of England? Didn't Parnell himself . . .[60]

—Parnell, said Mr Henchy, is dead. Now, here's the way I look at it. Here's this chap come to the throne after his old mother keeping him out of it till the man was grey.[61] He's a man of the world, and he means well by us. He's a jolly fine decent fellow, if you ask me, and no damn nonsense about him. He just says to himself: *The old one never went to see these wild Irish.*[62] *By Christ, I'll go myself and see what they're like.* And are we going to insult the man when he comes over here on a friendly visit? Eh? Isn't that right, Crofton?

Mr Crofton nodded his head.

—But after all now, said Mr Lyons argumentatively, King Edward's life, you know, is not the very . . .[63]

—Let bygones be bygones, said Mr Henchy. I admire the man personally. He's just an ordinary knockabout like you and me. He's fond of his glass of grog and he's a bit of a rake, perhaps, and he's a good sportsman. Damn it, can't we Irish play fair?

—That's all very fine, said Mr Lyons. But look at the case of Parnell now.

—In the name of God, said Mr Henchy, where's the analogy between the two cases?

—What I mean, said Mr Lyons, is we have our ideals. Why, now, would we welcome a man like that? Do you think now after what he did Parnell was a fit man to lead us? And why, then, would we do it for Edward the Seventh?

—This is Parnell's anniversary, said Mr O'Connor,

and don't let us stir up any bad blood. We all respect him now that he's dead and gone – even the Conservatives, he added, turning to Mr Crofton.

Pok! The tardy cork flew out of Mr Crofton's bottle. Mr Crofton got up from his box and went to the fire. As he returned with his capture he said in a deep voice:

—Our side of the house respects him because he was a gentleman.

—Right you are, Crofton! said Mr Henchy fiercely. He was the only man that could keep that bag of cats in order. *Down, ye dogs! Lie down, ye curs!* That's the way he treated them. Come in, Joe! Come in! he called out, catching sight of Mr Hynes in the doorway.

Mr Hynes came in slowly.

—Open another bottle of stout, Jack, said Mr Henchy. O, I forgot there's no corkscrew! Here, show me one here and I'll put it at the fire.

The old man handed him another bottle and he placed it on the hob.

—Sit down, Joe, said Mr O'Connor, we're just talking about the Chief.[64]

—Ay, ay! said Mr Henchy.

Mr Hynes sat on the side of the table near Mr Lyons but said nothing.

—There's one of them, anyhow, said Mr Henchy, that didn't renege him. By God, I'll say for you, Joe! No, by God, you stuck to him like a man!

—O, Joe, said Mr O'Connor suddenly. Give us that thing you wrote – do you remember? Have you got it on you?

—O, ay! said Mr Henchy. Give us that. Did you ever hear that, Crofton? Listen to this now: splendid thing.

—Go on, said Mr O'Connor. Fire away, Joe.

Mr Hynes did not seem to remember at once the piece to which they were alluding but, after reflecting a while, he said:

—O, that thing is it. . . . Sure, that's old now.

—Out with it, man! said Mr O'Connor.

—'Sh, 'sh, said Mr Henchy. Now, Joe!

Mr Hynes hesitated a little longer. Then amid the silence he took off his hat, laid it on the table and stood up. He seemed to be rehearsing the piece in his mind. After a rather long pause he announced:

THE DEATH OF PARNELL

6th October 1891

He cleared his throat once or twice and then began to recite:

> *He is dead. Our Uncrowned King is dead.*
>   *O, Erin, mourn with grief and woe*
> *For he lies dead whom the fell gang*
>   *Of modern hypocrites laid low.*
>
> *He lies slain by the coward hounds*
>   *He raised to glory from the mire;*
> *And Erin's hopes and Erin's dreams*
>   *Perish upon her monarch's pyre.*
>
> *In palace, cabin or in cot*
>   *The Irish heart where'er it be*
> *Is bowed with woe – for he is gone*
>   *Who would have wrought her destiny.*
>
> *He would have had his Erin famed,*
>   *The green flag gloriously unfurled,*
> *Her statesmen, bards and warriors raised*
>   *Before the nations of the World.*
>
> *He dreamed (alas, 'twas but a dream!)*
>   *Of Liberty: but as he strove*
> *To clutch that idol, treachery*
>   *Sundered him from the thing he loved.*

Shame on the coward caitiff hands
  That smote their Lord or with a kiss
Betrayed him to the rabble-rout
  Of fawning priests – no friends of his.

May everlasting shame consume
  The memory of those who tried
To befoul and smear th' exalted name
  Of one who spurned them in his pride.

He fell as fall the mighty ones,
  Nobly undaunted to the last,
And death has now united him
  With Erin's heroes of the past.

No sound of strife disturb his sleep!
  Calmly he rests: no human pain
Or high ambition spurs him now
  The peaks of glory to attain.

They had their way: they laid him low.
  But Erin, list, his spirit may
Rise, like the Phœnix from the flames,
  When breaks the dawning of the day,

The day that brings us Freedom's reign.
  And on that day may Erin well
Pledge in the cup she lifts to Joy
  One grief – the memory of Parnell.

Mr Hynes sat down again on the table. When he had finished his recitation there was a silence and then a burst of clapping: even Mr Lyons clapped. The applause continued for a little time. When it had ceased all the auditors drank from their bottles in silence.

Pok! The cork flew out of Mr Hynes' bottle, but Mr Hynes remained sitting, flushed and bareheaded on the table. He did not seem to have heard the invitation.

—Good man, Joe! said Mr O'Connor, taking out his cigarette papers and pouch the better to hide his emotion.

—What do you think of that, Crofton? cried Mr Henchy. Isn't that fine? What?

Mr Crofton said that it was a very fine piece of writing.

A MOTHER

Mr Holohan,[1] assistant secretary of the *Eire Abu*[2] Society, had been walking up and down Dublin for nearly a month, with his hands and pockets full of dirty pieces of paper, arranging about the series of concerts. He had a game leg and for this his friends called him Hoppy Holohan. He walked up and down constantly, stood by the hour at street corners arguing the point and made notes; but in the end it was Mrs Kearney who arranged everything.

Miss Devlin had become Mrs Kearney out of spite. She had been educated in a high-class convent where she had learned French and music. As she was naturally pale and unbending in manner she made few friends at school. When she came to the age of marriage she was sent out to many houses where her playing and ivory manners were much admired. She sat amid the chilly circle of her accomplishments, waiting for some suitor to brave it and offer her a brilliant life. But the young men whom she met were ordinary and she gave them no encouragement, trying to console her romantic desires by eating a great deal of Turkish Delight in secret. However, when she drew near the limit and her friends began to loosen their tongues about her she silenced them by marrying Mr Kearney, who was a bootmaker on Ormond Quay.[3]

He was much older than she. His conversation, which was serious, took place at intervals in his great brown beard. After the first year of married life Mrs Kearney perceived that such a man would wear better than a romantic person but she never put her own romantic ideas away. He was sober, thrifty and pious; he went to the altar every first Friday,[4] sometimes with her, oftener by himself. But she never weakened in her religion and was a good wife to him. At some party in a strange house when she lifted her eyebrow ever so slightly he stood up to take his leave and, when his cough troubled him, she put the eider-down quilt over his feet and made a strong rum punch. For his part he was a model father. By paying a small sum every week into a society[5] he ensured for both his daughters a dowry of one hundred pounds each when they came to the age of twenty-four. He sent the elder daughter, Kathleen, to a good convent, where she learned French and music and afterwards paid her fees at the Academy.[6] Every year in the month of July Mrs Kearney found occasion to say to some friend:

—My good man is packing us off to Skerries for a few weeks.

If it was not Skerries it was Howth or Greystones.[7]

When the Irish Revival[8] began to be appreciable Mrs Kearney determined to take advantage of her daughter's name[9] and brought an Irish teacher to the house. Kathleen and her sister sent Irish picture postcards to their friends and these friends sent back other Irish picture postcards. On special Sundays when Mr Kearney went with his family to the pro-cathedral[10] a little crowd of people would assemble after mass at the corner of Cathedral Street. They were all friends of the Kearneys – musical friends or Nationalist[11] friends; and, when they had played every little counter of gossip, they shook hands with one another all together, laughing at the crossing of so many hands and said good-bye to one another in Irish.[12] Soon the name of Miss Kathleen Kearney began to be heard often on people's lips. People said that she was very clever at music and a very nice girl and, more-over, that she was a believer in the language movement.

Mrs Kearney was well content at this. Therefore she was not surprised when one day Mr Holohan came to her and proposed that her daughter should be the accompanist at a series of four grand concerts which his Society was going to give in the Antient Concert Rooms.[13] She brought him into the drawing-room, made him sit down and brought out the decanter and the silver biscuit barrel. She entered heart and soul into the details of the enterprise, advised and dissuaded; and finally a contract[14] was drawn up by which Kathleen was to receive eight guineas for her services as accompanist at the four grand concerts.

As Mr Holohan was a novice in such delicate matters as the wording of bills and the disposing of items for a programme Mrs Kearney helped him. She had tact. She knew what *artistes* should go into capitals and what *artistes* should go into small type. She knew that the first tenor would not like to come on after Mr Meade's comic turn. To keep the audience continually diverted she slipped the doubtful items in between the old favourites. Mr Holohan called to see her every day to have her advice on some point. She was invariably friendly and advising – homely, in fact. She pushed the decanter towards him, saying:

—Now, help yourself, Mr Holohan!

And while he was helping himself she said:

—Don't be afraid! Don't be afraid of it!

Everything went on smoothly. Mrs Kearney bought some lovely blush-pink charmeuse[15] in Brown Thomas's[16] to let into the front of Kathleen's dress. It cost a pretty penny; but there are occasions when a little expense is justifiable. She took a dozen of two-shilling tickets for the final concert and sent them to those friends who could not be trusted to come otherwise. She forgot nothing and, thanks to her, everything that was to be done was done.

The concerts were to be on Wednesday, Thursday, Friday and Saturday. When Mrs Kearney arrived with her daughter at the Antient Concert Rooms on Wednesday night she did not like the look of things. A few young men, wearing bright blue badges in their coats, stood idle in the vestibule; none of them wore evening dress. She passed by with her daughter and a quick glance through the open door of the hall showed her the cause of the stewards' idleness. At first she wondered had she mistaken the hour. No, it was twenty minutes to eight.

In the dressing-room behind the stage she was introduced to the secretary of the Society, Mr Fitzpatrick. She smiled and shook his hand. He was a little man with a white vacant face. She noticed that he wore his soft brown hat carelessly on the side of his head and that his accent was flat. He held a programme in his hand and, while he was talking to her, he chewed one end of it into a moist pulp. He seemed to bear disappointments lightly. Mr Holohan came into the dressing-room every few minutes with reports from the box-office. The *artistes* talked among themselves nervously, glanced from time to time at the mirror and rolled and unrolled their music. When it was nearly half-past eight the few people in the hall began to express their desire to be entertained. Mr Fitzpatrick came in, smiled vacantly at the room, and said:

—Well now, ladies and gentlemen, I suppose we'd better open the ball.

Mrs Kearney rewarded his very flat final syllable with a quick stare of contempt and then said to her daughter encouragingly:

—Are you ready, dear?

When she had an opportunity she called Mr Holohan aside and asked him to tell her what it meant. Mr

Holohan did not know what it meant. He said that the Committee had made a mistake in arranging for four concerts: four was too many.

—And the *artistes!* said Mrs Kearney. Of course they are doing their best, but really they are no good.

Mr Holohan admitted that the *artistes* were no good but the Committee, he said, had decided to let the first three concerts go as they pleased and reserve all the talent for Saturday night. Mrs Kearney said nothing but, as the mediocre items followed one another on the platform and the few people in the hall grew fewer and fewer, she began to regret that she had put herself to any expense for such a concert. There was something she didn't like in the look of things and Mr Fitzpatrick's vacant smile irritated her very much. However, she said nothing and waited to see how it would end. The concert expired shortly before ten and everyone went home quickly.

The concert on Thursday night was better attended but Mrs Kearney saw at once that the house was filled with paper. The audience behaved indecorously as if the concert were an informal dress rehearsal. Mr Fitzpatrick seemed to enjoy himself; he was quite unconscious that Mrs Kearney was taking angry note of his conduct. He stood at the edge of the screen, from time to time jutting out his head and exchanging a laugh with two friends in the corner of the balcony. In the course of the evening Mrs Kearney learned that the Friday concert was to be abandoned and that the Committee was going to move heaven and earth to secure a bumper house on Saturday night. When she heard this she sought out Mr Holohan. She buttonholed him as he was limping out quickly with a glass of lemonade for a young lady and asked him was it true. Yes, it was true.

—But, of course, that doesn't alter the contract, she said. The contract was for four concerts.

Mr Holohan seemed to be in a hurry; he advised her to speak to Mr Fitzpatrick. Mrs Kearney was now beginning to be alarmed. She called Mr Fitzpatrick away from his screen and told him that her daughter had signed for four concerts and that, of course, according to the terms of the contract, she should receive the sum originally stipulated for whether the society gave the four concerts or not. Mr Fitzpatrick, who did not catch the point at issue very quickly, seemed unable to resolve the difficulty and said that he would bring the matter before the Committee. Mrs Kearney's anger began to flutter in her cheek and she had all she could do to keep from asking:

—And who is the *Cometty*,[17] pray?

But she knew that it would not be ladylike to do that: so she was silent.

Little boys were sent out into the principal streets of Dublin early on Friday morning with bundles of handbills. Special puffs appeared in all the evening papers reminding the music-loving public of the treat which was in store for it on the following evening. Mrs Kearney was somewhat reassured but she thought well to tell her husband part of her suspicions. He listened carefully and said that perhaps it would be better if he went with her on Saturday night. She agreed. She respected her husband in the same way as she respected the General Post Office,[18] as something large, secure and fixed; and though she knew the small number of his talents she appreciated his abstract value as a male. She was glad that he had suggested coming with her. She thought her plans over.

The night of the grand concert came. Mrs Kearney, with her husband and daughter, arrived at the Antient Concert Rooms three-quarters of an hour before the time at which the concert was to begin. By ill luck it was a rainy evening. Mrs Kearney placed her daughter's clothes and music in charge of her husband and went all over the building looking for Mr Holohan or Mr Fitzpatrick. She could find neither. She asked the stewards was any member of the Committee in the hall and, after a great deal of trouble, a steward brought out a little woman named Miss Beirne to whom Mrs Kearney explained that she wanted to see one of the secretaries. Miss Beirne expected them any minute and asked could she do anything. Mrs Kearney looked searchingly at the oldish face which was screwed into an expression of trustfulness and enthusiasm and answered:

—No, thank you!

The little woman hoped they would have a good house. She looked out at the rain until the melancholy of the wet street effaced all the trustfulness and enthusiasm from her twisted features. Then she gave a little sigh and said:

—Ah, well! We did our best, the dear knows.[19]

Mrs Kearney had to go back to the dressing-room.

The *artistes* were arriving. The bass and the second tenor had already come. The bass, Mr Duggan, was a slender young man with a scattered black moustache. He was the son of a hall porter in an office in the city and, as a boy, he had sung prolonged bass notes in the resounding hall. From this humble state he had raised himself until he had become a first-rate *artiste*. He had appeared in grand opera. One night, when an operatic *artiste* had fallen ill, he had undertaken the part of the king in the opera of *Maritana*[20] at the Queen's Theatre.[21] He sang his music with great feeling and volume and was warmly welcomed by the gallery; but, unfortunately, he marred the good impression by wiping his nose in his gloved hand once or twice out of thoughtlessness. He was unassuming and spoke little. He said *yous*[22] so softly that it passed unnoticed and he never drank anything stronger than milk for his voice' sake. Mr Bell, the second tenor, was a fair-haired little man who competed every year for prizes at the Feis Ceoil.[23] On his fourth trial he had been awarded a bronze medal. He was extremely nervous and extremely jealous of other tenors and he covered his nervous jealousy with an ebullient friendliness. It was his humour to have people know what an ordeal a concert was to him. Therefore when he saw Mr Duggan he went over to him and asked:

—Are you in it too?

—Yes, said Mr Duggan.

Mr Bell laughed at his fellow-sufferer, held out his hand and said:

—Shake!

Mrs Kearney passed by these two young men and went to the edge of the screen to view the house. The seats were being filled up rapidly and a pleasant noise circulated in the auditorium. She came back and spoke to her husband privately. Their conversation was evidently about Kathleen for they both glanced at her often as she stood chatting to one of her Nationalist friends, Miss Healy, the contralto. An unknown solitary woman with a pale face walked through the room. The women followed with keen eyes the faded blue dress which was stretched upon a meagre body. Someone said that she was Madam Glynn, the soprano.

—I wonder where did they dig her up, said Kathleen to Miss Healy. I'm sure I never heard of her.

Miss Healy had to smile. Mr Holohan limped into the dressing-room at that moment and the two young ladies asked him who was the unknown woman. Mr Holohan said that she was Madam Glynn from London. Madam Glynn took her stand in a corner of the room, holding a roll of music stiffly before her and from time to time changing the direction of her startled gaze. The shadow took her faded dress into shelter but fell revengefully into the little cup behind her collar-bone. The noise of the hall became more audible. The first tenor and the baritone arrived together. They were both well dressed, stout and complacent and they brought a breath of opulence among the company.

Mrs Kearney brought her daughter over to them, and talked to them amiably. She wanted to be on good terms with them but, while she strove to be polite, her eyes followed Mr Holohan in his limping and devious courses. As soon as she could she excused herself and went out after him.

—Mr Holohan, I want to speak to you for a moment, she said.

They went down to a discreet part of the corridor. Mrs Kearney asked him when was her daughter going to be paid. Mr Holohan said that Mr Fitzpatrick had charge of that. Mrs Kearney said that she didn't know anything about Mr Fitzpatrick. Her daughter had signed a contract for eight guineas and she would have to be paid. Mr Holohan said that it wasn't his business.

—Why isn't it your business? asked Mrs Kearney. Didn't you yourself bring her the contract? Anyway, if it's not your business it's my business and I mean to see to it.

—You'd better speak to Mr Fitzpatrick, said Mr Holohan distantly.

—I don't know anything about Mr Fitzpatrick, repeated Mrs Kearney. I have my contract, and I intend to see that it is carried out.

When she came back to the dressing-room her cheeks were slightly suffused. The room was lively. Two men in outdoor dress had taken possession of the fireplace and were chatting familiarly with Miss Healy and the baritone. They were the *Freeman* man and Mr O'Madden Burke. The *Freeman* man[24] had come in to say that he could not wait for the concert as he had to report the lecture which an American priest was giving in the Mansion House.[25] He said they were to leave the report for him at the *Freeman* office and he would see that it went in. He was a grey-haired man, with a plausible voice and careful manners. He held an extinguished cigar in his hand and the aroma of cigar smoke floated near him. He had not intended to stay a moment because concerts and *artistes* bored him considerably but he remained leaning against the mantelpiece. Miss Healy stood in front of him, talking and laughing. He was old enough to suspect one reason for her politeness but young enough in spirit to turn the moment to account. The warmth, fragrance and colour of her body appealed to his senses. He was pleasantly conscious that the bosom which he saw rise and fall slowly beneath him rose and fell at that moment for him, that the laughter and fragrance and wilful glances were his tribute. When he could stay no longer he took leave of her regretfully.

—O'Madden Burke will write the notice, he explained to Mr Holohan, and I'll see it in.

—Thank you very much, Mr Hendrick, said Mr Holohan. You'll see it in, I know. Now, won't you have a little something before you go?

—I don't mind, said Mr Hendrick.

The two men went along some tortuous passages and up a dark staircase and came to a secluded room where one of the stewards was uncorking bottles for a few gentlemen. One of these gentlemen was Mr O'Madden Burke, who had found out the room by instinct. He was a suave elderly man who balanced his imposing body, when at rest, upon a large silk umbrella. His magniloquent western name was the moral umbrella upon which he balanced the fine problem of his finances. He was widely respected.

While Mr Holohan was entertaining the *Freeman* man Mrs Kearney was speaking so animatedly to her husband that he had to ask her to lower her voice. The conversation of the others in the dressing-room had become strained. Mr Bell, the first item, stood ready with his music but the accompanist made no sign. Evidently something was wrong. Mr Kearney looked straight before him, stroking his beard, while Mrs Kearney spoke into Kathleen's ear with subdued emphasis. From the hall came sounds of encouragement, clapping and stamping of feet. The first tenor and the baritone and Miss Healy stood together, waiting tranquilly, but Mr Bell's nerves were greatly agitated because he was afraid the audience would think that he had come late.

Mr Holohan and Mr O'Madden Burke came into the room. In a moment, Mr Holohan perceived the hush. He went over to Mrs Kearney and spoke with her earnestly. While they were speaking the noise in the hall grew louder. Mr Holohan became very red and excited. He spoke volubly, but Mrs Kearney said curtly at intervals:

—She won't go on. She must get her eight guineas.

Mr Holohan pointed desperately towards the hall where the audience was clapping and stamping. He appealed to Mr Kearney and to Kathleen. But Mr Kearney continued to stroke his beard and Kathleen looked down moving the point of her new shoe: it was not her fault. Mrs Kearney repeated:

—She won't go on without her money.

After a swift struggle of tongues Mr Holohan hobbled out in haste. The room was silent. When the strain of the silence had become somewhat painful Miss Healy said to the baritone:

—Have you seen Mrs Pat Campbell [26] this week?

The baritone had not seen her but he had been told that she was very fine. The conversation went no further.

The first tenor bent his head and began to count the links of the gold chain which was extended across his waist, smiling and humming random notes to observe the effect on the frontal sinus. From time to time everyone glanced at Mrs Kearney.

The noise in the auditorium had risen to a clamour when Mr Fitzpatrick burst into the room, followed by Mr Holohan, who was panting. The clapping and stamping in the hall were punctuated by whistling. Mr Fitzpatrick held a few banknotes in his hand. He counted out four into Mrs Kearney's hand and said she would get the other half at the interval. Mrs Kearney said:

—This is four shillings short.

But Kathleen gathered in her skirt and said: *Now, Mr Bell*, to the first item, who was shaking like an aspen. The singer and the accompanist went out together. The noise in the hall died away. There was a pause of a few seconds: and then the piano was heard.

The first part of the concert was very successful except for Madam Glynn's item. The poor lady sang *Killarney*[27] in a bodiless gasping voice, with all the old-fashioned mannerisms of intonation and pronunciation which she believed lent elegance to her singing. She looked as if she had been resurrected from an old stage-wardrobe and the cheaper parts of the hall made fun of her high wailing notes. The first tenor and the contralto, however, brought down the house. Kathleen played a selection of Irish airs which was generously applauded. The first part closed with a stirring patriotic recitation delivered by a young lady who arranged amateur theatricals. It was deservedly applauded; and, when it was ended, the men went out for the interval, content.

All this time the dressing-room was a hive of excitement. In one corner were Mr Holohan, Mr Fitzpatrick, Miss Beirne, two of the stewards, the baritone, the bass, and Mr O'Madden Burke. Mr O'Madden Burke said it was the most scandalous exhibition he had ever witnessed. Miss Kathleen Kearney's musical career was ended in Dublin after that, he said. The baritone was asked what did he think of Mrs Kearney's conduct. He did not like to say anything. He had been paid his money and wished to be at peace with men. However, he said that Mrs Kearney might have taken the *artistes* into consideration. The stewards and the secretaries debated hotly as to what should be done when the interval came.

—I agree with Miss Beirne, said Mr O'Madden Burke. Pay her nothing.

In another corner of the room were Mrs Kearney and her husband, Mr Bell, Miss Healy and the young lady who had recited the patriotic piece. Mrs Kearney said that the Committee had treated her scandalously. She had spared neither trouble nor expense and this was how she was repaid.

They thought they had only a girl to deal with and that, therefore, they could ride roughshod over her. But she would show them their mistake. They wouldn't have dared to have treated her like that if she had been a man. But she would see that her daughter got her rights: she wouldn't be fooled. If they didn't pay her to the last farthing she would make Dublin ring. Of course she was sorry for the sake of the *artistes*. But what else could she do? She appealed to the second tenor who said he thought she had not been well treated. Then she appealed to Miss Healy. Miss Healy wanted to join the other group but she did not like to do so because she was a great friend of Kathleen's and the Kearneys had often invited her to their house.

As soon as the first part was ended Mr Fitzpatrick and Mr Holohan went over to Mrs Kearney and told her that the other four guineas would be paid after the Committee

A MOTHER

meeting on the following Tuesday and that, in case her
daughter did not play for the second part, the Committee
would consider the contract broken and would pay nothing.

—I haven't seen any Committee, said Mrs Kearney
angrily. My daughter has her contract. She will get four
pounds eight into her hand or a foot she won't put on
that platform.

—I'm surprised at you, Mrs Kearney, said Mr Holohan.
I never thought you would treat us this way.

—And what way did you treat me? asked Mrs Kearney.

Her face was inundated with an angry colour and she
looked as if she would attack someone with her hands.

—I'm asking for my rights, she said.

—You might have some sense of decency, said Mr Holohan.

—Might I, indeed? ... And when I ask when my
daughter is going to be paid I can't get a civil answer.

She tossed her head and assumed a haughty voice:

—You must speak to the secretary. It's not my business.
I'm a great fellow fol-the-diddle-I-do.[28]

—I thought you were a lady, said Mr Holohan, walking
away from her abruptly.

After that Mrs Kearney's conduct was condemned on
all hands: everyone approved of what the Committee had
done. She stood at the door, haggard with rage, arguing
with her husband and daughter, gesticulating with them.
She waited until it was time for the second part to begin
in the hope that the secretaries would approach her. But
Miss Healy had kindly consented to play one or two
accompaniments. Mrs Kearney had to stand aside to
allow the baritone and his accompanist to pass up to the
platform. She stood still for an instant like an angry stone
image and, when the first notes of the song struck her

147

ear, she caught up her daughter's cloak and said to her husband:

—Get a cab!

He went out at once. Mrs Kearney wrapped the cloak round her daughter and followed him. As she passed through the doorway she stopped and glared into Mr Holohan's face.

—I'm not done with you yet, she said.

—But I'm done with you, said Mr Holohan.

Kathleen followed her mother meekly. Mr Holohan began to pace up and down the room, in order to cool himself for he felt his skin on fire.

—That's a nice lady! he said. O, she's a nice lady!

—You did the proper thing, Holohan, said Mr O'Madden Burke, poised upon his umbrella in approval.

GRACE [1]

Two gentlemen who were in the lavatory at the time tried to lift him up: but he was quite helpless. He lay curled up at the foot of the stairs down which he had fallen. They succeeded in turning him over. His hat had rolled a few yards away and his clothes were smeared with the filth and ooze of the floor on which he had lain, face downwards. His eyes were closed and he breathed with a grunting noise. A thin stream of blood trickled from the corner of his mouth.

These two gentlemen and one of the curates [2] carried him up the stairs and laid him down again on the floor of the bar. In two minutes he was surrounded by a ring of men. The manager of the bar asked everyone who he was and who was with him. No one knew who he was but one of the curates said he had served the gentleman with a small rum.

—Was he by himself? asked the manager.

—No, sir. There was two gentlemen with him.

—And where are they?

No one knew; a voice said:

—Give him air. He's fainted.

The ring of onlookers distended and closed again elastically. A dark medal of blood had formed itself near the man's head on the tessellated floor. The manager, alarmed by the grey pallor of the man's face, sent for a policeman.

His collar was unfastened and his necktie undone. He opened his eyes for an instant, sighed and closed them again. One of the gentlemen who had carried him upstairs held a dinged silk hat in his hand. The manager asked repeatedly did no one know who the injured man was or where had his friends gone. The door of the bar opened and an immense constable entered. A crowd which had followed him down the laneway collected outside the door, struggling to look in through the glass panels.

The manager at once began to narrate what he knew. The constable, a young man with thick immobile features, listened. He moved his head slowly to right and left and from the manager to the person on the floor, as if he feared to be the victim of some delusion. Then he drew off his glove, produced a small book from his waist, licked the lead of his pencil and made ready to indite. He asked in a suspicious provincial accent:

—Who is the man? What's his name and address?

A young man in a cycling-suit cleared his way through the ring of bystanders. He knelt down promptly beside the injured man and called for water. The constable knelt down also to help. The young man washed the blood from the injured man's mouth and then called for some brandy. The constable repeated the order in an authoritative voice until a curate came running with the glass. The brandy was forced down the man's throat. In a few seconds he opened his eyes and looked about him. He looked at the circle of faces and then, understanding, strove to rise to his feet.

—You're all right now? asked the young man in the cycling-suit.

—Sha,[3] 's nothing, said the injured man, trying to stand up.

He was helped to his feet. The manager said something about a hospital and some of the bystanders gave advice. The battered silk hat was placed on the man's head. The constable asked:

—Where do you live?

The man, without answering, began to twirl the ends

of his moustache. He made light of his accident. It was nothing, he said: only a little accident. He spoke very thickly.

—Where do you live? repeated the constable.

The man said they were to get a cab for him. While the point was being debated a tall agile gentleman of fair complexion, wearing a long yellow ulster, came from the far end of the bar. Seeing the spectacle he called out:

—Hallo, Tom, old man! What's the trouble?

—Sha,'s nothing, said the man.

The new-comer surveyed the deplorable figure before him and then turned to the constable saying:

—It's all right, constable. I'll see him home.

The constable touched his helmet and answered:

—All right, Mr Power!

—Come now, Tom, said Mr Power, taking his friend by the arm. No bones broken. What? Can you walk?

The young man in the cycling-suit took the man by the other arm and the crowd divided.

—How did you get yourself into this mess? asked Mr Power.

—The gentleman fell down the stairs, said the young man.

—I' 'ery 'uch o'liged to you, sir, said the injured man.

—Not at all.

—'an't we have a little . . .?

—Not now. Not now.

The three men left the bar and the crowd sifted through the doors into the laneway. The manager brought the constable to the stairs to inspect the scene of the accident. They agreed that the gentleman must have missed his footing. The customers returned to the counter and a curate set about removing the traces of blood from the floor.

When they came out into Grafton Street[4] Mr Power

whistled for an outsider.[5] The injured man said again as well as he could:

—I' 'ery 'uch o'liged to you, sir. I hope we'll 'eet again. 'y na'e is Kernan.

The shock and the incipient pain had partly sobered him.

—Don't mention it, said the young man.

They shook hands. Mr Kernan was hoisted on to the car and, while Mr Power was giving directions to the carman, he expressed his gratitude to the young man and regretted that they could not have a little drink together.

—Another time, said the young man.

The car drove off towards Westmoreland Street.[6] As it passed the Ballast Office[7] the clock showed half-past nine. A keen east wind hit them blowing from the mouth of the river. Mr Kernan was huddled together with cold. His friend asked him to tell how the accident had happened.

—I' an't, 'an, he answered, 'y 'ongue is hurt.

—Show.

The other leaned over the well of the car and peered into Mr Kernan's mouth but he could not see. He struck a match and, sheltering it in the shell of his hands, peered again into the mouth which Mr Kernan opened obediently. The swaying movement of the car brought the match to and from the opened mouth. The lower teeth and gums were covered with clotted blood and a minute piece of the tongue seemed to have been bitten off. The match was blown out.

—That's ugly, said Mr Power.

—Sha, 's nothing, said Mr Kernan, closing his mouth and pulling the collar of his filthy coat across his neck.

Mr Kernan was a commercial traveller of the old school which believed in the dignity of its calling. He had never been seen in the city without a silk hat of some

decency and a pair of gaiters. By grace of these two
articles of clothing, he said, a man could always pass
muster. He carried on the tradition of his Napoleon, the
great Blackwhite,[8] whose memory he evoked at times by
legend and mimicry. Modern business methods had
spared him only so far as to allow him a little office in
Crowe Street[9] on the window blind of which was written
the name of his firm with the address – London, E.C.[10]
On the mantelpiece of this little office a little leaden
battalion of canisters was drawn up and on the table
before the window stood four or five china bowls which
were usually half full of a black liquid. From these bowls
Mr Kernan tasted tea. He took a mouthful, drew it up,
saturated his palate with it and then spat it forth into the
grate. Then he paused to judge.

Mr Power, a much younger man, was employed in the
Royal Irish Constabulary Office in Dublin Castle.[11] The
arc of his social rise intersected the arc of his friend's
decline but Mr Kernan's decline was mitigated by the fact
that certain of those friends who had known him at his
highest point of success still esteemed him as a character.[12]
Mr Power was one of these friends. His inexplicable
debts were a byword in his circle; he was a debonair
young man.

The car halted before a small house on the Glasnevin
road[13] and Mr Kernan was helped into the house. His
wife put him to bed while Mr Power sat downstairs in
the kitchen asking the children where they went to school
and what book they were in.[14] The children – two girls
and a boy, conscious of their father's helplessness and of
their mother's absence, began some horseplay with him.
He was surprised at their manners and at their accents[15]
and his brow grew thoughtful. After a while Mrs Kernan
entered the kitchen, exclaiming:

—Such a sight! O, he'll do for himself one day and

that's the holy alls of it.[16] He's been drinking since Friday.

Mr Power was careful to explain to her that he was not responsible, that he had come on the scene by the merest accident. Mrs Kernan, remembering Mr Power's good offices during domestic quarrels as well as many small, but opportune loans, said:

—O, you needn't tell me that, Mr Power. I know you're a friend of his not like some of those others he does be[17] with. They're all right so long as he has money in his pocket to keep him out from his wife and family. Nice friends! Who was he with to-night, I'd like to know?

Mr Power shook his head but said nothing.

—I'm so sorry, she continued, that I've nothing in the house to offer you. But if you wait a minute I'll send round to Fogarty's[18] at the corner.

Mr Power stood up.

—We were waiting for him to come home with the money. He never seems to think he has a home at all.

—O, now, Mrs Kernan, said Mr Power, we'll make him turn over a new leaf. I'll talk to Martin. He's the man. We'll come here one of these nights and talk it over.

She saw him to the door. The carman was stamping up and down the footpath and swinging his arms to warm himself.

—It's very kind of you to bring him home, she said.

—Not at all, said Mr Power.

He got up on the car. As it drove off he raised his hat to her gaily.

—We'll make a new man of him, he said. Good-night, Mrs Kernan.

.   .   .   .

Mrs Kernan's puzzled eyes watched the car till it was out of sight. Then she withdrew them, went into the house and emptied her husband's pockets.

She was an active, practical woman of middle age. Not long before she had celebrated her silver wedding and renewed her intimacy with her husband by waltzing with him to Mr Power's accompaniment. In her days of court-ship Mr Kernan had seemed to her a not ungallant figure: and she still hurried to the chapel door whenever a wedding was reported and, seeing the bridal pair, recalled with vivid pleasure how she had passed out of the Star of the Sea Church in Sandymount,[19] leaning on the arm of a jovial well-fed man who was dressed smartly in a frock-coat and lavender trousers and carried a silk hat gracefully balanced upon his other arm. After three weeks she had found a wife's life irksome and, later on, when she was beginning to find it unbearable, she had become a mother. The part of mother presented to her no insuperable difficulties and for twenty-five years she had kept house shrewdly for her husband. Her two eldest sons were launched. One was in a draper's shop in Glasgow and the other was clerk to a tea-merchant in Belfast.[20] They were good sons, wrote regularly and sometimes sent home money. The other children were still at school.

Mr Kernan sent a letter to his office next day and remained in bed. She made beef-tea for him and scolded him roundly. She accepted his frequent intemperance as part of the climate, healed him dutifully whenever he was sick and always tried to make him eat a breakfast. There were worse husbands. He had never been violent since the boys had grown up and she knew that he would walk to the end of Thomas Street[21] and back again to book even a small order.

Two nights after his friends came to see him. She brought them up to his bedroom, the air of which was impregnated with a personal odour, and gave them chairs at the fire. Mr Kernan's tongue, the occasional stinging pain of which had made him somewhat irritable during the day, became more polite. He sat propped up in the bed by pillows and the little colour in his puffy cheeks made them resemble warm cinders. He apologised to his guests for the disorder of the room but at the same time looked at them a little proudly, with a veteran's pride.

He was quite unconscious that he was the victim of a plot which his friends, Mr Cunningham, Mr M'Coy and Mr Power had disclosed to Mrs Kernan in the parlour. The idea had been Mr Power's but its development was entrusted to Mr Cunningham. Mr Kernan came of Protestant stock and, though he had been converted to the Catholic faith at the time of his marriage, he had not been in the pale [22] of the Church for twenty years. He was fond, moreover, of giving side-thrusts at Catholicism.

Mr Cunningham was the very man for such a case. He was an elder colleague of Mr Power. His own domestic life was not very happy. People had great sympathy with him for it was known that he had married an unpresentable woman who was an incurable drunkard. He had set up house for her six times; and each time she had pawned the furniture on him.

Everyone had respect for poor Martin Cunningham. He was a thoroughly sensible man, influential and intelligent. His blade of human knowledge, natural astuteness particularised by long association with cases in the police courts, had been tempered by brief immersions in the waters of general philosophy. He was well informed. His friends bowed to his opinions and considered that his face was like Shakespeare's.

When the plot had been disclosed to her Mrs Kernan had said:

—I leave it all in your hands, Mr Cunningham.

After a quarter of a century of married life she had very few illusions left. Religion for her was a habit and she suspected that a man of her husband's age would not change greatly before death. She was tempted to see a curious appropriateness in his accident and, but that she did not wish to seem bloody-minded, she would have told the gentlemen that Mr Kernan's tongue would not suffer by being shortened. However, Mr Cunningham was a capable man; and religion was religion. The scheme might do good and, at least, it could do no harm. Her beliefs were not extravagant. She believed steadily in the Sacred Heart[23] as the most generally useful of all Catholic devotions and approved of the sacraments. Her faith was bounded by her kitchen but, if she was put to it, she could believe also in the banshee[24] and in the Holy Ghost.

The gentlemen began to talk of the accident. Mr Cunningham said that he had once known a similar case. A man of seventy had bitten off a piece of his tongue during an epileptic fit and the tongue had filled in again so that no one could see a trace of the bite.

—Well, I'm not seventy, said the invalid.

—God forbid, said Mr Cunningham.

—It doesn't pain you now? asked Mr M'Coy.

Mr M'Coy had been at one time a tenor of some reputation. His wife, who had been a soprano, still taught young children to play the piano at low terms. His line of life had not been the shortest distance between two points and for short periods he had been driven to live by his wits. He had been a clerk in the Midland Railway,[25] a canvasser for advertisements for *The Irish Times* and for *The Freeman's Journal*,[26] a town traveller for a coal firm on commission, a private inquiry agent, a clerk in the office of the Sub-Sheriff[27] and he had recently become secretary to the City Coroner.[28] His new office made him professionally interested in Mr Kernan's case.

—Pain? Not much, answered Mr Kernan. But it's so sickening. I feel as if I wanted to retch off.

—That's the boose,[29] said Mr Cunningham firmly.

—No, said Mr Kernan. I think I caught a cold on the car. There's something keeps coming into my throat, phlegm or –

—Mucus, said Mr M'Coy.

—It keeps coming like from down in my throat; sickening thing.

—Yes, yes, said Mr M'Coy, that's the thorax.

He looked at Mr Cunningham and Mr Power at the same time with an air of challenge. Mr Cunningham nodded his head rapidly and Mr Power said:

—Ah, well, all's well that ends well.

—I'm very much obliged to you, old man, said the invalid. Mr Power waved his hand.

—Those other two fellows I was with –

—Who were you with? asked Mr Cunningham.

—A chap. I don't know his name. Damn it now, what's his name? Little chap with sandy hair. . . .

—And who else?

—Harford.

—Hm, said Mr Cunningham.

When Mr Cunningham made that remark people were silent. It was known that the speaker had secret sources of information. In this case the monosyllable had a moral intention. Mr Harford sometimes formed one of a little detachment which left the city shortly after noon on Sunday with the purpose of arriving as soon as possible at some public-house on the outskirts of the city where its members duly qualified themselves as *bona-fide* travellers.[30] But his fellow-travellers had never consented to overlook his origin. He had begun life as an obscure financier by lending small sums of money to workmen at usurious interest. Later on he had become the partner of a very fat short gentleman, Mr Goldberg, of the Liffey Loan Bank.[31] Though he had never embraced more than

the Jewish ethical code his fellow-Catholics, whenever
they had smarted in person or by proxy under his exactions, spoke of him bitterly as an Irish Jew and an
illiterate and saw divine disapproval of usury made manifest through the person of his idiot son. At other times
they remembered his good points.

—I wonder where did he go to, said Mr Kernan.

He wished the details of the incident to remain vague.
He wished his friends to think there had been some
mistake, that Mr Harford and he had missed each other.
His friends, who knew quite well Mr Harford's manners
in drinking, were silent. Mr Power said again:

—All's well that ends well.

Mr Kernan changed the subject at once.

—That was a decent young chap, that medical fellow,
he said. Only for him –

—O, only for him, said Mr Power, it might have been
a case of seven days without the option of a fine.

—Yes, yes, said Mr Kernan, trying to remember. I
remember now there was a policeman. Decent young
fellow, he seemed. How did it happen at all?

—It happened that you were peloothered,[32] Tom, said
Mr Cunningham gravely.

—True bill,[33] said Mr Kernan, equally gravely.

—I suppose you squared the constable, Jack, said Mr
M'Coy.

Mr Power did not relish the use of his Christian name.
He was not straight-laced but he could not forget that
Mr M'Coy had recently made a crusade in search of
valises and portmanteaus[34] to enable Mrs M'Coy to fulfil
imaginary engagements in the country. More than he
resented the fact that he had been victimised he resented
such low playing of the game. He answered the question,
therefore, as if Mr Kernan had asked it.

The narrative made Mr Kernan indignant. He was

keenly conscious of his citizenship, wished to live with his city on terms mutually honourable and resented any affront put upon him by those whom he called country bumpkins.

—Is this what we pay rates for? he asked. To feed and clothe these ignorant bostoons [35] . . . and they're nothing else.

Mr Cunningham laughed. He was a Castle official only during office hours.

—How could they be anything else, Tom? he said.

He assumed a thick provincial accent and said in a tone of command:

—65, catch your cabbage!

Everyone laughed. Mr M'Coy, who wanted to enter the conversation by any door, pretended that he had never heard the story. Mr Cunningham said:

—It is supposed – they say, you know – to take place in the depot where they get these thundering big country fellows, omadhauns,[36] you know, to drill. The sergeant makes them stand in a row against the wall and held up their plates.

He illustrated the story by grotesque gestures.

—At dinner, you know. Then he has a bloody big bowl of cabbage before him on the table and a bloody big spoon like a shovel. He takes up a wad of cabbage on the spoon and pegs it across the room and the poor devils have to try and catch it on their plates: 65, *catch your cabbage*.

Everyone laughed again: but Mr Kernan was somewhat indignant still. He talked of writing a letter to the papers.

—These yahoos [37] coming up here,[38] he said, think they can boss the people. I needn't tell you, Martin, what kind of men they are.

Mr Cunningham gave a qualified assent.

—It's like everything else in this world, he said. You get some bad ones and you get some good ones.

—O yes, you get some good ones, I admit, said Mr Kernan, satisfied.

—It's better to have nothing to say to them, said Mr M'Coy. That's my opinion!

Mrs Kernan entered the room and, placing a tray on the table, said:

—Help yourselves, gentlemen.

Mr Power stood up to officiate, offering her his chair. She declined it, saying she was ironing downstairs, and, after having exchanged a nod with Mr Cunningham behind Mr Power's back, prepared to leave the room. Her husband called out to her:

—And have you nothing for me, duckie?

—O, you! The back of my hand to you! said Mrs Kernan tartly.

Her husband called after her:

—Nothing for poor little hubby!

He assumed such a comical face and voice that the distribution of the bottles of stout took place amid general merriment.

The gentlemen drank from their glasses, set the glasses again on the table and paused. Then Mr Cunningham turned towards Mr Power and said casually:

—On Thursday night, you said, Jack?

—Thursday, yes, said Mr Power.

—Righto! said Mr Cunningham promptly.

—We can meet in M'Auley's,[39] said Mr M'Coy. That'll be the most convenient place.

—But we mustn't be late, said Mr Power earnestly, because it is sure to be crammed to the doors.

—We can meet at half-seven, said Mr M'Coy.

—Righto! said Mr Cunningham.

—Half-seven at M'Auley's be it!

There was a short silence. Mr Kernan waited to see whether he would be taken into his friends' confidence.

Then he asked:

—What's in the wind?

—O, it's nothing, said Mr Cunningham. It's only a little matter that we're arranging about for Thursday.

—The opera, is it? said Mr Kernan.

—No, no, said Mr Cunningham in an evasive tone, it's just a little . . . spiritual matter.

—O, said Mr Kernan.

There was silence again. Then Mr Power said, point-blank:

—To tell you the truth, Tom, we're going to make a retreat.[40]

—Yes, that's it, said Mr Cunningham, Jack and I and M'Coy here – we're all going to wash the pot.[41]

He uttered the metaphor with a certain homely energy and, encouraged by his own voice, proceeded:

—You see, we may as well all admit we're a nice collection of scoundrels, one and all. I say, one and all, he added with gruff charity and turning to Mr Power. Own up now!

—I own up, said Mr Power.

—And I own up, said Mr M'Coy.

—So we're going to wash the pot together, said Mr Cunningham.

A thought seemed to strike him. He turned suddenly to the invalid and said:

—Do you know what, Tom, has just occurred to me? You might join in and we'd have a four-handed reel.

—Good idea, said Mr Power. The four of us together.

Mr Kernan was silent. The proposal conveyed very little meaning to his mind but, understanding that some spiritual agencies were about to concern themselves on his behalf, he thought he owed it to his dignity to show a stiff neck. He took no part in the conversation for a long while but listened, with an air of calm enmity, while his friends discussed the Jesuits.

—I haven't such a bad opinion of the Jesuits, he said, intervening at length. They're an educated order. I believe they mean well too.

—They're the grandest order in the Church, Tom, said Mr Cunningham, with enthusiasm. The General of the Jesuits [42] stands next to the Pope.

—There's no mistake about it, said Mr M'Coy, if you want a thing well done and no flies about it you go to a Jesuit. They're the boyos have influence. I'll tell you a case in point. . . .

—The Jesuits are a fine body of men, said Mr Power.

—It's a curious thing, said Mr Cunningham, about the Jesuit Order. Every other order of the Church had to be reformed at some time or other but the Jesuit Order was never once reformed. [43] It never fell away.

—Is that so? asked Mr M'Coy.

—That's a fact, said Mr Cunningham. That's history.

—Look at their church, too, said Mr Power. Look at the congregation they have. [44]

—The Jesuits cater for the upper classes, said Mr M'Coy.

—Of course, said Mr Power.

—Yes, said Mr Kernan. That's why I have a feeling for them. It's some of those secular priests, [45] ignorant, bumptious –

—They're all good men, said Mr Cunningham, each in his own way. The Irish priesthood is honoured all the world over.

—O yes, said Mr Power.

—Not like some of the other priesthoods on the continent, said Mr M'Coy, unworthy of the name.

—Perhaps you're right, said Mr Kernan, relenting.

—Of course I'm right, said Mr Cunningham. I haven't

been in the world all this time and seen most sides of it without being a judge of character.

The gentlemen drank again, one following another's example. Mr Kernan seemed to be weighing something in his mind. He was impressed. He had a high opinion of Mr Cunningham as a judge of character and as a reader of faces. He asked for particulars.

—O, it's just a retreat, you know, said Mr Cunningham. Father Purdon[46] is giving it. It's for business men, you know.

—He won't be too hard on us, Tom, said Mr Power persuasively.

—Father Purdon? Father Purdon? said the invalid.

—O, you must know him, Tom, said Mr Cunningham, stoutly. Fine jolly fellow! He's a man of the world like ourselves.

—Ah, . . . yes. I think I know him. Rather red face; tall.

—That's the man.

—And tell me, Martin. . . . Is he a good preacher?

—Mmmno. . . . It's not exactly a sermon, you know. It's just a kind of a friendly talk, you know, in a common-sense way.

Mr Kernan deliberated. Mr M'Coy said:

—Father Tom Burke, that was the boy!

—O, Father Tom Burke,[47] said Mr Cunningham, that was a born orator. Did you ever hear him, Tom?

—Did I ever hear him! said the invalid, nettled. Rather! I heard him. . . .

—And yet they say he wasn't much of a theologian, said Mr Cunningham.

—Is that so? said Mr M'Coy.

—O, of course, nothing wrong, you know. Only sometimes, they say, he didn't preach what was quite orthodox.

—Ah! . . . he was a splendid man, said Mr M'Coy.

—I heard him once, Mr Kernan continued. I forget the subject of his discourse now. Crofton and I were in the back of the . . . pit,[48] you know . . . the –

—The body, said Mr Cunningham.

—Yes, in the back near the door. I forget now what . . . O yes, it was on the Pope, the late Pope. I remember it well. Upon my word it was magnificent, the style of the oratory. And his voice! God! hadn't he a voice! *The Prisoner of the Vatican*,[49] he called him. I remember Crofton saying to me when we came out –

—But he's an Orangeman, Crofton, isn't he? said Mr Power.

—'Course he is, said Mr Kernan, and a damned decent Orangeman[50] too. We went into Butler's in Moore Street[51] – faith, I was genuinely moved, tell you the God's truth – and I remember well his very words. *Kernan*, he said, *we worship at different altars*, he said, *but our belief is the same*. Struck me as very well put.

—There's a good deal in that, said Mr Power. There used always be crowds of Protestants in the chapel when Father Tom was preaching.

—There's not much difference between us, said Mr M'Coy. We both believe in –

He hesitated for a moment.

— . . . in the Redeemer. Only they don't believe in the Pope and in the mother of God.[52]

—But, of course, said Mr Cunningham quietly and effectively, our religion is *the* religion, the old, original faith.

—Not a doubt of it, said Mr Kernan warmly.

Mrs Kernan came to the door of the bedroom and announced:

—Here's a visitor for you!

—Who is it?

—Mr Fogarty.

—O, come in! come in!

A pale oval face came forward into the light. The arch of its fair trailing moustache was repeated in the fair eyebrows looped above pleasantly astonished eyes. Mr Fogarty was a modest grocer. He had failed in business in a licensed house in the city because his financial condition had constrained him to tie himself to second-class distillers and brewers.[53] He had opened a small shop on Glasnevin Road where, he flattered himself, his manners would ingratiate him with the housewives of the district. He bore himself with a certain grace, complimented little children and spoke with a neat enunciation. He was not without culture.

Mr Fogarty brought a gift with him, a half-pint of special whisky. He inquired politely for Mr Kernan, placed his gift on the table and sat down with the company on equal terms. Mr Kernan appreciated the gift all the more since he was aware that there was a small account for groceries unsettled between him and Mr Fogarty. He said:

—I wouldn't doubt you, old man. Open that, Jack, will you?

Mr Power again officiated. Glasses were rinsed and five small measures of whisky were poured out. This new influence enlivened the conversation. Mr Fogarty, sitting on a small area of the chair, was specially interested.

—Pope Leo XIII.,[54] said Mr Cunningham, was one of the lights of the age. His great idea, you know, was the union of the Latin and Greek Churches. That was the aim of his life.

—I often heard he was one of the most intellectual men in Europe, said Mr Power. I mean apart from his being Pope.

—So he was, said Mr Cunningham, if not *the* most so. His motto, you know, as Pope, was *Lux upon Lux*[55] – *Light upon Light*.

—No, no, said Mr Fogarty eagerly. I think you're wrong there. It was *Lux in Tenebris*, I think – *Light in Darkness*.[56]

—O, yes, said Mr M'Coy, *Tenebrae*.[57]

—Allow me, said Mr Cunningham positively, it was *Lux upon Lux*. And Pius IX. his predecessor's motto was *Crux upon Crux*[58] that is, *Cross upon Cross* – to show the difference between their two pontificates.

The inference was allowed. Mr Cunningham continued.

—Pope Leo, you know, was a great scholar and a poet.[59]

—He had a strong face, said Mr Kernan.

—Yes, said Mr Cunningham. He wrote Latin poetry.

—Is that so? said Mr Fogarty.

Mr M'Coy tasted his whisky contentedly and shook his head with a double intention, saying:

—That's no joke, I can tell you.

—We didn't learn that, Tom, said Mr Power, following Mr M'Coy's example, when we went to the penny-a-week school.[60]

—There was many a good man went to the penny-a-week school with a sod of turf under his oxter,[61] said Mr Kernan sententiously. The old system was the best: plain honest education. None of your modern trumpery. . . .

—Quite right, said Mr Power.

—No superfluities, said Mr Fogarty.

He enunciated the word and then drank gravely.

—I remember reading, said Mr Cunningham, that one of Pope Leo's poems was on the invention of the photograph – in Latin, of course.

—On the photograph! exclaimed Mr Kernan.

—Yes, said Mr Cunningham.

He also drank from his glass.

—Well, you know, said Mr M'Coy, isn't the photograph wonderful when you come to think of it?

—O, of course, said Mr Power, great minds can see things.

—As the poet says: *Great minds are very near to madness*,[62] said Mr Fogarty.

Mr Kernan seemed to be troubled in mind. He made an effort to recall the Protestant theology on some thorny points and in the end addressed Mr Cunningham.

—Tell me, Martin, he said. Weren't some of the Popes – of course, not our present man, or his predecessor, but some of the old Popes – not exactly . . . you know . . . up to the knocker?[63]

There was a silence. Mr Cunningham said:

—O, of course, there were some bad lots. . . . But the astonishing thing is this. Not one of them, not the biggest drunkard, not the most . . . out-and-out ruffian, not one of them ever preached *ex cathedra*[64] a word of false doctrine. Now isn't that an astonishing thing?

—That is, said Mr Kernan.

—Yes, because when the Pope speaks *ex cathedra*, Mr Fogarty explained, he is infallible.

—Yes, said Mr Cunningham.

—O, I know about the infallibility of the Pope. I remember I was younger then. . . . Or was it that –?

Mr Fogarty interrupted. He took up the bottle and helped the others to a little more. Mr M'Coy, seeing that there was not enough to go round, pleaded that he had not finished his first measure. The others accepted under protest. The light music of whisky falling into glasses made an agreeable interlude.

—What's that you were saying, Tom? asked Mr M'Coy.

—Papal infallibility, said Mr Cunningham, that was the greatest scene in the whole history of the Church.

—How was that, Martin? asked Mr Power.

Mr Cunningham held up two thick fingers.

—In the sacred college, you know, of cardinals and archbishops and bishops there were two men who held out against it while the others were all for it. The whole conclave except these two was unanimous. No! They wouldn't have it!

—Ha! said Mr M'Coy.

—And they were a German cardinal by the name of Dolling . . . or Dowling . . . or –

—Dowling was no German, and that's a sure five, said Mr Power, laughing.

—Well, this great German cardinal, whatever his name was, was one; and the other was John MacHale.[65]

—What? cried Mr Kernan. Is it John of Tuam?

—Are you sure of that now? asked Mr Fogarty dubiously. I thought it was some Italian or American.[66]

—John of Tuam, repeated Mr Cunningham, was the man.

He drank and the other gentlemen followed his lead. Then he resumed:

—There they were at it, all the cardinals and bishops and archbishops from all the ends of the earth and these two fighting dog and devil until at last the Pope himself stood up and declared infallibility a dogma of the Church *ex cathedra*. On the very moment John MacHale, who had been arguing and arguing against it, stood up and shouted out with the voice of a lion: *Credo!*[67]

—*I believe!* said Mr Fogarty.

—*Credo!* said Mr Cunningham. That showed the faith he had. He submitted the moment the Pope spoke.

—And what about Dowling? asked Mr M'Coy.

—The German cardinal wouldn't submit. He left the Church.

Mr Cunningham's words had built up the vast image of the Church in the minds of his hearers. His deep raucous voice had thrilled them as it uttered the word of belief and submission. When Mrs Kernan came into the room drying her hands she came into a solemn company. She did not disturb the silence, but leaned over the rail at the foot of the bed.

—I once saw John MacHale, said Mr Kernan, and I'll never forget it as long as I live.

He turned towards his wife to be confirmed.

—I often told you that?

Mrs Kernan nodded.

—It was at the unveiling of Sir John Gray's[68] statue. Edmund Dwyer Gray[69] was speaking, blathering away, and here was this old fellow, crabbed-looking old chap, looking at him from under his bushy eyebrows.

Mr Kernan knitted his brows and, lowering his head like an angry bull, glared at his wife.

—God! he exclaimed, resuming his natural face, I never saw such an eye in a man's head. It was as much as to say: *I have you properly taped, my lad*. He had an eye like a hawk.

—None of the Grays was any good,[70] said Mr Power.

There was a pause again. Mr Power turned to Mrs Kernan and said with abrupt joviality:

—Well, Mrs Kernan, we're going to make your man here a good holy pious and God-fearing Roman Catholic.

He swept his arm round the company inclusively.

—We're all going to make a retreat together and confess our sins – and God knows we want it badly.

—I don't mind, said Mr Kernan, smiling a little nervously.

Mrs Kernan thought it would be wiser to conceal her satisfaction. So she said:

—I pity the poor priest that has to listen to your tale.

Mr Kernan's expression changed.

—If he doesn't like it, he said bluntly, he can ... do the other thing. I'll just tell him my little tale of woe. I'm not such a bad fellow –

Mr Cunningham intervened promptly.

—We'll all renounce the devil, he said, together, not forgetting his works and pomps.

—Get behind me, Satan![71] said Mr Fogarty, laughing and looking at the others.

Mr Power said nothing. He felt completely outgeneralled. But a pleased expression flickered across his face.

—All we have to do, said Mr Cunningham, is to stand up with lighted candles in our hands and renew our baptismal vows.[72]

—O, don't forget the candle, Tom, said Mr M'Coy, whatever you do.

—What? said Mr Kernan. Must I have a candle?

—O yes, said Mr Cunningham.

—No, damn it all, said Mr Kernan sensibly, I draw the line there. I'll do the job right enough. I'll do the retreat business and confession, and . . . all that business. But . . . no candles! No, damn it all, I bar the candles![73]

He shook his head with farcical gravity.

—Listen to that! said his wife.

—I bar the candles, said Mr Kernan, conscious of having created an effect on his audience and continuing to shake his head to and fro. I bar the magic-lantern business.[74]

Everyone laughed heartily.

—There's a nice Catholic for you! said his wife.

—No candles! repeated Mr Kernan obdurately. That's off!

$\cdot$ $\cdot$ $\cdot$ $\cdot$ $\cdot$ $\cdot$ $\cdot$ $\cdot$

The transept of the Jesuit Church in Gardiner Street was almost full; and still at every moment gentlemen entered from the side-door and, directed by the lay-brother,[75] walked on tip-toe along the aisles until they found seating accommodation. The gentlemen were all well dressed and orderly. The light of the lamps of the church fell upon an assembly of black clothes and white collars, relieved here and there by tweeds, on dark mottled pillars of green marble and on lugubrious canvasses. The gentlemen sat in the benches, having hitched their trousers slightly above their knees and laid their hats in security. They sat well back and gazed formally at the distant speck of red light[76] which was suspended before the high altar.

In one of the benches near the pulpit sat Mr Cunningham and Mr Kernan. In the bench behind sat Mr M'Coy alone: and in the bench behind him sat Mr Power and Mr Fogarty. Mr M'Coy had tried unsuccessfully to find a place in the bench with the others and, when the party had settled down in the form of a quincunx,[77] he had tried unsuccessfully to make comic remarks. As these had not been well received he had desisted. Even he was sensible of the decorous atmosphere and even he began to respond to the religious stimulus. In a whisper Mr Cunningham drew Mr Kernan's attention to Mr Harford, the moneylender, who sat some distance off, and to Mr Fanning, the registration agent and mayor maker[78] of the city, who was sitting immediately under the pulpit beside one of the newly elected councillors of the ward. To the right sat old Michael Grimes, the owner of three pawnbroker's shops, and Dan Hogan's nephew, who was up for the job in the Town Clerk's[79] office. Farther in front sat Mr Hendrick, the chief reporter of *The Freeman's Journal*, and poor O'Carroll, an old friend of Mr Kernan's, who had been at one time a considerable commercial figure. Gradually, as he recognised familiar faces, Mr Kernan began to feel more at home. His hat, which had been rehabilitated by his wife, rested upon his knees. Once or twice he pulled down his cuffs with one hand while he held the brim of his hat lightly, but firmly, with the other hand.

A powerful-looking figure, the upper part of which was draped with a white surplice, was observed to be struggling up into the pulpit. Simultaneously the congregation unsettled, produced handkerchiefs and knelt upon them with care. Mr Kernan followed the general example. The priest's figure now stood upright in the pulpit, two-thirds of its bulk, crowned by a massive red face, appearing above the balustrade.

Father Purdon knelt down, turned towards the red speck of light and, covering his face with his hands, prayed. After an interval he uncovered his face and rose. The congregation rose also and settled again on its benches. Mr Kernan restored his hat to its original position on his knee and presented an attentive face to the preacher. The preacher turned back each wide sleeve of his surplice with an elaborate large gesture and slowly surveyed the array of faces. Then he said:

> For the children of this world are wiser in their generation than the children of light. Wherefore make unto yourselves friends out of the mammon of iniquity so that when you die they may receive you into everlasting dwellings.[80]

Father Purdon developed the text with resonant assurance. It was one of the most difficult texts in all the Scriptures, he said, to interpret properly. It was a text which might seem to the casual observer at variance with the lofty morality elsewhere preached by Jesus Christ. But, he told his hearers, the text had seemed to him specially adapted for the guidance of those whose lot it was to lead the life of the world and who yet wished to lead that life not in the manner of worldlings. It was a text for business men and professional men. Jesus Christ, with His divine understanding of every cranny of our human nature, understood that all men were not called to the religious life, that by far the vast majority were forced to live in the world and, to a certain extent, for the world: and in this sentence He designed to give them a word of counsel, setting before them as exemplars in the religious life those very worshippers of Mammon[81] who were of all men the least solicitous in matters religious.

He told his hearers that he was there that evening for no terrifying, no extravagant purpose; but as a man of the world speaking to his fellow-men. He came to speak to business men and he would speak to them in a business-like way. If he might use the metaphor, he said, he was their spiritual accountant; and he wished each and every one of his hearers to open his books, the books of his spiritual life, and see if they tallied accurately with con-science.

Jesus Christ was not a hard taskmaster. He understood our little failings, understood the weakness of our poor fallen nature, understood the temptations of this life. We might have had, we all had from time to time, our temptations: we might have, we all had, our failings. But one thing only, he said, he would ask of his hearers. And that was: to be straight and manly with God. If their accounts tallied in every point to say:

—Well, I have verified my accounts. I find all well.

But if, as might happen, there were some discrepancies, to admit the truth, to be frank and say like a man:

—Well, I have looked into my accounts. I find this wrong and this wrong. But, with God's grace, I will rectify this and this. I will set right my accounts.

THE DEAD

Lily,[1] the caretaker's daughter, was literally run off her feet. Hardly had she brought one gentleman into the little pantry behind the office on the ground floor and helped him off with his overcoat than the wheezy hall-door bell clanged again and she had to scamper along the bare hallway to let in another guest. It was well for her she had not to attend to the ladies also. But Miss Kate and Miss Julia had thought of that and had converted the bathroom upstairs into a ladies' dressing-room. Miss Kate and Miss Julia were there, gossiping and laughing and fussing, walking after each other to the head of the stairs, peering down over the banisters and calling down to Lily to ask her who had come.

It was always a great affair, the Misses Morkan's annual dance. Everybody who knew them came to it, members of the family, old friends of the family, the members of Julia's choir, any of Kate's pupils that were grown up enough and even some of Mary Jane's pupils too. Never once had it fallen flat. For years and years it had gone off in splendid style as long as anyone could remember; ever since Kate and Julia, after the death of their brother Pat, had left the house in Stoney Batter[2] and taken Mary Jane, their only niece, to live with them in the dark gaunt house on Usher's Island,[3] the upper part of which they had rented from Mr Fulham, the corn-factor on the ground floor. That was a good thirty years ago if it was a day. Mary Jane, who was then a little girl in short clothes, was now the main prop of the household for she had the organ in Haddington Road.[4] She had been through the Academy[5] and gave a pupils' concert every year in the upper room of the Antient Concert Rooms.[6] Many of her pupils belonged to better-class families on the Kingstown and Dalkey line.[7] Old as they were, her aunts also did their share. Julia, though she was quite grey, was still the leading soprano in Adam and Eve's,[8] and Kate, being too feeble to go about much, gave music lessons to beginners on the old square piano in the back room. Lily, the caretaker's daughter, did housemaid's work for them. Though their life was modest they believed in eating well; the best of everything: diamond-bone sirloins, three-shilling tea and the best bottled stout. But Lily seldom made a mistake in the orders so that she got on well with her three mistresses. They were fussy, that was all. But the only thing they would not stand was back answers.

Of course they had good reason to be fussy on such a night. And then it was long after ten o'clock and yet there was no sign of Gabriel[9] and his wife. Besides they were dreadfully afraid that Freddy Malins might turn up screwed.[10] They would not wish for worlds that any of Mary Jane's pupils should see him under the influence; and when he was like that it was sometimes very hard to manage him. Freddy Malins always came late but they wondered what could be keeping Gabriel: and that was what brought them every two minutes to the banisters to ask Lily had Gabriel or Freddy come.

—O, Mr Conroy, said Lily to Gabriel when she opened the door for him, Miss Kate and Miss Julia thought you were never coming. Good-night, Mrs Conroy.

—I'll engage they did, said Gabriel, but they forget that my wife here takes three mortal hours to dress herself.

He stood on the mat, scraping the snow from his goloshes,[11] while Lily led his wife to the foot of the stairs and called out:

—Miss Kate, here's Mrs Conroy.

Kate and Julia came toddling down the dark stairs at once. Both of them kissed Gabriel's wife, said she must be perished alive and asked was Gabriel with her.

—Here I am as right as the mail, Aunt Kate! Go on up. I'll follow, called out Gabriel from the dark.

He continued scraping his feet vigorously while the three women went upstairs, laughing, to the ladies' dressing-room. A light fringe of snow lay like a cape on the shoulders of his overcoat and like toecaps on the toes of his goloshes; and, as the buttons of his overcoat slipped with a squeaking noise through the snow-stiffened frieze, a cold fragrant air from out-of-doors escaped from crevices and folds.

—Is it snowing again, Mr Conroy? asked Lily.

She had preceded him into the pantry to help him off with his overcoat. Gabriel smiled at the three syllables she had given his surname[12] and glanced at her. She was a slim, growing girl, pale in complexion and with hay-coloured hair. The gas in the pantry made her look still paler. Gabriel had known her when she was a child and used to sit on the lowest step nursing a rag doll.

—Yes, Lily, he answered, and I think we're in for a night of it.

He looked up at the pantry ceiling, which was shaking with the stamping and shuffling of feet on the floor above, listened for a moment to the piano and then glanced at the girl, who was folding his overcoat carefully at the end of a shelf.

—Tell me, Lily, he said in a friendly tone, do you still go to school?

—O no, sir, she answered. I'm done schooling this year and more.

—O, then, said Gabriel gaily, I suppose we'll be going to your wedding one of these fine days with your young man, eh?

The girl glanced back at him over her shoulder and said with great bitterness:

—The men that is now is only all palaver and what they can get out of you.

Gabriel coloured as if he felt he had made a mistake and, without looking at her, kicked off his goloshes and flicked actively with his muffler at his patent-leather shoes.

He was a stout tallish young man. The high colour of his cheeks pushed upwards even to his forehead where it scattered itself in a few formless patches of pale red; and on his hairless face there scintillated restlessly the polished lenses and the bright gilt rims of the glasses which screened his delicate and restless eyes. His glossy black hair was parted in the middle and brushed in a long curve behind his ears where it curled slightly beneath the groove left by his hat.

When he had flicked lustre into his shoes he stood up and pulled his waistcoat down more tightly on his plump body. Then he took a coin rapidly from his pocket.

—O Lily, he said, thrusting it into her hands, it's Christmas-time, isn't it? Just . . . here's a little. . . .

He walked rapidly towards the door.

—O no, sir! cried the girl, following him. Really, sir, I wouldn't take it.

—Christmas-time! Christmas-time! said Gabriel, almost trotting to the stairs and waving his hand to her in deprecation.

The girl, seeing that he had gained the stairs, called out after him:

—Well, thank you, sir.

He waited outside the drawing-room door until the waltz should finish, listening to the skirts that swept against it and to the shuffling of feet. He was still discomposed by the girl's bitter and sudden retort. It had cast a gloom over him which he tried to dispel by arranging his cuffs and the bows of his tie. Then he took from his waistcoat pocket a little paper and glanced at the headings he had made for his speech. He was undecided about the lines from Robert Browning [13] for he feared they would be above the heads of his hearers. Some quotation that they could recognise from Shakespeare or from the Melodies [14] would be better. The indelicate clacking of the men's heels and the shuffling of their soles reminded him that their grade of culture differed from his. He would only make himself ridiculous by quoting poetry to them which they could not understand. They would think that he was airing his superior education. He would fail with them just as he had failed with the girl in the pantry. He had taken up a wrong tone. His whole speech was a mistake from first to last, an utter failure.

Just then his aunts and his wife came out of the ladies' dressing-room. His aunts were two small plainly dressed old women. Aunt Julia was an inch or so the taller. Her hair, drawn low over the tops of her ears, was grey; and grey also, with darker shadows, was her large flaccid face. Though she was stout in build and stood erect her slow eyes and parted lips gave her the appearance of a woman who did not know where she was or where she was going. Aunt Kate was more vivacious. Her face, healthier than her sister's, was all puckers and creases, like a shrivelled red apple, and her hair, braided in the same old-fashioned way, had not lost its ripe nut colour.

They both kissed Gabriel frankly. He was their favourite nephew, the son of their dead elder sister, Ellen, who had married T. J. Conroy of the Port and Docks. [15]

—Gretta tells me you're not going to take a cab back to Monkstown [16] to-night, Gabriel, said Aunt Kate.

—No, said Gabriel, turning to his wife, we had quite enough of that last year, hadn't we? Don't you remember,

Aunt Kate, what a cold Gretta got out of it? Cab windows rattling all the way, and the east wind blowing in after we passed Merrion.[17] Very jolly it was. Gretta caught a dreadful cold.

Aunt Kate frowned severely and nodded her head at every word.

—Quite right, Gabriel, quite right, she said. You can't be too careful.

—But as for Gretta there, said Gabriel, she'd walk home in the snow if she were let.

Mrs Conroy laughed.

—Don't mind him, Aunt Kate, she said. He's really an awful bother, what with green shades for Tom's eyes at night and making him do the dumb-bells,[18] and forcing Eva to eat the stirabout.[19] The poor child! And she simply hates the sight of it! . . . O, but you'll never guess what he makes me wear now!

She broke out into a peal of laughter and glanced at her husband, whose admiring and happy eyes had been wandering from her dress to her face and hair. The two aunts laughed heartily too, for Gabriel's solicitude was a standing joke with them.

—Goloshes! said Mrs Conroy. That's the latest. Whenever it's wet underfoot I must put on my goloshes. Tonight even he wanted me to put them on, but I wouldn't. The next thing he'll buy me will be a diving suit.

Gabriel laughed nervously and patted his tie reassuringly while Aunt Kate nearly doubled herself, so heartily did she enjoy the joke. The smile soon faded from Aunt Julia's face and her mirthless eyes were directed towards her nephew's face. After a pause she asked:

—And what are goloshes, Gabriel?

—Goloshes, Julia! exclaimed her sister. Goodness me, don't you know what goloshes are? You wear them over your . . . over your boots, Gretta, isn't it?

—Yes, said Mrs Conroy. Guttapercha things. We both have a pair now. Gabriel says everyone wears them on the continent.

—O, on the continent, murmured Aunt Julia, nodding her head slowly.

Gabriel knitted his brows and said, as if he were slightly angered:

—It's nothing very wonderful but Gretta thinks it very funny because she says the word reminds her of Christy Minstrels.[20]

—But tell me, Gabriel, said Aunt Kate, with brisk tact. Of course, you've seen about the room. Gretta was saying . . .

—O, the room is all right, replied Gabriel. I've taken one in the Gresham.[21]

—To be sure, said Aunt Kate, by far the best thing to do. And the children, Gretta, you're not anxious about them?

—O, for one night, said Mrs Conroy. Besides, Bessie will look after them.

—To be sure, said Aunt Kate again. What a comfort it is to have a girl like that, one you can depend on! There's that Lily, I'm sure I don't know what has come over her lately. She's not the girl she was at all.

Gabriel was about to ask his aunt some questions on this point but she broke off suddenly to gaze after her sister who had wandered down the stairs and was craning her neck over the banisters.

—Now, I ask you, she said, almost testily, where is Julia going? Julia! Julia! Where are you going?

Julia, who had gone halfway down one flight, came back and announced blandly:

—Here's Freddy.

At the same moment a clapping of hands and a final flourish of the pianist told that the waltz had ended. The drawing-room door was opened from within and some couples came out. Aunt Kate drew Gabriel aside hurriedly and whispered into his ear:

—Slip down, Gabriel, like a good fellow and see if he's all right, and don't let him up if he's screwed. I'm sure he's screwed. I'm sure he is.

Gabriel went to the stairs and listened over the banisters. He could hear two persons talking in the pantry. Then he recognised Freddy Malins' laugh. He went down the stairs noisily.

—It's such a relief, said Aunt Kate to Mrs Conroy, that Gabriel is here. I always feel easier in my mind when he's here. . . . Julia, there's Miss Daly and Miss Power will take some refreshment. Thanks for your beautiful waltz, Miss Daly. It made lovely time.

A tall wizen-faced man, with a stiff grizzled moustache and swarthy skin, who was passing out with his partner said:

—And may we have some refreshment, too, Miss Morkan?

—Julia, said Aunt Kate summarily, and here's Mr Browne and Miss Furlong. Take them in, Julia, with Miss Daly and Miss Power.

—I'm the man for the ladies, said Mr Browne, pursing his lips until his moustache bristled and smiling in all his wrinkles. You know, Miss Morkan, the reason they are so fond of me is –

He did not finish his sentence, but, seeing that Aunt Kate was out of earshot, at once led the three young ladies into the back room. The middle of the room was occupied by two square tables placed end to end, and on these Aunt Julia and the caretaker were straightening and smoothing a large cloth. On the sideboard were arrayed dishes and plates, and glasses and bundles of knives and forks and spoons. The top of the closed square piano served also as a sideboard for viands and sweets. At a smaller sideboard in one corner two young men were standing, drinking hop-bitters.

Mr Browne led his charges thither and invited them all, in jest, to some ladies' punch, hot, strong and sweet. As they said they never took anything strong he opened three bottles of lemonade for them. Then he asked one of the young men to move aside, and, taking hold of the decanter, filled out for himself a goodly measure of whisky. The young men eyed him respectfully while he took a trial sip.

—God help me, he said, smiling, it's the doctor's orders.

His wizened face broke into a broader smile, and the three young ladies laughed in musical echo to his pleasantry, swaying their bodies to and fro, with nervous jerks of their shoulders. The boldest said:

—O, now, Mr Browne, I'm sure the doctor never ordered anything of the kind.

Mr Browne took another sip of his whisky and said, with sidling mimicry:

—Well, you see, I'm like the famous Mrs Cassidy, who is reported to have said: *Now, Mary Grimes, if I don't take it, make me take it, for I feel I want it.*[22]

His hot face had leaned forward a little too confidentially and he had assumed a very low Dublin accent so that the young ladies, with one instinct, received his speech in silence. Miss Furlong, who was one of Mary Jane's pupils, asked Miss Daly what was the name of the pretty waltz she had played; and Mr Browne, seeing that he was ignored, turned promptly to the two young men who were more appreciative.

A red-faced young woman, dressed in pansy, came into the room, excitedly clapping her hands and crying:

—Quadrilles! Quadrilles![23]

Close on her heels came Aunt Kate, crying:

—Two gentlemen and three ladies, Mary Jane!

—O, here's Mr Bergin and Mr Kerrigan, said Mary Jane. Mr Kerrigan, will you take Miss Power? Miss Furlong, may I get you a partner, Mr Bergin. O, that'll just do now.

—Three ladies, Mary Jane, said Aunt Kate.

The two young gentlemen asked the ladies if they might have the pleasure, and Mary Jane turned to Miss Daly.

—O, Miss Daly, you're really awfully good, after playing for the last two dances, but really we're so short of ladies to-night.

—I don't mind in the least, Miss Morkan.

—But I've a nice partner for you, Mr Bartell D'Arcy, the tenor. I'll get him to sing later on. All Dublin is raving about him.

—Lovely voice, lovely voice! said Aunt Kate.

As the piano had twice begun the prelude to the first figure Mary Jane led her recruits quickly from the room. They had hardly gone when Aunt Julia wandered slowly into the room, looking behind her at something.

—What is the matter, Julia? asked Aunt Kate anxiously. Who is it?

Julia, who was carrying in a column of table-napkins, turned to her sister and said, simply, as if the question had surprised her:

—It's only Freddy, Kate, and Gabriel with him.

In fact right behind her Gabriel could be seen piloting Freddy Malins across the landing. The latter, a young man of about forty, was of Gabriel's size and build, with very round shoulders. His face was fleshy and pallid, touched with colour only at the thick hanging lobes of his ears and at the wide wings of his nose. He had coarse features, a blunt nose, a convex and receding brow, tumid and protruded lips. His heavy-lidded eyes and the disorder of his scanty hair made him look sleepy. He was laughing heartily in a high key at a story which he had been telling Gabriel on the stairs and at the same time rubbing the knuckles of his left fist backwards and forwards into his left eye.

—Good-evening, Freddy, said Aunt Julia.

Freddy Malins bade the Misses Morkan good-evening in what seemed an offhand fashion by reason of the habitual catch in his voice and then, seeing that Mr Browne was grinning at him from the sideboard, crossed the room on rather shaky legs and began to repeat in an undertone the story he had just told to Gabriel.

—He's not so bad, is he? said Aunt Kate to Gabriel.

Gabriel's brows were dark but he raised them quickly and answered:

—O no, hardly noticeable.

—Now, isn't he a terrible fellow! she said. And his poor mother made him take the pledge²⁴ on New Year's Eve. But come on, Gabriel, into the drawing-room.

Before leaving the room with Gabriel she signalled to Mr Browne by frowning and shaking her forefinger in warning to and fro. Mr Browne nodded in answer and, when she had gone, said to Freddy Malins:

—Now, then, Teddy, I'm going to fill you out a good glass of lemonade just to buck you up.

Freddy Malins, who was nearing the climax of his story, waved the offer aside impatiently but Mr Browne, having first called Freddy Malins' attention to a disarray in his dress, filled out and handed him a full glass of lemonade. Freddy Malins' left hand accepted the glass mechanically, his right hand being engaged in the mechanical readjustment of his dress. Mr Browne, whose face was once more wrinkling with mirth, poured out for himself a glass of whisky while Freddy Malins exploded, before he had well reached the climax of his story, in a kink of high-pitched bronchitic laughter and, setting down his untasted and overflowing glass, began to rub the knuckles of his left fist backwards and forwards into his left eye, repeating words of his last phrase as well as his fit of laughter would allow him.

.   .   .   .

Gabriel could not listen while Mary Jane was playing her Academy piece,[25] full of runs and difficult passages, to the hushed drawing-room. He liked music but the piece she was playing had no melody for him and he doubted whether it had any melody for the other listeners, though they had begged Mary Jane to play something. Four young men, who had come from the refreshment-room to stand in the doorway at the sound of the piano, had gone away quietly in couples after a few minutes. The only persons who seemed to follow the music were Mary Jane herself, her hands racing along the key-board or lifted from it at the pauses like those of a priestess in momentary imprecation, and Aunt Kate standing at her elbow to turn the page.

Gabriel's eyes, irritated by the floor, which glittered with beeswax under the heavy chandelier, wandered to the wall above the piano. A picture of the balcony scene in *Romeo and Juliet*[26] hung there and beside it was a picture of the two murdered princes in the Tower[27] which Aunt Julia had worked in red, blue and brown wools when she was a girl. Probably in the school they had gone to as girls that kind of work had been taught, for one year his mother had worked for him as a birthday present a waistcoat of purple tabinet,[28] with little foxes' heads upon it, lined with brown satin and having round mulberry buttons. It was strange that his mother had had no musical talent though Aunt Kate used to call her the brains carrier of the Morkan family. Both she and Julia had always seemed a little proud of their serious and matronly sister. Her photograph stood before the pierglass.[29] She held an open book on her knees and was pointing out something in it to Constantine[30] who, dressed in a man-o'-war suit, lay at her feet. It was she who had chosen the names for her sons for she was very sensible of the dignity of family life. Thanks to her, Constantine was now senior curate in Balbriggan[31] and. thanks to her, Gabriel himself had taken his degree in the Royal University.[32] A shadow passed over his face as he remembered her sullen opposition to his marriage. Some slighting phrases she had used still rankled in his memory; she had once spoken of Gretta as being country cute and that was not true of Gretta at all. It was Gretta who had nursed her during all her last long illness in their house at Monkstown.

He knew that Mary Jane must be near the end of her piece for she was playing again the opening melody with runs of scales after every bar and while he waited for the end the resentment died down in his heart. The piece ended with a trill of octaves in the treble and a final deep octave in the bass. Great applause greeted Mary Jane as, blushing and rolling up her music nervously, she escaped from the room. The most vigorous clapping came from the four young men in the doorway who had gone away to the refreshment-room at the beginning of the piece but had come back when the piano had stopped.

Lancers[33] were arranged. Gabriel found himself partnered with Miss Ivors. She was a frank-mannered talkative young lady, with a freckled face and prominent brown eyes. She did not wear a low-cut bodice and the large brooch which was fixed in the front of her collar bore on it an Irish device.[34]

When they had taken their places she said abruptly:

—I have a crow to pluck with you.

—With me? said Gabriel.

She nodded her head gravely.

—What is it? asked Gabriel, smiling at her solemn manner.

—Who is G. C.? answered Miss Ivors, turning her eyes upon him.

Gabriel coloured and was about to knit his brows, as if he did not understand, when she said bluntly:

—O, innocent Amy! I have found out that you write for *The Daily Express*.[35] Now, aren't you ashamed of yourself?

—Why should I be ashamed of myself? asked Gabriel, blinking his eyes and trying to smile.

—Well, I'm ashamed of you, said Miss Ivors frankly. To say you'd write for a rag like that. I didn't think you were a West Briton.[36]

A look of perplexity appeared on Gabriel's face. It was true that he wrote a literary column every Wednesday in *The Daily Express*, for which he was paid fifteen shillings. But that did not make him a West Briton surely. The books he received for review were almost more welcome than the paltry cheque. He loved to feel the covers and turn over the pages of newly printed books. Nearly every day when his teaching in the college was ended he used to wander down the quays to the second-hand booksellers, to Hickey's on Bachelor's Walk, to Webb's or Massey's on Aston's Quay,[37] or to O'Clohissey's in the by-street. He did not know how to meet her charge. He wanted to say that literature was above politics. But they were friends of many years' standing and their careers had been parallel, first at the University[38] and then as teachers: he could not risk a grandiose phrase with her. He continued blinking his eyes and trying to smile and murmured lamely that he saw nothing political in writing reviews of books.

When their turn to cross had come he was still perplexed and inattentive. Miss Ivors promptly took his hand in a warm grasp and said in a soft friendly tone:

—Of course, I was only joking. Come, we cross now.

When they were together again she spoke of the University question[39] and Gabriel felt more at ease. A friend of hers had shown her his review of Browning's poems. That was how she had found out the secret: but she liked the review immensely. Then she said suddenly:

—O, Mr Conroy, will you come for an excursion to the Aran Isles[40] this summer? We're going to stay there a whole month. It will be splendid out in the Atlantic. You ought to come. Mr Clancy is coming, and Mr Kilkelly and Kathleen Kearney.[41] It would be splendid for Gretta too if she'd come. She's from Connacht,[42] isn't she?

—Her people are, said Gabriel shortly.

—But you will come, won't you? said Miss Ivors, laying her warm hand eagerly on his arm.

—The fact is, said Gabriel, I have already arranged to go –

—Go where? asked Miss Ivors.

—Well, you know every year I go for a cycling tour with some fellows and so –

—But where? asked Miss Ivors.

—Well, we usually go to France or Belgium or perhaps Germany, said Gabriel awkwardly.

—And why do you go to France and Belgium, said Miss Ivors, instead of visiting your own land?

—Well, said Gabriel, it's partly to keep in touch with the languages and partly for a change.

—And haven't you your own language[43] to keep in touch with – Irish? asked Miss Ivors.

—Well, said Gabriel, if it comes to that, you know, Irish is not my language.

Their neighbours had turned to listen to the cross-examination. Gabriel glanced right and left nervously and tried to keep his good humour under the ordeal which was making a blush invade his forehead.

—And haven't you your own land to visit, continued Miss Ivors, that you know nothing of, your own people, and your own country?

—O, to tell you the truth, retorted Gabriel suddenly, I'm sick of my own country, sick of it!

—Why? asked Miss Ivors.

Gabriel did not answer for his retort had heated him.

—Why? repeated Miss Ivors.

They had to go visiting together[44] and, as he had not answered her, Miss Ivors said warmly:

—Of course, you've no answer.

Gabriel tried to cover his agitation by taking part in the dance with great energy. He avoided her eyes for he had seen a sour expression on her face. But when they met in the long chain he was surprised to feel his hand firmly pressed. She looked at him from under her brows for a moment quizzically until he smiled. Then, just as the chain was about to start again, she stood on tiptoe and whispered into his ear:

—West Briton!

When the lancers were over Gabriel went away to a remote corner of the room where Freddy Malins' mother was sitting. She was a stout feeble old woman with white hair. Her voice had a catch in it like her son's and she stuttered slightly. She had been told that Freddy had come and that he was nearly all right. Gabriel asked her whether she had had a good crossing. She lived with her married daughter in Glasgow[45] and came to Dublin on a visit once a year. She answered placidly that she had had a beautiful crossing and that the captain had been most attentive to her. She spoke also of the beautiful house her daughter kept in Glasgow, and of all the nice friends they had there. While her tongue rambled on Gabriel tried to banish from his mind all memory of the unpleasant incident with Miss Ivors. Of course the girl or woman, or whatever she was, was an enthusiast but there was a time for all things. Perhaps he ought not to have answered her like that. But she had no right to call him a West Briton before people, even in joke. She had tried to make him ridiculous before people, heckling him and staring at him with her rabbit's eyes.

He saw his wife making her way towards him through the waltzing couples. When she reached him she said into his ear:

—Gabriel, Aunt Kate wants to know won't you carve the goose as usual. Miss Daly will carve the ham and I'll do the pudding.

—All right, said Gabriel.

—She's sending in the younger ones first as soon as this waltz is over so that we'll have the table to ourselves.

—Were you dancing? asked Gabriel.

—Of course I was. Didn't you see me? What words had you with Molly Ivors?

—No words. Why? Did she say so?

—Something like that. I'm trying to get that Mr D'Arcy to sing. He's full of conceit, I think.

—There were no words, said Gabriel moodily, only she wanted me to go for a trip to the west of Ireland and I said I wouldn't.

His wife clasped her hands excitedly and gave a little jump.

—O, do go, Gabriel, she cried. I'd love to see Galway [46] again.

—You can go if you like, said Gabriel coldly.

She looked at him for a moment, then turned to Mrs Malins and said:

—There's a nice husband for you, Mrs Malins.

While she was threading her way back across the room Mrs Malins, without adverting to the interruption, went on to tell Gabriel what beautiful places there were in Scotland and beautiful scenery. Her son-in-law brought them every year to the lakes and they used to go fishing. Her son-in-law was a splendid fisher. One day he caught a fish, a beautiful big big fish, and the man in the hotel boiled it for their dinner.

Gabriel hardly heard what she said. Now that supper was coming near he began to think again about his speech and about the quotation. When he saw Freddy Malins coming across the room to visit his mother Gabriel left the chair free for him and retired into the embrasure of the window. The room had already cleared and from the back room came the clatter of plates and knives. Those who still remained in the drawing-room seemed tired of dancing and were conversing quietly in little groups. Gabriel's warm trembling fingers tapped the cold pane of the window. How cool it must be outside! How pleasant it would be to walk out alone, first along by the river and then through the park![47] The snow would be lying on the branches of the trees and forming a bright cap on the top of the Wellington Monument.[48] How much more pleasant it would be there than at the supper-table!

He ran over the headings of his speech: Irish hospitality, sad memories, the Three Graces,[49] Paris,[50] the quotation from Browning. He repeated to himself a phrase he had written in his review: *One feels that one is listening to a thought-tormented music.* Miss Ivors had praised the review. Was she sincere? Had she really any life of her own behind all her propagandism? There had never been any ill-feeling between them until that night. It unnerved him to think that she would be at the supper-table, looking up at him while he spoke with her critical quizzing eyes.

Perhaps she would not be sorry to see him fail in his speech. An idea came into his mind and gave him courage. He would say, alluding to Aunt Kate and Aunt Julia: *Ladies and Gentlemen, the generation which is now on the wane among us may have had its faults but for my part I think it had certain qualities of hospitality, of humour, of humanity, which the new and very serious and hypereducated generation that is growing up around us seems to me to lack.* Very good: that was one for Miss Ivors. What did he care that his aunts were only two ignorant old women?

A murmur in the room attracted his attention. Mr Browne was advancing from the door, gallantly escorting Aunt Julia, who leaned upon his arm, smiling and hanging her head. An irregular musketry of applause escorted her also as far as the piano and then, as Mary Jane seated herself on the stool, and Aunt Julia, no longer smiling, half turned so as to pitch her voice fairly into the room, gradually ceased. Gabriel recognised the prelude. It was that of an old song of Aunt Julia's – *Arrayed for the Bridal*.[51] Her voice, strong and clear in tone, attacked with great spirit the runs which embellish the air and though she sang very rapidly she did not miss even the smallest of the grace notes. To follow the voice, without looking at the singer's face, was to feel and share the excitement of swift and secure flight. Gabriel applauded loudly with all the others at the close of the song and loud applause was borne in from the invisible supper-table. It sounded so genuine that a little colour struggled into Aunt Julia's face as she bent to replace in the music-stand the old leather-bound song-book that had her initials on the cover. Freddy Malins, who had listened with his head perched sideways to hear her better, was still applauding when everyone else had ceased and talking animatedly to his mother who nodded her head gravely and slowly in acquiescence. At last, when he could clap no more, he stood up suddenly and hurried across the room to Aunt Julia whose hand he seized and held in both his hands, shaking it when words failed him or the catch in his voice proved too much for him.

—I was just telling my mother, he said, I never heard you sing so well, never. No, I never heard your voice so good as it is to-night. Now! Would you believe that now? That's the truth. Upon my word and honour that's the truth. I never heard your voice sound so fresh and so . . . so clear and fresh, never.

Aunt Julia smiled broadly and murmured something about compliments as she released her hand from his grasp. Mr Browne extended his open hand towards her and said to those who were near him in the manner of a showman introducing a prodigy to an audience:

—Miss Julia Morkan, my latest discovery!

He was laughing very heartily at this himself when Freddy Malins turned to him and said:

—Well, Browne, if you're serious you might make a worse discovery. All I can say is I never heard her sing half so well as long as I am coming here. And that's the honest truth.

—Neither did I, said Mr Browne. I think her voice has greatly improved.

Aunt Julia shrugged her shoulders and said with meek pride:

—Thirty years ago I hadn't a bad voice as voices go.

—I often told Julia, said Aunt Kate emphatically, that she was simply thrown away in that choir. But she never would be said by me.

She turned as if to appeal to the good sense of the others against a refractory child while Aunt Julia gazed in front of her, a vague smile of reminiscence playing on her face.

—No, continued Aunt Kate, she wouldn't be said or led by anyone, slaving there in that choir night and day, night and day. Six o'clock on Christmas morning! And all for what?

—Well, isn't it for the honour of God, Aunt Kate? asked Mary Jane, twisting round on the piano-stool and smiling.

Aunt Kate turned fiercely on her niece and said:

—I know all about the honour of God, Mary Jane, but I think it's not at all honourable for the pope to turn out the women out of the choirs[52] that have slaved there all their lives and put little whipper-snappers of boys over their heads. I suppose it is for the good of the Church if the pope does it. But it's not just, Mary Jane, and it's not right.

She had worked herself into a passion and would have continued in defence of her sister for it was a sore subject with her but Mary Jane, seeing that all the dancers had come back, intervened pacifically:

—Now, Aunt Kate, you're giving scandal to Mr Browne who is of the other persuasion.[53]

Aunt Kate turned to Mr Browne, who was grinning at this allusion to his religion, and said hastily:

—O, I don't question the pope's being right. I'm only a stupid old woman and I wouldn't presume to do such a thing. But there's such a thing as common everyday politeness and gratitude. And if I were in Julia's place I'd tell that Father Healy straight up to his face . . .

—And besides, Aunt Kate, said Mary Jane, we really are all hungry and when we are hungry we are all very quarrelsome.

—And when we are thirsty we are also quarrelsome, added Mr Browne.

—So that we had better go to supper, said Mary Jane, and finish the discussion afterwards.

On the landing outside the drawing-room Gabriel found his wife and Mary Jane trying to persuade Miss Ivors to stay for supper. But Miss Ivors, who had put on her hat and was buttoning her cloak, would not stay. She did not feel in the least hungry and she had already overstayed her time.

—But only for ten minutes, Molly, said Mrs Conroy. That won't delay you.

—To take a pick itself,[54] said Mary Jane, after all your dancing.

—I really couldn't, said Miss Ivors.

—I am afraid you didn't enjoy yourself at all, said Mary Jane hopelessly.

—Ever so much, I assure you, said Miss Ivors, but you really must let me run off now.

—But how can you get home? asked Mrs Conroy.

—O, it's only two steps up the quay.

Gabriel hesitated a moment and said:

—If you will allow me, Miss Ivors, I'll see you home if you really are obliged to go.

But Miss Ivors broke away from them.

—I won't hear of it, she cried. For goodness sake go in to your suppers and don't mind me. I'm quite well able to take care of myself.

—Well, you're the comical girl, Molly, said Mrs Conroy frankly.

—*Beannacht libh*,[55] cried Miss Ivors, with a laugh, as she ran down the staircase.

Mary Jane gazed after her, a moody puzzled expression on her face, while Mrs Conroy leaned over the banisters to listen for the hall-door. Gabriel asked himself was he the cause of her abrupt departure. But she did not seem to be in ill humour: she had gone away laughing. He stared blankly down the staircase.

At that moment Aunt Kate came toddling out of the supper-room, almost wringing her hands in despair.

—Where is Gabriel? she cried. Where on earth is Gabriel? There's everyone waiting in there, stage to let, and nobody to carve the goose!

—Here I am, Aunt Kate! cried Gabriel, with sudden animation, ready to carve a flock of geese, if necessary.

A fat brown goose lay at one end of the table and at the other end, on a bed of creased paper strewn with sprigs of parsley, lay a great ham, stripped of its outer skin and peppered over with crust crumbs, a neat paper frill round its shin and beside this was a round of spiced beef. Between these rival ends ran parallel lines of side-dishes: two little minsters of jelly, red and yellow; a shallow dish full of blocks of blancmange and red jam, a large green leaf-shaped dish with a stalk-shaped handle, on which lay bunches of purple raisins and peeled al-monds, a companion dish on which lay a solid rectangle of Smyrna figs, a dish of custard topped with grated nutmeg, a small bowl full of chocolates and sweets wrapped in gold and silver papers and a glass vase in which stood some tall celery stalks. In the centre of the table there stood, as sentries to a fruit-stand which upheld a pyramid of oranges and American apples, two squat old-fashioned decanters of cut glass, one containing port and the other dark sherry. On the closed square piano a pudding in a huge yellow dish lay in waiting and behind it were three squads of bottles of stout and ale and minerals, drawn up according to the colours of their uniforms, the first two black, with brown and red labels, the third and smallest squad white, with transverse green sashes.

Gabriel took his seat boldly at the head of the table and, having looked to the edge of the carver, plunged his fork firmly into the goose. He felt quite at ease now for he was an expert carver and liked nothing better than to find himself at the head of a well-laden table.

—Miss Furlong, what shall I send you? he asked. A wing or a slice of the breast?

—Just a small slice of the breast.

—Miss Higgins, what for you?

—O, anything at all, Mr Conroy.

While Gabriel and Miss Daly exchanged plates of goose and plates of ham and spiced beef Lily went from guest to guest with a dish of hot floury potatoes wrapped in a white napkin. This was Mary Jane's idea and she had also suggested apple sauce for the goose but Aunt Kate had said that plain roast goose without apple sauce had always been good enough for her and she hoped she might never eat worse. Mary Jane waited on her pupils and saw that they got the best slices and Aunt Kate and Aunt Julia opened and carried across from the piano bottles of stout and ale for the gentlemen and bottles of minerals for the ladies. There was a great deal of confusion and laughter and noise, the noise of orders and counter-orders, of knives and forks, of corks and glass-stoppers. Gabriel began to carve second helpings as soon as he had finished the first round without serving himself. Everyone protested loudly so that he compromised by taking a long draught of stout for he had found the carving hot work. Mary Jane settled down quietly to her supper but Aunt Kate and Aunt Julia were still toddling round the table, walking on each other's heels, getting in each other's way and giving each other unheeded orders. Mr Browne begged of them to sit down and eat their suppers and so did Gabriel but they said there was time enough so that, at last, Freddy Malins stood up and, capturing Aunt Kate, plumped her down on her chair amid general laughter.

When everyone had been well served Gabriel said, smiling:

—Now, if anyone wants a little more of what vulgar people call stuffing let him or her speak.

A chorus of voices invited him to begin his own supper and Lily came forward with three potatoes which she had reserved for him.

—Very well, said Gabriel amiably, as he took another preparatory draught, kindly forget my existence, ladies and gentlemen, for a few minutes.

He set to his supper and took no part in the conversation with which the table covered Lily's removal of the plates. The subject of talk was the opera company which was then at the Theatre Royal.[56] Mr Bartell D'Arcy, the tenor, a dark-complexioned young man with a smart moustache, praised very highly the leading contralto of the company but Miss Furlong thought she had a rather vulgar style of production. Freddy Malins said there was a negro chieftain singing in the second part of the Gaiety[57] pantomime who had one of the finest tenor voices he had ever heard.

—Have you heard him? he asked Mr Bartell D'Arcy across the table.

—No, answered Mr Bartell D'Arcy carelessly.

—Because, Freddy Malins explained, now I'd be curious to hear your opinion of him. I think he has a grand voice.

—It takes Teddy to find out the really good things, said Mr Browne familiarly to the table.

—And why couldn't he have a voice too? asked Freddy Malins sharply. Is it because he's only a black?

Nobody answered this question and Mary Jane led the table back to the legitimate opera. One of her pupils had given her a pass for *Mignon*.[58] Of course it was very fine, she said, but it made her think of poor Georgina Burns.[59] Mr Browne could go back farther still, to the old Italian companies that used to come to Dublin—Tietjens, Ilma de Murzka, Campanini, the great Trebelli, Giuglini, Ravelli, Aramburo.[60] Those were the days, he said, when there was something like singing to be heard in Dublin. He told too of how the top gallery of the old Royal[61] used to be packed night after night, of how one night an Italian tenor had sung five encores to *Let Me Like a Soldier Fall*,[62] introducing a high C every time, and of how the gallery boys would sometimes in their enthusiasm unyoke the horses from the carriage of some great *prima donna* and pull her themselves through the streets to her hotel.[63] Why did they never play the grand old operas now, he asked, *Dinorah*,[64] *Lucrezia Borgia*?[65] Because they could not get the voices to sing them: that was why.

—O, well, said Mr Bartell D'Arcy, I presume there are as good singers to-day as there were then.

—Where are they? asked Mr Browne defiantly.

—In London, Paris, Milan, said Mr Bartell D'Arcy warmly. I suppose Caruso,[66] for example, is quite as good, if not better than any of the men you have mentioned.

—Maybe so, said Mr Browne. But I may tell you I doubt it strongly.

—O, I'd give anything to hear Caruso sing, said Mary Jane.

—For me, said Aunt Kate, who had been picking a bone, there was only one tenor. To please me, I mean. But I suppose none of you ever heard of him.

—Who was he, Miss Morkan? asked Mr Bartell D'Arcy politely.

—His name, said Aunt Kate, was Parkinson.[67] I heard him when he was in his prime and I think he had then the purest tenor voice that was ever put into a man's throat.

—Strange, said Mr Bartell D'Arcy. I never even heard of him.

—Yes, yes, Miss Morkan is right, said Mr Browne. I remember hearing of old Parkinson but he's too far back for me.

—A beautiful pure sweet mellow English tenor, said Aunt Kate with enthusiasm.

Gabriel having finished, the huge pudding was transferred to the table. The clatter of forks and spoons began again. Gabriel's wife served out spoonfuls of the pudding and passed the plates down the table. Midway down they were held up by Mary Jane, who replenished them with raspberry or orange jelly or with blancmange and jam. The pudding was of Aunt Julia's making and she received praises for it from all quarters. She herself said that it was not quite brown enough.

—Well, I hope, Miss Morkan, said Mr Browne, that I'm brown enough for you because, you know, I'm all brown.[68]

All the gentlemen, except Gabriel, ate some of the pudding out of compliment to Aunt Julia. As Gabriel never ate sweets the celery had been left for him. Freddy Malins also took a stalk of celery and ate it with his pudding. He had been told that celery was a capital thing for the blood and he was just then under doctor's care. Mrs Malins, who had been silent all through the supper, said that her son was going down to Mount Melleray[69] in a week or so. The table then spoke of Mount Melleray, how bracing the air was down there, how hospitable the monks were and how they never asked for a penny-piece from their guests.

—And do you mean to say, asked Mr Browne incredulously, that a chap can go down there and put up there as if it were a hotel and live on the fat of the land and then come away without paying a farthing?

—O, most people give some donation to the monastery when they leave, said Mary Jane.

—I wish we had an institution like that in our Church, said Mr Browne candidly.

He was astonished to hear that the monks never spoke,

got up at two in the morning and slept in their coffins.⁷⁰
He asked what they did it for.

—That's the rule of the order, said Aunt Kate firmly.

—Yes, but why? asked Mr Browne.

Aunt Kate repeated that it was the rule, that was all. Mr Browne still seemed not to understand. Freddy Malins explained to him, as best he could, that the monks were trying to make up for the sins committed by all the sinners in the outside world. The explanation was not very clear for Mr Browne grinned and said:

—I like that idea very much but wouldn't a comfortable spring bed do them as well as a coffin?

—The coffin, said Mary Jane, is to remind them of their last end.

As the subject had grown lugubrious it was buried in a silence of the table during which Mrs Malins could be heard saying to her neighbour in an indistinct undertone:

—They are very good men, the monks, very pious men.

The raisins and almonds and figs and apples and oranges and chocolates and sweets were now passed about the table and Aunt Julia invited all the guests to have either port or sherry. At first Mr Bartell D'Arcy refused to take either but one of his neighbours nudged him and whispered something to him upon which he allowed his glass to be filled. Gradually as the last glasses were being filled the conversation ceased. A pause followed, broken only by the noise of the wine and by unsettlings of chairs. The Misses Morkan, all three, looked down at the tablecloth. Someone coughed once or twice and then a few gentlemen patted the table gently as a signal for silence. The silence came and Gabriel pushed back his chair and stood up.

The patting at once grew louder in encouragement and then ceased altogether. Gabriel leaned his ten trembling fingers on the tablecloth and smiled nervously at the company. Meeting a row of upturned faces he raised his eyes to the chandelier. The piano was playing a waltz tune and he could hear the skirts sweeping against the drawing-room door. People, perhaps, were standing in the snow on the quay outside, gazing up at the lighted windows and listening to the waltz music. The air was pure there. In the distance lay the park where the trees were weighted with snow. The Wellington Monument wore a gleaming cap of snow that flashed westward over the white field of Fifteen Acres.[71]

He began:

—Ladies and Gentlemen.

—It has fallen to my lot this evening, as in years past, to perform a very pleasing task but a task for which I am afraid my poor powers as a speaker are all too inadequate.

—No, no! said Mr Browne.

—But, however that may be, I can only ask you tonight to take the will for the deed and to lend me your attention for a few moments while I endeavour to express to you in words what my feelings are on this occasion.

—Ladies and Gentlemen. It is not the first time that we have gathered together under this hospitable roof, around this hospitable board. It is not the first time that we have been the recipients – or perhaps, I had better say, the victims – of the hospitality of certain good ladies.

He made a circle in the air with his arm and paused. Everyone laughed or smiled at Aunt Kate and Aunt Julia and Mary Jane who all turned crimson with pleasure. Gabriel went on more boldly:

—I feel more strongly with every recurring year that our country has no tradition which does it so much honour and which it should guard so jealously as that of its hospitality. It is a tradition that is unique as far as my experience goes (and I have visited not a few places abroad) among the modern nations. Some would say, perhaps, that with us it is rather a failing than anything to be boasted of. But granted even that, it is, to my mind, a princely failing, and one that I trust will long be cultivated among us. Of one thing, at least, I am sure. As long as this one roof shelters the good ladies aforesaid – and I wish from my heart it may do so for many and many a long year to come – the tradition of genuine warm-hearted courteous Irish hospitality, which our fore-fathers have handed down to us and which we in turn must hand down to our descendants, is still alive among us.

A hearty murmur of assent ran round the table. It shot through Gabriel's mind that Miss Ivors was not there and that she had gone away discourteously: and he said with confidence in himself:

—Ladies and Gentlemen.

—A new generation is growing up in our midst, a generation actuated by new ideas and new principles. It is serious and enthusiastic for these new ideas and its enthusi-asm, even when it is misdirected, is, I believe, in the main sincere. But we are living in a sceptical and, if I may use the phrase, a thought-tormented age: and sometimes I fear that this new generation, educated or hypereducated as it is, will lack those qualities of humanity, of hospitality, of kindly humour which belonged to an older day. Listening to-night to the names of all those great singers of the past it seemed to me, I must confess, that we were living in a less spacious age. Those days might, without exaggeration, be called spacious days: and if they are gone beyond recall let us hope, at least, that in gatherings such as this we shall still speak of them with pride and affection, still cherish in our hearts the memory of those dead and gone great ones whose fame the world will not willingly let die.[72]

—Hear, hear! said Mr Browne loudly.

—But yet, continued Gabriel, his voice falling into a softer inflection, there are always in gatherings such as this sadder thoughts that will recur to our minds: thoughts of the past, of youth, of changes, of absent faces that we miss here tonight. Our path through life is strewn with many such sad memories: and were we to brood upon them always we could not find the heart to go on bravely with our work among the living. We have all of us living duties and living affections which claim, and rightly claim, our strenuous endeavours.

—Therefore, I will not linger on the past. I will not let any gloomy moralising intrude upon us here to-night. Here we are gathered together for a brief moment from the bustle and rush of our everyday routine. We are met here as friends, in the spirit of good-fellowship, as colleagues, also to a certain extent, in the true spirit of *camaraderie*, and as the guests of – what shall I call them? – the Three Graces of the Dublin musical world.

The table burst into applause and laughter at this sally. Aunt Julia vainly asked each of her neighbours in turn to tell her what Gabriel had said.

—He says we are the Three Graces, Aunt Julia, said Mary Jane.

Aunt Julia did not understand but she looked up, smiling, at Gabriel, who continued in the same vein:

—Ladies and Gentlemen.

—I will not attempt to play to-night the part that Paris played on another occasion. I will not attempt to choose between them. The task would be an invidious one and one beyond my poor powers. For when I view them in turn, whether it be our chief hostess herself, whose good heart, whose too good heart, has become a byword with all who know her, or her sister, who seems to be gifted with perennial youth and whose singing must have been a surprise and a revelation to us all to-night, or, last but not least, when I consider our youngest hostess, talented, cheerful, hard-working and the best of nieces, I confess, Ladies and Gentlemen, that I do not know to which of them I should award the prize.

Gabriel glanced down at his aunts and, seeing the large smile on Aunt Julia's face and the tears which had risen to Aunt Kate's eyes, hastened to his close. He raised his glass of port gallantly, while every member of the company fingered a glass expectantly, and said loudly:

—Let us toast them all three together. Let us drink to their health, wealth, long life, happiness and prosperity and may they long continue to hold the proud and self-won position which they hold in their profession and the position of honour and affection which they hold in our hearts.

All the guests stood up, glass in hand, and, turning towards the three seated ladies, sang in unison, with Mr Browne as leader:

> *For they are jolly gay fellows,*
> *For they are jolly gay fellows,*
> *For they are jolly gay fellows,*
> *Which nobody can deny.*

Aunt Kate was making frank use of her handkerchief and even Aunt Julia seemed moved. Freddy Malins beat time with his pudding-fork and the singers turned towards one another, as if in melodious conference, while they sang, with emphasis:

> *Unless he tells a lie,*
> *Unless he tells a lie.*[73]

Then, turning once more towards their hostesses, they sang:

> For they are jolly gay fellows,
> For they are jolly gay fellows,
> For they are jolly gay fellows,
> Which nobody can deny.

The acclamation which followed was taken up beyond the door of the supper-room by many of the other guests and renewed time after time, Freddy Malins acting as officer with his fork on high.

·　　·　　·　　·　　·　　·　　·　　·

The piercing morning air came into the hall where they were standing so that Aunt Kate said:

—Close the door, somebody. Mrs Malins will get her death of cold.

—Browne is out there, Aunt Kate, said Mary Jane.

—Browne is everywhere, said Aunt Kate, lowering her voice.

Mary Jane laughed at her tone.

—Really, she said archly, he is very attentive.

—He has been laid on here like the gas,[74] said Aunt Kate in the same tone, all during the Christmas.

She laughed herself this time good-humouredly and then added quickly:

—But tell him to come in, Mary Jane, and close the door. I hope to goodness he didn't hear me.

At that moment the hall-door was opened and Mr Browne came in from the doorstep, laughing as if his heart would break. He was dressed in a long green overcoat with mock astrakhan cuffs and collar and wore on his head an oval fur cap. He pointed down the snow-covered quay from where the sound of shrill prolonged whistling was borne in.

—Teddy will have all the cabs in Dublin out, he said.

Gabriel advanced from the little pantry behind the office, struggling into his overcoat and, looking round the hall, said:

—Gretta not down yet?

—She's getting on her things, Gabriel, said Aunt Kate.

—Who's playing up there? asked Gabriel.

—Nobody. They're all gone.

—O no, Aunt Kate, said Mary Jane. Bartell D'Arcy and Miss O'Callaghan aren't gone yet.

—Someone is strumming at the piano, anyhow, said Gabriel.

Mary Jane glanced at Gabriel and Mr Browne and said with a shiver:

—It makes me feel cold to look at you two gentlemen muffled up like that. I wouldn't like to face your journey home at this hour.

—I'd like nothing better this minute, said Mr Browne stoutly, than a rattling fine walk in the country or a fast drive with a good spanking goer between the shafts.

—We used to have a very good horse and trap at home, said Aunt Julia sadly.

—The never-to-be-forgotten Johnny, said Mary Jane, laughing.

Aunt Kate and Gabriel laughed too.

—Why, what was wonderful about Johnny? asked Mr Browne.

—The late lamented Patrick Morkan, our grandfather, that is, explained Gabriel, commonly known in his later years as the old gentleman, was a glue-boiler.

—O, now, Gabriel, said Aunt Kate, laughing, he had a starch mill.

—Well, glue or starch, said Gabriel, the old gentleman had a horse by the name of Johnny. And Johnny used to work in the old gentleman's mill, walking round and round in order to drive the mill. That was all very well; but now comes the tragic part about Johnny. One fine day the old gentleman thought he'd like to drive out with the quality to a military review in the park.

—The Lord have mercy on his soul, said Aunt Kate compassionately.

—Amen, said Gabriel. So the old gentleman, as I said, harnessed Johnny and put on his very best tall hat and his very best stock collar and drove out in grand style from his ancestral mansion somewhere near Back Lane,[75] I think.

Everyone laughed, even Mrs Malins, at Gabriel's manner and Aunt Kate said:

—O now, Gabriel, he didn't live in Back Lane, really. Only the mill was there.

—Out from the mansion of his forefathers, continued Gabriel, he drove with Johnny. And everything went on beautifully until Johnny came in sight of King Billy's statue:[76] and whether he fell in love with the horse King Billy sits on or whether he thought he was back again in the mill, anyhow he began to walk round the statue.

Gabriel paced in a circle round the hall in his goloshes amid the laughter of the others.

—Round and round he went, said Gabriel, and the old gentleman, who was a very pompous old gentleman, was highly indignant. *Go on, sir! What do you mean, sir? Johnny! Johnny! Most extraordinary conduct! Can't understand the horse!*

The peals of laughter which followed Gabriel's imitation of the incident were interrupted by a resounding knock at the hall-door. Mary Jane ran to open it and let in Freddy Malins. Freddy Malins, with his hat well back on his head and his shoulders humped with cold, was puffing and steaming after his exertions.

—I could only get one cab, he said.

—O, we'll find another along the quay, said Gabriel.

—Yes, said Aunt Kate. Better not keep Mrs Malins standing in the draught.

Mrs Malins was helped down the front steps by her

son and Mr Browne and, after many manoeuvres, hoisted into the cab. Freddy Malins clambered in after her and spent a long time settling her on the seat, Mr Browne helping him with advice. At last she was settled comfortably and Freddy Malins invited Mr Browne into the cab. There was a good deal of confused talk, and then Mr Browne got into the cab. The cabman settled his rug over his knees, and bent down for the address. The confusion grew greater and the cabman was directed differently by Freddy Malins and Mr Browne, each of whom had his head out through a window of the cab. The difficulty was to know where to drop Mr Browne along the route and Aunt Kate, Aunt Julia and Mary Jane helped the discussion from the doorstep with cross-directions and contradictions and abundance of laughter. As for Freddy Malins he was speechless with laughter. He popped his head in and out of the window every moment, to the great danger of his hat, and told his mother how the discussion was progressing till at last Mr Browne shouted to the bewildered cabman above the din of everybody's laughter:

—Do you know Trinity College?[77]

—Yes, sir, said the cabman.

—Well, drive bang up against Trinity College gates, said Mr Browne, and then we'll tell you where to go. You understand now?

—Yes, sir, said the cabman.

—Make like a bird for Trinity College.

—Right, sir, cried the cabman.

The horse was whipped up and the cab rattled off along the quay amid a chorus of laughter and adieus.

Gabriel had not gone to the door with the others. He was in a dark part of the hall gazing up the staircase. A woman was standing near the top of the first flight, in the shadow also. He could not see her face but he could see the terracotta and salmonpink panels of her skirt which the shadow made appear black and white. It was his wife. She was leaning on the banisters, listening to something. Gabriel was surprised at her stillness and strained his ear to listen also. But he could hear little save the noise of laughter and dispute on the front steps, a few chords struck on the piano and a few notes of a man's voice singing.

He stood still in the gloom of the hall, trying to catch the air that the voice was singing and gazing up at his wife. There was grace and mystery in her attitude as if she were a symbol of something. He asked himself what is a woman standing on the stairs in the shadow, listening to distant music, a symbol of. If he were a painter he would paint her in that attitude. Her blue felt hat would show off the bronze of her hair against the darkness and the dark panels of her skirt would show off the light ones. *Distant Music* he would call the picture if he were a painter.

The hall-door was closed; and Aunt Kate, Aunt Julia and Mary Jane came down the hall, still laughing.

—Well, isn't Freddy terrible? said Mary Jane. He's really terrible.

Gabriel said nothing but pointed up the stairs towards where his wife was standing. Now that the hall-door was closed the voice and the piano could be heard more clearly. Gabriel held up his hand for them to be silent. The song seemed to be in the old Irish tonality[78] and the singer seemed uncertain both of his words and of his voice. The voice, made plaintive by distance and by the singer's hoarseness, faintly illuminated the cadence of the air with words expressing grief:

> *O, the rain falls on my heavy locks*
> *And the dew wets my skin,*
> *My babe lies cold . . .*[79]

—O, exclaimed Mary Jane. It's Bartell D'Arcy singing

and he wouldn't sing all the night. O, I'll get him to sing a song before he goes.

—O do, Mary Jane, said Aunt Kate.

Mary Jane brushed past the others and ran to the staircase but before she reached it the singing stopped and the piano was closed abruptly.

—O, what a pity! she cried. Is he coming down, Gretta?

Gabriel heard his wife answer yes and saw her come down towards them. A few steps behind her were Mr Bartell D'Arcy and Miss O'Callaghan.

—O, Mr D'Arcy, cried Mary Jane, it's downright mean of you to break off like that when we were all in raptures listening to you.

—I have been at him all the evening, said Miss O'Callaghan, and Mrs Conroy too and he told us he had a dreadful cold and couldn't sing.

—O, Mr D'Arcy, said Aunt Kate, now that was a great fib to tell.

—Can't you see that I'm as hoarse as a crow? said Mr D'Arcy roughly.

He went into the pantry hastily and put on his overcoat. The others, taken aback by his rude speech, could find nothing to say. Aunt Kate wrinkled her brows and made signs to the others to drop the subject. Mr D'Arcy stood swathing his neck carefully and frowning.

—It's the weather, said Aunt Julia, after a pause.

—Yes, everybody has colds, said Aunt Kate readily, everybody.

—They say, said Mary Jane, we haven't had snow like it for thirty years; and I read this morning in the newspapers that the snow is general all over Ireland.

—I love the look of snow, said Aunt Julia sadly.

—So do I, said Miss O'Callaghan. I think Christmas is never really Christmas unless we have the snow on the ground.

—But poor Mr D'Arcy doesn't like the snow, said Aunt Kate, smiling.

Mr D'Arcy came from the pantry, fully swathed and buttoned, and in a repentant tone told them the history of his cold. Everyone gave him advice and said it was a great pity and urged him to be very careful of his throat in the night air. Gabriel watched his wife who did not join in the conversation. She was standing right under the dusty fanlight and the flame of the gas lit up the rich bronze of her hair which he had seen her drying at the fire a few days before. She was in the same attitude and seemed unaware of the talk about her. At last she turned towards them and Gabriel saw that there was colour on her checks and that her eyes were shining. A sudden tide of joy went leaping out of his heart.

—Mr D'Arcy, she said, what is the name of that song you were singing?

—It's called *The Lass of Aughrim*, said Mr D'Arcy, but I couldn't remember it properly. Why? Do you know it?

—*The Lass of Aughrim*, she repeated. I couldn't think of the name.

—It's a very nice air, said Mary Jane. I'm sorry you were not in voice to-night.

—Now, Mary Jane, said Aunt Kate, don't annoy Mr D'Arcy. I won't have him annoyed.

Seeing that all were ready to start she shepherded them to the door where good-night was said:

—Well, good-night, Aunt Kate, and thanks for the pleasant evening.

—Good-night, Gabriel. Good-night, Gretta!

—Good-night, Aunt Kate, and thanks ever so much. Good-night, Aunt Julia.

—O, good-night, Gretta, I didn't see you.

—Good-night, Mr D'Arcy. Good-night, Miss O'Callaghan.

—Good-night, Miss Morkan.

—Good-night, again.

—Good-night, all. Safe home.

—Good-night. Good-night.

The morning was still dark. A dull yellow light brooded over the houses and the river; and the sky seemed to be descending. It was slushy underfoot; and only streaks and patches of snow lay on the roofs, on the parapets of the quay and on the area railings. The lamps were still burning redly in the murky air and, across the river, the palace of the Four Courts [80] stood out menacingly against the heavy sky.

She was walking on before him with Mr Bartell D'Arcy, her shoes in a brown parcel tucked under one arm and her hands holding her skirt up from the slush. She had no longer any grace of attitude but Gabriel's eyes were still bright with happiness. The blood went bounding along his veins; and the thoughts went rioting through his brain, proud, joyful, tender, valorous.

She was walking on before him so lightly and so erect that he longed to run after her noiselessly, catch her by the shoulders and say something foolish and affectionate into her ear. She seemed to him so frail that he longed to defend her against something and then to be alone with her. Moments of their secret life together burst like stars upon his memory. A heliotrope envelope was lying beside his breakfast-cup and he was caressing it with his hand. Birds were twittering in the ivy and the sunny web of the curtain was shimmering along the floor: he could not eat for happiness. They were standing on the crowded platform and he was placing a ticket inside the warm palm of her glove. He was standing with her in the cold, looking in through a grated window at a man making bottles in a roaring furnace. It was very cold. Her face, fragrant in the cold air, was quite close to his; and suddenly she called out to the man at the furnace:

—Is the fire hot, sir?

But the man could not hear her with the noise of the furnace. It was just as well. He might have answered rudely.

A wave of yet more tender joy escaped from his heart and went coursing in warm flood along his arteries. Like the tender fires of stars moments of their life together, that no one knew of or would ever know of, broke upon and illumined his memory. He longed to recall to her those moments, to make her forget the years of their dull existence together and remember only their moments of ecstasy. For the years, he felt, had not quenched his soul or hers. Their children, his writing, her household cares had not quenched all their souls' tender fire. In one letter that he had written to her then he had said: *Why is it that words like these seem to me so dull and cold? Is it because there is no word tender enough to be your name?*

Like distant music these words that he had written years before were borne towards him from the past. He longed to be alone with her. When the others had gone away, when he and she were in their room in the hotel, then they would be alone together. He would call her softly:

—Gretta!

Perhaps she would not hear at once: she would be undressing. Then something in his voice would strike her. She would turn and look at him. . . .

At the corner of Winetavern Street [81] they met a cab. He was glad of its rattling noise as it saved him from conversation. She was looking out of the window and seemed tired. The others spoke only a few words, pointing out some building or street. The horse galloped along wearily under the murky morning sky, dragging his old rattling box after his heels, and Gabriel was again in a cab with her, galloping to catch the boat, galloping to their honeymoon.

As the cab drove across O'Connell Bridge[82] Miss O'Callaghan said:

—They say you never cross O'Connell Bridge without seeing a white horse.

—I see a white man this time, said Gabriel.

Where? asked Mr Bartell D'Arcy.

Gabriel pointed to the statue,[83] on which lay patches of snow. Then he nodded familiarly to it and waved his hand.

—Good-night, Dan, he said gaily.

When the cab drew up before the hotel Gabriel jumped out and, in spite of Mr Bartell D'Arcy's protest, paid the driver. He gave the man a shilling over his fare. The man saluted and said:

—A prosperous New Year to you, sir.

—The same to you, said Gabriel cordially.

She leaned for a moment on his arm in getting out of the cab and while standing at the curbstone, bidding the others good-night. She leaned lightly on his arm, as lightly as when she had danced with him a few hours before. He had felt proud and happy then, happy that she was his, proud of her grace and wifely carriage. But now, after the kindling again of so many memories, the first touch of her body, musical and strange and perfumed, sent through him a keen pang of lust. Under cover of her silence he pressed her arm closely to his side; and, as they stood at the hotel door, he felt that they had escaped from their lives and duties, escaped from home and friends and run away together with wild and radiant hearts to a new adventure.

An old man was dozing in a great hooded chair in the hall. He lit a candle in the office and went before them to the stairs. They followed him in silence, their feet falling in soft thuds on the thickly carpeted stairs. She mounted the stairs behind the porter, her head bowed in the ascent, her frail shoulders curved as with a burden, her skirt girt tightly about her. He could have flung his arms about her hips and held her still for his arms were trembling with desire to seize her and only the stress of his nails against the palms of his hands held the wild impulse of his body in check. The porter halted on the stairs to settle his guttering candle. They halted too on the steps below him. In the silence Gabriel could hear the falling of the molten wax into the tray and the thumping of his own heart against his ribs.

The porter led them along a corridor and opened a door. Then he set his unstable candle down on a toilet-table and asked at what hour they were to be called in the morning.

—Eight, said Gabriel.

The porter pointed to the tap of the electric-light and began a muttered apology but Gabriel cut him short.

—We don't want any light. We have light enough from the street. And I say, he added, pointing to the candle, you might remove that handsome article, like a good man.

The porter took up his candle again, but slowly for he was surprised by such a novel idea. Then he mumbled good-night and went out. Gabriel shot the lock to.

A ghostly light from the street lamp lay in a long shaft from one window to the door. Gabriel threw his overcoat and hat on a couch and crossed the room towards the window. He looked down into the street in order that his emotion might calm a little. Then he turned and leaned against a chest of drawers with his back to the light. She had taken off her hat and cloak and was standing before a large swinging mirror, unhooking her waist. Gabriel paused for a few moments, watching her, and then said:

—Gretta!

She turned away from the mirror slowly and walked

along the shaft of light towards him. Her face looked so serious and weary that the words would not pass Gabriel's lips. No, it was not the moment yet.

—You looked tired, he said.

—I am a little, she answered.

—You don't feel ill or weak?

—No, tired: that's all.

She went on to the window and stood there, looking out. Gabriel waited again and then, fearing that diffidence was about to conquer him, he said abruptly:

—By the way, Gretta!

—What is it?

—You know that poor fellow Malins? he said quickly.

—Yes. What about him?

—Well, poor fellow, he's a decent sort of chap after all, continued Gabriel in a false voice. He gave me back that sovereign[84] I lent him and I didn't expect it really. It's a pity he wouldn't keep away from that Browne, because he's not a bad fellow at heart.

He was trembling now with annoyance. Why did she seem so abstracted? He did not know how he could begin. Was she annoyed, too, about something? If she would only turn to him or come to him of her own accord! To take her as she was would be brutal. No, he must see some ardour in her eyes first. He longed to be master of her strange mood.

—When did you lend him the pound? she asked, after a pause.

Gabriel strove to restrain himself from breaking out into brutal language about the sottish Malins and his pound. He longed to cry to her from his soul, to crush her body against his, to overmaster her. But he said:

—O, at Christmas, when he opened that little Christmas-card shop in Henry Street.[85]

He was in such a fever of rage and desire that he did

not hear her come from the window. She stood before him for an instant, looking at him strangely. Then, suddenly raising herself on tiptoe and resting her hands lightly on his shoulders, she kissed him.

—You are a very generous person, Gabriel, she said.

Gabriel, trembling with delight at her sudden kiss and at the quaintness of her phrase, put his hands on her hair and began smoothing it back, scarcely touching it with his fingers. The washing had made it fine and brilliant. His heart was brimming over with happiness. Just when he was wishing for it she had come to him of her own accord. Perhaps her thoughts had been running with his. Perhaps she had felt the impetuous desire that was in him and then the yielding mood had come upon her. Now that she had fallen to him so easily he wondered why he had been so diffident.

He stood, holding her head between his hands. Then, slipping one arm swiftly about her body and drawing her towards him, he said softly:

—Gretta dear, what are you thinking about?

She did not answer nor yield wholly to his arm. He said again, softly:

—Tell me what it is, Gretta. I think I know what is the matter. Do I know?

She did not answer at once. Then she said in an outburst of tears:

—O, I am thinking about that song, *The Lass of Aughrim*.

She broke loose from him and ran to the bed and, throwing her arms across the bed-rail, hid her face. Gabriel stood stock-still for a moment in astonishment and then followed her. As he passed in the way of the cheval-glass he caught sight of himself in full length, his broad, well-filled shirt-front, the face whose expression always puzzled him when he saw it in a mirror and his glimmering gilt-rimmed eyeglasses. He halted a few paces from her and said:

—What about the song? Why does that make you cry?

She raised her head from her arms and dried her eyes with the back of her hand like a child. A kinder note than he had intended went into his voice.

—Why, Gretta? he asked.

—I am thinking about a person long ago who used to sing that song.

—And who was the person long ago? asked Gabriel, smiling.

—It was a person I used to know in Galway when I was living with my grandmother, she said.

The smile passed away from Gabriel's face. A dull anger began to gather again at the back of his mind and the dull fires of his lust began to glow angrily in his veins.

—Someone you were in love with? he asked ironically.

—It was a young boy I used to know, she answered, named Michael[86] Furey. He used to sing that song, *The Lass of Aughrim*. He was very delicate.[87]

Gabriel was silent. He did not wish her to think that he was interested in this delicate boy.

—I can see him so plainly, she said after a moment. Such eyes as he had: big dark eyes! And such an expression in them – an expression!

—O then, you were in love with him? said Gabriel.

—I used to go out walking with him,[88] she said, when I was in Galway.

A thought flew across Gabriel's mind.

—Perhaps that was why you wanted to go to Galway with that Ivors girl? he said coldly.

She looked at him and asked in surprise:

—What for?

Her eyes made Gabriel feel awkward. He shrugged his shoulders and said:

—How do I know? To see him perhaps.

She looked away from him along the shaft of light towards the window in silence.

—He is dead, she said at length. He died when he was only seventeen. Isn't it a terrible thing to die so young as that?

—What was he? asked Gabriel, still ironically.

—He was in the gasworks,[89] she said.

Gabriel felt humiliated by the failure of his irony and by the evocation of this figure from the dead, a boy in the gasworks. While he had been full of memories of their secret life together, full of tenderness and joy and desire, she had been comparing him in her mind with another. A shameful consciousness of his own person assailed him. He saw himself as a ludicrous figure, acting as a pennyboy for his aunts, a nervous well-meaning sentimentalist, orating to vulgarians and idealising his own clownish lusts, the pitiable fatuous fellow he had caught a glimpse of in the mirror. Instinctively he turned his back more to the light lest she might see the shame that burned upon his forehead.

He tried to keep up his tone of cold interrogation but his voice when he spoke was humble and indifferent.

—I suppose you were in love with this Michael Furey, Gretta, he said.

—I was great with him[90] at that time, she said.

Her voice was veiled and sad. Gabriel, feeling now how vain it would be to try to lead her whither he had purposed, caressed one of her hands and said, also sadly:

—And what did he die of so young, Gretta? Consumption, was it?

—I think he died for me, she answered.

A vague terror seized Gabriel at this answer as if, at that hour when he had hoped to triumph, some impalpable and vindictive being was coming against him, gathering forces against him in its vague world. But he shook himself free of it with an effort of reason and continued to caress her hand. He did not question her again for he felt that she would tell him of herself. Her hand was warm and moist: it did not respond to his touch but he continued to caress it just as he had caressed her first letter to him that spring morning.

—It was in the winter, she said, about the beginning of the winter when I was going to leave my grandmother's [91] and come up here to the convent. [92] And he was ill at the time in his lodgings in Galway and wouldn't be let out and his people in Oughterard [93] were written to. He was in decline, they said, or something like that. I never knew rightly.

She paused for a moment and sighed.

—Poor fellow, she said. He was very fond of me and he was such a gentle boy. We used to go out together, walking, you know, Gabriel, like the way they do in the country. He was going to study singing only for his health. He had a very good voice, poor Michael Furey.

—Well; and then? asked Gabriel.

—And then when it came to the time for me to leave Galway and come up to the convent he was much worse and I wouldn't be let see him so I wrote a letter saying I was going up to Dublin and would be back in the summer and hoping he would be better then.

She paused for a moment to get her voice under control and then went on:

—Then the night before I left I was in my grandmother's house in Nuns' Island, [94] packing up, and I heard gravel thrown up against the window. The window was so wet I couldn't see so I ran downstairs as I was and slipped out the back into the garden and there was the poor fellow at the end of the garden, shivering.

—And did you not tell him to go back? asked Gabriel.

—I implored of him to go home at once and told him he would get his death in the rain. But he said he did not want to live. I can see his eyes as well as well! He was standing at the end of the wall where there was a tree.

—And did he go home? asked Gabriel.

—Yes, he went home. And when I was only a week in the convent he died and he was buried in Oughterard where his people came from. O, the day I heard that, that he was dead!

She stopped, choking with sobs, and, overcome by emotion, flung herself face downward on the bed, sobbing in the quilt. Gabriel held her hand for a moment longer, irresolutely, and then, shy of intruding on her grief, let it fall gently and walked quietly to the window.

She was fast asleep.

Gabriel, leaning on his elbow, looked for a few moments unresentfully on her tangled hair and half-open mouth, listening to her deep-drawn breath. So she had had that romance in her life: a man had died for her sake. It hardly pained him now to think how poor a part he, her husband, had played in her life. He watched her while she slept as though he and she had never lived together as man and wife. His curious eyes rested long upon her face and on her hair: and, as he thought of what she must have been then, in that time of her first girlish beauty, a strange friendly pity for her entered his soul. He did not like to say even to himself that her face was no longer beautiful but he knew that it was no longer the face for which Michael Furey had braved death.

Perhaps she had not told him all the story. His eyes moved to the chair over which she had thrown some of her clothes. A petticoat string dangled to the floor. One boot stood upright, its limp upper fallen down: the fellow of it lay upon its side. He wondered at his riot of emotions of an hour before. From what had it proceeded? From his aunt's supper, from his own foolish speech, from the wine and dancing, the merry-making when saying good-night in the hall, the pleasure of the walk along the river in the snow. Poor Aunt Julia! She, too, would soon be a shade with the shade of Patrick Morkan and his horse. He had caught that haggard look upon her face for a moment when she was singing *Arrayed for the Bridal*. Soon, perhaps, he would be sitting in that same drawing-room, dressed in black, his silk hat on his knees. The blinds would be drawn down and Aunt Kate would be sitting beside him, crying and blowing her nose and telling him how Julia had died. He would cast about in his mind for some words that might console her, and would find only lame and useless ones. Yes, yes: that would happen very soon.

The air of the room chilled his shoulders. He stretched himself cautiously along under the sheets and lay down beside his wife. One by one they were all becoming shades. Better pass boldly into that other world, in the full glory of some passion, than fade and wither dismally with age. He thought of how she who lay beside him had locked in her heart for so many years that image of her lover's eyes when he had told her that he did not wish to live.

Generous tears filled Gabriel's eyes. He had never felt like that himself towards any woman but he knew that such a feeling must be love. The tears gathered more thickly in his eyes and in the partial darkness he imagined he saw the form of a young man standing under a dripping tree. Other forms were near. His soul had approached that region where dwell the vast hosts of the dead. He was conscious of, but could not apprehend, their wayward and flickering existence. His own identity was fading out into a grey impalpable world: the solid world itself which these dead had one time reared and lived in was dissolving and dwindling.

A few light taps upon the pane made him turn to the window. It had begun to snow again. He watched sleepily the flakes, silver and dark, falling obliquely against the lamplight. The time had come for him to set out on his journey westward. Yes, the newspapers were right: snow was general all over Ireland.[95] It was falling on every part of the dark central plain, on the treeless hills, falling softly upon the Bog of Allen[96] and, farther westward, softly falling[97] into the dark mutinous Shannon[98] waves. It was falling, too, upon every part of the lonely church-yard on the hill where Michael Furey lay buried. It lay thickly drifted on the crooked crosses and headstones, on the spears of the little gate, on the barren thorns. His soul swooned slowly as he heard the snow falling faintly through the universe and faintly falling, like the descent of their last end, upon all the living and the dead.

APPENDIX I

The following is the order of composition and date of completion of the stories in *Dubliners*, as far as these have been ascertained. (Sources: Gifford op. cit. and Michael Groden, 'A Textual and Publishing History', in *A Companion to Joyce Studies*, eds. Zack Bowen and James Carens, 1984, pp. 78–9, The Viking Critical Library Edition, 1969):

1. 'The Sisters': completed in its first version in July, 1904, for publication in the *Irish Homestead* in August, 1904. Revised May–June, 1906.
2. 'Eveline': completed early autumn, 1904, for publication in the *Irish Homestead* in September, 1904.
3. 'After the Race': completed autumn, 1904, for publication in the *Irish Homestead* in December, 1904.
4. 'Clay': substantially completed January, 1905. Brought to final form in 1905 and 1906 (the story was first conceived as 'Christmas Eve', then re-cast as 'Hallow Eve', retitled as 'The Clay' before it became 'Clay').
5. 'The Boarding House': completed July, 1905 (manuscript is dated 1 July 1905).
6. 'Counterparts': completed mid–July, 1905.
7. 'A Painful Case': substantially completed July, 1905 (manuscript is dated 15 August, 1905). Brought to final form (the original title was 'A Painful Incident') 1906.
8. 'Ivy Day in the Committee Room': substantially completed August, 1905.
9. 'An Encounter': completed by September, 1905.
10. 'A Mother': completed late–September, 1905.
11. 'Araby': completed October, 1905.
12. 'Grace': substantially completed December, 1905.
13. 'Two Gallants': completed February 1906.

14. 'A Little Cloud': completed mid–1906.
15. 'The Dead': completed 1907.

APPENDIX II

Many of the characters in *Dubliners* appear or are referred to in Joyce's *Ulysses*. It is clear that Joyce thought of that novel and his earlier work as intimately interrelated. Stephen Dedalus of *A Portrait of the Artist as a Young Man* is one of the three central characters of the later novel, while *Ulysses* had its origin in a projected story for *Dubliners* about a Mr Hunter, instead of the Leopold Bloom who actually became the book's hero. It can accordingly be useful in reading *Dubliners* to know how the characters fare in the later work. The following is a list, story by story, of the characters from those stories in *Dubliners* who make a later appearance or appearances or who are referred to in *Ulysses* with the appropriate page references to *Ulysses*, London: Penguin Books, Twentieth-Century Classics edition, 1992. (Source: Shari Benstock and Bernard Benstock, *Who's He When He's at Home: A James Joyce Directory*, Urbana/Chicago/London: 1980).

'TWO GALLANTS'

Lenehan. This public-house parasite and racing man makes frequent appearances in *Ulysses*, in Aeolus, Wandering Rocks, Sirens, Cyclops, and Oxen of the Sun. 162–78, 181–2, 186, 188, 298–302, 325, 336–344, 420–49, 506–61. He is also referred to in Aeolus, 159, Lestrygonians, 221, in The Wandering Rocks, 294, Sirens, 328–30, Cyclops, 396–7, Eumaeus, 709, 752, Ithaca, 863. He appears also as a hallucination in Circe, 595, 611, 626, 669.
Corley. Appears in Eumaeus 708–11.
Holohan. Referred to in Lotus-Eaters and Aeolus, 89, 172, appears as hallucination in Circe, 611, 685.

'THE BOARDING HOUSE'

Mrs Mooney. Referred to in Cyclops, 391, 407.
Jack Mooney. Referred to in Lestrygonians, The Wandering Rocks and Cyclops, 220, 317, 407.
Polly Mooney. Referred to in Cyclops, 391, 407.
Mr Doran. Appears in Lestrygonians, The Wandering Rocks and Cyclops, 212, 317, 323, 385–449. He appears as a hallucination in Circe, 581.
Bantam Lyons. Appears in Lotus-Eaters, Lestrygonians, Oxen of the Sun, 105–6, 227–8, 558–9. He is referred to in Lotus-Eaters, The Wandering Rocks, Cyclops, Circe, Eumaeus, Ithaca, 89, 299, 391, 435, 685, 752, 789. He appears as a hallucination in Circe, 615.

'A LITTLE CLOUD'

Gallaher. He is referred to in Hades and Aeolus, 110, 172–4.

'COUNTERPARTS'

Crosbie and Alleynes. This company is mentioned in Hades, 113.
Leonard. Appears in Lestrygonians, 227–8. Referred to in Hades, Cyclops, 113, 407. He appears as a hallucination in Circe, 595, 609, 611.
Nosey Flynn. Appears in Lestrygonians, The Wandering Rocks, 218–28. 298. Referred to in Cyclops, Nausicaa, Penelope (in Penelope referred to simply as 'that longnosed chap'), 422, 481–2, 908. He appears as a hallucination in Circe, 595, 609, 611.
Little Peake. Referred to in Hades, 113.

'A PAINFUL CASE'

Mrs Sinico. Referred to in Hades, Ithaca, 145, 815, 835.

'IVY DAY IN THE COMMITTEE ROOM'

Joe Hynes. Appears in Hades, Aeolus and Cyclops, 126, 135,

141–3, 151–2, 376–449. He is referred to in Hades, Lestrygonians, Nausicaa, Eumaeus, Ithaca, Penelope, 111, 230, 489, 497, 751, 827, 872. He appears as a hallucination in Circe, 596, 608, 610, 685.

Mr Fanning. Appears in The Wandering Rocks, 317–9. Referred to in Aeolus (Long John), The Wandering Rocks ('sub-sheriff's office'), Sirens ('t'the long fellow'), Cyclops, Nausicaa, 151, 313, 315, 325, 344, 363, 374, 386, 407, 489. He appears as an hallucination in Circe, 596.

Crofton. Appears in Cyclops, 436–49. Mentioned in Hades, 116. He appears as a hallucination in Circe, 610, 686.

'A MOTHER'

Holohan. See above 'Two Gallants'.

Kathleen Kearney. Referred to in Penelope, 885, 905.

Mr O'Madden Burke. Appears in Aeolus, 167–82, 188. He is referred to in the Wandering Rocks and Sirens, 295, 338. He appears as a hallucination in Circe, 610.

'GRACE'

Mr Power. Appears in Hades, The Wandering Rocks and Cyclops, 107–28, 132, 143, 316–19, 436–49. Referred to in Lestrygonians, The Wandering rocks, Eumaeus, Ithaca, Penelope, 206, 306, 751, 827, 920. He appears as a hallucination in Circe, 595.

Mr Kernan. Appears in Hades, The Wandering Rocks, Sirens, 126–34, 305, 307–10, 324, 356–76. He is referred to in Lotus-Eaters, Hades, Lestrygonians, Sirens (Ker), Eumaeus, Ithaca and Penelope, 86, 111, 204, 218, 330, 751, 860, 919–20. He also appears as a hallucination in Circe, 595, 672.

Martin Cunningham. Appears in Hades, The Wandering Rocks, Cyclops, 107–26, 127–8, 135, 146–7, 316–19, 436–49. He is referred to in The Lotus-Eaters, Aeolus, The Wandering Rocks, Cyclops, Eumaeus, Ithaca, Penelope, 98, 154, 280, 391, 405, 432, 722, 751, 827, 920. Appears as a hallucination in Circe, 595, 672.

Mrs Cunningham. Referred to in Hades, 120–21. Appears as a hallucination in Circe, 672.

Mr M'Coy. Appears in The Lotus-Eaters, The Wandering Rocks, 89–92, 298–302, 325. He is referred to in Calypso, The Lotus-Eaters, Lestrygonians, Sirens, Nausicaa, Ithaca, Penelope, 82, 98, 212, 364, 479, 723, 751, 920. He also appears as a hallucination in Circe, 395, 685.

'THE DEAD'

Gabriel Conroy. Referred to in Aeolus and Nausicaa, 159, 492.

Gretta Conroy. Referred to in Calypso, 84.

Julia Morkan. Referred to in Lestrygonians and Ithaca, 205–6, 782.

Kate Morkan. Referred to in Ithaca, 781–2.

Bartell D'Arcy. Referred to in Lestrygonians, The Wandering Rocks, Penelope, 196–7, 300, 863, 881, 921. Appears as a hallucination in Circe, 685.

APPENDIX III

The following is taken from a Victorian edition of Balfe's opera, frequently referred to in the text.

THE BOHEMIAN GIRL.

DRAMATIS PERSONÆ.

Count Arnheim (*Governor of Presburg*) .... Baritone.
Thaddeus (*a proscribed Pole*) .... Tenor.
Florestein (*Nephew of the Count*) .... Tenor.
Devilshoof (*Chief of the Gipsies*) .... Bass.
Captain of the Guard .... Bass.
Officer .... Tenor.
Arline (*Daughter of the Count*)....................... Soprano.
Buda (*her Attendant*).. Soprano.
Queen of the Gipsies .... Soprano.

Chorus.

This Opera is founded on a ballet called 'La Gipsy,' derived from Cervantes' tale 'Preciosa'. Its action is as follows:—Count Arnheim, loyal to the Austrian Empire, entertains certain guests at his castle, where they raise the National Standard above the Emperor's statue, the Count meanwhile extolling a soldier's life. The guests depart for the chase without him, his daughter, Arline, a child six years old, accompanying them with her nurse. Thaddeus, an exiled Polish rebel, enters seeking refuge, which he finds in the company of a tribe of passing gipsies, who disguise him by order of their leader, Devilshoof, just in time to escape his pursuers. The huntsmen, with Florestein, a foolish nephew of Count Arnheim, return in terror with the tidings that Arline is attacked by a stag; Thaddeus rushes to her assistance, and restores her unhurt to the Count, whose gratitude induces him to invite the apparent gipsy to join the feast of rejoicing. At this feast Arnheim proposes the Emperor's health, which is declined boldly by Thaddeus, whose life is in danger for this act, but he is protected by the Count; Devilshoof, however, who has shared the republican enthusiasm of Thaddeus, is arrested and confined in the castle. He escapes, and is seen by the distracted company bearing away in his arms Arline, whose abduction suggests his revenge. In Act 2, twelve years have been past in sorrow by the Count; the gipsies are stationed at Presburg ready for a fair, led still by Devilshoof, who catches and robs Florestein, an incautious intruder; the GIPSY QUEEN, however, commands the restoration of his property; Devilshoof obeys, but reserves a diamond medallion for himself. Arline, reared among the gipsies and tended gently by Thaddeus, wakes from a sleep, and relates a strange dream, which Thaddeus knows is retrospective.* She asks the history of her birth, which he hesitates to relate fearing lest her love should leave him. The Gipsy Queen who also loves Thaddeus now irritates Arline into jealousy, whereupon Thaddeus implores her to marry him. Their betrothal is witnessed by the tribe, who now set out for the fair. Here Arline attracts hosts of admirers, amongst them Florestein, who suddenly recognizes

---

* It is at this point in the opera that Arline sings 'I Dreamt that I Dwelt in Marble Halls'.

The cancelled stanza which Maria in 'Clay' does not sing reads:

> I dreamt that suitors sought my hand,
>   That knights upon bended knee,
> And with vows no maiden heart could withstand,
>   They pledged their faith to me,
> And I dreamt that one of that noble host
>   Came forth my hand to claim;
> But I also dreamt, which charmed me most,
>   That you loved me still the same.

his medallion on Arline's neck, where it has been cunningly placed by the Gipsy Queen. In spite of Thaddeus and the tribe, she is seized and conveyed to the Count's castle. Here an accident reveals to the father that the prisoner is his child. Thaddeus implores Arline (Act 3) in a secret interview not to desert him, but the Count spurns the supposed vagabond; when Thaddeus declares himself, and Arnheim is induced to give his daughter to the noble exile. At the feast in their honour, the Gipsy Queen with Devilshoof attempts Arline's life, but the gipsy diverts the shot which strikes her who aimed it. The festival proceeds to commemorate the happy fortunes of The Bohemian Girl.

The scene is laid in Presburg and its neighbourhood.

Descriptions of this and other operas mentioned in the text and in the notes can be found in Kobbés *Complete Opera Book*, ed. and rev. by the Earl of Harewood, London: Putnam and Company, 1976.

NOTES

In preparing these annotations, as well as to standard reference works, dictionaries, Partridge on slang, biographies and histories, and so on, I have been significantly indebted to Don Gifford, *Joyce Annotated: Notes to* Dubliners *and* A Portrait of the Artist as a Young Man, Second Edition, revised and enlarged, (Berkeley/Los Angeles/London: University of California Press, 1982). Where my debt to Gifford has been more than simply a common employment of similar sources and a shared fascination for that Joycean cornucopia, Thom's *Directory*. I have indicated as much in the text by the use of the letter G. with relevant page reference or references. I have accepted Gifford's division of the city into four quadrants which allows directions and locations to be given in relation to points of the compass.

I have also been significantly helped by the following: Clive Hart, ed. *James Joyce's* Dubliners: *Critical Essays* (London: Faber and Faber, 1969) (referred to in the text as C. H.); Donald Torchiana, *Backgrounds for Joyce's* Dubliners (Boston/London/Sydney: Allen and Unwin, 1986), (referred to in the text as T.); Brendan O'Hehir, *A Gaelic Lexicon For* Finnegans Wake *and Glossary for Joyce's Other Works* (Berkeley and Los Angeles: University of California Press, 1967), (referred to in the text as O'H.) and by Richard Wall, *An Anglo–Irish Dialect Glossary for Joyce's Works* (Gerrards Cross: Colin Smythe, 1986) (referred to in the text as W.). Invaluable as always was Richard Ellmann, *James Joyce* (New and revised edition, Oxford/New York/Toronto/Melbourne: Oxford University Press, 1982, issued as Oxford University Press paperback with corrections, 1983) (this latter volume referred to in the text as J. J.). Also useful were Shari Benstock and Bernard Benstock, *Who's He When He's at Home: A James Joyce Directory* (Urbana/London/Chicago: University of

Illinois Press, 1980) (referred to in the text as B. and B.) and Thomas F. Staley, *An Annotated Critical Bibliography of James Joyce*, (New York/London/Toronto/Sydney/Tokyo: Harvester Wheatsheaf, 1989). I have also employed *The Letters of James Joyce*, ed. Stuart Gilbert (London: Faber/New York: Viking, 1957; reissued with corrections, 1966); vols. *II* and *III*, ed. Richard Ellmann (London: Faber/New York: Viking, 1966) (referred to in the text as *Letters* and *Letters, II, III*).

NAMES IN THE NOTES

Unless otherwise stated it may be assumed that the names of characters, locations, and so on are fictional (or must be reckoned such in the absence of an identification). From time to time, however, it seemed helpful to comment on the significance of the fictional or apparently fictional name of a character or names of a group of characters. On the many occasions in *Dubliners* where the name of a character or a place is an explicit reference to an actual person or place I have stated relevant facts, often noting a debt to Gifford.

Some of the characters possessing fictional names are, as I indicated in the introduction, based on actual persons whom Joyce knew or knew of in the Dublin and Ireland of his day (or are based indeed on aspects of his own life). I have not usually thought it proper to indicate these in the notes except in such cases as that of Michael Furey/Michael Bodkin/Gretta Conroy/Nora Barnacle in 'The Dead' where knowledge of the origins of the story in Joyce's complex personal experience seems highly pertinent. Elsewhere in a text so attentive to social actuality, Joyce's decision to supply some of his characters with fictional names, should, I believe, be respected, allowing them to exist as the fictional phenomena they essentially are.

THE SISTERS

1. gnomon. The remainder of a parallelogram after removal of a similar parallelogram containing one of its corners. The stylus of a sundial that throws the shadow which

indicates the hours of the day is also known as a gnomon. Also, a rule, canon of belief or action.

2. *Euclid*. Alexandrian Greek geometer of about 300 BC. The narrator here refers to Euclid's treatise on geometry, *Elements*, by the name of the author.

3. simony. In Roman Catholic Church law, the selling or giving in exchange of a temporal thing for a spiritual thing, such as the buying of a blessing, the purchase of ecclesiastical favour, or of pardons. It is also understood as infringing the natural law as defined by Roman Catholic teaching. It originates from Simon Magus in the Acts of the Apostles who sought to gain spiritual powers by payment.

4. *Catechism*. Instructions in Christian doctrine, usually of the question and answer form, by which elements of the faith or belief are taught to children. Also a collection of questions and answers, usually a book or booklet, used for instruction in Christian doctrine. Gifford states that simony is not defined in any of the Irish catechisms he consulted to prepare his notes and suggests that the narrator here refers to the 'courses in religious instruction' he has undergone in school. (G., p. 29)

5. *stirabout*. A porridge of oatmeal boiled in water or milk and stirred.

6. *faints and worms*. A reference to processes in the distillation of whiskey. Faints is the weak and impure spirit which comes over last in the process. A worm is the spiral condensing tube of a still in which the liquor is distilled.

7. *a great wish for him*. Hiberno-English (deriving from the Irish) idiom meaning great esteem, respect (W., p. 29). It may also suggest in this context that the priest hoped the boy would follow him into the priesthood.

8. *that Rosicrucian there*. A jocular if slightly derisive reference to the narrator's interest, as a dreamer and as a possible future ordinand, in the esoteric mysteries of religion. By associating with Father Flynn he seems as if he is receiving an introduction, not completely healthy for one of his tender years, to the cultic and magical aspects of the Church's power, already setting him apart from the rest of

mortals. A Rosicrucian is a member of a fraternity of religious mystics which traces its origins to ancient Egypt by way of the probably fictitious fifteenth-century German monk Father Christian Rosenkreutz. There was a revival of interest in the cult in the nineteenth century as conventional religion seemed increasingly unsatisfactory to many minds hungering for mystery and occult powers. The Irish poet W. B. Yeats was deeply interested in such matters; he published his essay 'The Body of the Father Christian Rosencrux' in 1895, the year in which this story is set. See W. B. Yeats, *Essays and Introductions* (1961) pp. 196–7.

9. *as if to absolve the simoniac of his sin.* Absolution is the remission of sin by an authorized priest in the Roman Catholic sacrament of Penance. Absolution from censures is the removal of penalties imposed by the Church; it grants reconciliation with the Church. As the penalty for simony is excommunication, depriving one of the sacraments, excluding one from divine services, prayers of the Church, Christian burial, and canonical rights, a judgement which is reserved to papal authority, it must be assumed that it is absolution of censures to which the narrator here apparently refers. Absolution of censures for a sin so serious as simony could be granted, when the sinner is a priest, only by higher ecclesiastical authority.

10. *Great Britain Street.* Street in North Central Dublin, north of the river Liffey, in a part of the city inhabited by many of the city's poor. Now Parnell Street.

11. Drapery. A shop dealing in cloth and dry goods.

12. *July 1st, 1895.* It has been noted by several critics that Father Flynn dies on the Church Feast of the Most Precious Blood. Another also notes that July 1st was the date of the Battle of the Boyne in which Catholic Ireland was defeated by William Prince of Orange and the subsequent King William the Third of England.

13. *S. Catherine's Church.* A Roman Catholic church in Meath Street in central Dublin to the south of the river Liffey, in a more socially acceptable part of the city, where however there were many poor parishioners living in slum conditions.

14. *R.I.P.* Stands for Latin *Requiescat In Pacem*, or Rest In Peace, brief prayer for the dead.

15. *High Toast.* Brand of snuff, i.e. pulverized tobacco to be snuffed up the nostrils.

16. *the Irish college in Rome.* An Irish seminary in Rome founded in 1628. In the nineteenth century only the most promising of Irish ordinands for the priesthood were educated there.

17. *to pronounce Latin properly.* Presumably Father Flynn was an advocate of the 'Roman method' of pronunciation of Latin in church services. This was a nineteenth-century attempt to pronounce Latin as Cicero might have done in the first century BC. It differed in pronunciation both from medieval church Latin and from the 'English method' in use in schools throughout the Anglo-Saxon world. The matter remained controversial in the period when Joyce set his stories. (G., p. 31)

18. *the catacombs.* Subterranean places of burial consisting of galleries with recesses for tombs. In first- and second-century Rome the early Christians sought to escape religious persecution by hiding in the catacombs beneath the city.

19. *Napoleon Bonaparte.* The French emperor (1769–1821) closed the Irish college in Rome in 1798, which perhaps accounts for Father Flynn's interest in tales about him. Among such in Ireland was the legend that Napoleon considered the day of his first communion in church the happiest day of his life.

20. *the meaning of the various ceremonies of the Mass.* The Mass is the supreme act of worship in the Roman Catholic Church which is offered up by the priest in the place of Christ Himself. At Mass the acts of Jesus at the Last Supper, in breaking bread and drinking wine, are reproduced making present his sacrificial grace through the sacrament. There are many Masses associated with different times in the liturgical year and Masses for different ecclesiastical occasions (as, for example, a votive Mass, which is celebrated according to the wish of the celebrant or of his superior, or of the person for whose intention the Mass is

being offered). It is probably these complex regulations that Father Flynn explains to the boy narrator.

21. *the different vestments worn by the priest.* During the course of the liturgical year the outer garments of the priest at Mass are of different colours in a complex religious symbology.

22. *sins were mortal or venial.* In Roman Catholic doctrine a mortal sin is a morally bad human act which, undertaken with full consent of the will, is grievously offensive to God and which makes the soul deserving of eternal punishment. To die in mortal sin without the absolution which only a priest can give in confession is accordingly a fate to be feared above all others. A venial sin is an offence against God in a light matter or without full consent of the will that does not destroy the right to eternal happiness. The difference is obviously crucial.

23. *the Eucharist.* In Roman Catholic teaching the Sacrament of the body and blood of Christ in the Mass, truly present under the species of bread and wine; the Sacrament re-enacts the Sacrifice of Christ at Calvary; the Real Presence (by which is meant the real presence of Christ in the Sacrament and the Sacrifice under the appearances of bread and wine). Also the sacrifice of Christ's body and blood.

24. *the secrecy of the confessional.* The confessional is the seat or place used by a priest in a church when hearing the confessions of the faithful. It is traditionally a place of two compartments separated by a screen in one of which the priest is seated and in the other the penitent kneels. In the Sacrament of Penance, which involves confession of sins and absolution, an obligation of complete confidentiality is enjoined upon the confessor, the duly ordained priest who hears the penitent's confession.

25. *the fathers of the Church.* The name by which Christian writers of the first seven centuries are designated.

26. Post Office Directory. An annual Dublin publication giving city addresses and names of residents and occupants.

27. *responses.* Verses, phrases or words sung or said by the

congregation or choir after or in reply to the priest in divine worship.

28. *Persia*. Now Iran. Throughout the nineteenth century the Orient was associated with romance and mystery, but also with sensuality, opulence and exoticism.

29. *altar*. The table in a church used for the celebration of the Sacrifice of the Mass. On the table must be placed the altar stone which has been consecrated by a bishop.

30. *chalice*. The cup-shaped vessel (made up of cup, node, base) used in the Mass in which the wine is consecrated. The vessel must be of gold or silver or the cup should be silver and gold-lined. The chalice must be consecrated with chrism (a mixture of olive oil and balsam) by a bishop and must be touched only by those in Holy Orders or by those to whom special permission has been given.

31. *blessed ourselves*. The mourners make the sign of the cross upon their persons as an indication of a private prayer asking for God's favour and in recognition of Christ's sacrifice.

32. *And everything . . . ?* The questioner seems to express concern here as to whether Father Flynn received Extreme Unction before his death. Extreme Unction is the Sacrament of anointing a person in danger of death accompanied by designated prayers. It is administered by a priest for the salvation through grace of the soul of the dying person. The rite would only be refused in exceptional circumstances. Accordingly the doubt about Father Flynn's end augments the mystery which surrounds him in the story. For only in the case of something very disgraceful indeed could it be imagined that a dying priest could be refused this last Sacrament of his Church.

33. *notice for the* Freeman's General. A death notice to be placed in a daily national newspaper published in Dublin, the *Freeman's Journal and National Press*. This newspaper (here referred to in a malapropism) was an organ of middle-class Catholic nationalist opinion and notable for its respectful and ample reports on ecclesiastical matters, including funerals.

34. *papers for the cemetery and poor James's insurance.* The reference here is to the papers proving Father Flynn's entitlement to a grave plot in a cemetery and possibly to an insurance policy in respect of funeral and burial expenses. Such provision for his death suggests a characteristic middle-class Irish preoccupation with dignified and impressive obsequies. A priest like Father Flynn, whose origins were in the lower-class Dublin district of Irishtown, yet who trained at the Irish College in Rome, might have been expected to be particularly concerned about such matters.

35. *beef-tea.* A juice made from beef cooked in water, often associated with invalidism and illness.

36. *breviary.* The collection in book form of prescribed prayers and readings contained in the divine office. As a priest Father Flynn would have been required to recite prayers daily from the breviary.

37. *Irishtown.* A poor area of Dublin just south of the river Liffey.

38. *rheumatic wheels.* Presumably a malapropism for pneumatic wheels, i.e. for wheels with pneumatic tyres. But Eliza may also be unconsciously employing a piece of inventive Dublin slang of a kind common in the city in Joyce's time as now, where an apparent solecism or bull is adopted with affectionate zest.

39. *Johnny Rush's.* 'Francis (Johnny) Rush, cab and car proprietor, 10 Findlater's Place'. (G., p. 34)

40. *it contained nothing.* The Sacrament of the Mass and the chalice employed therein are here the objects of pious superstition. The speaker is expressing a fear that the consecrated wine might have been spilt thereby doing profound disrespect to the body and blood of Christ. This of course is to confuse substance with accidence in a theologically unsophisticated fashion.

41. *they say it was the boy's fault.* The boy is an altar boy, server or acolyte who assists the priest in the Mass. Here the speaker reports an effort to ascribe the blame for a possible sacrilege to the altar boy, thereby exonerating the priest himself. But the speaker remains unconvinced.

AN ENCOUNTER

1. *Wild West*. The Western United States in the period of lawless development. It was the setting for many adventure stories of cattle rustlers, bandits, sheriffs and of the wars between European Americans and Amerindian tribes. In the popular imagination it represented romance, danger, opportunity and rugged individualism.

2. The Union Jack, Pluck *and* The Halfpenny Marvel. Popular boys' magazines, published in England to 'replace sensational trash with good clean instructive stories of adventure for boys' (G., pp. 34–5). The title of *The Union Jack* refers to the national ensign of the United Kingdom of Great Britain and Ireland. Together with the title *Pluck* is suggested the imperial vision of adventurous British boyhood that played a significant part in late-Victorian British culture, to which publications of this kind contributed. The fact that the publications referred to in this story were published by an Irishman (Alfred C. Harmsworth, G., p. 34) may have struck Joyce as significant. A halfpenny in the title of the third periodical mentioned, was one of the smallest units of British coinage (the farthing or quarter penny was the smallest). The title promises great adventure at small expense.

3. *Indian battles*. Mock battles as between cowboys and Indians in the Wild West.

4. *His parents went to eight-o'clock mass every morning*. Even in the notably pious climate of late-nineteenth-century Dublin such daily attendance at Mass, at what in Ireland is a significantly early hour of the day, would have signalled special dedication or at least the desire to be reckoned as a married couple of advanced piety.

5. *Gardiner Street*. Street in Dublin's north side which contains the Jesuit church of St Francis Xavier. The fact that the Dillons choose to fulfil their religious obligations in a Jesuit church possibly suggests social ambition, for the Jesuits (i.e. members of the Society of Jesus, an order of religious men who follow the particularly rigorous way of

religious life laid down by their founder, St Ignatius of Loyola, in 1534) in Ireland are looked upon as the most intellectually and socially admirable of the regular clergy.

6. *Ya! yaka, yaka, yaka!* Amerindian cry used in religious ceremony. (G., p. 36)

7. *a vocation for the priesthood.* The sense that God is calling one to become a priest.

8. *Father Butler was hearing the four pages of Roman History.* The reference is to regular translation classes from the classical Latin authors' accounts of ancient Roman history. A compendium volume (probably with extracts from classical authors) entitled *Roman History* was apparently employed in Father Butler's classes. The classics played a highly significant part in the curriculum in British and Irish schools in the late nineteenth century and analogies between Roman and British imperial experience were often drawn by imperialist ideologues. In Ireland, Latin was also the language of the Roman Church's imperium, so instruction in the classical texts carried a heavy weight of ambiguous political and cultural implication. The teaching however was often of the rote kind suggested in this reference.

9. Hardly had the day . . . Hardly had the day dawned. Translationese for stock phrases which occur in Caesar's account of his Gallic wars in *Commentarii de Bello Gallico*.

10. The Apache Chief. Title of a story in *The Halfpenny Marvel*, dealing, one supposes, with the Amerindian wars. An Apache is a member of a nomadic warlike Athapascan tribe who formerly ranged vast tracts of land in south-western North America.

11. *this college.* From the setting this would have been understood by Dublin readers as Belvedere College, a Jesuit-run day school for boys, in Great Denmark Street on the north side of the city. Joyce himself attended this school and his experiences are re-created in fiction in *A Portrait of the Artist as A Young Man* (1916). The school was renowned for its soundly based education and for the intellectual rigour of the instruction offered there.

12. *National School.* Primary School. The national school

system in Ireland was established by British legislation in 1831–34. The national schools supplied a basic education, with something of a practical emphasis for the majority of Irish children. Reckoned anti-national by Irish nationalists since they were blamed, as English language institutions, for the near-extirpation of the Irish language, they also were suspect in the eyes of the Catholic hierarchy since the English administration had sought at their inception to devise a religious curriculum which would be suitable for Catholic and Protestant pupils alike, allowing them to be educated together. The schools were viewed as agents of proselytism and Anglicization by respectable Catholic nationalist opinion and as socially unsuitable by the middle classes.

13. *The summer holidays were near at hand.* Gifford notes Luke 21: 29–31, 'And he spake unto them a parable; Behold the fig tree, and all the trees; When they now shoot forth, ye see and know of your own selves that summer is now at hand. So likewise ye, when ye see these things come to pass, know ye that the kingdom of God is nigh at hand' (G., p. 37).

14. *miching.* Slang: playing truant.

15. *sixpence.* Small silver coin worth six pennies. Probably about a week's pocket-money (or allowance) for a middle-class boy at the time the story is set.

16. *Canal Bridge.* Bridge on the north side of the city which crosses the Royal Canal.

17. *Wharf Road.* Road running along the top of a sea-wall which protects part of north Dublin from submergence in the waters of the river Tolka delta and of the tides of Dublin bay (G., p. 37).

18. *the ferryboat.* A Liffey ferry which carried passengers across the river close to its mouth. It left from the North Wall Quay (T., p. 41).

19. *Pigeon House.* At the time of composition the Pigeon House was the electricity and power station which served the city of Dublin. The site had been sold to Dublin Corporation in 1897 (T., p. 42). So if this story is set at roughly the same time as 'The Sisters' (where Father Flynn's date of death

alerts us to the temporal setting), then the Pigeon House in 'An Encounter' must be reckoned the military dock it was at the date of sale. Certainly at the time of composition the site's recent history would have been readily present in Dubliners' minds. By the (delayed) date of publication it may well have become more immediately associated with the light and power it gave. Perhaps this has allowed the many critics (in a story dominated by triune details suggestive of the Christian Trinity and where punishment is imagined as inflicted at three o'clock in the afternoon, the hour of Jesus's death on the cross at Calvary) to read references to the Holy Spirit in the name of the power station, linking it with the dove of Gospel imagery (Matthew 3:16, John 1:32) and of Christian iconography where the third person of the Trinity, the Holy Spirit, is represented in the guise of a dove. The Pigeon House which is situated on a finger of land which points out into Dublin bay on the south side of the city (it is in fact a continuation of the south bank of the Liffey) takes its name from the caretaker and watchman, one John Pidgeon, who transformed a watch-house and the rough wall formed of pilings upon which it stood into a place of refreshment (Pidgeon's House) for passengers from packet ships. It also became in his time (the mid-eighteenth century) a place for Sunday excursion for the citizenry of Dublin. For details of the geography and history of the area in which this story is set see also H. A. Gilligan, *A History of the Port of Dublin* (1988).

20. *pipeclayed*. Cleaned with pipeclay, a clay often used in the manufacture of pipes for smoking tobacco, but in this case employed to clean white canvas shoes.

21. *the mall*. Street on the south side of the Royal Canal which runs through the north side of the city.

22. *to have some gas with*. Slang: to have fun with.

23. *Bunsen Burner*. A gas burner which produces an extremely hot blue flame, often used in chemistry experiments in the classroom. A play on Father Butler's name, but also one supposes a disrespectful reference to his temperament.

24. *a bob*. Slang: a shilling, a small silver coin worth twelve pence.

25. *a tanner*. Slang: a small silver coin worth six pence.

26. *North Strand Road*. A major thoroughfare on the north side of the city.

27. *Vitriol Works*. A chemical factory on the north side of the city.

28. *Wharf road*. See note 17 above.

29. *ragged boys ... ragged girls ... the ragged troop*. Possibly a reference to pupils of charitable schools run by Catholic and Protestant agencies for the education of the city's poor. There were a number of these fairly near this area of Dublin, for example St Brigid's Orphanage at 46 Eccles Street (founded 1857) and run by the Sisters of the Holy Faith and St Joseph's Female Orphanage at 61 Mountjoy Street, Dublin's oldest orphanage, run by the Sisters of Charity.

30. Swaddlers. Dublin slang: Protestants. Pejorative. Derivation obscure. Originally applied to Methodists and may be a response to the apparently inhibited quality of puritan life. May also contain satiric allusion to the Authorised Version of the Bible, popularly known as the 'Protestant' Bible, and to Luke 2:7 where Jesus as a newborn baby is described as being wrapped in 'swaddling clothes'.

31. *cricket*. The English game of cricket was associated in Ireland with the garrison and with the English conquest. It was viewed as non-national by the supporters of the Gaelic games of football and hurling. The Gaelic Athletic Association was founded in 1884 to encourage support of national sports and, after 1902, included among its regulations a rule banning participation in 'foreign games' by its members.

32. *Smoothing Iron*. A well-known bathing place on the north side of Dublin bay. No longer in existence because of building development.

33. *Ringsend*. Working-class district of Dublin just south of the mouth of the river Liffey. Virtually a self-contained village at the time this story is set.

34. *right skit*. Slang: great fun.

35. *Liffey*. The principal river upon which the city of Dublin is built. It divides the city into its north and south sides, a distinction which is never lost on the native Dubliner.

36. *green eyes*. Possibly an allusion in this context of seafaring and adventure to the medieval tradition that Ulysses, the hero of Homer's *Odyssey* was said to have green eyes.

37. *the Dodder*. A river which flows into the Liffey close to its mouth.

38. *jerry hat*. Stiff felt hat.

39. *Thomas Moore*. Irish poet (1779–1852). Author of *Irish Melodies* (published between 1807 and 1834). Moore's *Melodies* (as they were known) set verses to Irish airs which he acquired from the collector Edward Bunting, were enormously popular in Victorian and Edwardian Dublin.

40. *Sir Walter Scott*. Scottish poet and historical novelist (1771–1832). His work was notably romantic about the past.

41. *Lord Lytton*. Edward Bulwer-Lytton, Baron Lytton, English politician and novelist (1803–73). Author of historical novels and sensational romances. His works and his life were considered morally dubious by the prudish.

42. *totties*. Slang: girlfriends (derivation from Hottentot). Also vulgar term for expensive prostitutes.

43. *josser*. Slang: a simpleton, or simply a fellow, when used as in this case with 'old'. Gifford, presumably following Partridge, suggests a derivation from pidgin English for a worshipper of a joss (a god) and 'suggestive of the burning of joss (sticks of incense)'. (G., p. 40) This might add a sense of the unknown and suspect to the term.

44. *in my heart I had always despised him a little*. Gifford cites II Samuel 6:21, 6:16 and 6:23. In this Biblical incident Saul's daughter is punished by God with childlessness because of her unrepentantly scornful attitude to King David.

ARABY

1. Araby. Poetic name for Arabia. Throughout the nineteenth century the orient was a principal object of European romance and fantasy, in which images of exoticism, sensual-

ity, prodigious wealth and refined cruelty were all involved. The bazaar in this story was identified by Richard Ellmann (J. J., p. 40) as taking place between 14 and 19 May, 1894 in aid of Jervis Street Hospital. The bazaar's theme song was 'I'll sing thee songs of Araby' (G., pp. 40–42) Gifford also cites Thomas Moore's ballad 'Farewell – farewell to thee, Araby's daughter' as an example of period orientalism (G., p. 42).

2. *North Richmond Street.* Street on the north side of the city.

3. *blind.* A *cul de sac* or dead-end.

4. *Christian Brothers' School.* A Roman Catholic school for boys run by a teaching order founded by Ignatius Rice in Waterford in 1802. They were renowned for their strenuous if not always humane educational efforts on behalf of the sons of the nation's poor. Joyce himself attended briefly at the Christian Brothers' School in North Richmond Street in 1893, a fact he chose to omit from his autobiographical fictions. His father John Joyce referred to the Brothers as 'Paddy Stink and Mickey Mud' (E., p. 35). Torchiana reminds us that the Christian Brothers' Schools were known in Joyce's youth as the O'Connell schools and that the school in North Richmond Street was founded by the Liberator, Daniel O'Connell, in 1828. (T., p. 66)

5. *brown.* In *Stephen Hero* Joyce refers to 'one of those brown brick houses which seem the very incarnation of Irish paralysis', p. 211 (G., p. 43). The brown bricks used to construct such Dublin houses were in fact known as Dolphin's Barn bricks, since they were manufactured in a brickery in that part of the city.

6. *The Abbot by Walter Scott.* Novel which idealizes Mary Queen of Scots by Scottish novelist and poet Sir Walter Scott (1771–1832).

7. *The Devout Communicant.* Work of Catholic devotional literature by English Franciscan, Pacificus Baker (1695–1774).

8. *The Memoirs of Vidocq.* Very popular account of the exploits of a criminal turned detective, notable for the author, François–Eugène Vidocq's (1775–1857) blend of

invention, sensationalism and prurience. The memoirs were translated into English by the Irishman William Maginn (1793–1842) in 1828, the year of their publication.

9. *the areas.* Sunken spaces affording access, air and light to the basements of houses.

10. *Mangan's sister.* Joyce's use of this name in the story may have been intended to bring to readers' minds the nineteenth-century Irish romantic poet of doomed love and agonized despair James Clarence Mangan (1803–1849). Joyce presented a paper on Mangan at the Literary and Historical Society at University College, Dublin in February 1902 (E., pp. 98–101). His paper was published in a student literary magazine, *St Stephen's*, in May 1902.

11. come-all-you. Popular song or ballad which employed the conventional phrase 'Come all you gallant Irishmen and listen to my song' to gain an audience's attention.

12. *O'Donovan Rossa.* Jeremiah O'Donovan (1831–1915), Fenian revolutionary and member of Parliament elected in 1869 when serving a life sentence for treason-felony. He came from Ross Carberry in County Cork and was nick-named Dynamite Rossa.

13. *a ballad about the troubles in our native land.* Revolutionary nationalism in nineteenth- and early-twentieth-century Ireland depended in part for popular support on a vast repository of songs and ballads which recounted the wrongs suffered by the nation and the daring deeds of her patriots.

14. *my chalice.* A goblet; especially the cup used in the Eucharist. Here the suggestion of bearing a venerated object through a crowd of foes brings to mind the quest romance tale of the Holy Grail (the cup used at the Last Supper) which was popularized in Tennyson's *Idylls of the King*. *The Holy Grail* was published as part of this ongoing poetic work in 1869.

15. *a retreat.* A period of a few days' retirement from normal life for prayer, reflection and religious services.

16. *some Freemason affair.* A function organized by a lodge of the Society of Freemasons. The Masons were highly influen-

tial in the professional and business life of Victorian Protestant Dublin. They were suspected by Roman Catholics of atheism, anti-Catholicism and Protestant bigotry.

17. *collected used stamps for some pious purpose.* This refers to the practice whereby used postage stamps are sold to collectors and the proceeds are employed to support some church cause, the foreign missions being the most likely.

18. *this night of our Lord.* Popular pious conventional reference to the present evening.

19. The Arab's Farewell to his Steed. Poem by the Irish poet Caroline Norton (1808–77). Very popular as a piece for recitation.

20. *a florin.* A silver coin worth two shillings. For the boy in the story it would have been an awe-inspiring sum.

21. *Buckingham Street.* Street on the north side of the Liffey in central Dublin.

22. *Westland Row Station.* Railway station on the south side of the river Liffey.

23. Café chantant. French. Literally 'singing café'; that is a coffee house which also offers entertainment. Such a name for a café in Dublin suggests a provincial attempt to evoke the romance and risqué temptations of the Paris of the gay nineties.

24. *two men were counting money on a salver.* Gifford cites Matthew 21:12–13. (G., p. 48).

EVELINE

1. Eveline. Gifford cites Thomas Moore's poem 'Eveleen's Bower', (G., p. 48) as a possible source for the name of the principal figure in this story. However a Victorian pornographic novel (well-known to those interested in such matters), in which the heroine has sexual intercourse with her father (among other members of her family) and whose speciality is *fellatio*, was entitled *Eveline*. See Peter Gay, *The Bourgeois Experience, Victoria To Freud: Education of the Senses* (1984), p. 373. When it is remembered that this story was written in an earlier form at the suggestion of

George Russell for the *Irish Homestead* (the journal of agricultural co-operation, which was one of Russell's enthusiasms) and that Russell advised Joyce that he should not shock his readership, the possibility arises that the young author was playing a mischievous joke in using this name and perhaps implying sexual abuse as a subterranean theme.

2. *a man from Belfast*. A man from the industrial and largely Protestant city in the north of the country. The commercial aggressiveness and philistine bumptiousness of the stereotypical Belfastman is perhaps suggested in this reference.

3. *nix*. Slang: to keep guard.

4. *the promises made to Blessed Mary Alacoque*. St Margaret Mary Alacoque (1647–90). French nun who after a series of visions introduced devotion to the Sacred Heart of Jesus. She was beatified in 1864 and canonized in 1920. Many Irish Catholic homes in the time of this story would have contained a print of the Sacred Heart with a list of promises of domestic security and blessing in life for those who maintain devotion to it and are regular in attendance at Mass.

5. *Melbourne*. City in Victoria State, Australia. In the nineteenth century many Irish were transported as criminals to Australia while many emigrants settled there. The Catholic priesthood in Australia was significantly Irish in personnel and ethos.

6. *in the Stores*. The shop in which she works. Gifford notes that a Quaker family named Pim owned a general dry goods store in Great George's Street South in south-central Dublin, which was termed their 'Stores' in popular parlance (G., p. 57).

7. *down somewhere in the country*. A common Dublin mode of reference to the rest of Ireland which bespeaks the city's essential indifference to life outside the capital.

8. *night-boat*. A ferry left Dublin every night for Liverpool in England. It must be assumed (that is, if his intentions are honourable) that Frank intends to embark there for South America.

9. *Buenos Ayres*. Capital of Argentina, in the nineteenth and

early twentieth century a thriving and wealthy city which attracted many European immigrants and adventurers. The phrase 'Going to Buenos Ayres' was also slang for taking up a life of prostitution.

10. The Bohemian Girl. Very popular romantic light opera (1843) with music by the Dublin musician and composer Michael William Balfe (1808–1870). See Appendix III.

11. *the lass that loves a sailor*. Popular song by English song-writer Charles Dibdin (1745–1814). See G., p. 51.

12. *Allan Line*. A passenger shipping line out of Liverpool in England that served the Pacific coast of North America by way of a voyage which involved sailing round Cape Horn, calling at Buenos Aires *en route*. The Allan Line was associated with exile. See for example Percy French's well-known song 'The Emigrant's Letter' with its lines 'In the grand Allan liner we're sailing in style/But I'm sailing away from the Emerald Isle'.

13. *the terrible Patagonians*. Notoriously uncivilized, nomadic tribes-people, inhabitants of the southern part of Argentina. Almost unknown in Europe, they were a Victorian byword for wildness and barbarity.

14. *Hill of Howth*. Headland nine miles to the north-east of Dublin on Dublin Bay with pleasant cliff walks and areas suitable for picnicking.

15. *Damned Italians! coming over here*. Italian immigration to Ireland was in fact very slight, which fact must add to the intemperance of this xenophobic outburst. As it happens Argentina was a main focus of Italian emigration in the period.

16. *Derevaun Seraun! Derevaun Seraun*! A famous crux. Possibly mere nonsense. It has been generally assumed that this is corrupt Gaelic. Among suggestions as to possible meanings have been that it may mean 'the end of pleasure is pain' or 'the end of song is raving madness'. (G., p. 52) Others have proposed that the phrase is a corruption of a phrase meaning 'Worms are the only end' (T., p. 75 and p. 76). Brendan O'Hehir (*A Gaelic Lexicon for* Finnegans Wake *And Glossary For Joyce's Other Works*, 1967) is much less

positive stating that the phrase is 'probably gibberish but phonetically like Irish'.

17. *the North wall*. A dock on the river Liffey from where the ferry boat to Liverpool left each evening.

AFTER THE RACE

1. After the Race. Joyce's readers would readily have recognized that the motor race described in this story was the widely reported annual Gordon–Bennett automobile race, which was held in Ireland on 2 July in 1903, when this story is set.

2. *the Naas Road*. The road from the town of Naas, County Kildare, to the south-west of the city. The Gordon–Bennett race was a road race of 370 miles (G., p. 52), mostly in County Kildare. It finished about five miles from Kilcullen, so, as the story opens, the participants are returning to Dublin from whose port, presumably, their cars will be shipped back to England and the continent.

3. *Inchicore*. A lower-middle-class suburb to the west of the city.

4. *their friends, the French*. Reference to the Irish crowd's support for the French team, but also possibly to Ireland's traditional expectations of French help in her time of trial, which were disappointed both in the seventeenth-century wars and during the Rebellion of 1798 when the landing of French Republican troops in County Mayo in the West of the country was too late to aid the cause of the United Irish insurrection. That second French adventure on Irish soil had however enjoyed momentary success at a famous battle, where the English were temporarily defeated, known as the Races of Castlebar (T., pp. 80–81).

5. *Gallicism*. In this context, spirited *élan* expected of members of the Gallic or French nation.

6. *advanced Nationalist*. A fervent supporter or member of the Irish Parliamentary Party at Westminster which, under the leadership of Charles Stewart Parnell (1846–91), sought legislative independence for Ireland.

7. *Kingstown*. Town with harbour six miles south of Dublin. Now Dun Laoghaire, in 1903 it remained a predominantly Protestant town, markedly English in style and pretension. Its name was changed from Dun Laoghaire in 1821 to record George IV's departure from Ireland on the royal yacht after a brief visit. The Dublin/Holyhead (a port in Anglesea in Wales) mailboat left from Kingstown.

8. *police contracts*. There were two police forces that Jimmy's father might have supplied with meat products: the Dublin Metropolitan Police and the Royal Irish Constabulary. Apparently his 'modified' nationalism did not advance as far as refusing to provision one or other or both of these two staunch bodies of men, upholders of British law and order in Ireland.

9. *a big Catholic college*. Probably Stonyhurst, a Jesuit-run secondary school in Lancashire.

10. *Dublin University*. Trinity College, Dublin was (and remains) the only constituent college of the University of Dublin. In nationalist Ireland in the late nineteenth century it was associated with Anglicization, Unionist politics and Protestantism. Since about 1875 Catholics had been permitted to attend the college only with special permission from a bishop of their church. Ironically it was in 1873 that all discriminatory religious tests in relation to membership of the college were abolished.

11. *Cambridge*. The University of Cambridge in England. It would have been a simple matter in the late nineteenth century for a matriculated student of Trinity College (even one as dilatory as Jimmy) to transfer to a college in Oxford or Cambridge. Even without graduating from Cambridge he could thereafter have enjoyed the social distinction conferred almost universally on the 'Oxbridge man'.

12. *Dame Street*. A main thoroughfare in central Dublin on the south side of the river.

13. *the Bank*. The Bank of Ireland in College Green, which served as the Irish Parliament building until the Act of Union in 1801.

14. *Grafton Street*. A fashionable street in south central Dublin.

15. *northward*. To the northside, the less socially fashionable

side of the city. Apparently Jimmy's father, although accounted a merchant prince, has not chosen to invest in a southside address.

16. *electric candle lamps*. Electric bulbs shaped to look like lit candles. In 1903 only the most pretentious of hotels would have boasted such amenities.

17. *the English madrigal*. The early twentieth century saw a revival of interest in the music of the English Elizabethan era, when the madrigal, a five- or six-part polyphonic song, was popular. (G., p. 54)

18. *old instruments*. In the Renaissance madrigal the vocal parts were often doubled by instruments, many of which (for example the lute, viol and the most highly prized Elizabethan instrument, the cornet) had fallen into disuse by the nineteenth century. The revival of interest in Renaissance music was accompanied by an enthusiasm for replicas of the old instruments.

19. *the mask of a capital*. Dublin, although the capital of Ireland, did not exercise legislative authority over the country in 1903. The Act of Union in 1801 had established that power in London.

20. *Stephen's Green*. A large public park in a square of elegant and fashionable Georgian houses south of the river in central Dublin.

21. *Westland Row*. A street in central Dublin south of the river. It contained a railway station which served Kingstown harbour and the town.

22. *Kingstown Station*. The railway station in Kingstown.

23. Cadet Roussel. A French marching song associated with the revolutionary 1790s, about a volunteer in the republican army named Rousselle.

24. Ho! Ho! Hohé, vraiment. Part of the refrain of the song. (See T., p. 84)

25. *Bohemian*. Wildly unconventional in a manner which would suggest the indifference to respectable mores believed to be characteristic of artists and intellectuals.

26. *the Queen of Hearts and the Queen of Diamonds*. The red queens in the pack.

27. The Belle of Newport. The yacht is named for the opulent yachting centre of the American plutocratic rich in Newport, Rhode Island.

TWO GALLANTS

1. *Rutland Square*. Now Parnell Square. A square on the north side of the river Liffey at the head of Sackville Street (now O'Connell Street), Dublin's principal thoroughfare Named in 1791 after Charles Manners, fourth Duke of Rutland, Lord-Lieutenant of Ireland, in the early twentieth century the headquarters of the Orange Order was located at number 10. (T., pp. 94–5) For information on the Ascendancy significance of the street names in this story see Torchiana, op. cit., pp. 91–108.

2. *rotundity*. Dublin readers would have been aware that at this moment the pair would have been passing by the Maternity Hospital known (appropriately as Brendan Behan once remarked) as the Rotunda because of the circular form of a building within its grounds.

3. recherché. French: Sought out with care; choice; of rare quality.

4. *Dorset Street*. A main thoroughfare in north central Dublin.

5. *racing tissues*. Cheap publications about horse racing. In the Aeolus episode in *Ulysses* Lenehan is reported as coming out of the inner office of a newspaper 'with *Sport's* tissues' (Penguin *Ulysses*, p. 162).

6. *Dame Street*. A thoroughfare in central Dublin just south of the Liffey. In 1904 it was a business street.

7. *Waterhouse's clock*. Reference to the clock outside the premises of a goldsmith, silversmith, jeweller and watchmaker on Dame Street.

8. *the canal*. The Grand Canal on the south side of the city. They have in fact walked some considerable distance.

9. *slavey*. A skivvy or maid-of-all-work.

10. *Baggot Street*. A street of fashionable Georgian houses and expensive shops in the south-east of the city.

11. *Donnybrook*. A suburb of the city about two miles to the

south-south-east of the city centre. Until 1855 an annual fair took place there, notorious for riotous excesses of all kinds. To this day the phrase 'Donnybrook Fair' evokes scenes of debauch and gratuitous violence. The fair was abandoned in 1855.

12. *the real cheese*. Slang: the real thing, the authentic experience.

13. *up to the dodge*. Able to avoid pregnancy. Or, possibly, capable of criminal activity.

14. *Pim's*. Pim Brothers Limited was a well-known Dublin commercial concern, manufacturing and dealing in household goods such as furniture, carpets and cloth. They had a retail outlet in Great George's Street, where they also dealt in clothing and leather goods. Among their employees at one time, as well as Joyce's Eveline, was the Irish poet, prophet and agricultural organizer George Russell (AE). The Pims were a Quaker family and a Dublin byword for Protestant probity and high ethical standards. It is unlikely that a dissolute like Corley would have lasted long in their employment.

15. *hairy*. Slang: cute or cunning.

16. *an inspector of police*. Presumably Corley's father was a senior officer in the Dublin Metropolitan Police, which was responsible for the policing of the capital, while the Royal Irish Constabulary was responsible for law and order in the rest of the country. It seems likely that Corley's father is now dead since a senior officer would probably have been able to arrange some kind of sinecure for his son. In the Eumaeus episode of *Ulysses* he is described as 'lately deceased' (Penguin *Ulysses*, p. 709) and as formerly a member of G. Division, the plain-clothes branch of the D. M. P.

17. *about town*. Making the social round. Euphemism for out of work and surviving on the edge of the law.

18. *to give him the hard word*. That is pass on the disagreeable information that a job was available which might have meant some real work for the work-shy Corley.

19. *walking with policemen in plain clothes, talking earnestly*.

The implication would appear to be that Corley is a police informer, who for payment keeps the police supplied with useful information. The spy or informer of course plays an ignominious role in the history of Irish rebellion. Joyce himself was obsessed with the theme of betrayal and treachery.

20. *he aspirated the first letter of his name after the manner of Florentines*. The Florentines (that is citizens of the Italian city of Florence) aspirate *c* as *h*. Hence Corley pronounces his name as Horely, or more appropriately in this context (in, for Corley, an unconscious pun) Whorely. Florence was the city of Dante and this reference can bring to mind the truly gallant relationship of Dante and Beatrice.

21. *Lothario*. A libertine. In *The Fair Penitent* (1703) by the English dramatist Nicholas Rowe, Lothario is a gay (meaning merry and carefree but also with the implication of sexual licence) unscrupulous rake and seducer.

22. *girls off the South Circular*. Girls who promenaded in the evenings along the South Circular road, a ring road on the south side of the city. In Ascendancy Dublin this road had been a place of 'elegant upper-class promenade' (T., p. 98). By the early twentieth century its reputation was altogether less exalted.

23. *on the turf*. Slang: engaged in prostitution.

24. *down Earl Street*. Earl Street is part of a principal east-west thoroughfare in central Dublin. It led to the notorious red-light district just north of the river. The implication may be that Corley is in the company of one of the ladies of the night who conducted her business in the area.

25. *on a car*. That is on an outrider, the Irish horse-drawn jaunting-car.

26. *the railings of Trinity College*. The main buildings of the university which front on College Green are set back from the street behind a wall topped with high railings. For Trinity College, Dublin see note 10 'After the Race'.

27. *Nassau Street*. They are walking along the railings of the street which runs east on the southern side of Trinity. The

name of this street is perhaps the most obvious allusion in this story, which began close to the headquarters of the Orange Order (for Orange Order see note 50 'Grace'), to that protestant Ascendancy Ireland which owed its contemporary status and political power to the Williamite victories of the seventeenth century; for Henry Nassau (1641–1708), Count and Lord of Auverqueque fought at the Boyne on the victorious side with William of Orange in 1690 and subsequently occupied Dublin with nine troops of horse.

28. *Kildare Street*. Street of fine houses and buildings which runs south from Nassau street to Stephen's Green.

29. *the club*. The Kildare Street Club, on the corner of Nassau Street and Kildare Street was an exclusive gentlemen's club whose membership was almost completely Protestant and Anglo-Irish. It was a byword for caste superiority and reactionary attitudes and a key element in the nexus of individuals, families and institutions which constituted Anglo-Ireland.

30. *harp*. The harp as symbolic of Ireland and her legendary past was popularized by the poet Thomas Moore in his *Irish Melodies*. See, for example, 'The Harp that once through Tara's Halls'.

31. *heedless that her coverings had fallen about her knees*. Ireland in tradition, poetry and ballad is often portrayed as a wronged or abused woman.

32. *strangers*. Traditional mode of reference to the English invasion and occupation of Ireland.

33. Silent O Moyle. One of the *Irish Melodies* by Thomas Moore. Entitled 'The Song of Fionnuala', it alludes to the enchantment of the children of Lir in the Irish legend. To this poem Moore appended the following footnote: 'Fionnuala, the daughter of Lir, was by some supernatural power transformed into a swan, and condemned to wander, for many hundreds of years, over certain lakes and rivers in Ireland, till the coming of Christianity; when the sound of the mass bell was to be the signal of her release.' Joyce was very fond of this song and he sang it often. (*Letters, III*, p. 348)

34. *Stephen's Green*. A large public park in a square of elegant and fashionable Georgian houses south of the river in central Dublin.

35. *Hume Street*. Street off the eastern side of Stephen's Green.

36. *a blue dress and a white sailor hat*. Blue and white are the colours associated with the Virgin Mary in Catholic tradition.

37. *Are you trying to get inside me?* Slang: trying to shove me aside or take my place. The phrase derives from the game of bowls in which players seek to score by casting a bowl as close as possible to a target ball or 'jack' (G., p. 59).

38. *the chains*. At that time chains separated the footpath which ran around Stephen's Green from the streets which surrounded it.

39. *Corner of Merrion Street*. Where Merrion Row intersects with Merrion Street Upper and gives on to Baggot Street.

40. *the road*. They are on Stephen's Green East.

41. *Hume Street Corner*. Where Hume Street gives on to Stephen's Green.

42. *Stems upwards*. According to etiquette the stems of a corsage should be pointed downwards. This is of a piece with the vulgar ostentation of her 'Sunday finery', all cheap scent and ragged black fur scarf or boa.

43. *Shelbourne Hotel*. Elegant and expensive hotel on the north side of Stephen's Green.

44. *turned to the right*. They turned to their right *en route* to Merrion Square.

45. *he followed them*. Twice in the tale Lenehan is described as following Corley and the slavey. In contemporary newspaper advertisements for domestic labour in Dublin it was common to include the phrase 'No followers', meaning that young women seeking such employment should not allow young men to court them or to become romantically involved with them. The slavey is obviously ignoring this oppressive prohibition. See *Ulysses*, 'Calypso' (Penguin, p. 70) where Bloom, lusting after his neighbour's servant girl, recalls the phrase 'no followers allowed'. See also Mona Hearn, 'Life for Domestic Servants in Dublin' in *Women*

Surviving, eds. M. Luddy and C. Murphy, Dublin: 1990, p. 156, who informs us that the term follower for a servant's boyfriend was 'the subject of jokes and cartoons'.

46. *Merrion Square*. One of Dublin's principal squares of fine Georgian Houses. Now almost entirely occupied by commercial and professional offices it was, at the time of this story, one of the most desirable residential areas in the city, inhabited by professional people.

47. *the Donnybrook tram*. The tram for Donnybrook which stopped at a halt in Merrion Square.

48. *the railings of Duke's Lawn*. The railings which surrounded a grassed area in front of Leinster House on Merrion Square. Leinster House in the early twentieth century was the headquarters of the Royal Dublin Society. It now houses the Dáil and Seanad of the Irish Parliament. It is part of a group of elegant buildings which then, as now, included the National Library, Museum and Gallery.

49. *round Stephen's Green and then down Grafton Street*. Lenehan is turning now in the direction of the river in a lengthy stroll which will take him back to the northside to Rutland Square where the story began.

50. *to the left*. Into Great Britain Street (now Parnell Street).

51. *curates*. Slang: under-barmen. Term derives from the role of those clergy who assist at the celebration of the Mass.

52. *Three halfpence*. Even in the early 1900s a very small sum to expend on an evening meal. The *Refreshment Bar* is obviously a fairly basic establishment frequented by working-class patrons and hard-up would-be respectable folk like Lenehan.

53. *ginger beer*. A ginger-flavoured non-alcoholic gaseous beverage. Lenehan's repast must be one of the most dismal in all of literature.

54. *pulling the devil by the tail*. Slang: living on the brink of financial catastrophe.

55. *a little of the ready*. Slang: with immediate access to significant funds.

56. *Capel Street*. Lenehan now begins to wander southwards again in a journey which will bring him across the Liffey by way of Grattan Bridge into Parliament Street.

TWO GALLANTS

57. *the City Hall.* The building in south central Dublin which houses the city government, Dublin Corporation. It is part of a complex of buildings which also includes Dublin Castle, from which the British administration ruled the country.

58. *Dame Street.* Lenehan is walking down this principal thoroughfare towards College Green and Trinity College.

59. *At the Corner of George's Street.* Great George's Street South gives on to Dame Street from the south.

60. *Westmoreland Street.* Street that runs from College Green to O'Connell Bridge.

61. *Egan's.* A public house. 'John J. Egan ran a pub called the Oval at 78 Abbey Street Middle off O'Connell Street just north of the river Liffey' (G., p. 61). The Oval is still in business.

62. *Holohan.* A character of this name, presumably the same individual, appears in 'A Mother' in *Dubliners.*

63. *the City Markets.* A section of the city which contained many retail stalls. Lenehan is *en route* for Grafton Street once more.

64. *the clock of the College of Surgeons.* The clock on the façade of the building of the College of Surgeons, which is on the west side of Stephen's Green. The college was responsible for the control of surgical education and practice in Ireland.

65. *the corner of Merrion Street.* Lenehan's peregrination becomes repetitive.

66. *Baggot Street.* See above.

67. *into the area of a house.* Corley's slavey is obviously entering her employee's house by way of the area (or the sunken space in front of the house which allows access and light to the basement rooms). It is there that the kitchens and laundry in which she does some of her work would have been located.

68. *A woman came running down the front steps.* We swiftly learn that this is the slavey. Why she enters by one door and exits by another (the main door of the house placed above street level at the top of a set of steps) is puzzling. It

may be that she has entered by the servants' quarters (though it is more likely that she has her room in the attic in a garret) and has then entered the main part of the house where she steals the coin and makes a swift exit through the main door. Or it may be that she has a key for the basement work rooms 'below stairs', where she enters and that she then climbs the internal stairs to her own room in the attic where she has secreted the saved or more likely stolen coin, making her exit by the most convenient door, the front door of the house.

69. *Ely Place*. A small street of fashionable houses off Baggott Street. It is appropriately enough, at the dismal close of this grim tale, a *cul de sac* or dead-end.

70. *A small gold coin*. This would have been a sovereign, the only gold coin in use. It was worth twenty shillings or £1, a very considerable sum for a slavey and more than even the likes of Corley and Lenehan could reasonably have hoped for. General servants at this date in a Dublin household could have expected to earn between £4 and £8 per annum, though young girls from the country (as the slavey would seem to be in her rude good health) might have been paid even less (Luddy and Murphy, op. cit.). However wages for domestic service compared favourably with wages in the industrial and labouring sectors especially when room and board is included in the equation, which accounts for the fact that the slavey in this story can afford her 'Sunday finery'.

THE BOARDING HOUSE

1. *foreman*. In other words she had married one of her father's employees, a man appointed to oversee his other employees. Mrs Mooney probably married beneath her.

2. *Spring Gardens*. A street on the north side of the city between the Royal Canal and the River Tolka.

3. *take the pledge*. Forswear drinking alcohol by taking an oath not to do so.

4. *a separation*. Even the limited opportunities for divorce

afforded by British law in England and Wales in the early twentieth century were unavailable to the Irish since the provisions of the Divorce Act of 1857 (in an attempt to placate Catholic opinion) were not extended to Ireland. This left only divorce by private Act of Parliament which was very expensive and not open to wives 'except in cases of aggravated enormity'. In situations of marital breakdown it was possible to enter into a legal agreement of separation, in which case a Church court could grant a judicial separation. Separated individuals were unable to remarry since in the eyes of Church and State they remained married to the separated partner.

5. *sheriff's man.* He worked for the office responsible for the collection of debts and revenues due to the city.

6. *Hardwicke Street.* Street of respectable terraced houses on the north side of the city.

7. *Liverpool.* Port and city on the north-west coast of England. The Dublin to Liverpool sea route by packet steamer was a chief means of travel between England and Ireland.

8. *the Isle of Man.* Small inhabited island, west of Liverpool.

9. artistes *from the music halls.* Touring performers in the popular vaudeville and musical entertainments which respectable society viewed as morally suspect.

10. The Madam. Term of respect, but also slang for the female overseer of a brothel.

11. *the chances of favourites and outsiders.* The characters are discussing form and bookies' odds in forthcoming horse races.

12. *a commission agent.* One who does business on another's behalf for commission or a percentage of the takings or profits.

13. *Fleet Street.* Street in central Dublin, off Westmoreland Street just south of the river. It was an office area in which many law firms and business agents operated.

14. *handy with the mits.* Slang: good with the fists and inclined to use them.

15. I'm a . . . naughty girl. *etc.* A mildly salacious music-hall song. See Zack Bowen, *Musical Allusions in the Works of James Joyce* (1974) pp. 16–17. For lyrics see G., pp. 63–4.

16. *corn-factor's*. A trader in corn.
17. *George's Church*. St George's, a Protestant (Church of Ireland) church in Hardwicke Place off Temple Street on the north side of the city.
18. *the little volumes in their gloved hands*. Bibles and prayer books. The wearing of gloves *en route* to worship was a mark of decent respectability among Protestant folk.
19. *Mr Doran*. It has been noted by several commentators on this story that *Doran* means exile or stranger in the Irish language.
20. *catch short twelve at Marlborough Street*. Mrs Mooney hopes to arrive in time for Mass in St Mary's, the pro-Cathedral in Marlborough Street in central Dublin north of the river. Low Mass was the shortest of the day, celebrated at noon at the side altar. It was much favoured by those recovering from the excesses of a late Saturday night.
21. *sit*. Slang: abbreviation for 'situation', respectable post in employment.
22. *screw*. Slang: salary.
23. *a bit of stuff put by*. Slang: savings.
24. *pier-glass*. A large high mirror usually narrow enough to occupy the pier or wall space between windows.
25. *reparation*. In Church teaching making amends for material or spiritual wrong committed against another; also restitution. In the rite of confession the penitent is invited to perform acts in reparation of sin.
26. Reynolds's Newspaper. A radical London Sunday newspaper which reported on scandalous events. (G., p. 65)
27. *religious duties*. The obligations imposed upon the Christian by the Church to obey Church law in the matters of attendance at Mass, confession, etc.
28. *to get a certain fame*. A dubious reputation, suggestive of sexual irregularity.
29. *combing-jacket*. A bathrobe or dressing-gown.
30. Bass. A strong, English-brewed brown ale.
31. *the return-room*. A room added to the wall of a house. Usually small. In Dublin a return-room is often found on the first landing of the stairs which seems to be the case in Mrs Mooney's house.

A LITTLE CLOUD

1. A Little Cloud. Possible allusion to the Biblical tale of Elijah and the prophets of Baal and more particularly to 1 Kings 18:44.
2. *North Wall.* The quay on the docks on the north side of the Liffey from which a packet steamer to England departed.
3. *the King's Inns.* The buildings in a small park on the north side of the river in central Dublin that were occupied by the societies which called individuals to the bar, thereby allowing them to practise as barristers or advocates in the Irish courts. The King's Inns also included the Law Library, the Deeds Registry Office, Stamp Office, and Local Registry of Title Office, in any of which Little Chandler might have worked as a scrivener or clerk.
4. *on the London Press.* As a journalist writing for the English national newspapers.
5. *when his hour had struck.* When his working day had ended.
6. *Henrietta Street.* Street in central Dublin leading to the rear of the King's Inns, which, at the time this story is set, was lined by tenement dwellings, inhabited by the poor.
7. *in which the old nobility of Dublin had roistered.* The tenements of Dublin where many of the poor dwelt in slum conditions, were often the Georgian mansions, which, in the popular mythology about eighteenth-century life, had seen the riotous excesses of a brilliantly self-indulgent aristocracy, whose young bucks were a byword for Bacchanalian exploit.
8. *memory of the past.* Possible allusion (G., p. 68) to sentimental song from the opera *Maritana* (1845, with music by the Irish-born composer William Vincent Wallace), 'There is a flower which bloometh' with its repeated phrase 'the memory of the past'. For lyrics see G., p. 68.
9. *Corless's.* Famous restaurant in central Dublin. Its full name was the Burlington Hotel, Restaurant and Dining Rooms. It was in fact owned by the Jammet Brothers by

the time Joyce came to compose this story but many Dubliners still knew it by the name of the preceding owner, Thomas Corless (G., p. 68).

10. *Atalantas*. In Greek mythology Atalanta would marry no one who could not beat her in a foot-race. She followed any suitor and speared him in the back if she could not catch him. She eventually married Hippomenes, who delayed her by throwing three golden apples, which he had received from Aphrodite, in her path. Hippomenes failed to thank Aphrodite and the couple, when they impiously lay together in a holy place, were turned into lions by the angered goddess. In archaic art Atalanta is often shown as a huntress and as an athlete in short tunic.

11. *Capel Street*. Street in central Dublin north of the river which gives on to Grattan Bridge over the Liffey.

12. *Half time*. Brief break between the two halves of a football match, in which teams prepare for the challenges to come. Phrase means 'hold on a minute'.

13. *considering cap*. A wily character, Silas Wegg, in Charles Dickens's *Our Mutual Friend*, employs this phrase when about to gull his intended victim. The phrase suggests the unabashed cunning of Ignatius Gallaher when confronted by financial embarrassment.

14. *That was Ignatius Gallaher all out*. Hiberno-English, expressing grudging admiration, despite manifest faults.

15. *Grattan Bridge*. Liffey bridge which spans the river from Capel Street on the north side to Parliament Street on the south.

16. *nearer to London*. Both figuratively (for he is to meet Gallaher who bears news of the English metropolis) and actually, since he walks south and then east, which would take him a very short distance of a journey to London. East is the direction associated with escape from Dublin s oppressive life in many of the stories in the book.

17. *The Celtic note*. Since Matthew Arnold in his *Study of Celtic Literature* (1867) identified the Celt as possessing 'natural magic' and had popularized the notion of the Celt as being incapable of submitting to 'the despotism of fact', many Irish poets had satisfied English stereotypical expecta-

tion by supplying verses on Irish mythology and the melancholy past in lines of tremulous mediocrity. Twilight with its suggestion of transience and pathos was a frequent theme which allowed this mode to be described as 'Celtic Twilight' poetry. The early work of W. B. Yeats had exploited such Celticism for distinctive purposes, but by 1904 he had largely abandoned it. Many lesser poets still sought literary success within the convention and in 1904 AE (George Russell) was involved in the publication of an anthology *A Celtic Christmas* which met with Joyce's considerable contempt (T., pp. 131–6).

18. *It was a pity that his name was not more Irish looking.* It was common for poets who intended to strike the Celtic note to adopt names which suggested an Irish spiritual authenticity, which Chandler (English term for a candlemaker and also for a general dealer in groceries, provisions and small wares) could never do with its all-too-material and Anglo-Saxon associations. And most unfortunately for the aspirant poet, Chandler in Hiberno-English also means 'meat-maggot'.

19. *Malone.* Little Chandler chooses a name which is indubitably Irish, for the Malones in the seventeenth century were distinguished Catholic Irish landowners.

20. *across the water.* Common Irish mode of reference to the neighbouring island of Britain, most frequently employed by those like Gallaher for whom England is the primary focus of attention.

21. *Lithia.* A mineral water characterized by the presence of lithium salts. Gallaher is offering Little Chandler the choice of common mixers which were often drunk with whisky. Gallaher of course prefers his whisky neat, which suggests the hard-drinking journalist. The text gives 'whisky' rather than the more usual Irish form 'whiskey' (though some Irish whiskeys were spelt 'whisky'). But Gallaher's remarks imply that it is 'Irish' he has ordered.

22. *garçon.* French: boy. Also a mode of address when summoning a waiter in a French restaurant, though less likely to attract immediate attention than the more courteous, '*M'sieur*' or 'Sir'.

23. *dear dirty Dublin.* Common affectionate reference to the city, first popularized by the Irish novelist (author of *The Wild Irish Girl*, 1806) Lady Sydney Morgan (c. 1783–1859).

24. *gone to the dogs.* Slang: deteriorated markedly, especially in moral and personal matters.

25. *a good sit.* Diminutive for good situation, or secure paid employment.

26. *Land Commission.* The Irish Land Commission Court, the British Gcvernment agency which gave effect to land reform whereby tenant purchase of farmland (aided by substantial government credits) transferred ownership from landlord to tenant. This policy had resulted from the land agitation of the 1880s and made the commission a disburser of considerable sums of money.

27. *very flush.* Slang: with lots of spending money.

28. *Boose.* Slang: alcohol.

29. *Isle of Man.* Island in the Irish Sea between Dublin and Liverpool: a less than exciting destination despite the rough reputation of its inhabitants (G., p. 70).

30. *the Moulin Rouge.* A famous Paris music hall, the very embodiment of gay Paree for the Anglo-Saxon puritan mind.

31. *Bohemian cafés.* Cafés, many of them in Montmartre, patronized by writers, artists and denizens of the *demi-monde*. They enjoyed a dubious reputation in respectable society.

32. *gay.* A reference to the city's reputation as a centre of uninhibited pleasure-seeking and *joie de vivre* in the gay nineties. The word also had connotations of sexual licence and prostitution.

33. *a catholic gesture.* That is a gesture which in its breadth implied a comprehensive knowledge of a subject. Joyce may intend us also to imagine a more specifically Catholic gesture whereby a pious believer might make the sign of the cross in contemplation of such widespread sin.

34. *the students' balls.* Dances in Parisian restaurants and cafés, which enjoyed a reputation as hot-beds of sexual vice. Some were genuine Left-bank student haunts, but others

were more populously frequented by ladies who had already embarked upon the oldest of professions.

35. cocottes. French: hens. Slang: flirtatious young women, prostitutes.

36. *many of the secrets of religious houses on the Continent.* Sexual orgies in European Catholic convents and monasteries were a frequent sensationalist motif in Victorian English pornography and in the gutter press. These combined salaciousness with anti-Catholic bigotry.

37. *story about an English duchess.* The English aristocracy were popularly presumed to live lives of colourfully profligate disregard for Victorian bourgeois proprieties.

38. *parole d'honneur.* French: word of honour. Gallaher is affecting cosmopolitan sophistication in his use of the French phrase.

39. *an a.p.* Possibly slang: an appointment. Also possibly diminutive for author's proof, a printer's final version of a text which is sent to an author for checking before the work is published (G., p. 71).

40. deoc an doruis. Irish: a door-drink, hence a final round or one for the road.

41. *Bewley's.* A famous chain of tea and coffee houses, owned by a well-known Dublin Quaker family.

42. *ten and eleven pence.* Ten shillings and eleven pence, almost eleven shillings (twelve pence in the shilling), a substantial sum for one such as Little Chandler.

43. *on the hire system.* By hire-purchase: on credit with the loan repaid in instalments and at considerable interest.

44. *Byron's poems.* The English Romantic poet George Gordon Byron (1788–1824) was a byword for romantic excess in a life touched by Satanic grandeur, and for the heroism of his poetic *personae.*

45. Hushed are the winds ... dust I love. First stanza of Byron's poem 'On the Death of a Young lady, Cousin of the Author, and Very dear to Him'. Written in 1802, this was published as the first poem in the poet's volume of 1807, *Hours of Idleness.* The poem is Byron at his most affectingly sentimental and scarcely represents him as the

romantic he was. Rather it is a piece of emotional trifling, in a wearisomely conventional mode.

46. *Lambabaun.* Irish term of affection: lamb-child.

47. *lamb of the world.* Jesus in the Gospel of St John is described by John the Baptist as 'the lamb of God' (John 1:29).

COUNTERPARTS

1. *Miss Parker.* Unidentified, apparently fictional, but the name is obviously of English origin.

2. *the tube.* A device for communicating between offices.

3. *North of Ireland accent.* In Dublin the accent of the nine counties of Ulster (often referred to somewhat dismissively as the North of Ireland) is reckoned peculiarly unpleasant and is often associated with brash discourtesy and displeasing directness of manner.

4. *Mr Alleyne.* Gifford identifies a solicitor C. W. Alleyne who 'had offices at 24 Dame Street (on the corner of Eustace Street) in central Dublin just south of the Liffey' (G., p. 74).

5. *a copy of that contract between Bodley and Kirwan.* Farrington works as a scrivener or copy clerk in a law firm whose duties are to copy legal documents in long-hand (which include a contract between the apparently fictional parties here named; G., p. 74) since typewritten documents at the time of this story were not legally binding.

6. *Mr Shelley.* Apparently fictional (G., p. 74). But perhaps it is worth reminding oneself that the chief clerk in this depressing working environment bears an English name, that of no less a figure than the romantic poet Percy Bysshe Shelley (1792–1822) whose short life and works were the antithesis of the grinding tedium of Farrington's existence.

7. *Mr Crosbie.* Unidentified. Possibly fictional.

8. *an order on the cashier.* A note of authorization for an advance on his wages.

9. *the objective of his journey.* Presumably Farrington makes

some gesture to indicate (perhaps suggesting a natural necessity) that he is not leaving the building which would be suspicious behaviour in an employee who is obviously less than satisfactory in the performance of his duties.

10. *the snug of O'Neill's shop.* A pub in Essex Street in central Dublin on the south side of the river. Many Dublin pubs in the early twentieth century had a small enclosed space or a parlour (known as the snug) beside or behind the bar where customers could drink and talk in intimate privacy.

11. *g. p.* A glass of porter, with suggestions of drink consumed for medicinal purposes since G. P. is also short for a general medical practitioner. In Dublin a half pint of beer or porter is referred to as a glass.

12. *curate.* Dublin term for an under-barman (since he attends on customers in a pub like a curate who attends the priest at Mass).

13. *caraway seed.* A particularly pungent seed of a herbal plant of the carrot family. Useful in disguising the smell of alcohol on the breath, so available in the pub.

14. *Miss Delacour.* Unidentified, apparently fictional. It is notable that all the names of those associated with the firm for whom Farrington works (including his own) would suggest that they are of non-Catholic background, though Farrington's wife and child are clearly Catholic. It is likely that Alleyne and Crosbie is a Protestant firm which employs Protestants almost exclusively, and deals with a largely non-Catholic clientele (in this instance the client is apparently Jewish) in the sectarian fashion of the period. It has been observed however that the first syllable of Farrington's name is pronounced like the Irish word *fear*, a man. Farrington is referred to as 'the man' in the text. But the name is not an explicitly Irish one.

15. *hot punches.* A beverage usually made of whisky mixed with hot water, sugar and lemon juice and, often, spice or mint or cloves.

16. *manikin.* Little man or dwarf.

17. *a bob.* Slang: a shilling.

18. *Terry Kelly's pawn shop in Fleet Street.* Street in central
    Dublin just south of the river. Terry Kelly was a pawnbro-
    ker, (48 Fleet Street, G., p. 74) one who loans money on the
    security of personal property pledged in his keeping.

19. *the dart.* The way it could be managed.

20. *Temple Bar.* Street in south central Dublin which leads into
    Fleet Street.

21. A crown! Five shillings.

22. *six shillings.* A considerable sum for a man in Farrington's
    position, with a wife and family to support on a clerk's
    wages. To spend such a sum on an alcoholic binge suggests
    he has a significant drink problem.

23. *Westmoreland Street.* Street in south central Dublin which
    leads to College Green and to Grafton Street, the principal
    fashionable thoroughfare of the city.

24. *evening editions.* Evening editions of the daily national news-
    papers.

25. *Davy Byrne's.* Public house at 21 Duke Street, just off
    Grafton Street. Still in business.

26. *a half-one.* A half-measure of whiskey.

27. *tailors of malt.* Measures of malt, that is of unblended, whis-
    key.

28. *Callan's of Fownes's Street.* Presumably a law firm in this
    street in central Dublin. Gifford has not identified it, though
    records that there was a firm of Callan and Murphy in
    nearby St Andrew's Street (G., p. 75).

29. *after the liberal manner of the shepherds in the eclogues.* In
    Virgil's (70–19 BC) ten pastoral poems *Bucolica* the Roman
    poet characterized rustic life as essentially innocent. A
    remark after their manner, whatever its ostensible import,
    could not have been expected to cause any offence. In
    Shakespeare's *Hamlet* (Act IV, Scene 7) Gertrude refers
    however to 'liberal shepherds' in a more suggestive context.

30. *poisons.* Slang: alcoholic drinks.

31. *my nabs.* Dialect: jocularly pejorative term of reference for
    a person.

32. *At the corner of Duke Street.* That is the corner where
    Duke Street gives on to Grafton Street.

33. *bevelled*. Moved off at an angle or in a slantwise direction.

34. *the Ballast Office*. Building on the west side of Westmoreland Street on the south side of the city. It was on the corner where it gave on Aston Quay beside the Liffey. From this building the Dublin Port and Docks Board supervised the commercial life of Dublin port. In 'The Dead' T. J. Conroy, Gabriel's father is recorded as having been employed by this body.

35. *Scotch House*. Public house on Burgh Quay on the south side of the river.

36. *the Tivoli*. Theatre on Burgh Quay where music hall entertainments were presented.

37. *small Irish and Apollinaris*. A measure of Irish whiskey mixed with a German mineral water.

38. *too Irish*. All too generous.

39. *some nice girls*. Euphemistic and ironic reference to girls of less than respectable reputation, likely to prove sexually accommodating.

40. *tincture*. Literally a slight trace; euphemism for a drink which is hardly a drink at all and scarcely counts.

41. *Mulligan's of Poolbeg Street*. Pub in a nearby street just south of the river. Still in business.

42. *When the Scotch House closed they went round to Mulligan's*. Drinking in the city's public houses was governed by the licensing laws. The Scotch House operated, it seems, under a licence which required it to close early.

43. *small hot specials*. Small measures of whiskey mixed with water and sugar.

44. *a glass of bitter*. A half pint of beer.

45. *a sponge*. Slang: one who cadges favours.

46. *gab*. Dialect (Scots): mouth.

47. *Pony up*. Slang: pay up.

48. *smahan*. Irish: a taste, used with some of the same self-deluding implications as 'a tincture'.

49. *O'Connell Bridge*. Liffey Bridge which gives on to the city's principal street, Sackville Street (now O'Connell Street).

50. *Sandymount tram*. The tram which carried passengers to Sandymount, a suburb about three miles east-south-east of the city centre.

51. *Shelbourne Road*. Street about two miles east-south-east of the city centre. In the early twentieth century it was a street of mixed lower-middle-class houses and slum tenements.

52. *the barracks*. British Military barracks on Shelbourne Road.

53. *at the chapel*. At a Roman Catholic Church. In Ireland the word chapel almost always refers to a church of the Roman Catholic persuasion.

54. *a Hail Mary*. Roman Catholic prayer to the Virgin Mary which begins with the salutation of the Angel Gabriel at the Annunciation.

CLAY

1. *barmbracks*. From Irish *bairín breac*: speckled cake. Fruit breads or cakes used in Hallowe'en games of divination. In such games a coin or a ring or a nut are baked with the bread. Whoever gets a particular item could be assured of a specific future, marriage for example.

2. *a veritable peace-maker*. See Matthew 5:9. The ready reference to Biblical texts was a commonplace of daily speech among the kind of zealous Protestants with whom Maria finds employment.

3. *the Board ladies*. The *Dublin By Lamplight* laundry at which, we learn, Maria works, was a Protestant charitable institution which sought to rescue fallen women and drunkards. It was run by a board of governors (two of whom are referred to here) with its Chaplain and Secretary, one Rev. J. S. Fletcher D. D. and it set the women in its charge (who otherwise might have been in gaol) to useful work in the laundry. It is clear that Maria is not such a one, since she is granted permission to go out for the evening. She would in fact seem to have a job as a scullery maid in this less than genteel environment.

4. *Ballsbridge*. The laundry was in Ballsbridge, a prosperous and significantly Protestant suburb about two miles southeast of the city centre.

5. *the Pillar*. Nelson's pillar in Sackville Street (now O'Connell Street). This memorial to Admiral Horatio Lord Nelson (1758–1805) was a principal focal point in the city until it was destroyed by a bomb in 1966.

6. *Drumcondra*. Suburb about one-and-a-half miles north of the city centre. It was (and remains) an area with many ecclesiastical and Catholic associations (T., p. 160).

7. *Whit-Monday*. A day of public holiday, following the seventh Sunday after Easter which in the liturgical year marks the descent of the Holy Spirit on the Apostles (Acts 2:1–6).

8. *two half-crowns*. Two silver coins together worth five shillings.

9. *coppers*. Slang: penny coins.

10. *tracts on the walls*. Religious and Biblical texts hung on the walls for the purposes of proselytism and the moral improvement of the inmates. Among these may well have been the institution's Biblical motto 'That they may recover themselves out of the snare of the devil, who are taken captive by him at his will'. (II Timothy: 26).

11. *already mixed with milk and sugar*. In the genteel rituals of tea-drinking it is the individual's prerogative (denied here) to add milk and sugar to taste.

12. *get the ring*. In the game of divination referred to here the person who got the ring could hope to marry within the year.

13. *Hallow Eves*. The story takes place on All Hallow's Eve, or Hallowe'en, the night before the Church feast of All Saints (celebrated on the first of November in commemoration of all the Saints of the Church, whether canonized or not). All Hallow's Eve falls at the same time of the year as the old Celtic festival of summer's end, *Samhain. Samhain* was a three-day feast of the dead when the fairy folk were said to walk and divination was attempted.

14. *a mass morning*. All Saints' Day for the faithful is a Holy Day of Obligation with attendance at the liturgical feast of the Mass a duty which must be discharged.

15. *changed the alarm from seven to six*. It seems that Maria is permitted by her Protestant employers to practise her

religion only if it does not interfere with her other duties; so she is forced to rise at an earlier hour than usual on a Mass morning and sets her alarm-clock accordingly.

16. *Downes's cake shop.* Gifford gives Sir Joseph Downes's, confectioner, 6 Earl Street North, near Nelson's Pillar (G., p. 80). Joyce's contemporaries could have been expected to identify this shop near such a well-known landmark and to have remembered the social distinction of its titular proprietor.

17. *apples and nuts.* Traditionally served at Hallowe'en parties and used in various games, such as ducking for apples.

18. *Henry Street.* Street in central Dublin running west from Sackville Street.

19. *Two-and-four.* Two shillings and four pence, a significant expenditure for one in such lowly and undoubtedly ill-paid employment.

20. *a colonel-looking gentleman.* The implication is that he has the air of a retired British army officer. As such he would most likely have been an Anglo–Irish Protestant member of the upper or upper-middle class.

21. *the Canal Bridge.* Bridge over the Royal Canal on the north side of the city where Maria descends from the tram in Drumcondra.

22. *along the terrace.* Maria walks along a street which is flanked by a row of terrace houses.

23. *a drop taken.* Euphemism which in Dublin can cover a multitude of alcoholic sins, from mild inebriation to outright intoxication.

24. *Hallow Eve games.* The games of divination which follow involve blindfold participants selecting by touch from items proffered to them in a saucer. These can include a prayer book which presages entry to a convent or monastery, the ring which promises marriage, water which assures continued life and clay which indicates death before too long.

25. *Miss McCloud's reel.* Irish fiddle tune.

26. I Dreamt that I Dwelt. A favourite aria from Balfe's opera *The Bohemian Girl*. In the opera the nobly born heroine who has been kidnapped by gypsies, dreams of a scarcely

remembered life of luxury to which in the opera she is (at first not so happily) restored. See Appendix III.

27. *her mistake.* Maria sings the first stanza of the aria twice (which has offered criticism a notable crux). The second stanza intensifies the heroine's commitment to a love that she hopes will remain true in any social circumstances, whether those of a gypsy Bohemia or aristocratic splendour (see Appendix III). The interpretative possibilities in relation to Maria's diminished experience are many. Adaline Glasheen was responsible for the printing of this set of verses without a break to make them two stanzas. They had appeared as two stanzas in all editions before Robert Scholes and A. Walton Litz's Viking Critical Library *Dubliners*, 1969. Glasheen argued 'This *seeming* to print two verses of the song makes nonsense of: ". . . and when she came to the second verse she sang again . . ."' (C. H., p. 104).

28. *poor old Balfe.* Balfe during his lifetime had enjoyed an almost universal reputation as a composer, but since his death his name had suffered an eclipse.

A PAINFUL CASE

1. *Duffy.* The name derives from the Irish *Dubh*: black or dark.

2. *Chapelizod.* A village that spans the Liffey about three miles down river to the west of the city centre. It borders on the Phoenix Park. Both places are associated with the legend of Tristan and Iseult (Chapelizod derives from the French, *Chapel d'Iseult*), (G., p. 81). The doomed love of that enchanted pair has offered the critics many interpretative opportunities in their reading of Joyce's tale of rejected love. (T., p. 165–75) Chapelizod is of course where the Earwicker family reside in Joyce's *Finnegans Wake.*

3. *the disused distillery.* This is the Dublin and Chapelizod Distilling Company in which, in fact, Joyce's father John Joyce had once held shares (J. J., p. 16). The company had gone bankrupt during John Joyce's involvement with it, but

by the time of this story the building on the bank of the river was back in service as the Phoenix Park Distillery.

4. *a double desk.* A desk-like store for papers and documents which has a sloped upper surface which can be used as a writing desk.

5. *a complete Wordsworth.* A complete edition of the poems of the English romantic poet William Wordsworth (1770–1850) whose works once thought to be revolutionary and radical had by late Victorian times achieved canonical respectability and were often published in deluxe editions.

6. Maynooth Catechism. The catechetical instrument of religious instruction used by the Catholic Church in Ireland. The Royal College of St Patrick is the principal Irish seminary. Situated in Maynooth about fifteen miles west of Dublin, it hosted a National Synod which issued this catechism in 1883. It is 64 pages in its long version and 32 in the shorter version (C. H., p. 89).

7. *Hauptmann's* Michael Kramer. Play written in 1900 by German writer Gerhart Hauptmann (1862–1946). It dramatizes the conflict between a highminded, reclusive father and his bohemian and artistically gifted son which ends in the suicide of the latter and the realization by the former that his demanding treatment of his offspring has contributed to his son's tragic fate. Joyce himself did a translation into English of this work in 1901 which he hoped would be presented by the Irish Literary Theatre (subsequently the Abbey) in Dublin, but it was rejected in 1904 by W. B. Yeats. At the time when this story is set (it was completed in July 1905) no English translation of the play had been published (the first appeared in 1911) so we must assume that the manuscript is imagined as being in Mr Duffy's own hand.

8. Bile Beans. A popular patent cure for various bilious afflictions.

9. *saturnine.* Medieval medicine attributed psychological states to the influence of the bodily fluids or humours, the balance of which was believed to be affected by the influence of the planets. The Saturnine man, born under the influence of the

watery planet Saturn, is afflicted by an excess of bile and is a gloomy heavy-spirited sort of fellow whose constitutional *melancholia* can only be lifted by music.

10. *a stout hazel*. A stick cut from the hazel tree, which was associated in Celtic mythology and tradition with the magical powers of the poet.

11. *a cashier of a private bank in Baggot Street*. Mr Duffy holds a senior and highly responsible position in a bank in central Dublin in a street which runs south-east off St Stephen's Green.

12. *Dan Burke's*. A public house in Baggot Street.

13. *George's Street*. That is Great George's Street South, a thoroughfare on the south side of the Liffey in central Dublin. It is on Mr Duffy's route home from Baggot Street to Chapelizod and runs through a largely commercial district where Mr Duffy can feel himself safe, as he dines, from the fashionable young who might disturb the even tenor of his days.

14. *Mozart's music*. Wolfgang Amadeus Mozart (1756–91). Austrian composer whose works were acclaimed in late Victorian times for their genial good spirits.

15. *the Rotunda*. A series of buildings on the south-east corner of Rutland Square which included a concert hall. The complex includes the famous maternity hospital on the same site (also known as the Rotunda).

16. *Earlsfort terrace*. The Dublin International Exhibition Building was used for concerts and public meetings at the time this story is set. It is situated on the west side of a street of that name in central Dublin which runs south from St Stephen's Green.

17. *Leghorn*. Italian city of Livorno in Tuscany.

18. *an Irish Socialist Party*. At the time this story is set there was no fully fledged Irish left-wing political party. Individuals interested in socialism and left-wing political thought gathered in what were essentially discussion groups rather than anything akin to the seriously active revolutionary cells of other European countries. Nevertheless it was in Thomas Street in the west of the city not very far from

where Mr Duffy lives that the Irish Socialist Republican Party was founded with James Connolly (the 1916 martyr and revolutionary) as Secretary on 29 May, 1896.

19. *Parkgate*. The main entrance to Phoenix Park, the large park north of the river on the western side of the city.

20. *Nietzsche*: Thus Spake Zarathustra *and* The Gay Science. The German philosopher Friedrich Nietzsche (1844–1900) published *Die fröhliche Wissenschaft* ('*la gaya scienza*') in 1881–2 and *Also Sprache Zarathustra* in 1883–4. Although Mr Duffy seems to have produced a translation of *Michael Kramer* and must therefore have known some German, it must be assumed since Joyce gives the English titles of Nietzsche's two works in his library, that he has the English language versions. It was only in the second half of the 1890s that Nietzsche's thought made any impact in England (and then only in comparatively advanced circles) when A. Tille's incomplete editions *The Collected Works of Friedrich Nietzsche* (three volumes) and *The Works of Friedrich Nietzsche* (four volumes) appeared. Mr Duffy is therefore fairly well abreast of thought in his interest in this writer. Patrick Bridgewater has noted (*Nietzsche in Anglosaxony*, Leicester, 1972) quoting an article of 1913 that those 'who were most drawn to Nietzsche' were like Mr Duffy 'the "socialistically inclined"'. Op. cit., p. 17.

21. *the buff* Mail. The *Dublin Evening Mail*. A Unionist daily newspaper printed on light brown paper (G., p. 86).

22. *reefer over-coat*. A tight-fitting, usually double-breasted, jacket of thick cloth.

23. *the prayers* Secreto. Latin: secret. The prayer or prayers in the liturgy of the Mass corresponding in form and number to the Collects (prayers said aloud), which the priest reads silently or quietly between the Offertory and the Preface; they vary according to the feast.

24. *the City of Dublin Hospital*. Royal City of Dublin Hospital in Baggot Street on the south side of the city near the Grand Canal. It had a round-the-clock casualty department to which all accident victims in the city were taken (T., p. 173).

25. *the Deputy Coroner*. An official charged with determining cause of death in cases due to other than natural causes.

26. *Sydney Parade Station*. The railway station in Sydney Parade Avenue, a street in the comfortably middle-class village of Merrion (where Mrs Sinico lived), three miles roughly south-east of the city centre.

27. *Kingstown*. Town and harbour about six miles south-east of central Dublin. Formerly Dun Laoghaire, by which name it is now known.

28. *Leoville*. The name of the house in which the Sinicos resided. The name means 'city of the lion'. Pope Leo XIII was of course one of the most renowned nineteenth-century popes. The Joyce family had in fact lived in a house of that name in 1892, but that was located at 23, Carysfort Avenue in Blackrock (J. J., p. 34) some miles south of the Sinicos' home.

29. *Rotterdam*. City port in Holland.

30. *a league*. A temperance league or association which would have required members to forswear alcohol.

31. *the Lucan road*. The road which runs along the south bank of the river from Chapelizod to the village of Lucan which is about six miles west of the city centre.

32. *the public house at Chapelizod Bridge*. A pub beside the bridge which crosses the river in Chapelizod.

33. *a gentleman's estate in County Kildare*. County Kildare to the west and south-west of County Dublin is a rich, agricultural county that in the early twentieth century was home to many Anglo-Irish families who owned considerable tracts of prime land.

34. The Herald. The *Evening Herald*. A Dublin daily paper of nationalist sympathies.

35. *Magazine Hill*. A hill in the park which overlooks the river. From here the observer can enjoy a famous view of the river and the city.

36. *Kingsbridge Station*. Railway station close to the southern bank of the river near the park, which served the south and south-west of the country. It is now named Heuston Station.

IVY DAY IN THE COMMITTEE ROOM

1. *Ivy Day*. The death of Charles Stewart Parnell on 6 October 1891 is remembered each year on Ivy Day, so called because at his funeral to Glasnevin Cemetery the mourners who awaited the cortège (delayed because of the huge crowd which followed it through the streets of Dublin) wore ivy leaves in their lapels picked from the ivy plants in the graveyard.

2. *the Committee Room*. In December 1890 the Irish Parliamentary failed to support Parnell as leader because of his role in the divorce action taken by Captain O'Shea against his wife, who was also Parnell's mistress, Katherine O'Shea. This controversy split the party and destroyed Parnell's political career. The meeting took place in Committee Room 15 in the Palace of Westminster in London, the seat of the parliament of Great Britain and Ireland.

3. *MUNICIPAL ELECTIONS*. The election which is the main business of the characters in this story is for the Municipal or city council which had charge over the activities of the City of Dublin Corporation. The Corporation was responsible for the daily life of the city: the upkeep of services, parks, roads etc. The election in this story is in fact a by-election, probably as a result of a death or a resignation. Mr Tierney is apparently fictional.

4. *Royal Exchange Ward*. A municipal electoral area in central Dublin south of the river.

5. *P.L.G.* Poor Law Guardian. An official charged with the operation of the extremely severe laws on the disbursement of niggardly public relief funds to the poor.

6. *Wicklow Street*. Street just south of the river in central Dublin. It is from here that the Nationalist Party organizes its campaign. Avondale, Parnell's home, was in County Wicklow.

7. *Christian Brothers*. The teaching order of Catholic male religious founded by Ignatius Rice in 1802, renowned both for its dedication in providing primary education for the

disadvantaged and for the robustness of its pedagogic methods. (See note 4, 'Araby').

8. *cocks him up*. Slang: gives him exaggerated ideas about himself.

9. *a sup taken*. Euphemism: alcoholic drink obviously taken. A sup is a mere mouthful.

10. *bowsy*. Slang: a ruffian or low fellow.

11. *a Freemasons' meeting*. A meeting of the secret society of Freemasons whose activities are always shrouded in mystery and some of which are presumed to take place in darkness. In Ireland Freemasonry is associated in the popular mind with Protestantism and anti-Catholicism.

12. *Has he paid you yet?* It is clear that the electioneering is performed for payment and not because of any particular political zeal.

13. *tinker*. Term of vulgar abuse. The tinkers in Ireland are travelling people who are regarded by the settled community as vicious, villainous and irredeemably disreputable.

14. *shoneens*. Pejorative reference (from the Irish *Seoinin*, little John Bull) to Irish people who 'attempt to improve their status by rejecting their own heritage and aping English ways' (W., p. 31).

15. *with a handle to his name*. Slang: a title.

16. *hunker-sliding*. Slang: shirking, performing a task in a half-hearted or dishonest fashion.

17. *a German monarch*. The King of England (and indeed Ireland), Edward the Seventh as son of Queen Victoria and Prince Albert was a descendant of German princely families. He had ascended the throne of England upon the death of his mother in early 1901. He in fact visited Ireland in July 1903, so the events in this story may be reckoned to occur on 6 October, 1902. We know furthermore that Joyce drew on his brother Stanislaus's experience of a Dublin election in 1902 in which Joyce's father, John Joyce, was temporarily employed as an election agent.

18. *they want to present an address of welcome*. For Dublin Corporation to welcome the King in this formal fashion would fly in the face of nationalist opinion which explicitly

questioned Britain's right to rule Ireland under the provisions of the Act of Union of 1801.

19. *the Nationalist ticket*. On behalf of the Irish Parliamentary Party which ostensibly sought Home Rule.

20. *spondulics*. Slang: money.

21. *Musha*. Hiberno-English interjection from Irish *muise*, well, indeed.

22. *serve Aungier Street*. Canvass a street in central Dublin just south of the Castle.

23. *'Usha*. Contraction of Musha.

24. Mr Fanning. Fictional name for the sub-sheriff of Dublin. He appears in 'Grace'. See note 27, 'Grace'.

25. *shoeboy*. Pejorative: a flatterer.

26. *hand-me-down shop*. A shop, that deals in second-hand clothing.

27. *Mary's Lane*. Street in poor district of the city just north of the river.

28. *the houses*. Public houses which opened late on Sundays.

29. *moya*. As it were! An ironic interjection. From the Irish *mar bh'eadh* (W., p. 31).

30. *tricky little black bottle up in a corner*. He sells drink illegally when the pubs are closed.

31. *a decent skin*. Frequently used Dublin phrase which suggests that an individual is essentially decent whatever his manifest faults.

32. *hillsiders and fenians*. Rebels. The term Fenian derives from the Fenian rebellion of the 1860s, in which the revolutionaries identified with the warriors of the Fenian cycle. Gifford suggests (G., p. 93) that they were termed 'hillsiders' because the British pilloried them as hillside men, dangerous and barbarian outsiders in the body politic. Malcolm Brown (*The Politics of Irish Literature*, London: 1972) writes that 'An exciting aura surrounded their raids, their escapes, their deaths, their colossal funerals, their colourful minor mechanisms of conspiracy – their disguises, codes, and secret movements "on the hillside" or "in their own keeping"'. Op. cit., pp. 6–7. The point of the reference here is that Parnell's career was marked by a skilled use of parliamen-

tary tactics employed with the implicit threat that he could if he wished draw on the support of the 'Hillside men' (to whom he referred in his speeches) if he didn't get satisfaction. It was of course a risky strategy and sometimes the 'Hillsiders', the tiger which Parnell rode with such skill, threatened to devour him.

33. *Castle hacks*. Informers in the pay of the British authorities who governed from Dublin Castle. The informer has played a dismal role in the long history of Irish rebellion. In Ireland to be reckoned a spy or informer is a very grave matter.

34. *Major Sirr*. Henry Charles Sirr, (1764–1841). The Irish-born British army officer who helped to suppress rebellion in 1798 and 1803. He was notorious for his role in the arrest of Lord Edward Fitzgerald in 1798 and for his hand in the arrest of Robert Emmet whose apprehension he organized in 1803. Born in Dublin Castle from which as town-major he ran the policing of the city, his name is synonymous in nationalist demonology with treachery and suppression of liberty. Even as late as the twentieth century his name was used as a kind of bogey-man, as when one might say 'the Major used it' to prevent someone taking a taxi-cab one wished to use oneself.

35. *the* Black Eagle. The name of Tierney's pub. Apparently fictional.

36. *Kavanagh's*. Another pub. 'Kavanagh's pub was located just north of the City Hall and the Castle and was a gathering place for Dublin politicians and for those in search of political favours' (G., p. 93).

37. *a black sheep*. It seems Father Keon has fallen out of favour with his ecclesiastical superiors. It may be in this context of politics and Parnellism that he is an 'out and outer', an uncompromising supporter of extra-Parliamentary politics (a Fenian no less) and therefore he has been disciplined by the Church, the Irish hierarchy of which opposed Fenianism vigorously. On the other hand, he may simply be an alcoholic.

38. *knock it out*. Slang: survive financially.

39. *travelling on his own account*. The speaker indicates that Father Keon has no particular priestly duties or ecclesiastical

attachments. The implication is that he has been deprived of these because of some fairly serious breach of discipline.

40. *goster*. Hiberno-English, talk, conversation, gossip. From Irish *gasrán* (W., p. 31).

41. *Yerra*. But, Now, Really. Used at the beginning of a clause with the force of a mild oath. From Irish *ara* in which it is often preceded by *a Dhia*, (O God) and 'the whole contracted to *dheara*' (W., p. 31). Hence 'Yerra'.

42. *hop-o'-my-thumb*. Pejorative reference to person of diminutive stature or to a young man.

43. *Suffolk Street corner*. A corner about two minutes' walk from the committee room in Wicklow Street.

44. *the Mansion House*. The official residence of the city's Lords Mayor in Dawson Street just south of the river.

45. *vermin*. A malapropism, or satiric reference to the ermine with which the Lord Mayor's official robe is trimmed.

46. a Lord ... pound of chops. Scornful reference to the Lord Mayor of Dublin who in 1902 was Timothy Charles Harrington, a man of lowly origins 'well known for his simple tastes and for his unswerving loyalty to Parnell' (G., p. 94).

47. *Wisha*. Variant of Musha.

48. *Any bottles?* Empties which can presumably be reused.

49. *a loan of him*. Influence on him.

50. *tinpot way*. Ineffective fashion.

51. *the thin end of the wedge*. In logging the thin end of the wedge opens the wood to prepare for the thicker end which finishes the job. The implication of this proverbial phrase is that, the first step taken, there is no going back.

52. *Dawson Street*. Street of offices and shops in central Dublin just south of the river. See note 44 above.

53. *Crofton*. J. T. A. Crofton an employee of the Collector General's or tax office (B. and B., pp. 72–3) is referred to in 'Grace' where he is identified as an Orangeman (but see note 50, 'Grace'). In the 'Cyclops' episode in *Ulysses* he is referred to as 'presbyterian'. His politics would most probably have been Unionist but not so extremely so as to prevent him working for the Nationalist candidate as the lesser of two evils.

54. *boose*. Slang: alcohol.

55. *Did the cow calve?* In other words is there a cause for celebration?

56. *Lyons.* A 'Bantam Lyons' is referred to as one of Mrs Doran's lodgers in 'The Boarding House'.

57. *the Conservatives.* The Irish Conservative group which with the Tory party in England upheld the Union of Great Britain and Ireland which the Home Rule Party sought to bring to an end.

58. *Parkes...Atkinson...Ward...* Names of English origin and therefore likely to be Protestants with Unionist political sympathies. To get their support is therefore something of a coup.

59. *a big rate-payer.* A propertied man and therefore to be trusted.

60. *Didn't Parnell himself.* Mr O'Connor is remembering that when Edward had visited Ireland in 1885 as Prince of Wales, Parnell had advised his supporters to ignore the royal presence.

61. *till the man was grey.* Queen Victoria's longevity kept Edward from the throne until an advanced age.

62. *The old one never went to see these wild Irish.* Not in fact true. The English Queen visited Ireland on four occasions, the last being in 1900.

63. *King Edward's life ... is not the very....* Edward was a notorious womaniser.

64. *the Chief.* Common appellation for Parnell among his devout supporters.

65. fawning priests. Parnell was denounced from many Catholic pulpits in Ireland when knowledge of his affair with Katherine O'Shea came to public attention.

A MOTHER

1. *Holohan.* Referred to in 'Two Gallants'.

2. *Eire Abu.* Irish: Ireland to Victory, a well-known nationalist slogan.

3. *a bootmaker on Ormond Quay.* Quay on the northern bank of the river in central Dublin where Mr Kearney is in business as a manufacturer of boots. In marrying him Miss Devlin has opted for petit-bourgeois security.

4. *every first Friday*. The pious Catholic was encouraged to receive communion in honour of the Sacred Heart of Jesus on the first Friday of every month. Christ was believed to have assured Margaret Mary Alacoque that an individual who maintained such devotion for nine consecutive Fridays could be assured that he or she would not die without the blessing of the sacraments. See note 4, 'Eveline'.

5. *a society*. An assurance scheme.

6. *the Academy*. The Royal Irish Academy of Music in Westland Row in central Dublin on the south side of the river.

7. *Skerries . . . Howth . . . Greystones*. Three popular seaside resorts near Dublin. Skerries is about eighteen miles to the north, Howth about nine miles to the north-east of the city and Greystones is about fourteen miles to the south.

8. *the Irish Revival*. The Irish literary and cultural renaissance, a movement which since the 1880s had sought to raise Irish national awareness through cultivation of aspects of Celtic and Gaelic civilization. Some supporters of the movement sought to revive the Irish language as a vernacular for the entire island.

9. *her daughter's name*. Kathleen ni Houlihan is a traditional figure for Ireland. W. B. Yeats's famous nationalistic play *Cathleen ni Houlihan* was first performed to acclaim in Dublin in 1902. Kathleen Kearney is referred to in 'The Dead'.

10. *pro-cathedral*. The Catholic pro-Cathedral in Marlborough Street in central Dublin on the north side of the river. It is on a corner where Cathedral Street gives on to Marlborough Street.

11. *Nationalist*. A supporter of Home Rule for Ireland and in this context an enthusiast for Irish cultural independence from English influence.

12. *said good-bye to one another in Irish*. It was a common practice for those who supported the revival of the Irish language to employ a few phrases in Irish whenever possible, even if their command of the language was minimal.

13. *Antient Concert Rooms*. Public meeting hall in central Dublin in what was then Brunswick Street Great and is

now Pearse Street. It was frequently used for musical concerts and recitals.

14. *a contract*. In the context of such a concert in which an unproven artist sought recognition this would have been more of a promise to pay a certain amount if box-office takings justified it, than a legally binding document (G., p. 99).

15. *charmeuse*. French: alluring, winning, fetching. In this context trimming for a garment.

16. *Brown Thomas's*. Fashionable and expensive lace and linen and general drapery shop in Grafton Street the city's principal shopping street in central Dublin just south of the river.

17. Commetty. Mrs Kearney snobbishly finds Mr Fitzpatrick's 'flat', Dublin Hiberno-Irish pronunciation unacceptable. As Wall points out this is the only occasion in *Dubliners* that Joyce attempts to represent Hiberno-English pronunciation phonetically (W., p. 32).

18. *the General Post Office*. A large building with an impressive classical façade in the heart of Dublin on Sackville (now O'Connell) Street, the principal thoroughfare of the city, just north of the river.

19. *the dear knows*. Common Irish expression. So mild as to scarcely constitute an oath, it usually expresses sad resignation to the inevitable disappointments of life. A corrupt derivation from the Irish for 'God knows'.

20. Maritana. Popular light opera by the Irish composer William Vincent Wallace (1812–65) with libretto by Edward Fitzball. It had its first Dublin performance in 1846.

21. *the Queen's Theatre*. One of the city's main theatres. Situated in Brunswick Street Great (now Pearse Street) it was a large theatre which catered for the considerable audiences who enjoyed melodramas and light entertainments.

22. Yous. An ungrammatical form of the plural address which suggests a poor education.

23. *Feis Ceoil*. An annual festival of music which, inaugurated in 1897, sought to popularize the Irish musical tradition.

24. *the* Freeman *man*. A reporter from the *Freeman's Journal* which as a nationalist daily newspaper might have been

expected to notice such a concert as this is. He appears and is named in 'Grace' (see note 78, 'Grace').

25. *the Mansion House.* The official residence on Dawson Street (just south of the river) of Dublin's Lord Mayor. Adjacent to the residential building is a large public hall which could be hired for public meetings and lectures, etc.

26. *Mrs Pat Campbell.* Mrs Patrick Campbell (1865–1940). One of the most famous actresses of her day on the English stage. She included Dublin on her many tours of provincial theatrical centres. Her presence in town would scarcely have helped the unfortunate *artistes* in this story to attract a large audience.

27. Killarney. A popular song of great sentimentality by the Irish composer Michael William Balfe (1808–70). It comes from his opera *Inisfallen* (date unknown) (G., p. 100).

28. *fol-the-diddle-I-do.* Nonsense phrase which implies truculence and devil-may-care contempt. Mrs Kearney imputes arrogant self-satisfaction to Mr Holohan in this exchange.

GRACE

1. Grace. In Roman Catholic theology, grace is a supernatural gift freely given by God to rational creatures to enable them to obtain eternal life. Grace in less specific English usage can refer to personal style and graciousness of manner. It can also mean the period of grace granted to a debtor by a person who is owed money.

2. *curates.* Slang: under-barmen.

3. *Sha.* From Irish *'seadh*: it is, yes; interjection indicating satisfaction (O'H., p. 335).

4. *Grafton Street.* The principal shopping street in central Dublin just south of the river.

5. *an outsider.* Two-wheeled horse-drawn car: the Irish jaunting-car.

6. *Westmoreland Street.* Street in central Dublin just south of the river which gives on to O'Connell Bridge across the river. Mr Kernan is being taken to his home on the northside.

7. *the Ballast Office*. Building on the corner of Westmoreland Street and Aston Quay beside the river.

8. *his Napoleon, the great Blackwhite*. Mr Kernan is apparently inspired in his commercial life by a salesman of Napoleonic fame and success. The original of Blackwhite, if there was one, is unknown to scholarship.

9. *Crowe Street*. Street in central Dublin just south of the river. It gives on to Dame Street.

10. *E.C.* East Central, a postal district in London.

11. *Royal Irish Constabulary in Dublin Castle*. The R.I.C. an armed militia-like police force that was responsible for the security of the state in the country at large. Its headquarters were in central Dublin just south of the river in Dublin Castle, the seat of British power in Ireland.

12. *a character*. In Dublin the last expedient of the defeated is to aspire to an eccentricity or excess of personality which endows the individual with a degree of social acceptability and some small measure of not-entirely-spurious dignity.

13. *the Glasnevin road*. In the direction of Glasnevin, the suburban village about two miles north of the city centre where Mr Kernan resides.

14. *what book they were in*. That is to what year or class they had advanced in school, since the curriculum involved specific books for specific years.

15. *their accents*. Mr Kernan's social decline is accentuated by the obviously low-class accents of his offspring.

16. *the holy alls of it*. Slang from the Irish: the truth of the matter, all that's to be said about it.

17. *he does be*. From the Irish for the present tense of the verb 'to be' (*bíonn sé*). This is known as the habitual present tense of the Irish verb, appropriate enough for a man of such habitual excesses as Mr Kernan. Such usage is however considered a 'mark of uneducated speech' (W., p. 32).

18. *Fogarty's*. A local shop. Gifford suggests 'P. Fogarty, grocer and tea, wine and spirits merchant, 35 Glengarrif Parade, off North Circular Road on the then northern outskirts of metropolitan Dublin' (G., p. 102).

19. *the Star of the Sea Church in Sandymount*. Catholic Church

dedicated to the Blessed Virgin Mary (*Stella Maris*: Star of
the Sea) in the suburban village of Sandymount about two
miles south-east of central Dublin.

20. *Glasgow ... Belfast*. Mr Kernan's sons are perhaps true to
their father's original denominational loyalty, choosing to
work in the largely Protestant cities of Glasgow in Scotland
and Belfast in the north of Ireland.

21. *Thomas Street*. Street in west-central Dublin just south of
the river where Guinness's famous brewery is situated.

22. *the pale*. An enclosure. In Ireland the pale was the area
around Dublin within which the English legal writ ran
before the final conquest of Ireland in the seventeenth
century. Employed in this context, where a Protestant has
converted to the faith of the native majority, it is deeply
ironic.

23. *the Sacred Heart*. The promises made to the Blessed (now
Saint) Margaret Mary Alacoque (1647–90), a visionary
French nun, assured the faithful who displayed in their
homes an image of the sacred heart of Jesus and who took
communion regularly on the first Friday of the month that
they would would receive many blessings. Most Irish Catholic homes in the early twentieth century would have contained such an image or icon even where piety did not
extend to the observance of the sacramental duties associated with this devotional tradition.

24. *the banshee*. From the Irish: woman of the fairy folk or
Sidhe. In folkloric tradition she appears, wailing, when
death is about to visit a household.

25. *the Midland Railway*. The Great Western and Midland
Railway which served Galway in the west from Dublin.
Joyce imagined this story as taking place in 1901 or 1902
(*Letters II*, p. 193). Mr M'Coy seems to have retained an
association with his former employers for in 1904 in *Ulysses*
Joyce has Bloom remark to himself after meeting M'Coy
(who is still secretary to the City Coroner) 'Damn it. I
might have tried to work M'Coy for a pass to Mullingar'
(Penguin *Ulysses*, p. 98) on the western route. A historian
of Irish railway development records that by the end of the

nineteenth century there was one official for every fifteen miles of track in the three-thousand-mile railway system. (J. C. Conroy, *A History of Railways In Ireland*, London: 1928, p. 178). Mr M'Coy's duties with the company cannot have been onerous.

26. The Irish Times ... The Freeman's Journal. Two daily Dublin newspapers. Both conservative. The *Times* was predominantly Protestant and Unionist in politics, the *Freeman* was Catholic and Nationalist and supported Home Rule. Like Bloom in *Ulysses* Mr M'Coy, who has shared an insecure trade as an advertising canvasser with the hero of that work, finds a living where he can.

27. *the office of the Sub-Sheriff*. The office responsible for redeeming bad debts, for evictions etc.

28. *the City Coroner*. The chief official responsible for conducting inquests as to cause of death in cases other than by natural causes.

29. *boose*. Slang: alcohol.

30. bona-fide *travellers*. According to the licensing laws, inns and public houses were able to sell alcoholic drinks to genuine travellers (travellers in good faith: Latin *bona fide*) outside the regulated hours. It was assumed that as travellers (that is individuals who had journeyed five miles from the place where they had spent the previous night) they would have been unable to dine and refresh themselves during the normal hours of legal business. A tradition inevitably developed whereby journeys to suburban public houses were undertaken with the sole intent of drinking outside hours, genuine thirst being, one supposes, a form of good faith.

31. *the Liffey Loan Bank*. In a city inhabited by as many poor as Dublin, there were and are many unscrupulous individuals prepared to lend money at usurious rates. Mr Harford, in partnership with the Jewish Mr Goldberg in the impressively named (but apparently fictional) Liffey Loan Bank, as a Catholic and a Gentile has apparently nothing to learn from his partner who, as a Jew, would have been associated in Dublin as elsewhere with stereotypical images of usurious

exactions on the poor. Joyce's own attitude to anti-Semitism may be adjudged when we note that he has Stephen Dedalus aver in *Ulysses* 'A merchant . . . is one who buys cheap and sells dear, jew or gentile, is he not?' (*Ulysses*, p. 41)

32. *peloothered*. Slang: comprehensively drunk. More usually the term is phlootered, so perhaps this is a comic mis-pronunciation of 'polluted' which in Dublin also denotes a state of thorough-going inebriation.

33. *True bill*. Legal term: sufficient evidence to require a trial before a court.

34. *a crusade in search of valises and portmanteaus*. M'Coy borrows luggage, ostensibly for his wife's imaginary singing engagements outside Dublin. Presumably he sells or pawns the borrowed goods.

35. *bostoons*. From the Irish *bastun*: a switch of rushes, hence pejoratively a spineless no-good, 'poltroon, blockhead, bounder' (O'H., p. 335).

36. *omadhauns*. From Irish *amadán*: a fool, an idiot.

37. *yahoos*. The simian creatures in the fourth book of Jonathan Swift's *Gulliver's Travels* (1726) whose repulsive and recognizably human forms and habits contrast shockingly with the gracious rationality of the horses or Houyhnhnms. In Dublin the term is employed quite frequently, often without consciousness of its Swiftian source, to mean a graceless and ill-mannered fellow, usually, but not invariably, from rural Ireland.

38. *coming up here*. From the country to the city. Many members of the Dublin Metropolitan Police were countrymen. The presence of so many countrymen in the city was resented by native Dubliners, although the force itself was not uniformly unpopular, unlike the Royal Irish Constabulary, which was much disliked in many parts of the country.

39. *M'Auley's*. Gifford gives 'A pub, Thomas M'Auley, grocer and wine merchant, 39 Dorset Street Lower, about a block north-west of the Jesuit Church of Saint Francis Xavier in Gardiner Street Upper where the retreat is to be held' (G., p. 103).

40. *to make a retreat*. To retire for a few days of prayer, reflection and special instruction, usually in the company of others.

41. *to wash the pot*. Slang: to cleanse the soul in Confession.

42. *The General of the Jesuits*. The head of the religious order organized on military lines by St Ignatius of Loyola (1491–1556) in 1534. The order possesses an enviable reputation for the formidable quality of its intellectual life and in Ireland is reckoned the most socially elevated of the regular clergy. Much of the comedy of the ensuing conversation between the intending penitents of this tale involves the half-truths and downright errors that their talk contains. In this case the error is that the superior or General of the Jesuit order does not 'stand next to the Pope' as he has no formal role in the Church's hierarchy. He is however directly responsible to the Pope and is therefore a man of considerable power.

43. *never once reformed. It never fell away*. Again an ill-informed gloss on the facts. The orders of monks and friars that required reformation were much older than the Jesuit order which is comparatively young as the Church reckons age. So Mr Cunningham's opinion is historical nonsense. Furthermore it did fall under Papal displeasure on a number of occasions and was suppressed for a period at the end of the eighteenth century.

44. *their church ... the congregation they have*. The Jesuit Church of Saint Francis Xavier in Gardiner Street in northeast central Dublin was popular with middle-class Catholics of social pretension. Joe Dillon's parents attend eight o'clock Mass there every day in 'An Encounter'.

45. *secular priests*. The priesthood of the Roman Catholic Church is divided into the secular clergy (that is priests who live in the world with appointments in parishes) and regular clergy who belong to an order and live together in a monastery or house.

46. *Purdon*. Joyce may well mischievously intend his readers to associate Father Purdon's name with Purdon Street in central Dublin just north of the river which was at the heart of

NOTES

the red-light or brothel district (the 'Nighttown' of *Ulysses*) at the time this story is set.

47. *Father Tom Burke*. (1830–83). A famous Irish Dominican priest whose homiletic style was anything but gracious being marked by vulgar oratorical tricks, crass metaphors and an unabashed xenophobic Irish nationalism. He was immensely popular as a preacher in Ireland, Britain and the United States, but suspect as a theologian since his stylistic carelessness tended to introduce doctrinal error into his published work. The Jesuits and the Dominicans do in fact disagree on theological interpretations of the relationship between grace and liberty, so it should not surprise that Mr Cunningham, the devout advocate of the Ignatian fathers, should report on the suspicion of heterodoxy that hangs over Father Burke's remarkable reputation in the English-speaking Catholic world.

48. *pit*. The less than churchy Mr Kernan does not know the ecclesiastical term for the body of the church, 'the nave', comically drawing on the theatrical 'pit'. 'The Pit' is also of course 'Hell' in popular Evangelical and Catholic retreat homiletics.

49. The Prisoner of the Vatican. The temporal powers of the Vatican were seized by the Italian state led by King Victor Emmanuel II in 1870. The Popes Pius IX (reigned 1846–78) and Leo XIII (reigned 1878–1903) regarded themselves as prisoners in Vatican City in Rome. Hence the term, used in reference to them both.

50. *Orangeman*. Strictly a member of a lodge of the Orange Order, a militant Protestant organization founded in the north of Ireland in 1795 and dedicated to the protection of the Protestant faith in Ireland and to the maintenance of the political, social and economic privileges associated with that profession. It is named for William of Orange, King William III of England whose defeat of James II at the Battle of the Boyne in 1690 consolidated Protestant rule in Ireland. But the term was also sometimes used in Dublin to refer simply to a Protestant with Unionist sympathies who may have no links with an Orange lodge whatsoever. The

fact that Mr Kernan allows that Crofton is 'a decent Orangeman' implies the latter, for no full-blooded Orangeman could quite be deemed 'decent' in such a Catholic circle. 'Decent' in this context suggests 'acceptable', not inclined to make too much of his Protestantism, or to press sectarian points. The fact that Crofton was willing to attend a sermon delivered by the Catholic Father Tom Burke further suggests that he is not an Orangeman by membership, since attendance at such an event (and indeed his support of the Nationalist candidate in 'Ivy Day in the Committee Room') would have made a true-blue Orangeman liable to expulsion from his lodge.

51. *Butler's in Moore Street.* A pub in central Dublin, just north of the river. Moore Street runs north and south parallel to Sackville Street.

52. *the Pope and the Mother of God.* A garbled version of the differences on the role of the Papacy and on the role as mediator between God and Man of the Blessed Virgin Mary between orthodox Catholicism and Protestantism. While Protestants respect Mary as Mother of Jesus, the Redeemer, they do not generally make her a focus of supplicatory prayer or of special veneration.

53. *tie himself to second-class distillers and brewers.* In other words he was restricted to purchasing less expensive but inferior products since he lacked the capital to start and service his business with first-rate stock. Public houses had contracts with specific producers and were therefore 'tied' to these.

54. *Leo XIII.* One of the most renowned popes of the nineteenth century. Famed for learning, his papacy was marked by reactionary defence of conservative forces in the European social order.

55. Lux upon Lux. Clearly absurd as a motto combining as it does Latin and English. What is more the popes do not in fact take mottoes for themselves, as this conversation suggests. What the speakers may have in mind here is a half-remembered version of the spurious *The Prophecy of Popes* supposedly by St Malachy, the twelfth-century Archbishop

of Armagh, which listed mottoes for popes as yet unborn. It is also possible that the characters are inaccurately recalling to mind the titles of individual papal encyclicals issued by nineteenth-century popes and confusing these with mottoes.

56. *Lumen in Coelo.* Light in the sky or in Heaven was associated with Pope Leo and *Crux de cruce* (Cross from a cross) with Pius IX (G., p. 106).

57. Tenebrae. Here M'Coy is confusing the motto with the liturgical *Tenebrae*, a ceremony in Holy Week in which all lights in the church were extinguished to symbolize both Christ's passion and death and the disciples' desertion, the world left dark.

58. Crux upon Crux. Once again, a linguistic absurdity.

59. *great scholar and a poet.* Pope Leo, although he enjoyed this reputation, was not a particularly impressive scholar. He did write Latin verse however and produced in 1867, before he had in fact been elevated to the papacy, a poem in that language on the invention of the photograph.

60. *penny-a-week school.* Schools for the Irish poor run on the same lines as the hedge-schools of eighteenth-century and early-nineteenth-century Ireland, where pupils paid the teacher on a weekly basis.

61. *sod of turf under his oxter.* The pupils were expected to contribute to the heating of the establishment. 'Oxter': dialect for armpit.

62. Great minds are very near to madness. Inevitably a misquotation of Dryden's lines in *Absalom and Achitophel*: 'Great wits are sure to madness near allied/And thin partitions do their bounds divide'.

63. *up to the knocker.* Slang: up to standard. Mr Kernan here is referring, in a manner not uncommon among Irish Protestants, to the disreputable, morally substandard, lives of some of the medieval and Renaissance popes.

64. ex cathedra. In 1870 the Vatican Council declared the Infallibility of the Pope when he speaks on matters of faith and doctrine *ex cathedra* (from his chair). For Mr Kernan's imagined career in the context of nineteenth-century church history, see *Letters II*, p. 193.

65. *Dolling ... John MacHale.* Two bishops did in fact vote against the promulgation of the doctrine of Infallibility, but they were not the men named or referred to in this text. Our Dublin Church historians have once more got it wrong. Mr Cunningham is in fact recalling the German Johann Dollinger (1799–1890) who opposed the dogma. But he was neither a cardinal nor was he present at the Vatican Council where it was proclaimed. And he did not leave the church but was excommunicated in 1871. John MacHale, (1791–1881) was Archbishop of Tuam in Connacht and a vigorous nationalist (and famously a product of a penny-a-week or hedge-school). Although he opposed the promulgation of the dogma, once it was promulgated he accepted it. But he was absent from the vote at the Council.

66. *some Italian or American.* Mr Fogarty has a dim sense of the true facts. The two bishops who voted against the decree were the Italian Bishop Riccio and the American Bishop Fitzgerald.

67. Credo. Latin: I believe.

68. *Sir John Gray.* (1816–1875). A famous Irish journalist and public figure. As owner of the *Freeman's Journal* he supported the repeal movement led by Daniel O'Connell. As a member of Dublin City Council he was instrumental in bringing clean drinking water to the citizenry in the Vartry water supply scheme. As a Member of Parliament (1865–75) he advocated disestablishment of the Protestant Church of Ireland and supported land reform. A Protestant patriot, his statue stands on O'Connell Street in Dublin (on the Sackville Street of *Dubliners*).

69. *Edmund Dwyer Gray.* (1845–1888). The second son of Sir John Gray whom he succeeded as proprietor of the *Freeman's Journal*. He was also an advocate of repeal of the Union between Ireland and Great Britain and a supporter of Parnell. Like his father he was both a member of Dublin City Council and a Member of Parliament. As a councillor he promoted public health reform.

70. *none of the Grays was any good.* In view of the Gray family record and their notable contributions to civic and national

life this is an especially ungracious remark, crudely sectarian in its implications and sadly ignorant. However, Mr Power is probably recalling the fact that in 1891 Edmund Gray's son deserted the Parnellite cause.

71. *Get behind me, Satan!* See Matthew 16:21–3.

72. *baptismal vows.* Promises made by a child's godparents on his or her behalf at baptism which is performed in infancy. Adults must accordingly renew these promises from time to time.

73. *I bar the candles.* The Church of Ireland in which Mr Kernan has undoubtedly been raised is markedly low church in its liturgical practices, eschewing candles for their suggestion of papist superstition and sacerdotalism.

74. *I bar the magic-lantern business.* A possible allusion to the Catholic belief in apparitions and sacred shrines. An apparition of the Blessed Virgin Mary together with St Joseph and what was taken to be St John the Evangelist was believed to have taken place in 1879 in Knock, County Mayo (in MacHale's arch-diocese). The village and shrine there became a popular pilgrimage destination. At the time it was suggested by the irreverent and sceptical that the apparitions had been contrived by magic lantern images and this became a common enough explanation of the matter among sectarian Protestants who suspected Catholics of primitive superstition. A John MacPhilpin (a newspaper editor in Tuam, County Galway) in 1880 published his *The Apparitions and Miracles at Knock: also the Official Depositions of the Eye-Witnesses* in which he sought to refute the claim that the apparitions were a hoax perpetrated by the local parish priest with the aid of a magic lantern and slides. Recollection of this controversy is enough it seems to stimulate Mr Kernan's residual distaste for the devotional practices and traditions of his adopted church.

75. *the lay-brother.* A member of a religious order who is not a priest. They often perform menial tasks in the church's affairs. Here a lay-brother is a church usher.

76. *speck of red light.* The sanctuary lamp which burns to indicate the presence of the Blessed Sacrament, in the wafer

blessed at the Sacrament of the Eucharist, contained within the chalice in the locked tabernacle on the altar. The red-light district of a city is of course the brothel area, like Purdon Street in Dublin.

77. *quincunx*. A set of objects arranged so that four occupy the corners and the fifth is the centre of the square or rectangle. In ecclesiastical practice such an arrangement is reckoned to symbolize the five sacrificial wounds of Christ and to encourage reflection on His suffering undertaken for the redemption of human sin.

78. *the registration agent and mayor maker*. Mr Fanning's job involves him in taking charge of the annual election for the Lord Mayor of the city. He is referred to in an electoral context in 'Ivy Day in the Committee Room'. All the names of members of the congregation here are of apparently fictional individuals. Mr Hendrick appears about his business as a reporter at the concert in 'A Mother'.

79. *Town Clerk's*. The office of a city official.

80. For the children . . . into everlasting dwellings. Luke 16:8–9. This text is from one of Jesus' more enigmatic parables and is a notable hermeneutic crux. Father Purdon, it seems, has no interpretative difficulties. He is however aided in his reading of this mysterious text by the fact that he alters it slightly. Here the Rheims-Douay version (from which he is quoting) gives 'fail'. Father Purdon substitutes 'die' (T., p. 220).

81. *Mammon*. In the New Testament Mammon (the pagan deity of the Old Testament or Hebrew Bible) represents wealth and cupidity.

THE DEAD

1. *Lily*. The flower of that name is symbolically associated with the Archangel Gabriel who, in the gospel account, informs Mary at the Annunciation of her role in the Incarnation. In church tradition the Virgin is associated with Lily of the Valley or Madonna lily and in Renaissance art the Virgin's chaste purity at the Annunciation is often

represented by a lily growing in a pot or vase. In a tale set at, or just before the feast of the Epiphany (see Introduction, p. xxxiv), whose protagonist is named Gabriel, Joyce's choice of name for the caretaker's daughter has inevitably generated much interpretative speculation.

2. *Stoney Batter*. A single street which gives its name to a district on a north-west thoroughfare, on the north side of the Liffey.

3. *Usher's Island*. The Misses Morkan live in a house which fronted on a quay named Usher's Island, on the south bank of the river to the west of central Dublin.

4. *she had the organ in Haddington Road*. She was employed as organist in the Catholic Saint Mary's Church in Haddington Road on the fashionable south side of the river. The congregation there was notably Unionist in outlook.

5. *the Academy*. The Royal Irish Academy of Music in Westland Row on the south side of the river in central Dublin.

6. *Antient Concert Rooms*. A hall in Brunswick Street Great (the modern Pearse Street) in central Dublin just south of the river, where concerts were often held (as in 'A Mother').

7. *the Kingstown and Dalkey line*. A railway ran from Dublin to the fashionable suburbs and seaside resorts that had developed in the nineteenth century on the southern shores and headland of Dublin bay. Kingstown is now known by its earlier name of Dun Laoghaire.

8. *Adam and Eve's*. Popular Dublin name for the Church of Immaculate Conception, a well-known Franciscan Church in Merchant's Quay near Usher's Island. It is frequently referred to in *Finnegans Wake*.

9. *Gabriel*. In the Biblical account the angel Gabriel, one of the four great archangels, announces the birth of John the Baptist to Zacharias and the coming of the Messiah to the Virgin Mary. In Hebrew the name means 'Man of God'.

10. *screwed*. Slang: drunk.

11. *goloshes*. India rubber or gutta-percha (Malay: tree of the gum) over-shoes which became popular at the end of the nineteenth century.

12. *smiled at the three syllables she had given his surname.*
    Gabriel is patronizing her because of her 'flat' Dublin
    accent in which his name would be pronounced *Con-er-roy.*

13. *Robert Browning.* (1812–89). English Victorian poet. Al-
    though his passionate wooing of his wife, the poet Elizabeth
    Barrett Browning, was a famous love story, his poetry was
    often reckoned by Victorian and Edwardian readers to be
    obscure and difficult.

14. *the Melodies.* The altogether more readily comprehensible
    Irish Melodies of Thomas Moore. (See note 39, 'An Encoun-
    ter'.)

15. *the Port and Docks.* The Dublin Port and Docks Board
    (newly constituted in 1868) which was responsible for the
    control of the port, shipping and customs. In the late
    nineteenth century the Board retained a distinctly Protestant
    complexion. If we are to assume that the impressively
    named T. J. Conroy was in fact a member of the Board and
    not simply an official employed by it, then we must imagine
    that he was one of a panel of representatives on the Board
    elected by Traders and Manufacturers (no Conroy was
    actually a member of the Board). Whatever his exact role,
    association with the powerful and respectable Board gave
    him social significance in Victorian Dublin.

16. *Monkstown.* Comfortable suburban village about five miles
    south-east of central Dublin on the shore of Dublin bay.
    That Gabriel and Gretta are able to live in this pleasant
    fairly fashionable place to the south of the city, suggests a
    certain social achievement which sets them apart from the
    other guests at the party.

17. *Merrion.* Suburban village about three miles roughly south-
    east of central Dublin on the shore of Dublin bay.

18. *dumb-bells.* Weights used for callisthenic exercises.

19. *stirabout.* A porridge of oatmeal boiled in water or milk
    and stirred.

20. *Christy Minstrels.* A theatrical entertainment devised by the
    American Edwin T. Christy, in which Afro-Americans were
    represented in stereotypical fashion for supposedly humor-
    ous purposes often by white 'blacked-up' performers. By the

early twentieth century any show which exploited such 'Negro' minstrels would have been named a Christy Minstrel Show.

21. *the Gresham.* Fashionable and expensive hotel in Sackville Street (now O'Connell Street), Dublin's principal thorough-fare on the north side of the river, in the centre of the city.

22. *the famous Mrs Cassidy . . . for I feel I want it.* Gifford suggests possible reference to ·stock characters from the repertoire of Irish jokes of the Pat ·and Mike variety. The reference here may also invoke a character and a catch phrase from a popular and probably vulgar review sketch (G., p. 115).

23. *Quadrilles.* A square dance popular in Victorian and Ed-wardian times.

24. *the pledge.* A religious oath to forswear alcohol. Freddy has fallen from grace all too swiftly.

25. *her Academy piece.* A challenging piece of music prescribed by the Royal Irish Academy of Music to test the technical proficiency of musicians and teachers of music.

26. *the balcony scene in* Romeo and Juliet. Act 2, Scene 2 of Shakespeare's play of star-crossed lovers, where Romeo declares his love from a garden as Juliet takes the night air on the balcony of her father's house. The fated love of Michael Furey for Gretta, recounted later in the story, involved a not dissimilar scene.

27. *the two murdered princes in the tower.* The two young sons of the English King Edward IV were murdered in the Tower of London probably on the instructions of their uncle Richard who became Richard III in 1483. Portrayal of the unsuspecting innocents asleep or dead in the Tower, where they were suffocated, was a common Victorian genre piece.

28. *tabinet.* A silk and wool watered fabric which resembles poplin.

29. *pierglass.* A tall mirror usually placed on a wall between win-dows.

30. *Constantine.* The fact that Mrs Conroy has named her other son after the Roman Emperor Constantine the Great

(AD c. 285–337), who effectively brought Christianity to supremacy in the religious life of the Roman empire, bespeaks both the piety and ambition for her offspring of the brothers' mother.

31. *Balbriggan.* Town about twenty miles north of Dublin where Constantine is a priest working as a curate in a parish. The brothers live at some distance from one another.

32. *the Royal University.* The examining and degree granting body which awarded degrees to students of University College, Dublin, at which no doubt Gabriel attended. As the name implies it was established by the British Government, as an effort to meet the educational needs of Catholic Ireland.

33. *Lancers.* A kind of quadrille dance. The name is appropriately military in this story of frequent martial allusion, where even the dishes and drinks on the festive board are described as if they were armies in serried ranks.

34. *She did not wear a low-cut bodice . . . the large brooch . . . an Irish device.* The Celtic revival of the 1880s onwards encouraged the self-conscious adoption of Celtic design in fashions and costume jewellery. Individuals who espoused the separatist cause and the Irish Ireland movement were often notably puritanical in sexual matters, which may account for Miss Ivors' modest evening wear.

35. The Daily Express. A Dublin published newspaper of pronounced Conservative and Unionist sympathies, though it hoped for national development within the British Empire.

36. *West Briton.* A member of the English nation in Ireland; an Anglo-Irishman; one who sympathizes with the Unionist cause. Originally a strictly descriptive term employed by those who felt proud to be such, by the early twentieth century it was a term of opprobrium employed by Home Rulers and separatists.

37. *Bachelor's Walk, Aston's Quay.* Quays on both sides of the river Liffey immediately west of O'Connell Bridge where there were a number of booksellers (Webb's on Aston's Quay on the south bank is still trading in books).

38. *at the University*. University College did not admit women at the time when Gabriel and Miss Ivors might be reckoned to have attended university, so she must have studied at one of two other institutions which prepared candidates for the examinations of the Royal University. These were St Mary's University College, established by the Dominican nuns and Loreto College established by Loreto nuns. Both colleges were affiliated to the Royal University, so their students took their degrees within that institution. St Mary's is the more likely since it had a reputation for 'its teaching of the Gaelic language' and was 'committed to women who needed to or planned to make their way in the world'. Bonnie Kime Scott, *Joyce And Feminism*, Bloomington/Sussex, 1984, p. 41. It was Saint Mary's that Joyce's Dublin acquaintance, Hanna Sheehy, attended and she may have supplied a model for Miss Ivors.

39. *the university question*. A contentious issue in nineteenth- and early-twentieth-century Ireland was how to cater for the university needs of the Catholic majority when the major university in the country, Trinity College, Dublin, was distinctly Anglican in ethos (although all its offices and privileges had been opened to Catholic and dissenting men in 1873 and to women of any religious profession in 1904) and the secular institutions which the British government had founded in various centres had been largely deemed unacceptable by Catholic lay opinion and especially so by ecclesiastical edict.

40. *the Aran Islands*. This group of islands off the west coast of County Galway were predominantly Irish-speaking. As such they were the focus of much nationalist mythologizing. A visit there was *de rigueur* for any *echt* Gael.

41. *Kathleen Kearney*. See 'A Mother' to learn the kind of company Miss Ivors suggests they should keep.

42. *Connacht*. One of the four provinces of Ireland. It is almost entirely a western province and is bounded on its western shores by the Atlantic Ocean.

43. *your own language ... Irish*. The Irish Ireland movement considered that Gaelic was the national language of Ireland

and that all self-respecting Irish people should learn it as soon as possible. It was part of the movement's propagandist endeavour to ensure that the language was called Irish, and not Gaelic or Celtic, thereby affording it the same status as English enjoyed in England: Irish for the Irish, English for the English.

44. *They had to go visiting together*. A reference to a movement in the dance which involved Gabriel partnering Miss Ivors for a time. It is ironic in this context, where he has no intention of accompanying her on holiday to the Aran Islands.

45. *Glasgow*. Scottish industrial city. Many Protestant and Catholic Irish immigrants lived there (as they still do) in mutual distaste.

46. *Galway*. Presumably she means Galway city, the principal city of County Galway and of the province of Connacht.

47. *the park*. The Phoenix Park whose eastern gate is a short walk away from where they are meeting for the party.

48. *Wellington Monument*. Large monument in Phoenix Park in memory of Arthur Wellesley, Duke of Wellington (1769–1852), the hero of Waterloo. Wellington was born in Dublin but refused to consider himself as Irish, famously declaring that to be born in a stable does not make one a horse. Possibly his distinctive contribution to Irish debates on identity is in Gabriel's mind after his encounter with Miss Ivors.

49. *the Three Graces*. In Greek mythology the daughters of Zeus and Eurynome as Aglaia (Brilliance), Euphrosyne (Joy), and Thalia (Bloom) are reckoned the patrons of pleasant, gracious social intercourse.

50. *Paris*. In Greek mythology Paris was required to choose to which of three goddesses (Hera, Athena, and Aphrodite) he would award the golden apple mischievously thrown by Eris (Discord). He chose Aphrodite (the goddess of Love) and was awarded Helen with all the discordant consequences for the Greeks and the Trojans.

51. Arrayed for the Bridal. From an English language version of a song from Vincenzo Bellini's opera *I Puritani*, 1835 (see G., p. 118).

52. *women out of the choirs.* Pope Pius X in his *Motu Proprio* of 1903 tried to bring order to the liturgy of the church. Among his measures was to forbid the use of musical instruments other than organs in divine worship and to exclude women from church choirs.

53. *of the other persuasion.* Euphemistic, and in this context courteous, reference to the fact that Mr Browne is a Protestant.

54. *to take a pick itself.* Colloquial and encouraging in a friendly fashion: to eat a little.

55. Beannacht libh. Irish: Goodbye (literally: a blessing with you).

56. *Theatre Royal.* One of Dublin's three principal contemporary theatres. It was situated in Hawkins Street in central Dublin just south of the river.

57. *the Gaiety.* Another Dublin theatre on South King Street, south of the river. South King Street runs away from St Stephen's Green at the point where Grafton Street gives on to the Green.

58. *a pass for* Mignon. That is free entry to a performance of the French composer Ambroise Thomas' opera (immensely popular in the nineteenth century) *Mignon* which was first performed in Paris in 1866.

59. *poor Georgina Burns.* Unknown. But possibly Mary Jane is referring to one of her pupils who has suffered a mental breakdown, for in *Mignon* the heroine undergoes a period of insanity. (G., p. 120) The reference to the opera may have brought her equally unfortunate pupil to mind.

60. *Tietjens . . . etc.* Famous operatic stars. The discussion here indicates the high level of appreciation for grand opera that existed in Dublin in the Victorian and Edwardian periods. However it is significant that this conversation is a nostalgic one for the high period of opera in Dublin (when the public's taste was almost entirely for Italian opera apart from the Irish favourites *Maritana* and *The Bohemian Girl*) was between 1840 and 1880. And since that date more English opera had been performed in Dublin and the role of the great opera star was significantly diminished: 'For a time, at least, the importance of the great singer in Dublin

THE DEAD

opera, like the light of other days, had faded.' T. J. Walsh,
'Opera in Nineteenth Century Dublin' in *Four Centuries of
Music in Ireland*, ed. Brian Boydell, London, 1979, p. 49.

61. *the old Royal*. The original Theatre Royal had been de-
    stroyed by fire in 1880. This event played its part in the
    changes in operatic fashion which the speakers here regret.

62. Let Me Like a Soldier Fall. From William Vincent Wallace's
    opera *Maritana* (1845).

63. *unyoke the horses . . . to her hotel*. This in fact happened to
    one of the singers mentioned in this series of recollections,
    Therese Tietjens (1831–77), a German soprano, who was
    afforded this accolade in December 1874 (Walsh, op. cit.,
    p. 46).

64. Dinorah. Opera by Giacomo Meyerbeer (1791–1864) first
    performed in 1859. More properly known by its French title
    Le Pardon de Ploermel.

65. Lucrezia Borgia. Opera (1833) by Gaetano Donizetti (1797–
    1848).

66. *Caruso*. The internationally acclaimed Italian tenor Enrico
    Caruso (1874–1921).

67. *Parkinson*. Unknown. Possibly Joyce is allowing us to infer
    that she is confused in her memories, and that Mr Browne,
    in his demonstratively overstated fashion, is trying to save
    her blushes. It seems unlikely that such a group of *aficiona-
    dos* would have known nothing of so remarkable a tenor
    voice as that evoked by Aunt Kate.

68. *I'm all brown*. Possibly a familiar catchphrase or piece of
    advertising copy which allows Mr Browne to crack a rather
    forced joke. The critic Bernard Benstock has suggested that
    the words may even be 'an intentional echo of an off-colour
    joke involving a man named Browne (spelled with the same
    final 'e'); it ends with a deflation of Browne's Anglo-Saxon
    chauvinism' (C.H., p. 179). It's a pity Professor Benstock
    did not see fit to share this drollerie with his readers.

69. *Mount Melleray*. Site of reformed Cistercian ('Trappist')
    monastery in County Waterford. Monastic hospitality in
    Ireland allowed respectable folk to seek a cure for alcohol-
    ism without social obliquy.

70. *slept in their coffins*. A popular misconception about the rigours of the Trappist order. As scrupulous followers of the rule of St Benedict the monks in fact sleep in their habits. This, together with the fact that they are buried in open coffins, has, possibly, led to the fanciful idea invoked here.

71. *Fifteen Acres*. An open grass space in Phoenix Park.

72. *the world will not willingly let die*. Gabriel is quoting the English poet John Milton who hoped in *The Reason of Church Government* that he would leave writings 'to after times as they would not willingly let die' (G., p. 122).

73. For they are . . . tells a lie. Gifford allows us to hear in this well-known traditional song an addition to the many military references which this story contains. For he identifies its source as a French popular song which makes reference to the English general the Duke of Marlborough (1650–1722), the hero of Blenheim (G., p. 122). The word 'gay' here of course means only merry and bright.

74. *laid on here like the gas*. Installed, like the gas supply which was thereby permanently available. Though not of course so permanently welcome or useful.

75. *Back Lane*. Street in central Dublin just south of the river. The district in which Gabriel imagines Grandfather Morkan to have lived was a distinctly shabby one and we can take it that he was not possessed of 'an ancestral mansion' as Gabriel sarcastically suggests.

76. *King Billy's statue*. At the time of this story an equestrian statue of William, Prince of Orange and King William III of England, the Protestant victor of the Battle of the Boyne (1690) stood in College Green in the centre of Dublin. It has since been removed.

77. *Do you know Trinity College?* A fatuous question to address to a Dublin cabman since the college is a principal city landmark.

78. *the old Irish tonality*. The folk music of Scotland, Ireland, Wales and Brittany employed a pentatonic scale. Melodies which exploited this five-note scale often embraced a range of two octaves and were a challenge to the singer, especially

for one more accustomed to the eight-tone octave of the diatonic scale.

79. O, the rain falls . . . lies cold. From the folk song *The Lass of Aughrim*, a version of a widely dispersed Scots and Irish ballad. See Child Ballad, 76 and Hugh Shields, 'The History of *The Lass of Aughrim*', in *Irish Musical Studies, 1: Musicology in Ireland*, eds. Gerard Gillen and Harry White, Dublin, 1990, pp. 58–73. Aughrim is a village in County Galway and the site of the catastrophic Irish defeat at the Battle of Aughrim (in the Irish tradition the place is known as *Eachroim an áir* – Aughrim of the slaughter) in 1691. The title of this song adds therefore a note of national significance to the ballad's affecting tale of the seduction, betrayal, rejection and death of a young girl. The name Aughrim is an Anglicization of the Irish *Each-druim*: horse's back. The Williamite victory certainly broke the back of Gaelic civilization when a stray bullet decapitated the mounted Jacobite general St Ruth.

80. *the palace of the Four Courts*. An imposing eighteenth-century building, designed by James Gandon, on the north bank of the river which houses the central courts of Ireland.

81. *Winetavern Street*. Street close to Usher's Island which gives on to the south bank of the river.

82. *O'Connell Bridge*. Bridge over the Liffey which gave on to Sackville Street (now O'Connell Street), the city's principal thoroughfare.

83. *the statue*. Statue of Daniel O'Connell (1775–1847) which stands at the head of what is now named O'Connell Street. O'Connell achieved Catholic Emancipation in 1829. Known as 'The Liberator' he was also popularly or satirically referred to as 'Dan'.

84. *sovereign*. A gold coin worth £1, quite a substantial sum, the amount involved indeed in 'Two Gallants'.

85. *when he opened that little Christmas-card shop in Henry Street*. As Gifford informs us, Christmas cards were traditionally sold from temporary card shops and the profits were usually devoted to a charity (G., p. 125). Freddy Malins has sought to catch the Christmas trade in a shop

near the General Post Office in central Dublin, but we can assume that he was his own best charity, even though he has managed to keep by enough to repay Gabriel.

86. *Michael*. Many critics have noted that Gretta's love in this story like her husband bears the name of an Archangel. His name in Hebrew means 'Who is like God?'

87. *delicate*. Frequently employed Irish euphemism of the period for a victim of consumption or tuberculosis, which at the time of this story had no certain cure.

88. *go out walking with him*. In the Ireland of the period such a public gesture of courtship usually implied the possibility of a serious relationship.

89. *in the gasworks*. Was employed in a plant which manu- factured town gas from coal, a distinctly unromantic occupation and one scarcely conducive to good health for the 'delicate'.

90. *great with him*. Slang: got along very well with him to the point where the relationship might well have become serious, though as yet without any great sexual connotation. Irish equivalent *mór le* (W., 33).

91. *my grandmother's*. Gretta lived with her grandmother in Galway city. This might imply that she had been orphaned, but it was not uncommon in the period for the parents of a large family to foster out one or more of their children with an aunt or a grandmother.

92. *up here to the convent*. This suggests that Gretta was dispatched by her family to a convent school in Dublin. This might suggest that they had some social ambition for her (for such schools were distinctly middle-class institu- tions) or they may have been concerned that her relationship with Michael Furey had gone too far and that she needed the protective care of the nuns in a distant city to protect her virtue or to save her from an unfortunate marriage with a working-class lad. On the other hand she may simply have lived in a convent hostel while employed in Dublin, which was not uncommon. Such detail as the story offers about Gretta's background implies that Gabriel, according to his mother's scale of values, probably married beneath

him, for there is no mention of either family distinction or university education.

93. *Oughterard*. Village about seventeen miles to the north of Galway. Michael Furey was accordingly a countryboy despite his city job.

94. *Nuns' Island*. A district of Galway city, known as such because of a convent situated there on one of the city's several river islands created by the Galway River which runs through the city.

95. *snow was general all over Ireland*. A very rare occurrence indeed given Ireland's generally temperate climate.

96. *Bog of Allen*. Large turf bog twenty-five miles to the southwest of Dublin.

97. *falling softly . . . softly falling*. This poetic inversion anticipates Joyce's poem 'She weeps over Rahoon' (Rahoon is a small village just outside Galway) composed in 1913 and published in *Pomes Pennyeach* (1927). That poem of darkly melancholic ambiguity about love and death begins 'Rain on Rahoon falls softly, softly falling/Where my dark lover lies.' It was written after a visit by Joyce in 1912 to the grave of Nora's Galway sweetheart, Michael Bodkin, who was buried in the cemetery in Rahoon. Bodkin is the inspiration for Michael Furey in this story. It is possibly worth noting that in 'The Dead' Joyce invests Gabriel's consciousness with the poeticism which later seemed apt for Nora/Gretta/the imagined female voice of 'She weeps over Rahoon'. See also Joyce's notes for his play *Exiles*: 'She weeps over Rahoon, over him whom her love has killed, the dark boy whom, as the earth, she embraces in death and disintegration.'

98. *Shannon*. One of Ireland's principal rivers. To cross the Shannon is to enter or leave the west of Ireland. The river has a broad estuary.